HANS COULD SEE THE BANTAG DEPLOYING OUT ALONG THE RIDGE,

forming into assault lines, battle standards held aloft. The standards were bloodred, and from a distance reminded Hans of Rebel battle flags from the war back on Earth. There was almost a nostalgic feeling at the sight of them. At least against the Rebs, the fight would be an honorable one and if overwhelmed, surrender was still a possibility. He looked down at the line of his "army" and could see the fear on their faces. But they were committed now, knowing what would happen if the Bantag should ever break in.

"Here they come!"

A line of skirmishers started to deploy out from the ridge facing the eastern wall. Hans raised his glasses to study them. Their lines were well intervaled, spaced half a dozen yards apart, moving deliberately. They knew what they were doing, he realized grimly. . . .

"Bill Forstchen's works have flair and power."—Joel Rosenberg

"Some of the best science fiction writing in years!"—*Science Fiction Chronicle*

THE LOST REGIMENT

BATTLE HYMN

William R. Forstchen

A ROC BOOK

ROC
Published by the Penguin Group
Penguin Books USA Inc., 375 Hudson Street,
New York, New York 10014, U.S.A.
Penguin Books Ltd, 27 Wrights Lane,
London W8 5TZ, England
Penguin Books Australia Ltd, Ringwood,
Victoria, Australia
Penguin Books Canada Ltd, 10 Alcorn Avenue,
Toronto, Ontario, Canada M4V 3B2
Penguin Books (N.Z.) Ltd, 182–190 Wairau Road,
Auckland 10, New Zealand

Penguin Books Ltd, Registered Offices:
Harmondsworth, Middlesex, England

First published by Roc, an imprint of Dutton Signet,
a division of Penguin Books USA Inc.

First Printing, January, 1997
10 9 8 7 6 5 4

FOR TWO FRIENDS
WHO HELPED KEEP ME ON TRACK—
BILL FAWCETT AND MAURY HURT

BATTLE HYMN

Preface

In recording the history of the Human-Horde Wars on Valennia, confusion often arises over military, technical, and political terminology. The difficulty of this issue is compounded by the multiplicity of languages involved, both Human and Horde.

To simplify this issue the author has taken the liberty of applying a common terminology for both sides, based upon definitions used in America at the time of the Civil War.

The reader will therefore note that in this and subsequent works members of the Horde will refer to units as regiments, to steam-driven machines on iron track as railroads, and to ships sheathed in armor as ironclads. The use of the actual Horde words for these items—*kagth-umen, vagga ca qugarmak,* and *vagga ca x'qiere*—would only result in confusion.

Regarding the organization of the Army of the Republic, it was structured along lines similar to the Union Army during the Civil War. Two key exceptions are the field strengths of regiments and batteries. American Civil War regiments in the Union Army had a paper strength of one thousand enlisted men and thirty-five officers, and batteries almost always had six guns. Regiments in the Army of the Republic had a paper strength of five hundred enlisted men and twenty-six officers, while batteries were organized into four-gun units.

During the Tugar and Merki Wars, infantry regiments of the Republic also had two four-pound artillery pieces, an idea borrowed by the architect of this army, Andrew Lawrence Keane, from the European armies of the seventeenth and early eighteenth centuries. This system was abolished two years after the end of the Merki War because of the increased firepower available to infantry regiments with the standardized issuing of rifled muskets and the introduction of breechloaders. Four-pound artillery pieces were in general phased out of the army at this time.

Units in the Army of the Republic were recruited locally and designated in the official rolls by the community they came from—i.e., First Murom, Third Capri, Eighth Suzdal. During peacetime two to four companies of the unit became the "active battalion," and the remaining companies were the "reserve battalion." The active battalion served as the training unit for new recruits, who after two years of service were transferred to the reserve.

By the end of the Merki War the vast majority of units had suffered casualty rates as high as 50 to 60 percent, and three to four years later were still attempting to rebuild their strength; thus in reality most regiments could field only three hundred fifty to four hundred men.

Five regiments were organized into a brigade, two brigades formed a division, and three divisions formed a corps, which on paper should have a strength of fifteen thousand men, along with a battalion of artillery and a regiment of cavalry.

First through Fifth Corps were in general made up of units from Rus, and Sixth through Eleventh Corps were made up of units from Roum. These separate formations were designated as the First and Second Armies.

A note should be made here as well of the interesting political structure created in the year after the end of the Merki War. Rus and Roum joined together as a single political unit called the Republic. A general election was held, and the president of the Republic of Rus, Kalencka, took office for six years, with Pro Consul Marcus Licinius Graca as vice president. Congress was of two houses, with representatives elected based upon population and senators based upon states. As a concession to Rus's position as the founding state, the Second Constitution of Valennia declared that it was entitled to fifteen senators and Roum to ten senators. This inequity was balanced in part by the fact that Roum, with nearly double the population, dominated the lower house. Any new states that joined the Republic, coming in with a population of more than one million, would be entitled to five senators. Again, the terminology applied here is based upon English usage, although Rus was the official language of the government.

The issue of dates has caused significant confusion at times. Thus this note of clarification: Rus, Roum, Bantag, Merki, and Tugar each used different calendars based upon the 340-day year of Valennia. The Republic of Rus, upon its founding after the Rebellion against the Boyars, declared that its calendar would start at year 1 beginning with the next midwinter day. It should be noted that the rebellion occurred six months after the arrival of the Thirty-fifth Infantry and the Forty-fourth New York Artillery. Thus the first day of year 1 roughly coincided with late summer of 1865 A.D.

Upon the drafting of the Second Constitution, incorporating the Republics of Rus and Roum into a single political entity, the Rus calendar was adopted. Therefore the Battle of Hispania was fought in the fifth year of the Republic and the Second Constitution was signed in the sixth year.

Regarding Horde organization, the term "umen," which applies to a unit of ten thousand warriors, will continue to be used, since it has found general acceptance, even among the humans living on Valennia.

Horde military organization was based on the umen, which generally was organized from a given subclan within a horde and commanded by a subclan Qarth. Umens were divided into ten subunits, and the American concept of a regiment is most applicable to this formation and will thus be used, but it should be kept in mind that Horde regiments tended to have twice the numbers of a human regiment.

Ha'ark the Redeemer found that the umen organization was so ingrained into Horde society that it could not be changed, though he did move to create a corps system, with three umens to a corps and then three corps to an army.

A final note regarding language: Human captives of the Hordes tended to adopt the dialect of their captors as a common language, thus enabling people from a wide variety of nationalities to communicate.

In closing, I again wish to thank John Keane, president of the Thirty-fifth Maine Historical Society for valuable insights and a most generous access to the society's magnificent archival resources. Additional thanks must go to Professor Dennis Showalter, who had an ancestor serving with the Thirty-fifth, for the opportunity to examine his yet to be published work "The Impact of Rifles and Railroads on Bantag Military-Political Reform" and to Professor Gunther Rothenberg for the guidance provided by his noted study, *The Military Border of the Republic and the Bantag Empire.*

Prologue

Fifth Year of the Republic of Rus—
Summer of the Battle of Hispania

Long he fell through the fire, until he believed that this was, indeed, the punishment for his sins. That thought alone was nearly beyond his ability to accept. A life of war, of struggle and annihilation, had inured him to such philosophical concerns. There was life and there was nothingness. He had sent more than his share into the nothingness, watching the life drain out of their eyes ... and now it was his turn.

Funny, he could not remember being hit. Even now he could yet sense his body. No wounds. I'm still whole. Strange.

My uxar, my command of ten? What of them? And as he wondered he could hear screams. Are they with me in this torment now as well?

Four were dead. That he knew. Falling in the first moments of the ambush, torn apart by the fusillade that erupted from the jungle. Are their spirits now around me? Am I a spirit as well?

"Kasar!"

He turned. It was Ha'ark, the new recruit, but he could not see him. The idiot. It would be my fate to have him as my companion in the afterworld. The new recruit, a book reader, a fool who was useless except to be beaten to relieve the boredom. Absurd that he had survived the ambush. No, Ha'ark was still with me, running through the jungle, heading into the ruins of the temple.

But what next? We clawed our way into the bowels of the temple, slithering through weed-choked jumbles of rock, the damned forces of the Traitor behind us. They had stopped, though; he could remember their fearful voices outside the ruins. And then there was the flash of light, the tunnel of fire, and now this.

How long have I fallen thus? he wondered. Is this eternity?

The growing fear of it threatened mastery, and he spat out an angry curse at the gods whom he had never believed in. "If this is your punishment, then the hell with you!"

"Kasar. Don't!"

Ha'ark again. So the weakling, the pious one, is with me as well. The thought of it made him throw back his head and roar with laughter. So it was all meaningless—good or evil, warrior or philosopher, we are all doomed to torment.

Even as he laughed he slammed into the ground, a grunt of surprise escaping him. He rolled, still clutching his rifle, and came to his feet.

The fire still swirled around him, but there was no heat, only a pulsing glow. From out of the fire a form appeared ... it was Ha'ark, dropping his gun. Eyes wide with terror, Ha'ark scurried back from the cold flames until Kasar grabbed him by the collar and pulled him to his feet.

"Get your gun, you damned idiot!" Kasar roared. Ha'ark looked up at him, terrified.

"Your gun, damn you!" He kicked Ha'ark toward the pillar of light. Stiff with fear, Ha'ark staggered forward, snatched the weapon from the ground, and scurried back. An instant later four more appeared— Jamul the radio operator, Uthak the heavy weapons man, doggedly clinging to his Vark 32 machine gun,

Bakkth, and Machka, the last two both draftees like Ha'ark and both just about as useless.

Kasar stood mesmerized, but only for an instant, until the old instincts again took hold. He quickly scanned the ground around him, which was lit now by the light of what appeared to be either dawn or sunset.

"Check your weapons," Kasar hissed, even as he ran his fingers along the side of the gun, checking to make sure that the muzzle was clear. Just holding the rifle made him feel somehow secure, and he worked the bolt, which clicked reassuringly as a round chambered out and a new round slapped in. If we're in the afterlife, he thought, at least we've come armed.

He looked at Jamul, who was speaking hurriedly into his radio microphone and reaching around to his back, turning dials arrayed along the side panel.

Jamul shook his head. "Where are we? Either the set's shot or all radio traffic, theirs and ours, is simply gone."

Kasar said nothing. Where were they? There was no telling. The air was different, and his nostrils were distended as he breathed in short pants. Dry, desert dry ... what in the name of the gods, we were in the jungle?

"*Huk Varani ga!*"

Kasar swung around, crouching low.

In the shadows he could see someone standing silhouetted by the moonlight. Then the hair down his back rose on edge. There were two moons!

"*Huk! Huk! Varani ga!*"

Others came out of the shadows, moving cautiously, but he kept his rifle aimed at the first one, even as he struggled with his terror.

"Uthak, cover right. The rest of you, left."

Soldiers of the Traitor? No, and the realization of it, rather than comforting him, redoubled his fear.

They were armed with bows and lances, their weapons poised.

I can drop one, maybe two, he realized, but then I'm dead. At least it's better than falling into the hands of the Traitors and having your ribs cracked open while you are still alive and watching as your heart is drawn out to be devoured. Even though he had practiced the ritual a hundred times on those he had taken, still it had a certain barbarity to it when it was you on whom it was about to be practiced. I thought I was dead, and now I am.

"Don't move, sir."

It was Ha'ark, and the order, coming from the draftee, startled him.

"Aim at the one on the left," Kasar hissed. "When I give the word, drop him. Maybe we can still get out of here."

"Out of where?" Ha'ark replied, and there was the edge of a taunt in his reply. "Look at the sky. Two moons, not one, like home."

"Just get ready."

"We're somewhere else," Ha'ark replied coolly. "They're telling us to drop our weapons. I understand them, they're speaking the ancient tongue."

Kasar snorted with disdain. The recruit had always thought himself better than the rest of them. He was educated, coming from a family that could wear the red cloak of middle rank, drafted into the army only because of a minor offense that gave him the choice of jail or the ranks. And now he thought he could give orders. Like hell.

"On three, get ready," Kasar growled.

"Umaga vikaria. Bantag vu!"

Kasar spared a quick glance to his side. It was Ha'ark speaking. What the hell was the fool doing?

"On three," Kasar snapped. "One, two . . ."

The impact of the bullet doubled him over. As he spun around, Kasar saw the swirl of smoke cloaking

Ha'ark. He struggled to raise his gun toward the recruit. Smiling, Ha'ark chambered another round and squeezed the trigger, knocking Kasar to the ground.

"The rest of you! Don't move!"

"Ha'ark?" It was Jamul. "Why?"

"He was about to get us killed! Let me handle this if you want to live. . . . *Umaga vikaria, Bantag vu!*"

Kasar looked up at the stars overhead. Not of home. A great wheel of stars dimming now in the twilight . . . or was it his vision that was fading?

"Where am I?"

"The home of the ancients, that's where."

Ha'ark was standing over him, looking down, his eyes pitiless.

"Legends," Kasar sighed.

Ha'ark shook his head.

"You thought me an idiot, a fool," Ha'ark hissed, the anger so long suppressed now boiling out. "I wanted to stay with my mentors, but I was forced into your hands instead. But you taught me well, Kasar." And as he spoke, Ha'ark chambered another round.

The world, whichever world it was, was growing distant. Kasar lay his head back, watching the others. His command stood silent, watching the drama play out.

"Kill him." At least he thought he said the words, but no one moved.

Ha'ark looked away from him, shouted something, and the others went down on their knees, murmuring in a strange tongue.

"I was nothing to you, but here"—and his smile turned to a wolfish grin—"here I can be a king."

Ha'ark touched the muzzle of his gun to Kasar's forehead, and in that instant Kasar discovered whether his musings about nothingness were right after all.

Sixth Year of the Republic of Rus

Poking tentatively at his meal, Sergeant Major Hans Schuder of the Thirty-fifth Maine Volunteer Infantry sat in silence. He looked carefully at the bowl of gruel, studying it intently in the dim light that filtered into the yurt. The meal looked clean. A memory of serving out on the Plains against the Comanche came to mind, and he shook his head sadly. Didn't care what the meat looked like back then, just damn grateful to get it, maggots and all. But now . . .

The bastards had tried to force him to eat "cattle" flesh. They viewed it as part of the ritual of breaking a pet. Get you to eat of your own kind, and the ultimate taboo is broken. Even if you escape, you are never the same, a pariah among your own. He had fought against it, even when they held him down and jammed the cooked flesh into his mouth. When they left he forced himself to vomit it back up.

They had tricked him, to be sure. Shortly after his capture, the contents of a tasty soup had been revealed to him the following morning—a dead Cartha, part of a haul of prisoners as the remnants of the Merki Horde swept southwest after their defeat. That was the first time he tried to kill himself. There had been other attempts afterward. He had desperately wanted to succeed, at least at first. But now, after a year of captivity, the wish to die had flickered away. He had been tricked, but in the back of his mind he knew he would remain unbroken, as long as he did not knowingly eat of his own kind. There was something else as well now that held him. It was all so curious, this strange new emotion.

At the other side of the yurt, she was asleep, curled up in a dirty blanket, almost childlike. Strange, she is almost a child, not more than twenty or twenty-two years, and me in my fifties, he thought. He sat down by her side. She stirred in her sleep, murmured something, a troubled look wrinkling her brow. He watched her intently. She sighed, her brow unknitting, her features relaxing into untroubled sleep.

He kissed her lightly on the forehead and stood up.

How did I allow this to happen, he wondered. Never before ... why now? Was it the constant fear, the dread, a wish for some spark, some tenderness, the touch of another by your side as you stand at the edge of the abyss? He looked at her again, wondering. No, no matter where I met her—here, Rus, the States—it would have been the same, something in her pale brown features, gold almond eyes. Where were her people from, back on Earth? Now if Andrew or that damnable Emil was here, he could tell me. India, or maybe one of the heathen isles of the Pacific.

He smiled, remembering sailor stories about the tropical isles and the native girls and jumping ship never to come home. Looking at Tamira, he could understand why. And why me? Was it the fear? After all, I'm old enough to be her father. But no, it wasn't that. There was something instinctive between them, an unspoken word that could communicate volumes.

If I had met her back home, back in the States, or further back, in Germany, would I have become a soldier? Ridiculous thought. It is what I am—Hans Schuder, Sergeant Major, *bei Gott*.

So she's the one who keeps me alive now, a desire to live in hell.

She stirred again, curling up and covering her face with a nervous gesture, a whimper escaping her lips. He was tempted to kiss her lightly on the brow, to awaken her. But no, let her sleep.

Again he looked around the yurt. Why are we here? He sensed that there had been some sort of trade, of which he was a part. Otherwise why would he and hundreds of prisoners from the wars be culled out from what was left of the Merki and driven hundreds of miles to the east? This morning he had glimpsed a vast Horde encampment on the far horizon, yurts by the thousands dotting the prairie. The scene reminded him of the buffalo herds that were such a common sight on the plains.

When the two of them were led to a separate yurt, Tamira became rigid with fear that they were being set aside for the Moon Feast. He had lied to her convincingly, stilling his own conviction that they had been driven all this way just to be used for ritual torture, most likely to calm the spirit of some damnable ancestor of some petty chieftain. Perhaps it was part of the tribute that the Bantag Horde now exacted on the shattered remains of the Merki, and the bastards wanted some prisoners to roast alive to cement the deal.

He reached into the right pocket of his tattered sky-blue trousers and felt up along the reinforced waistband. The thin sliver of razor-sharp steel was still reassuringly there, tucked into its hiding place. It was the one assurance he still had that he could at least spare Tamira. If, when the bastards came back to get him there was a sense that they were to be dragged out to provide entertainment, one quick slash, a momentary flicker of pain, a look in her eyes almost of thankfulness, and she at least would be spared.

Why had they even allowed her to come with him? That was a mystery as well. The bastards had no sense, no pity for any of the bonds of human affection. A couple, two pets, might be together for years, even indulged in their affection by their owner, only to be split apart forever on a whim. When the Merki had separated him off to be led away, Tamira had clung tightly to his side . . . and no one had stopped her from going along.

That alone had filled him with curiosity, and a sense of dread. He knew his status as a prisoner was of the highest. Before Tamuka, the former Qar Quarth, had disappeared, riding back westward with the few that remained loyal to him, he had promised a long and agonizing death, as befitted his rank. He had heard that the issue of his survival had even been debated by the clan chieftains who had taken him away from Tamuka's circle and then shortly afterwards sent him east with so many other prisoners of the war.

Maybe it was curiosity to see what would come next that had prevented him from simply ending Tamira's life and then taking his own. Why had they kept him alive—that alone was beyond understanding. Their hatred of Yankees, and especially of Andrew Lawrence Keane, knew no bounds. They must know that subjecting him to an agonizing death, and then making sure that Andrew knew about it, would be a way of striking back.

He closed his eyes and again allowed "the dream" to form . . .

They were on campaign—sometimes it was here, other times back on Earth, but everyone was there . . . Pat, Emil, and, of course, Andrew. It was after a fight, the tension easing off, the bottle of whiskey sliding back and forth across the table. Pat would tell the latest joke, usually about some less than virtuous innkeeper's wife; Emil would complain about the drinking even as he sipped from his glass; and Andrew—Andrew would sit quietly, the occasional flicker of a smile appearing as their gazes locked.

Always there would be that unspoken something, a feeling, an understanding beyond words . . . again we've survived and won. And something much beyond that, a camaraderie, a trust, a love that would never be voiced but that was a bond unlike all others.

Funny, he's still a boy to me in a way, Hans thought with a smile as "the dream" took on a reality that blocked out all others. The memories swirled like images in a kaleidoscope. Andrew, the scared young professor who had gone to see the elephant and had become a leader of a nation on this strange, accursed world. And I remember him when he didn't even know how to get a company from column into line. He chuckled softly at the thought of it, their old Colonel Estes swearing at Andrew, "Gods! What am I to do with a book-learning professor?" Andrew taking it, eyes straight ahead, the crestfallen look emerging only when he thought he was alone.

Pity him I did at first, figured he'd get killed in the first fight, like so many young lieutenants.

Hans let the memories engulf him. Andrew in his first fight at Antietam, the regiment trapped in the West Woods. At that moment I could see the fighter instinct behind the bookish features and I knew, Hans thought with a smile, I knew what he could be. That grand, glorious moment at Gettysburg, when Andrew assumed command of the regiment and held the rear guard as First Corps retreated . . . and losing his arm in the process. Wilderness, that nightmare morning at Cold Harbor, the trenches of Petersburg, they were still real inside, as if only this morning.

Antietam—why, Antietam must be ten years ago now, nearly eight of those years here on this world. Back home, 1872. That would make Andrew almost forty, and me halfway between fifty and sixty. And all that had happened in those eight years. Coming through the Tunnel of Light, the rebellion of the Rus, first against their own nobility and then the First War of the Horde, that one against the Tugars. Then the war against the Cartha, followed by the Second War of the Horde, the bitter, nearly yearlong struggle against the Merki.

And what since then, since the day I was captured, more than a year ago and at least two thousand miles away? The vast distance of time and space weighed down on him yet again, and sighing, he tasted the gruel. No, it was just grain, mullet, no meat in it.

He heard a rustling behind him, the sound of the curtain door to the yurt being pulled aside. He did not bother to turn around. Let the bastard announce his presence. Hans continued to eat, waiting, while his left hand slipped into his pocket, fingers touching the hilt of the blade.

"Yankee, stand up."

The words were in Rus. Surprised, Hans looked up. The warrior was dressed as a Bantag, wearing the chain mail jerkin favored by the southern clans, his dark scarlet cape reaching to his ankles. What was startling, though, was that this creature's face was clean-shaven, revealing the flat face, high cheekbones, and mashed-in nose of a Horde rider. Hans examined him cautiously, and then his eyes dropped to what the Bantag was holding.

The Bantag chuckled softly at Hans's startled expression.

"Come to your feet. I am Ha'ark Kathul, Qar Qarth of the Bantag Horde."

The words were not quite a command, but they did carry an insistence that expected instant obedience. Hans, grinning softly, did not move.

"I could have you killed for such insolence."

"Go ahead—it'd be a pleasant end to the day," Hans replied coolly.

Ha'ark threw back his head and laughed. "You aren't like the other cattle I've seen."

"I'm not cattle," Hans replied slowly, his voice filled with a barely concealed rage. "I am a soldier of the Army of the Potomac, by God."

The Bantag did not reply, studying him carefully, and then to Hans's amazement the warrior came forward and sat down by his side.

"I wanted to meet you."

"The feeling is not mutual."

The Bantag leaned forward, his breath washing over Hans. "Don't bandy insults about, cattle. You live or die only by my wishes, and I can choose any manner of death."

Hans fixed him with an icy glare. Even the fact that he looked into the Bantag's eyes was cause enough for death, but he had a sense that at the moment it might have quite the opposite effect.

Ha'ark looked over at Tamira, who was still asleep, and Hans moved ever so imperceptibly to slip the knife out, ready to go for the Bantag or, if need be, to turn on Tamira.

"Your mate?"

Hans looked at him coldly. "Wife—there's a difference."

The Bantag looked at him appraisingly, a wolfish grin flickering across his features.

"Let us understand something here. To everyone outside this yurt you are a pet, cattle that could be consumed at any time. I don't necessarily see you in that light. I see you as a warrior, the same as I."

Hans wanted to come back with a sarcastic reply but held his tongue.

"If you cooperate, your"—he hesitated as if trying to remember the word—"wife will be spared the slaughter pit. Do you understand me?"

Hans said nothing, trying not to let the bastard sense the flood of emotion and relief that the comment had unleashed.

"I see I've got your attention," the Bantag announced softly.

"Where did you learn Rus?"

"From two of your cattle. The one called Hinsen and another that we recently took."

Hans spat angrily on the floor at the mention of the traitor who had gone into the service of the Merki before the Cartha War.

"I share the same opinion; he is a sniveling coward."

"But useful to you," and as he spoke Hans looked again at the rifle that was still in the Bantag's right hand.

Ha'ark smiled.

"When I came to this world, I brought this with me. Care to examine it?"

Shocked, Hans looked straight at the Bantag. "Came to this world? You're not a Bantag?"

A ripple of laughter greeted the question.

"I came here as you did, through the Tunnel of Light."

"Not of this world, then?" Hans asked softly. There was a momentary flood of relief. Perhaps, just perhaps. He said he was not of this world, and yet he is the Qar Qarth, ruler of the Bantag Horde. Was there a hope, that he would see everything differently, see that humans were not cattle? But then he looked at the weapon. The rifle was heavy, built to fit a Horde Rider, with a barrel and stock nearly six feet in length. But what caught his attention was the working mechanism at the breech.

He looked back at Ha'ark.

"Go on, you may hold it."

Hans hefted the weapon and felt a surging thrill. Again he had a gun in his hand, and for a fleeting instant he felt free, but then he looked at Ha'ark again and saw the cool gaze of appraisal and wariness, ready to spring if he made the slightest mistake. Hans held the weapon up to examine it. It was heavy, at least eighteen to twenty pounds, but he knew the weight was a matter of scale. For a Horde warrior the gun would be a comfortable weapon to hold. He examined the breech; it reminded him of a Prussian needle gun, and taking hold of the bolt, he worked it back. A bright shell casing ejected onto the floor of the yurt, and Hans slammed the bolt forward. He stole another look at the Bantag. For the first time since his capture he had a real weapon in his hand. If only the barrel were shorter, I could swing it around . . .

"Don't even consider it," the Bantag replied smoothly. "Though I do want to speak to you, I'll kill you if you make a wrong move."

Hans saw the glint of a dagger in the Bantag's left hand, poised to strike.

Hans smiled.

He slid the breech open again. It worked smoothly. It was precision work, and he sensed it was far better than anything that could currently be made by the Rus. For that matter it was better than anything he had seen on Earth. The thought was chilling . . . the bastards are ahead of us with this. What else do they know that we don't?

With the breech open, he lifted the gun up, turning it to look straight down the barrel. By the dim reflected light shining into the breech he saw the tight, spiraling bands of rifling. The bands were smaller, tighter than in a Springfield, or his old Sharps carbine. Watching Ha'ark, he carefully lifted the gun, with the breech open, to his shoulder, and sighted down it. In spite of the weight, the gun had a good balance to it, and he aimed at the flickering lamp hanging in the center of the yurt. There was a single levered rear sight, and as he squinted, he realized that the sight was an adjustable peephole that could slide up and down for range. The only weapon he had ever seen with a peephole rear sight was the precision Sharps rifle issued to Berdan's Sharpshooters.

The writing etched into the rear sight was unintelligible, but he supposed that the gradient markings would each represent roughly a hundred yards, since trajectory had to be adjusted at approximately that distance to compensate for the drop of a bullet.

"Strange. The gravity must be slightly less on this

planet," Ha'ark said. "I've noticed the sights aren't quite accurate."

Hans looked at him in surprise. He had heard Ferguson talk about that and remembered feeling a bit lighter when they had first arrived on this world. But the thought had never concerned him.

Hans laid the gun down on the floor of the yurt and then picked up the bullet. It was definitely brass cartridge, caliber seemed to be around a fifty, but the bullet was hard and pointed. He sensed it carried a lot more power to it than the old minié ball of the Springfield.

"You brought the gun from where?" Hans asked.

"My own world."

Hans said nothing.

"That is why, in part, I wanted to speak to you. I, like you, am not of this world. I came through the Tunnel of Light."

"And you had this gun?"

"A soldier as well, though at the time I did not want to be. And you?"

"A soldier. How we got here ..." he shrugged, "I don't know. Do you?"

Hans was surprised he was even speaking to the creature before him. Maybe it was the simple joy of hearing a familiar tongue again. German was still his native language, and seventeen years in the States had made English far more familiar, but with Rus being the common speech, he found that that language had become the one that he finally thought in. What was disturbing was that of late he had acquired enough skill with the language of the Hordes that on occasion he now dreamed in it. It was a delight not to have to articulate his thoughts in a language that struck him as being nothing more than grunts and animal growls. To hear someone of the Horde speak Rus was indeed curious, the language coming out rough and guttural.

"I don't know either," Ha'ark replied. "I was hoping you could explain."

"Why, do you want to go home?"

Ha'ark leaned back and laughed deeply.

"Home. To what? To be a student, or worst yet, a drafted soldier? Here—why, here I am Kathul. Do you know the word?"

Hans shook his head.

"The Redeemer, the one of prophecy."

Hans felt a chill at the way he said it.

"No. I'll stay. But if I could find a way back, there are things I need."

"Such as?"

The Bantag smiled as if deciding whether to share a secret or not.

"What I would give for a book on refining. Or even some good tungsten steel tool bits. As for engines, I never could understand how internal combustion worked, though one of my Companions worked on—what is the word you use?—railroads."

Hans was silent.

"So we do know steam. Tell me, did you have flying machines on your world?"

Hans felt a cold chill creep into his soul. "Of course."

The Bantag smiled again and shook his head. "I doubt it. Your machines are generations behind what I knew. There are artifacts here on this world, however, that are useful. I think the ancients, before the fall, even had atomic power. At least that's what I suspect from the description of the engines the Merki used for their flying machines. We're digging in gravesites right now for more of these ancient devices. Unless the fuel has decayed, they should still be useful for flyers."

He stopped for a moment. "Atomic? Do you understand the word?"

"Who doesn't?"

"Then explain it."

Hans fell silent, angry with himself. Whatever it was this creature was rambling about, Hans knew that he had already revealed too much. He felt he should say nothing more, but his curiosity compelled him not simply to turn away and retreat into silence.

The Bantag chuckled. "You're not revealing anything I didn't suspect. Your friend Hinsen told me everything of your world. Primitive. If we could but use a portal from my world to yours we would squash you."

"I doubt it."

"By defending yourselves with what?" Ha'ark laughed. "Rifled muskets against machine guns. Airships against jets and rockets. Do you even know what a radio is?"

"Go ahead and try it," Hans spat, feeling increasingly angry, as if this creature were taunting him with his ignorance.

The Bantag smiled and shook his head. "Don't worry. There are other things to do first."

"Such as?"

"End this war between you"—he hesitated for a moment—"you humans and us."

Hans felt a surge of hope that he knew had to be misplaced. There would never be an end to the war until one race, or the other, was annihilated.

"How?"

"Maybe an accommodation could be made—a division, perhaps."

"I doubt it."

"Why?"

"First of all, why should we?" Hans replied coldly. "We all but destroyed the Tugars, and the Merki were shattered as well. What's left?"

"The Bantag, with over sixty umens. The Harangi to the south of the Bantag, with another forty umens. That's a million warriors we can put in the field."

"We defeated forty umens of the Merki."

"And nearly destroyed yourselves in the process. Even now your people are still recovering and, I hear, are divided as well."

In his year of captivity Hans had not heard a single word of what had happened to his old comrades. He tried not to show interest. The Bantag smiled.

"Curious, aren't you? Maybe later I'll share more. For that matter, you might even see your friends before you die."

"That doesn't matter to me. I assumed I was dead the moment I was taken prisoner. Hope of a different ending is a fool's dream."

"You know, I might actually like you."

Hans found himself weakening. He felt almost as if he were talking with another soldier rather than a hated enemy.

"I'll grant that if those barbarians you called the Bantag marched against you as they were, they'd most likely lose. But"—and Ha'ark patted the rifle on his lap—"that's changed."

"The Merki had weapons like ours."

"Primitive, and besides, not enough. Things have changed since I've come. We have a factory east of here, turning out three hundred rifles a week."

"Like yours?" Hans asked cautiously.

"No, muzzle loaders like yours. We used a Merki weapon as a pattern, but I think we'll be up to breechloaders in a year or so." He snorted with disdain. "Damn primitives, these tribes. Taking them over was child's play. They feared me. I spouted some ancient legends about the Redeemer, killed half a dozen, and was soon Qar Qarth. That was the easy part. Getting them to work, another thing altogether."

"So you used humans."

"You know there's a city of them east of here, Yellow-skinned, call themselves Chin. A million in one city. We promised them exemption from the feast if they'd do my bidding. They're excellent workers. But my gun—that's beyond them for the moment, at least. So I drew on older designs. Breechloaders next. We have the weapon that was taken with you."

Hans thought fondly of his cherished Sharps carbine and unconsciously he flexed his hand, as if the reassuring weight of the gun was again balanced in his grip. Ha'ark smiled. "The same with artillery, even airships," he continued. "Steam power as well. Not very efficient at the moment, but we're learning. Even showed them how to making a printing press, so technical books can be printed, and harvesting machines, so more laborers can work in the factories I plan."

"So what do you want of me? If it's understanding machines, I know nothing, but even if I did, you can go to hell."

"Spoken like a soldier. No, not that, though it was suggested that if we slowly burned you to death you'd talk. A waste, though."

"So what do you want?"

"You will be, how do they say it, my *ragma*."

Hans stiffened angrily. "A pet? Be damned to you."

Ha'ark extended his hand. "A poor choice of words. Let us say 'companion,' then. We'll talk at times."

"You'll get no help from me."

"Most likely not. But I would like to ask a question."

"What?"

"Tell me about Keane."

Hans smiled. "You'll never beat him. No one ever has. I should know—I was with him from the beginning. A dozen battles in our war back on Earth, in every campaign here until I was captured. Even if he knew he was facing final defeat, he'd spit in your eye and die fighting."

"You're proud of him, aren't you?"

"You're damn right I'm proud of him," Hans snapped.

"I understand you were as his father to him. You trained him in war. Perhaps in knowing you I can know him."

Ha'ark smiled and Hans suddenly sensed that perhaps he had said too much.

"Come with me."

Hans looked at Tamira, who was still fast asleep.

"She's safe," Ha'ark said softly. "You are now of my circle, and so is she."

Hans tried not to let his relief show.

Ha'ark stood up and motioned Hans to follow. Stepping out of the yurt, Hans squinted from being shut up for so long. The evening sun was low on the horizon, bathing the rolling steppe in a blood-red light. The encampment of the Bantag stretched to the far horizon, coils of smoke wafting up from the dung campfires. The scent of roasting meat drifted on the breeze. He had long ago learned to suppress the horror that the smell engendered. In the distance he could hear the plaintive screams of someone about to be slaughtered. Ha'ark had momentarily put him at his ease, but the sound of the cries caused an icy chill to run through the aging sergeant major.

"As long as that continues," Hans snarled bitterly, "the war between us will be to the death."

Ha'ark looked at Hans, puzzled, not understanding at first. The screams grew louder and the realization dawned.

"Maybe someday it will change. I hear the Tugar have forsworn human flesh. Some are even riding with your Keane."

Hans shook his head and mumbled a curse. The idea was absurd.

Two guards approached, each leading a horse, and to Hans's surprise one was offered to him. He reached up, struggling to get in the saddle of the Clydesdale-like mount. It felt good to have a horse beneath him again, and for an instant he almost felt free.

I could spur it and be gone, he thought, the vision forming in his mind of galloping free across the steppe, heading north and west. But then the memory of Tamira seized him, and he felt a wave of guilt that even for an instant he had imagined abandoning her. Not a chance in a million anyhow that he could escape, he realized as well, but at least for a moment, he might be free.

"You won't get fifty strides," Ha'ark announced calmly. "And besides, what of your companion?"

Hans looked over at him, startled. Can this one read thoughts, he wondered. Andrew believed they could. Was it true? He looked at Ha'ark, who smiled cryptically.

Hans followed Ha'ark's lead and they set off at a leisurely canter, weaving through the maze of yurts. More than once they passed a family clan sitting around a fire, and in more than one boiling pot Hans saw part of a human body.

At the approach of the Qar Qarth, all rose and then bowed low, many openly curious at the sight of a human riding.

"They're primitives," Ha'ark announced.

"You hold them in contempt?"

"No. Not really. More in tolerance. According to our legends, the ones of my world, these are the ancestors, who once bestrode the universe—until the Great War. They were the builders of the Tunnels that let one leap between worlds. It was a shock to discover them reverted, decadent. But we shall raise them up to their former glory once again."

The way Ha'ark had said, "We shall raise them up" had a certain chill to it. Hans knew that Ha'ark was not speaking in his native tongue, but the use of the plural was unsettling.

Once out of the camp, Ha'ark urged his mount to a gallop and Hans followed. The surging of the horse beneath him and the wind in his hair set his pulse to pounding. He closed his eyes for a moment, and he was twenty-five years younger, galloping across the Texas plains, chasing Comanche in his first charge. The vast steppe rolled by beneath him. Cresting a low hill, they galloped down into a hollow that was already filling with the damp mist of early evening and then back up another rise. Now Ha'ark gained the crest ahead of him, and reined in, his mount rearing up. Hans came to a stop beside him. He was about to speak, to make a comment about the pleasure of riding, when he felt his heart constrict.

Ha'ark smiled at him.

Hans looked disbelievingly at the thousands of humans who labored in the valley below. Then in the distance came a low mournful sound that chilled his blood.

"You're building a railroad," Hans whispered.

Ha'ark again smiled. "Twenty miles already back to the city of the Chin. Thousands of humans are laboring upon it in the mines and foundries, turning out rails, cutting ties, building bridges. We're laying a quarter mile of track a day."

Ha'ark edged his mount in closer to Hans.

"It was the one advantage you had in your last war that the Merki lacked. You could move strategically by rail. You could support an army hundreds of miles away. The Merki were dependent on the grass around them, on what food they could harvest within a few days' march. Your Keane chose his ground well to fight upon and burned everything as he retreated. Now, that will not help."

Hans sat meditatively, watching the labor gangs working under the threat of Bantag overseers. He found an old craving coming back and wished more than anything for a good chew. Ha'ark extended his hand to Hans. In it was a tightly bound twist of tobacco. Amazed, Hans looked at his companion, who smiled.

"At times I can," Ha'ark replied coolly. "The Merki had the tradition of the *tu* and the *ka*. The spirit walker and the warrior spirit. If we practice, some of us do have the ability to see as I now see you."

Hans felt a ripple of fear. Was all that he was thinking, the fear created at the sight of the railroad, the sense of doom it created—had Ha'ark picked up on that as well? He hesitated for an instant and then reached for the plug, nodding his thanks as he took a bite. The jolt of nicotine made him light-headed for a moment, and he could not stifle a sigh of contentment. An old instinct to offer a chew to Andrew momentarily caused him to forget where he was, and he almost extended his hand to Ha'ark but then stopped. The Qar Qarth was looking straight into his eyes.

"Why?" Hans asked softly.

"Just curious about you," Ha'ark replied calmly. "You were one of the designers of the defeat of the Merki. I paid well for the trade of you and the other survivors taken in the war against you and the Cartha, nearly five thousand in all."

Hans spit a stream of tobacco juice onto the ground.

"Merki. Dumb bastards."

"But we're not," Ha'ark said, his voice now edged with a brittle hardness.

"Why are you even bothering? Hell, where we live is fifteen hundred, maybe two thousand miles away. Can't you let it be?"

Hans was afraid that his tone had a note of pleading in it. He fell silent and chewed, staring straight at Ha'ark.

"You're planning to renew the war."

"When we are ready," Ha'ark replied calmly.

"To what end?"

Ha'ark laughed and reined his horse around in front of Hans. "First you defeat the Tugars. Unthinkable: A despised race rises up, in less than two seasons arms itself, goes to war, and defeats nearly twenty umens of a proud Horde. That should have been the alarm. At that moment Bantag and Merki should have forgotten their differences, should have prepared, and should have eradicated you. But the fools left themselves divided. I have studied the campaign the Merki launched. If but ten umens of the Bantag had swept up from the south, between what you call the Inland and the Great Seas, Roum would have been flanked from the south. You could not have held two fronts. You would have been destroyed."

"But you didn't, and we won."

Ha'ark nodded. "You wouldn't have if I had been there."

He held up his rifle.

"I understand this. I understand where it comes from. I know where you come from. Two, perhaps three generations at most behind my own world. But fifty, a hundred generations ahead of what these savages I now rule could ever dream of. I know the rule of it all, that when a superior culture meets an inferior one, the inferior one is doomed either to adapt or to die. The choice is that simple: Either you will die or we will die."

Hans stared at Ha'ark. He wanted to tell the bastard to go to hell, but he knew that Andrew would handle it differently, would want him to handle it differently. He took a deep breath.

"It could have been different. It doesn't have to be that way even now. If you saw a race that slaughtered your own children and devoured them, would you not fight to the death?"

Ha'ark nodded slowly in agreement. "Of course. Ask me to change them? Impossible."

"Then it will be war. That abomination we will never accept."

"Don't you think I know that?"

"You are Qar Qarth. You can command anything and it shall be so."

"Not all things. I sit lightly upon the golden throne. Many of the clan Qarths already doubt that I am the Kathul."

Hans continued to stare at him.

"A prophecy of the Hordes says that a leader will come through the Tunnel of Light, sent by the Ancestors, to return his people to the stars."

"And are you this Kathul?"

Ha'ark smiled and Hans felt distant and alone. He believes it, Hans realized. Now we've got a religious fanatic to deal with.

"I'm not a fanatic," Ha'ark whispered and Hans averted his eyes, a response that elicited a soft, growling chuckle.

"What do you want from me?"

Ha'ark sighed and leaned forward in the saddle. He motioned for the tobacco plug and Hans offered it. It felt so damn strange, a ritual he had practiced with Andrew for years, repeated now—he wondered if Ha'ark did it for just that reason.

Ha'ark took the plug, bit off a chew, and handed it back.

"We have a similar leaf on my world. It's called *lakh gudak*, soldier's weed. More potent than yours, it stills nerves yet keeps you awake for the long night watches."

"So there's war on your home world?"

Ha'ark nodded, his gaze distant. "Wars you could little dream of. Constant war, dynastic struggles, war just because we feel we need one. Weapons you could not even imagine, though the ones you carried are the beginnings of them."

Ha'ark chewed, looking off to the horizon as if lost in thought. "This world, the wars here. Stuff of legends, child's play. I want you to run my factories for turning out iron and steel. You are respected and known. You can organize and lead."

Hans snorted and spat on the ground. "Like hell."

Ha'ark nodded and motioned for Hans to follow him. He set off at a trot along the low ridgeline. As they rode Hans noticed the rail line under construction. It struck him as something right out of the old etchings of slaves working on some wonder of the ancient world. Thousands of laborers dressed in rags moved in slow, shuffling gangs, flanked by Horde overseers. Whip cracks snapped the air. Even as he watched, a slave faltered. A guard walked over and in a casual gesture picked the man up by the throat with one hand. The rest of the work gang continued on, carrying a rail, their eyes averted. The guard shook the man several times, but there was only a feeble response. With frightening ease, the guard snapped the man's neck, then threw him to one side.

Hans had slowed down to watch. Though he had seen such acts hundreds of times in the last year, he felt rage building within him. He saw that Ha'ark was looking at him.

"To help continue that?" Hans snarled. "Let's just be done with it, you bastard."

Ha'ark motioned for Hans to follow. At first he refused. Ha'ark swung his rifle around.

"Go ahead and be done with it."

"And what of your mate?"

Hans looked at him silently. We're doomed anyhow. We're fooling ourselves to think differently.

"Come. Indulge me and then decide."

Ha'ark turned around and continued his ride. Hans looked down at the body and saw that the guard was staring straight at him, casually flicking his whip, letting its coils drift back and forth across the twisted corpse. Tamira . . . and he found yet again the bitter conflict, the sense of love, countered by something edging on bitter resentment of her, for his life, and that what he would do with it was no longer completely his to decide.

He jerked his bridle sharply, and flinging the foulest of curses in English at the Bantag guard, he galloped to catch up with Ha'ark. At the top of the next rise Ha'ark had already reined in. Before him was arrayed the center of the vast Bantag host. As the sun touched the horizon, all faced the blood-red light of the sunset. The call of the chanters echoed on the breeze, and Hans felt a corkscrew shiver run down his back. The steppe, as far as he could see, was filled with Bantag warriors raising their swords heavenward to catch the last light of the dying day. Ha'ark, as was appropriate for his rank, remained astride his mount, and rather than a sword he held his rifle aloft, an ululation erupting from his throat and mingling with the cries of his host.

As the sun disappeared, all now turned eastward and within seconds the first faint sliver of a moon broke the horizon, followed immediately by a second moon, appearing only a hand's span to the right. Wild cheering broke out, with the strange accompaniment of a steam whistle and a booming cannon.

Ha'ark said to Hans, "It is the night of the Moon Feast. You know that."

Hans nodded.

"Shall I tell you the names of the prisoners I bartered for with the Merki?"

"No need to," Hans replied, knowing what was coming.

"More than fifty Rus from your army, taken at Hispania and in the skirmishing that followed the Merki withdrawal. We have more than four thousand

Cartha." He hesitated. "And you and your—what did you call her—your wife."

Hans watched him as he continued. "I have Hinsen, but I know you'd love to see him go to the Moon Feast. As for the others, the offer is simple. Many of them worked in the iron factories, a few even on the railroads and in armories. We've even taken half a hundred prisoners of our own, in skirmishes with your army in the lands between what you call the Great Sea and the Inland Sea. I promise every one of them life for as long as they are willing to work."

"Or?"

"They will go to the Moon Feast this very evening if you refuse to cooperate."

Hans sat in silence, his heart torn. If it were only himself, he knew the answer: He would have almost welcomed it. Why did Tamira come into my life? he wondered. There was a small part of him that still thought that the lovely young woman now asleep in the yurt must somehow have a pact with the Horde, that she was sent to him for just this purpose, to seduce him. But he knew that could not be. He had looked too often into her eyes, had held her close to him too many nights, not to know her love and to know his own as well, a love he had never dreamed would come to him.

But we could be free. There would be only the moment of final terror for her, and we would be free, rather than being among the living dead.

"All of them," Ha'ark said again. "I understand that at the funeral of the Merki Qar Qarth you witnessed the slaughter of a hundred thousand and you alone were spared."

Hans tried to force the memory away . . . the blood-filled pit, the insane hysteria of killing, and I alone the Lazarus to remember it.

"You will see it again, Sergeant. Know that I can

get others to do the labor, so nothing will change. The machines will be built, the war will come, and you will watch the agonizing torture of your wife. And I promise you, when it is revealed who you are and who she is, there are many who will delight in dragging out the torment till dawn."

As if to add weight to his argument, a hysterical scream sounded from the encampment below—the first victim being dragged to the pit.

"You've not seen a Bantag Moon Feast, have you, Sergeant?"

"The Merki do it well enough."

"They do some extra forms of entertainment in my Horde," Ha'ark said quietly. "They believe that the torment, the screaming, the struggle, make the meat taste better when it finally comes time to cut open the skull and consume the brain. Slow roasting over a simmering fire for half the night while still alive is the preferred method to start the festivities. Your wife has such lovely brown skin, it would be a shame to see it roasted black while she was still alive."

Hans looked bitterly at Ha'ark, who was staring straight at him. "Bastards, you are all bastards," Hans snarled.

"Decide, human. I have no more time. And remember, even if you die, nothing will change for me. Others will simply fill your place. The machines will be built. But for you, your wife—the agony this night will be beyond your worst imaginings."

More screams came from the camp, each one tearing into his soul. He could somehow sense that Tamira must now be awake, huddled in the yurt, terrified. The thought of looking into her eyes as she died in agony was more than he could bear.

"Food. I want adequate food for the workers," he said gruffly.

The thin crease of a smile lit Ha'ark's features.

"One day in seven to rest. You'll get more work

that way in the long run. Proper shelter, barracks for my people to live in. And exemption from the Moon Feast and, for that matter, from the pits at all times. If they work for you they live, if they have children the mothers are exempt from work while pregnant and the children are too until old enough."

"Agreed."

Hans sagged forward, feeling sick. They had finally broken him.

"And one final thing," his tormentor said. "We will talk, from time to time, human. There is something about you I like."

"The feeling is not mutual."

"But still we will talk. You choose well, human. It is better than having to kill you."

"So others will die in our place tonight."

"They are not your concern. Fifty thousand will die this night of feasting. It could have been you, your companions; now it is someone else. You will see tomorrow, as will the woman who waits for you." He paused for a moment. "And an old friend as well."

And others will die in my place, Hans thought bitterly.

"There is no room for pity in this world," Ha'ark snapped. "You have chosen to live, to choose otherwise is the act of a fool. Go and hold your woman tonight and know she will not scream in agony."

Ha'ark reined his horse around, and then almost as an afterthought he extended his hand, offering the plug of tobacco again. Hans took it.

"You know the way back. Now go. We will talk more another time. Tomorrow you will go to the place where the new factory is to be built. You and your people will build it and make it run. Do that and you will live. Fail me and . . ." He nodded down the hill, where the feasting had already begun.

With a soft laugh Ha'ark rode off into the gathering darkness, and half a dozen guards, who throughout the conversation had remained at a discreet distance, fell in around him.

Hans was tempted to throw the plug of tobacco to the ground but instead put it in his pocket. With his head low, he turned his mount, choking back tears of humiliation and rage.

"Hans?"

Startled, he looked up. "My God! Gregory?"

A lean and battered figure, dressed in the baggy white tunic and trousers of the Rus infantry, stepped from the side of his yurt and approached him nervously.

"Sir, is it really you?"

Hans slid off his horse and with hand extended raced up to the boy who had once been his chief of staff for Third Corps but was even better known as a budding Shakespearean actor, a Rus soldier who had become enamored of a copy of the plays brought from another world.

Gregory came to attention and started to salute, but Hans grabbed his hand, clutching it tight.

"Son, how the hell?"

Gregory shook his head. "I was taken about six months ago. We were running patrols out, pushing south and east, probing to find out whatever happened to the Merki and also trying to find out where these bastards were."

He hung his head, as if ashamed. "My unit, we fell right into a trap. It got wiped out, sir. I wish I'd been killed." His voice started to falter. "I woke up after the fight and they had me. I had a hundred men with me, sir. All of them . . ."

"Nothing to be ashamed of, son," Hans replied. "The same with me."

"They took me to this Ha'ark, or Redeemer, or whatever it is he thinks he is. He treated me well enough, sir, just wanted to learn the language. He told me this morning I might see you, but I didn't believe it until they brought me here a couple of minutes ago."

"This might not sound right," Hans replied eagerly, "but I'm almost glad to see you."

Gregory tried to smile.

"There's a couple other men here from Rus. Alexi Davidovich, he used to be an engineer, was in my unit—they got him as well. I also saw Hinsen. I never knew him before he deserted, but I kind of figured out it was him. He's in good with them, has his own yurt, a horse, even women. It'd be worth dying just to get him."

Hans shook his head. "Let it go. He'll get his reward. The main thing is to stay alive for now."

"What will they do to us?"

"In the end, they'll kill us," Hans said quietly, and he looked at his yurt, thinking of her inside. "But for now, we survive. We survive and find a way to escape. We have to get back to tell Andrew, even if it takes years to do it."

Chapter One

"Hans!"

Colonel Andrew Lawrence Keane sat bolt upright in his bed, his sheets soaked with sweat.

"Andrew, you all right?"

For a moment he couldn't speak. The image had been so clear.

"Andrew?"

"All right, Pat."

Andrew swung out from his bunk and stood up, shifting his feet to maintain balance as the train thundered around a sharp curve.

"It was Hans, wasn't it?"

Pat O'Donald, commander of the First Army of the Republic, sat up and tossed his blankets aside. Andrew nodded.

"Thought so. The old bugger came to me in my dreams as well." Sighing, Pat slipped out of the bunk. "Could use a spot of the cruel right now. Stills the nerves of an old soldier."

"I was thinking the same."

Andrew walked down the swaying corridor and stepped into the back parlor of his command car. Fortunately the room was empty. The staff was sleeping soundly in the next car forward. Andrew sat down on a hard-back bench while Pat threw a shovelful of coal into the stove and stoked it. Andrew started to shiver and Pat, seeing his discomfort, went back up to the bunks and returned with Andrew's sky-blue cape, which he draped over his shoulders.

Andrew nodded his thanks, wishing he had put his jacket on, but he hadn't wanted to deal with it. It had taken him a long time to get used to the fact that with only one arm, putting on a jacket could be something of a bother. At home Kathleen always helped him to dress, an almost comforting ritual, but he hated to impose on Pat, or anyone else, especially in the middle of the night. Pat next handed Andrew his glasses, which he worked open with his one hand and put on. Not being able to see, even when sitting in a darkened room, bothered him.

Pat settled down beside him and pulled a flask of vodka from his hip pocket, uncorked it, and ceremoniously passed it to Andrew.

"For Hans, God bless him."

"For Hans," Andrew whispered, and raising the flask, he took a long pull, grimacing as the fiery liquid burned his throat. He handed the flask back to Pat, who seemed to be praying. The old artilleryman quickly made the sign of the cross, raised the flask, and took a long pull himself.

"If Doctor Weiss gets up and sees you doing that on an empty stomach," Andrew said, "we'll both be in for it."

"I'm already up."

Emil Weiss, chief surgeon of the armies, stepped into the parlor, wearing a dressing gown and a nightcap. Yawning, he went over to the stove and opened the lid of the coffee pot to sniff its contents. Emil poured a steaming cup and sat down by Andrew. After sampling the brew, he wordlessly upended Pat's flask into his cup, then took another long sip.

"Almost like the old days," Emil grumbled. "Hard to believe it's been more than four years since our last campaign."

"We were dreaming of Hans," Andrew announced quietly.

"And?"

Andrew sighed and looked out the window at the steppe rolling by, shimmering silver beneath the glow of the twin moons. After the disaster to the Third Corps in the Battle of the Potomac, he had always assumed that Hans had died fighting. But since then there had been disquieting rumors. A Cartha merchant reporting seeing him, and several escaped slaves of the Merki and one from the Bantag came bearing reports of a "Yankee." It was well known that the traitor Hinsen had gone into the service of the Bantag, and Andrew always preferred to believe that such reports were about him. But the last escapee to come through the lines had insisted that the "Yankee's" name was "Ghanz." Given the guttural pronunciations of the Horde language, he could easily see that as a corruption of his mentor's name.

"He's dead, Andrew. I assumed that on the day he was lost," Emil said coldly. "It was the best way to think of him."

"I never could. He has drifted in my dreams for four years now. But tonight it was stronger. I saw him in what looked like hell, flames all around him." Andrew lowered his head, his voice thick. "He was in hell and alive."

The low, mournful whistle of the train interrupted his thoughts. He turned to look out the window as they thundered across a bridge and past a station. Village lights whisked by.

"Where are we?" Emil asked.

Andrew strained to see the station sign, but it shot past in the shadows. "I think we're out of Roum. Could be Asgard."

Pat grinned and stood up to look out the window. "Now there's folks who know how to brew beer."

"Barbarians," Emil sniffed.

"Good fighters," Andrew replied. "Damn, this is a strange world. Descendants of ancient Germany next to Romans, and medieval Japan eight hundred miles ahead. How many damn gates were there back home?"

"Well, the Vikings must have come through the same one we did, down near Bermuda," Emil said. "There's the one in the Mediterranean—that explains the Romans and Carthaginians, Egyptians and Greeks. The one that got the Rus, that's beyond me. It could have been a weird one that opened up only once. I've even been thinking that maybe there's only one, somewhere out in space above our world. As the world rotates on its axis, the gate above is pointed at different places."

Pat looked at him wide-eyed. "In space, you say. Why, what would keep it up?"

"It's orbiting."

"Don't be foolish. There's nothing out there except the stars. How could anyone get something up there? You're daft."

Andrew was barely listening as Emil and Pat launched into an argument about the Tunnels while finishing off the rest of the vodka.

Damn, how I miss the old days, Hans, Andrew thought sadly. You'd be sitting in the corner, matching Pat drink for drink, usually saying nothing, just watching, smiling occasionally, but always thinking.

The old days ... Funny, the old days were years of unrelenting fear, staring disaster in the face and knowing that you didn't stand a chance of survival. Of the more than five hundred men who had come through the Tunnels into this world, members of the old Thirty-fifth Maine, Forty-fourth New York Artillery, and the crew of the *Ogunquit*, fewer than two hundred were still alive. And as for the Rus who had started the human rebellion on this planet, more than half were dead.

"Strange," Andrew whispered.

"What?" Emil asked, breaking away from his argument with Pat, which was being expressed with an increasingly choice selection of obscenities.

"Oh, just that we look back now on the wars and somehow miss them."

Emil nodded sagely. "I guess we're getting older. Hell, even Pat here is starting to lose his blessed red hair for gray."

Pat stroked his heavy beard, which was now peppered with long streaks of white, and laughed. "Ah, but the lasses still love it."

"When are you ever going to settle down and get respectable?" Emil asked.

"Never! And have three squawking young ones like Andrew here? No wonder he wanted to go on this inspection tour."

Andrew smiled. Every minute away from Kathleen and the three little ones was a torture to him. No, it wasn't to escape that he had come ... it was to find something again.

"Do you miss the old times, Pat?"

Pat upended his flask after snatching it away from Emil and gave the doctor a mock angry look. He retreated to his sleeping berth and returned a minute later with a full bottle of vodka. Uncorking it, he took a long pull and then passed it over to Emil.

"Ah, now those were the days. Shielding the northern flank with Fourth Corps as we retreated. And that first day of Hispania, now there was a fight to be proud of."

"But do you miss it?"

"Guess it's the Irish in me, to be certain. I miss it, Lord, how I miss it. I miss old Hans forever chewing, and me beauties, my Napoleon twelve-pounders. Firing them in battery, ramming double canister down the throats of them heathens, now there was a moment to remember."

Andrew looked over at his old friend and smiled.

"And you, Andrew?" Emil asked quietly, his voice slurring after another drink from Pat's bottle.

"I don't know anymore," Andrew replied. "During all of it, all I wanted was an end to the fighting. Lord knows—and I can say it now, no matter what I said or did at the time—I feared that in the end we'd lose. More than anything, I fought to try and give my friends—and my Kathleen—a little more time to live, to let my daughter and now my two boys have a chance.

"But for myself . . ." He hesitated. "I felt like a sacrifice, someone to be used up for others. I never found in it the same joy you did, Pat."

"As you look back upon it now, though?" Emil pressed.

"It was easier then. There was only one focus, one goal, to make it to the next day, the next campaign. Beyond that, there was no time to think about."

"It was the preciousness of it all that I miss," Pat interjected.

Startled, Andrew stared at him.

"You know. Us being together." He fumbled for words for a moment. "It was good. We trusted each other, knew each other. Now the years are passin', new faces taking over, like Hawthorne. But I miss old Hans, I do. It's never been quite the same."

He shook his head.

"The old days were precious, they were."

All that has transpired since, Andrew thought. In the year after the end of the war, all were united by the common goal of simply getting through the winter and rebuilding. But then, somehow, it seemed to get sidetracked. The alliance with Roum, forged in blood, would endure as long as Proconsul Marcus lived. That, at least, was secure. The Cartha were a different story. In the winter after the war they endured devastating raids from the scattered bands of

Merki, who finally drifted off to the west. Fighting a regular campaign was one thing, but the army was not designed for protracted counterinsurgent warfare. A division of troops was all that could be spared to help the Cartha, and by the following spring Hamilcar severed any hope of an alliance. The Cartha, at least for now, were lost.

The dream of building a transcontinental railroad—that seemed to be dissolving as well. The line had been run nearly a thousand miles east, through the region of the Asgard, and then it came to a halt, stopped by negotiations with the next neighbors, the Nippon, and more frustratingly, the vote in Congress to cut back funding.

Now there was the constant skirmishing to the south, on the open steppe frontier between the two seas. Patrols were constantly going out from the defensive line, currently under construction where the Great Sea jutted westward, coming within a hundred fifty miles of the Inland Sea. Probing patrols of cavalry would have occasional run-ins with Bantag patrols. Never anything major—a few casualties traded on both sides—but the numbers slowly added up. Nearly five hundred dead this year alone. It reminded him so much of the Indian wars on the frontier before the Civil War. The land had once been Merki, but now the Bantag laid claim to it.

He had hoped that the Bantag would continue migrating and move on, but they were staying put, and he surmised that the reason was the Republic. They were preparing, and at some point the blow would come.

Young Admiral Bullfinch's long-coveted Second Fleet was finally coming into existence. At present it comprised only one ironclad and a newly commissioned side-wheeler gunboat, the *Petersburg*. There were half a dozen wooden three-masted sloops, which were keeping watch mainly over an estuary on the eastern shore of the sea, four hundred miles southeast of the defensive line. There was a small city at the mouth of the river, apparently occupied by Bantag, and indications of a larger town up the river, but the approach was guarded by more than a dozen galleys.

He had wanted to run a patrol up the river, if need be risk an encounter with the galleys, but the president had firmly overruled that idea. The problem was to keep the constant state of watch, to convince Congress, and now even the president, that this was not the time to let one's guard down and, more than ever, to keep pushing the railroad forward.

In the years since he had come here, the railroad had caused his first real falling-out with the president, the wily old peasant Kal. No amount of lobbying on Andrew's part regarding the military necessity of projecting a potential line of conflict as far forward as possible could sway Kal and his party from wanting to cut back on military spending and, with it, the railroad. It was now shaping up as the key issue in the fall congressional elections.

Just thinking about it gave Andrew reason to want another drink, and he reached over and took the bottle from Emil.

"Damn Congress," Andrew muttered.

Emil sat back and laughed.

"What's so damn funny?"

"Ah, the Republic. You're the one who created it here, and now that you can't get your own way, you damn them. You know, you could have made yourself dictator for life and they would have loved you for it."

Andrew looked at Emil as if he had just muttered the foulest obscenity.

"Why, he was dictator," Pat chimed in, "a regular Julius by God Caesar back during the first war. And a damn good one he was. Too bad he threw it away."

Andrew looked from one to the other and finally saw the grins of amusement.

"You're a born Republican and Abolitionist," Emil said. "Guess that's why I came to America from the old country—'cause of folks like you. If you had tried to keep it, I think I would have poisoned you."

Andrew laughed and shook his head.

"It's a soldier's prerogative to mumble against the government in private," he replied. "The best system humanity's ever created, but still, a pox on it at times. Always so damn shortsighted. We really didn't win a war, just a battle. There's still two other tribes out there, and the Merki, what's left of them, lurking on the western border. It could start again at any time."

"I bet old Grant and Lincoln back home made sure the army was treated just fine," Pat interjected.

Emil laughed and shook his head.

"I bet they don't have twenty thousand men in the army now. Unless something good got stirred up in Mexico or the Rebs decided to kick up another fuss. No, my friends, you're anachronisms once the fighting's stopped. You're dealing now with politicians and peasants, neither of which have much use for an army except when the wolf is at the door."

"Well, something is brewing," Andrew replied coldly.

"The Bantag," Pat announced, and there was an edge of hopefulness in his voice. "I tell you, I believe what that old Muzta told us, even if he is a bloody Tugar."

Andrew nodded, saying nothing. The understanding that had developed between the Tugar leader, Muzta, and Andrew was something he would never have dreamed possible. Such a strange irony, he reflected. Seven years ago they damn near destroyed us. In the war with the Merki, they actually wound up on our side. And now, because of some strange quirk of their code of honor, they actually admire me. They were drifting off on the edge of the frontier to the east, settling into a half-million-square-mile range of empty land, living by herding and, though he hated to turn a blind eye to it, by the occasional exacting of tribute from human neighbors. But there were no more slaughter pits, and Muzta was sending warnings as well that something was astir with the Bantag.

Andrew went out the back door of the train onto the platform. Overhead, the stars were obscured by the sooty plume of smoke trailing behind the locomotive as it thundered eastward.

The open steppe was gradually giving way to a scattering of trees as the rail line edged northward to skirt the fever-laden marshlands and tributaries that bordered the Great Sea to the south. Like the Inland Sea, now five hundred miles to the west, the Great Sea formed a defensive barrier to anchor a right flank on. If something should turn and come out of the east, this could be the outer defensive line this time.

In the shadows he saw villages drift past, marked by the distinctive wooden huts and feasting halls of the Asgard. They could prove tough fighters in a pinch but were totally lacking in the discipline that had been instilled in the regiments of Rus and Roum. Hans would have liked them, given their Teutonic origin from what he guessed was Roman Germania.

The door opened behind him, and Emil joined him in the chilled night air. "Come on in here, damn it, or you'll catch your death of cold."

"You really believe that?" Andrew asked.

"No, but it sounds good."

"In a minute."

"Still thinking of Hans."

"Wish he were here."

"If it's any comfort, I think he always will be."

"That's something Father Casmar would say."

"No, I don't mean it that way. I mean in you. Hans trained you, he trained most of the boys with the old Thirty-fifth. You and the regiment shaped this world. If ever there was a soldier who represented the grand old Army of the Potomac it's Sergeant Major Hans Schuder. That army created the Republic here on this world. It had to create the Republic to mirror what it was and always will be. Draw on that, Colonel Keane, whenever you feel like you now do."

Andrew smiled at Emil. "Again the philosopher."

"What old Jew like me isn't a philosopher?" Emil said with an answering smile.

Andrew nodded. "I know something's coming." He hesitated. "There's been the other dreams. Somewhat the same as with Jamuka."

Emil looked closely at Andrew.

"It was a look inside of me, the same way I told you Tamuka tried to do during the war. Some of the Horde seem to have that, and this one is strong, far stronger. His mind is different," Andrew paused, as if looking for the right word. "Modern. That's it, modern. He thinks differently and that, my friend, frightens me."

Emil looked at him, his features drawn. "If you are frightened, Andrew, then maybe we all should be."

"Battalion . . . attenshun!"

Major General Vincent Hawthorne scanned the line as the troops arrayed before him snapped to shoulders. He felt a cool shiver of delight at the sound. The Fifth Suzdal, "Hawthorne's Guards," stood arrayed before him. With access to blue dye gained by trading with the Asgard, the Army of the Republic was gradually adopting the traditional uniform of their mentors—sky-blue trousers, navy-blue four-button jacket, and black felt slouch caps. The sight of his regiment dressed in the cherished blue made his heart beat faster. He looked up at the colors snapping in the breeze, his gaze lingering on the shot-torn standard of the regiment emblazoned with the names of half a dozen hard-fought battles.

Deployed next to them was a company of sailors wearing the blue trousers, blue-and-white-checkered shirts, and white neckerchiefs of the navy, with Admiral Bullfinch proudly standing in front of them in his finest double-breasted blue frock coat, his handsome features made exotic and slightly dangerous-looking by the black eye patch.

As the train drifted to a stop, venting steam, the band gave a single ruffle and flourish as befitted the commander of the armies, and then broke into "Battle Cry of Freedom."

Vincent, joined by Bullfinch, turned and walked to the last car and, coming to attention, saluted as Andrew stepped out onto the platform. Andrew, smiling, snapped off a salute to the colors and then to Vincent and Bullfinch. He climbed off the train, and walked down the line of troops, followed by Pat and Emil, who peered curiously at the men, as if looking for a telltale cough or a sign of fever.

"The men look good," Andrew stated, loud enough so his words could be heard, "but then again, I wouldn't expect anything less from the old Fifth."

Behind the line of troops Andrew saw the crowd of curious onlookers, the hundreds of railroad men, dockhands, shipbuilders, and factory workers who were laboring at what was now the railhead of the eastward expansion of the Republic. As they left the platform Andrew smiled at Vincent.

"It's been how long?"

"Four months since I was last in Suzdal."

"Good to see you, Vincent."

"And you too, sir. My family?"

"That poor girl," Pat laughed. "Good heavens, is she pregnant!"

"She's all right, isn't she?" He looked at Emil.

"Don't worry. Another two months. She's doing fine."

"Maybe you should stay out here another year and give her some rest," Pat interjected.

Vincent fixed his old friend with a cool stare, and Pat held up his hands in surrender.

"Ah, those Quaker sensibilities of yours. All right, but good heavens, the way you make babes I'd think you were an Irishman."

"How's my father-in-law?"

Andrew shook his head.

"Our president is proving to be a president."

"He's a pain, he is," Pat interjected. "Wants to cut the budget again, divert rail development back into Rus, and Marcus agrees—as long as it means extra lines inside Roum. And he wants to cut the training and field assignment of new troops down to one year from two."

"Damn! We need it out here," Vincent replied sharply. "We're nearly a thousand miles past Roum now, in the middle of nowhere. I've only got five thousand mounted patrolling a frontier more than five hundred miles across to the east and another five thousand on the defensive line to the south. They could slip ten umens through that cordon and be halfway here before we'd even notice."

He nodded toward the two hundred fifty men lined up to receive Andrew. "And look at those boys. I've got exactly twenty-two vets with this battalion. The rest of them are recruits who were underage kids when the Merki came. We need two years to get them in shape before sending them into the reserve. What the hell is Kal thinking?"

"Ah, politics, my lad," Emil interrupted. "Remember now, they're voters back home, not a bunch of terrified peasants with the bogeyman at the gate. The danger's past, at least according to some in Congress. The Merki are scattered, the Tugars have gone east, and the Bantag are a thousand miles away and supposedly moving east as well. The wars are over, and they don't need us old soldiers now."

"And it's another four hundred miles to the capital of the Nippon," Andrew replied. "Four hundred miles of rail and bridges, to Kal's thinking, can help link a lot of towns together before the next election. The votes are back there, not out here. Kal's party is facing opposition, and that's their complaint. And getting across that next river thirty miles ahead. That's a mile of bridging, and Ferguson's talking about a thousand-foot span in the middle. That same material could build a dozen rail bridges back home."

"We need that bridge," Vincent snapped. "Forward projection. That was the whole idea, which we agreed upon if the Bantag should turn north. We fortify the narrows south of Roum between the Inland Sea and the Great Sea, use that as a barrier. But even that's more than a hundred fifty miles across, and the rail to that position still has eighty miles to go. By God, sir, if they should come at us from that direction, how in hell are we to hold a front, with the railhead so far in the rear? We'll lose it all, and if the army deploys out, we'll lose that as well."

Andrew nodded in agreement. "I think we'll get the appropriation to finish running the rail line south, but that's it."

Hawthorne threw up his hands in exasperation. "Sir. It's not just that. We need a rail line running parallel to where we want to fortify. We need stockpiles of equipment there. And I've been screaming for half a year to build a new airship base down there. If we base our air fleet out of there, build that airship resupply vessel that Bullfinch here has been talking about, we might even be able to push an airship into their territory."

"Provocative act, there," Pat said dryly.

"Provocative or not, it needs to be done," Bullfinch interjected. "I'd like to see an airship in there right now, especially up that river. You saw the report I forwarded about that escaped slave the sloop picked up. They're building ships up there, sir, and here we've barely got a proper naval base and nothing much more than an anchoring spot down on the defensive line."

"I'm still arguing for it, Admiral, but we have to face facts. The money, the resources are stretched beyond the breaking point. If we had not been blessed with a damn good harvest last year, which gave us some surplus to trade with Cartha, we'd be in the barrel now. Everyone in Congress is screaming internal improvements first. They need more harvesting machines, every congressman is crying for a rail line to his town and the hell with wasting track in the wilderness, and the pensions for disabled soldiers are staggering."

"Then push on to Nippon and get them allied with us," Vincent shot back. "That could be another ten corps worth of troops, and damn good ones at that. I've been there. I know."

"And it was your report, I think, that scared some people in Congress," Emil replied. "Remember, Rus lost half its population in the wars. There's barely seven hundred thousand still alive. Roum outnumbers them nearly two to one. But Nippon has more people than Roum and Rus put together."

"Precisely why we need them," Vincent replied heatedly. "We could double the army. At best we'll get a corps out of the Asgard and it will take years to get them adapted. Right now they're next to useless except as raiding troops and scouts."

"Vincent! And here you're married to the president's daughter," Emil said with a shake of his head. "Don't you get the political ramifications? If we bring Nippon in as a state of the Republic it'll control half the seats in Congress. Come next election it might even be able to put a president in."

Vincent shook his head angrily. "To base a cutback decision on that is obscene. The ideal of the Republic is that all men are created equal regardless of race. Didn't we join the Army of the Potomac for that? Lord knows, I did, even though I was a Quaker. We fought and a hell of a lot of our comrades died for an ideal. Now let's live up to it."

"Idealism," Pat interjected with a smile. Vincent flinched and then saw the admiration in Pat's eyes.

"Me bucko, you're a wonder. Too bad not everyone is as high-minded and book-learned as you."

Andrew smiled at Pat's words. Shortly after he had joined the army in '62, Colonel Estes, the first commander of the Thirty-fifth, had snapped, "Just what the hell am I supposed to do with a book-learned professor?"

And now look at me, he thought with a twinge of irony. General of the Armies. The life and death of human civilization on this insane world resting on my shoulders for nearly eight years. He fully agreed with Vincent.

"There'd still be the balance in the Senate, though," Vincent finally replied. "Nippon will get only five seats, the same as Asgard, once it becomes a state of the Republic, and Rus and Roum will each hold their fifteen and ten seats."

"Well, now," Emil replied, as if lecturing a student, "so what? Right now the balance is there between Roum and Rus even though Roum controls the House by virtue of population. But the alliance between us, so far, is one of blood spilled on the battlefield, and we still trust each other. Nippon is an unknown. Maybe after the next presidential election, when Kal is secure for six more years, maybe then we'll push the railhead, but not before."

Vincent looked at Andrew appealingly. "You wrote the bloody Constitution. Didn't you see this?"

"I figured it might be a possibility," Andrew replied. "That's why we put in that the two founding states of the Republic, Rus and Roum, each had more senators than the five granted to new states as they join. We'll maintain control in the Senate for a long time to come, but it's the House that will be up for grabs if Nippon joins us, and that has them spooked."

"Can't you convince Kal?"

"Oh, eventually."

"The damn thing's nuts," Vincent stormed, his voice growing louder. "During the war we got what we needed and the hell with politics. This damn Constitution will get our asses in the wringer."

Andrew, in a fatherly fashion, put his hand on Vincent's shoulder and led him off the platform, beyond the hearing of their three comrades and the troops deployed along the depot siding.

"If I ever hear you say that in public again I'll strip you of command," Andrew said quietly. "Do I make myself clear, General?"

Vincent looked straight up into Andrew's eyes. "But, sir, you see the problem it's created."

"Do I make myself clear, General?" Andrew repeated, his voice growing hard.

Vincent stared at him, wanting to raise a protest, but the growing anger evident in Andrew's eyes stilled his voice. He snapped to attention. "Yes, sir."

Andrew knew that several of Vincent's men had overheard the comment and were now watching the dressing-down. He had to maintain discipline but at the same time not cause Vincent to lose too much face.

"You are not in McClellan's army, Mr. Hawthorne. That talk might have been tolerated back in sixty-two, but it will *never* be tolerated here. Do I make myself clear?"

"Yes, sir."

He now raised his voice slightly so the men, who were undoubtedly straining to catch every word, would hear. "I don't care if you are the best fighting general in the army. When it comes to this issue, in this country, the military must take its orders from the civilian government, like it or not. That is the oath we swore to uphold."

Vincent nodded, his face turning red.

"Fine. We understand each other, then."

"Yes, sir. I apologize, sir."

Andrew nodded. Handling Hawthorne was always something of a tricky job. There was, of course, the political connection. Though Kal would never interfere in the way Vincent was disciplined, he knew that the boy—after all, he was only twenty-seven—could not help but feel that the presence of his father-in-law gave him certain leverage.

Beyond that, Vincent simply was the best he had. His defense of the center at the second and third day of Hispania was now the stuff of legend. One of the most popular paintings to emerge from the war was that of Vincent standing like an immovable rock on a flatbed car, the Merki host storming around him. The painting rivaled Showalter's *Last Stand* as the most popular illustration hanging in bars throughout the Republic.

Andrew hoped that there would come a day when Vincent became general of the armies. He mused on that for a moment and found the thought troubling. But it was an option that might become necessary before much longer. Though Pat could possibly fill the post, he did not have the charismatic appeal of Vincent, especially with the Roum, who viewed Vincent as their hero as well for his defense of the palace during the Cartha War. If it came to that choice, Pat could serve publicly as direct commander of all Rus troops but in private he would be the brake and steady hand, a Hans for a new general.

Hans. Again the troubling memory. Wish you were here, old friend, Andrew thought sadly, and then he focused again on Vincent. The boy would need more grooming, especially when it came to his temper and his often impetuous actions.

"Fine. We understand each other, then," Andrew said again, letting his voice go softer.

"Yes, sir, we do."

Andrew could sense the embarrassment in Vincent's tone. Good, let it stay there for a while.

He looked back at Bullfinch, who had respectfully withdrawn while his friend was being chewed out. "Mr. Bullfinch, shall we start this inspection tour?"

"Aye, aye, sir."

Pat chuckled at the nautical terminology, feeling, as most soldiers did, that the vocabulary of sailors was nothing but an affectation.

"How much time do we have before the meeting with the Nippon military liaison?"

Vincent pulled out his pocket watch. "We have a couple of hours, sir. Last report from the telegraph station said he crossed the river shortly after dawn. We should have plenty of time."

Though Andrew still wore the pocket watch given to him by the men of the Thirty-fifth after he was wounded at Gettysburg, he didn't even bother to wind it anymore. The days on this planet were fifty minutes shorter, and trying to reset the timing had caused endless confusion. A team under Chuck Ferguson, the scientific wizard who, perhaps more than anyone else, had helped to save them all, had worked out a new twenty-four-hour standard after endless debate about going to a ten-hour rather than twenty-four-hour day, just how long was a second, and should there be sixty or a hundred minutes in an hour. In the end, no matter how illogical it really was, the Republic had adopted the twenty-four-hour day, with the seconds just slightly shorter than back home to make up the difference. One of the new watchmakers, a former Rus artillery major, had offered to regear Andrew's watch, but he had yet to get around to having it done. Besides, he realized, one of the prerogatives of command was that he could simply rely on his staff for the time.

"Fine, then. Let's go see Mr. Bullfinch's new ship."

Following Vincent and Bullfinch's lead, Andrew fell back in with Emil and Pat, both of them watching Vincent, who stayed several feet ahead. Andrew could see that Pat wanted to make a wisecrack, but he shook his head.

"Ah, youth," Pat muttered, loud enough for Vincent to hear. Vincent turned angrily, and Pat, with a smile, went up and slapped him on the shoulder, moving him forward and away from Andrew.

"They'll make a good team," Emil said softly. "Reminds me of you and Hans."

Andrew smiled and nodded as he watched the two of them, Pat's hand on Vincent's shoulder and Vincent obviously pouring out his frustration. As they walked down the main street of the town that had sprung up around the railhead and port, Andrew could not help but feel a certain sense of awe.

At one of the sidings a crew was unloading cut railroad ties off a narrow gauge line that ran northward for fifty miles up into the forest, where a steam-powered mill operated. The laborers were a mixed lot of Rus and Roum, with a few Cartha refugees and Asgard thrown in. He could hear the polyglot language they spoke, a mixture of medieval Russian and ancient Latin, with a fair sprinkling of English, especially for military and technical terms. Gates, the editor of the Republic's most popular paper, *Gates's Illustrated Weekly*, had even written a couple of articles speculating that because of the rapid rise in literacy, the speed of transportation, and the mixing of formally isolated societies through the army and politics a new language might eventually emerge.

The laborers paused upon seeing Andrew, and several of the men came to attention, snapping off salutes.

Andrew smiled and saluted in turn.

"Bloody Seventh Murom!" one of them shouted. "Twenty-third Roum," another chimed in proudly as he pulled up his sleeve to show a jagged white scar. Andrew waved in reply.

"Roll his sleeve, and bare his scars, and say these wounds I won on Chrispen's Day."

Andrew felt a cool shiver of memory at Emil's words, remembering young Gregory's stirring recitation of *Henry V* on the second night of Hispania when all believed that the battle was lost.

Another one lost, he thought sadly. Gregory had disappeared the spring after the end of the war while on patrol down the western coast of the Great Sea. It was a frustrating blow. He had shown so much promise, having acted as corps commander for what was left of the old Third. Interestingly, his avocation had given him much fame as well. In the months after the battle he had been called upon repeatedly to appear on the stage, playing Henry V to critical acclaim.

Andrew gazed at the veterans, who were now standing around the lumber pile, talking in an animated manner, the veteran of the Seventh Murom starting to pull his shirt up while the Asgard workers watched with obvious envy.

"It's about the only good thing that comes out of a war," Emil said. "It united us like nothing else ever could. That, and the fact that we won, of course."

"Let's hope we don't forget it too soon."

With a piercing shriek a train at the far end of the rail yard announced that it was leaving, the engineer playing out the first bar of an bawdy Roum tavern song on the whistle. The train lurched forward, pulling a long line of empty flatcars that had most likely been loaded down with rails when it came east. Andrew watched the train as it slowly built up speed and thundered past. The brass work on the engine was polished to a brilliant gleam, "City of Roum" painted in bright red letters beneath the cab. The engineer, posing like a highborn lord, leaned out of the cab and saluted as he passed. The engine was one of the new 4-6-0 designs, rated at just over 1,500 horsepower, twice what the main engines in use during the war had been capable of.

The string of fifteen cars behind the engine rattled past and switched onto the main line heading back west.

"You know, I can almost see their point," Emil said. "Day after day, trains heading out into unknown, carrying the wealth of Rus. More than two hundred fifty thousand tons of iron and steel since the end of the war. That could go to a lot of other things right now."

Andrew didn't reply as the train passed the switch and started the climb toward the low ridge to the west of town. Here was the edge of the frontier. He imagined it was a fair mimic of the frontier back home on Earth. The town had a rough-hewn look about it, smelling of unwashed bodies, fresh-cut pine lumber, horses, ship's tar, and cheap liquor. There was even a form of buffalo out in this part of the steppe, bigger, some of them almost elephant-size and covered with fur. They looked like elephants, with their long trunks, and Andrew wondered if they were native to this world or somehow had been imported from another planet, perhaps even from Earth thousands of years ago.

The thought was intriguing to him, though he would not have debated it too openly back at Bowdoin, since such a theory did fly in the face of accepted religious thought about the age of the planet. There were no records of such beasts. He supposed he could argue that they had simply failed to make the boat and thus were antediluvian.

Several of the flatcars on the train rumbling past were stacked high with cured hides for the new market in fashionable winter coats that was catching on in Rus. Some of the Asgard, led by one of his retired soldiers from the sniper detachment and armed with custom-made heavy-caliber Sharps rifles, were making quite a good living hunting the beasts, providing food for the army and a tidy return shipping the woolly hides back to Rus. It wasn't just the wool, hides, Asgar mead, and changes to the language that were moving on the rails, though. There was something else happening as well, something indefinable.

The historian in him had been musing on this of late. Perhaps it was the frontier that was the definer of a society. It was shaping the America he remembered even before the war. A sense of destiny, a sense of limitless possibilities, even a safety valve for those who couldn't quite fit in with conventional norms. It was interesting to him how many of his old soldiers, men who had been First Corps, the founding unit of the army, had attached themselves to the railroad and moved with it. Maybe they had seen too much, had lived on the edge too long, to go quietly home now. Out here they could be free. Maybe it was the frontier that would define the Republic rather than the notion so many had that the railroad was bringing the definition of what they were into new lands. Perhaps it was that which was triggering the sense of fear in Congress, that things would somehow change even more.

If Congress should put a permanent end to his dream of building a railroad completely around the world, they would retreat back upon themselves. As he walked along with Vincent, the thought crystallized and he realized that perhaps here was part of the answer to why he had decided to come out on an inspection tour. It was to escape from Suzdal, to see what it was they were really doing, and somehow touch it and let it flow into him, reminding him of all that once was. And with it came the chilling thought as well that if they should stop and turn inward again sooner or later the Hordes would win.

As they approached the dockyard Andrew slowed in front of a shed where a new ship was just beginning to take form. Stacks of cured oak were piled outside the building, along with strips of one-inch iron plate. All of it had been shipped from Suzdal, marked and numbered. The crew here had only to assemble it according to the plans.

"Sir, here's our new beauty," Bullfinch announced, and he pointed down toward the water.

At first impression Andrew thought it an ugly monstrosity. His image of ships had been formed in Maine. Bowdoin College was in Brunswick, a major shipbuilding town, and nearby was Bath, famed for its clipper ships. A ship should have masts raked back at a provocative angle, canvas as white as snow to capture the wind. He tried to muster a smile of approval as Bullfinch led him down to the dock.

The crew was lined up along the starboard side, standing on the narrow open deck between the railing and the armored blockhouse. At their approach pipes trilled and the ship's company snapped to attention. Remembering naval ritual, Andrew stepped aboard and turned to first salute the colors, then the officer on deck.

He knew he was expected to give a speech, and so he ran through his short inspiration one, citing the proud record of the navy, then expressing confidence that the men of this ship would carry on the tradition. The hands were dismissed and Andrew surveyed the scene curiously.

"She's an interesting design, sir," Bullfinch stated, taking him forward to stand at the bow so he could have a clear view aft. "She's a twin paddle-wheel design, those twin humps aft, each of them twenty-five feet high, are the armored housing for the wheels."

"I thought screw propellers were better," Emil interjected.

"For deepwater operations I agree, but the Great Sea's an interesting body of water. It's barely been charted. We don't even know yet if you can continue sailing southward on into the Inland sea, down past the Cartha narrows, and somehow eventually swing east and north."

Andrew could sense that Bullfinch was leading up to one of his pet proposals. A ship had already been sent out to explore that possibility and it never returned. There had been no appropriations for another.

"Stick to the question of this ship, Mr. Bullfinch," he said quietly.

"Ah-hmm, of course, sir. As I was going to say, the east coast has a lot of shoals, and approaches to some of the rivers are all but impassable. This ship was designed like some of the ships used during the Civil War. Capable of some deepwater work when necessary, but excellent for poking up rivers, hugging the coast—in general, getting in close. She only draws six feet, is basically flat-bottomed, with three small keels running fore and aft and a rudder that can be raised if we get in too shallow."

Bullfinch, now in his element, started to rattle off the design details. "She's just under a thousand tons, and the armored blockhouse here"—as he spoke he led them back toward the squat black structure that ran nearly the length of the ship—"has two inches of iron backed with two feet of oak. Should keep out anything we've run up against so far."

He led them through an open hatchway into the blockhouse. Pat admiringly approached one of the guns. "These are real beauties!" he exclaimed. "I always did envy you sailors for the metal you can carry."

"Four guns per broadside port, and starboard all of them six-inch smoothbores, but the real treat's up forward."

Andrew followed his lead, ducking low in the confined space of the gun deck.

"Our first hundred-pound rifled Parrott gun," Bullfinch exclaimed proudly, slapping the massive breech. "We can hit at four miles with this."

Pat stood behind the gun, sighting down the barrel through the open gun port, grinning with delight.

Bullfinch finally convinced Pat to leave the gun and led them aft. They climbed a narrow ladder and stepped into the armored bridge. Andrew squatted down to look through the narrow slits.

"Normally we'll sail her topside on the open bridge and use this only if we're in action. Since we don't draw that much for a full lower deck, the engine room's directly behind us, most of it above the waterline. Actually that's where we put the most armor, an inner layer of iron and oak, with coal bunkers around the engine as well. Crew's quarters, additional coal and ammunition are all down below, but normally the men will string hammocks right on the gun deck."

Andrew could see the pride in Bullfinch's face. It was not normally an admiral's job to go on the shakedown cruise for a new ship, but for a navy that had only half a dozen active ironclads with the so-called First Fleet on the Inland Sea, the launching of the first true fighting ship on this sea was an event he could not very well miss.

"Once we get *Franklin* back there in the boat shed launched next month, we'll have a deepwater ship on this ocean as well, sir. Having only half a dozen sloops to patrol everything out there was stretching it way too thin."

"I know, Bullfinch. Remember, I'm on your side."

"Sorry, sir. It's just that I'd love to see that idea that Jack Petracci and I have been kicking around, to build a ship that could handle the docking and re-supply of airships. It would really give us the range to explore and keep a check on those heathens out there."

"Maybe next year's appropriations."

Bullfinch nodded sadly.

"Would you care to join my crew and me for tea, sir?"

Andrew registered Vincent's impatient agitation at the mention of staying for tea.

"Later," Andrew said with a smile. "I think General Hawthorne here wants to get his official part of this visit over with first. Perhaps this evening we'll bring the Nippon liaison officer on board for a tour."

"I'd be delighted, sir."

Following Bullfinch's lead, they went back down to the gun deck and from there to the outer deck, where Andrew had to endure yet another round of trilling pipes and exchanges of salutes before stepping back onto the dock.

"Them navy fellas must have to blow them blasted pipes and salute everything in sight before they're even allowed to dump a chamber pot," Pat growled.

With Vincent guiding them, the group climbed the hill away from the navy yard and headed back through the town. Cresting a low rise, Andrew could see spread out before him half a dozen warehouses of rough framed lumber, buildings more than a hundred yards long and forty feet high. A row of workshops was arrayed halfway down the slope, and coming out of the one closest to the road Andrew saw Chuck Ferguson.

Ferguson started up the hill to meet them, grinning, and came to attention, snapping off a salute.

"Ferguson, how's those lungs of yours?" Emil snapped, stepping in front of Andrew. Without waiting for a reply, the old doctor put his head against Ferguson's chest to listen.

"Fine, sir, fine."

"Be quiet. Now breathe deeply."

Ferguson did as ordered and then coughed slightly.

"Uncle Drew!"

Andrew smiled as a boy of three, dressed in a Union-blue jacket and sky-blue trousers trimmed with the white piping of the air corps, burst out of a cabin and raced up to his side, standing with mock seriousness, right hand at his brow, until Andrew returned his salute.

"He's still coughing, doctor."

The child's mother, Varinia, came out the cabin door, an infant in her arms. Andrew tipped his cap, and she smiled a reply but then hurried to Emil's side.

"He still goes into that damnable workshop, even when they're making gas for the airships," she told the doctor, with a worried glance at her husband.

As Andrew watched the young couple he felt warm inside at the love that bound the two. Varinia was the daughter of Marcus's bodyservant, a man who had risen to serve on the Senate. She had been one of the most beautiful women he had ever seen . . . until the explosion at the powder mill seared her face, arms, and legs. Her very survival was a testament to Emil's skill and to his own wife's ability as a doctor as well. Kathleen had hovered over the girl for weeks and had come away convinced that it was Chuck's love for her that gave her the will to live in spite of her disfigurement. "I know the beauty within," Chuck had said, "and that's all I'll ever see."

Nursing her back to health had created a close bond, and Kathleen and Andrew had stood as their witnesses when the two were married, and now they stood as godparents for their two children as well.

Andrew watched Emil anxiously as he continued to listen and then frowned. Finally Emil straightened up. "Son, I'm making this plain to you. I told you before I thought you had consumption, and I'm telling you now that you do."

Ferguson nodded calmly. "I knew that all along, sir."

"Well, now. You can live to a ripe old age if you take good care of yourself and follow my orders exactly. We'll talk more about it later."

"Sir, a few things I'd like you to see," Chuck said, ignoring Emil.

"All right, but you're too valuable to be out here in the middle of nowhere," Andrew replied. "You're heading back to Rus with me tomorrow."

Chuck looked as if he wanted to protest, but a sidelong glance to Varinia, who was smiling at Andrew's orders, stilled him.

"This way, sir."

Andrew and his companions followed Chuck down the hill and into the shops. Ferguson had insisted on working out at the new airship station, but Andrew could see from Emil's worried expression that it was time to end that.

Ferguson led them into a room that was brightly lit by a row of kerosene lamps hanging from the ceiling. Half a dozen draftsmen labored at long tables.

"We're working on some new airship designs," Ferguson announced, pointing to a drawing.

"This one here will be twin-engined, giving us an estimated speed of twenty-five miles an hour at cruise and forty in a pinch. It's designed for quicker maneuvering, sort of a fighting ship to hunt down other ships. We'd also have a fallback if there's an engine failure. I'm planning this with a three-man crew—a pilot, an engineer who would act as a rear gunner, and a gunner on top."

"How far along are you?" Andrew asked, leaning over the table to study the drawings.

Ferguson smiled. "Nearly done, out in hangar five right now."

"Let's go see it."

"But there's something else first," Chuck added. He reached into a drawer in his table, pulled out a roll of paper, and pinned it to the board.

"This is the real beauty."

The reality of it didn't hit until Andrew saw the scale line at the bottom of the drawing. "Good heavens, Chuck! You're talking about an airship over four hundred feet long."

Chuck grinned. "It'll be powered by four engines mounted two fore and two aft. Now that we've got a good supply of hydrogen we can completely eliminate the hot-air bag. That'll give us even more lift. It'll have a pilot, an engineer, and three gunners."

"But whatever for?" Andrew asked.

"Range and lift, sir. Our old ships had a radius of operation of less than two hundred miles. I expect the two-engine machine can do four hundred. I'm looking at eight hundred miles with this, maybe twelve hundred when the new engines are perfected. We could fly it clear from here to Rus and carry close to a ton of either passengers or munitions at forty miles an hour."

"Trains do it better," Pat sniffed, "and a damn sight safer."

"Trains don't go south or east yet," Ferguson replied. "Sir, even with the older engines we could fly this damn near all the way down into Bantag country. If it was stripped down to just a pilot, an engineer, and one gunner and all the rest of the weight was fuel, I guarantee you it'd get there and back. We'd have photographs sitting on your desk of what they were doing in their camp less than forty-eight hours after they were taken. It could solve once and for all the question of whether they were heading east and leaving us alone or stopped and preparing to turn north. And another thing, sir. We can't send a boat up any of them rivers without maybe triggering a fight. If we fly this thing and keep it at ten thousand feet, hell, sir, there's nothing they can do. No shots are exchanged and those worrywarts back in Congress won't have a fit."

Ferguson leaned forward.

"Sir, it'll end the questioning once and for all about what's going on down there. With luck, maybe we'll find nothing and that will end it. That will mean their patrols are just trying to make sure we stay at a distance. Hell, it might even mean they're afraid we're coming after them. But if we do find something, it will end this deadlock with Congress and we can be ready for whatever comes."

"You're talking one hell of a distance, Chuck."

Ferguson nodded toward the back of the room, where Jack Petracci, chief pilot of the air corps, stood expectantly.

"Colonel Petracci, get over here!" Pat shouted, and Jack came over with a grin.

Pat slapped him hard on the back. "I keep betting you're dead," Pat laughed, "and losing my money."

Andrew shook Jack's hand and then motioned toward the drawing. "What do you think?"

"I'd be scared to death to fly it," Jack said quietly, "but then again I've always been afraid of flying."

Andrew grinned, but he could see the truth in Jack's eyes. By an odd set of circumstances, Jack, having once worked for a circus that had a balloon, had wound up being the planet's first pilot, handling an observation balloon. From there the balloon evolved into airships. Though he admitted to his fear, there was no denying that when need be Jack consistently tempted the fates and came out ahead.

"The four engines suit me just fine. I like the backup, especially when flying downwind. That'd be the problem with going for a look at the Bantag. Heaven knows what the weather and winds would be like. We could get down there and never get back if the weather was against us. Always been a problem on this world. Prevailing winds come from the west. It's the return trip that makes you worry, since you're bucking the wind all the way."

"What about the range?"

"Nearly sixteen hundred miles round trip. That'd be nearly two days in the air. There's that rough air station started down on the defensive line. If we could at least get some fuel stockpiled down there, along with a hydrogen gas generator, I'd feel a bit more secure. That would cut the run down to less than four hundred miles southeasterly across the sea before fetching up on that river we're curious about."

"Hauling all that equipment down there without the railroad would be devilish," Pat interjected.

"You're forgetting the *Petersburg*, Bullfinch's new boat," Jack replied. "It's going down that way anyhow."

"Well, that point is moot right now," Andrew replied. "Though maybe it would a good idea to have that equipment there for our light airships."

He saw an exchange of significant glances between Jack and Chuck, which set off a bit of an alarm bell for him.

"How much?" Andrew asked.

"Sir?"

"How much will this cost?"

"Well, sir, it's like this."

"Remember Chuck, it's not the old days, when we just built what we damn well pleased. The Cartha control the silk trade to the south and the bamboo you've been using for framing."

"I'm trying out some ideas using canvas painted with this mixture we've been getting out of the oil we're refining. As for the bamboo, there's something like it growing up in the north woods. It's like nothing we've got back on Earth. Cut it into thin strips, soak it and bend it to shape, then laminate it several layers thick, and you've got something darn near as strong as steel but as light as bamboo."

He hesitated.

"Problem is, not many have been trained how to work it yet."

"The cost, Mr. Ferguson."

"Fifty thousand."

Andrew exhaled noisily.

"Laddie, you can build locomotives for five thousand Rus dollars each," Pat reminded him, shaking his head. "Last year's budget for the entire air corps was damn near sixty thousand. And half your ships were lost or crashed and turned into junk."

"Not to mention twelve pilots and crew dead," Emil interjected.

"We need it, sir. If it gives us early warning, we'll have months to get ready, instead of only weeks or days, as it now stands."

Andrew nodded, saying nothing, and walked out of the room, heading into the adjacent workshop. The room was humming with activity. Leather belts attached between the lathes and drive shaft whirred, metal and wood shavings were deep around the machines. The workers paused to see the distinguished visitor. Andrew, feeling almost like a politician, worked his way through the room, shaking hands, looking into the eyes of old veterans who gazed at him proudly as they named the regiments they had served with. Again there was the mix of Rus and Roum workers here, something Andrew was proud of.

Ferguson came to his side. "This is the new machine shop for the airships. Right now we're turning out a new set of engines for all the ships, based on the improved design tested last month."

"And I take it this was in the budget?"

Ferguson smiled and nodded his head. "It's all fair and square, sir."

"But you do have a couple of things up your sleeve, Chuck. I know you better than that. If old John Mina was still alive, he'd have ferreted it out by now."

Chuck lowered his head and started to cough, covering his mouth with a handkerchief that Andrew noticed had a few flecks of blood on it.

"You're worse off then you're letting on."

"A lot of work to get done, sir. There's something brewing out there, and I want us to have the edge."

"You think we don't?"

"You've heard the rumors, sir. Even the name of this new Qar Qarth."

"The Redeemer," Andrew said. "I've heard them all. Remember, Chuck, I do have access to intelligence reports, something you're not supposed to have."

"Well, sir, it adds up that there'll be trouble sooner or later. I want to push things."

"While there's still time, is that it?"

Chuck nodded and coughed again. Andrew realized that Ferguson had not understood the context of what he had just said.

"While there's still time for you," Andrew said quietly.

The thought frightened Andrew. Almost every major invention or reinvention on this world had come from Chuck—the railroad, telegraphs, standardized mass production, ironclads, airships, and even photography. If he should die now, the world could go dark.

He looked carefully at Ferguson.

"You're going home with us. You need some rest, and there's that teaching position at the new college."

Chuck laughed. "Me? A professor? Hell, sir, I never finished my degree back home."

"Well, we've got to start somewhere and you're it. Someone's got to train the younger ones around here to think the way you do. So amongst the other powers I have, I'm going to call you Doctor of Engineering and you can settle on being a professor."

"Before I'm gone, is that it?"

"I didn't say that, son, but you are going home."

Chuck looked at him imploringly. "Just a couple of things first."

"All right. Let's see them."

Chuck led him to a room adjacent to the machine shop. Andrew stopped at the sight of the artillery piece pointed toward the door. He looked at the gun carriage, which came only up to his knees, and bent over to examine it.

"It's quarter scale, sir"—Chuck hesitated—"so I'd save on cost."

"Breechloading artillery?" Andrew asked.

"Yes, sir. When the idea hit me, it was so damn simple. It's an interrupted screw breech. Turn the handle a quarter turn, it unlocks, shove a shell in, turn it back a quarter turn and it's sealed."

"What about the problem of gas escape?"

"The shell does it, sir," and Chuck went over to a wooden case, opened it up, and lifted out a brass cartridge.

"It's like the cartridge for a Spencer rifle, only bigger. The rim of the cartridge is locked in between the breech and the barrel, making it airtight. It's simple, it works, and it can fire up to ten rounds a minute with a trained crew."

Andrew took the shell and hefted it.

"Brilliant. Ten rounds a minute, you say?"

"Absolutely, sir. And range, sir. We can get a tighter fit between shell and barrel than with a muzzle loader. There's a lot more pressure as a result, but I think we've licked the problem we had with brittle steel by injecting oxygen straight into the crucible to burn off the impurities, then adding a trace of nickel. I think a full-scale gun would shoot three to four miles. I've been fooling around with some improved fuses as well, and for close range a new type of canister round. Actually it's a tin packed with hundreds of nails mounted in resin."

"There's a problem, though," Andrew replied.

"Yes, sir. Brass. I already thought about that. A battery of six guns could fire off a couple of thousand rounds in an hour. They'd burn their barrels out, but they could pump out the firepower of a full battalion of Parrott guns. If we had had fifty of these at Hispania the Merki would never have gotten across the river."

"And we would have needed a stockpile of a hundred thousand shells."

Vincent nodded. "That's what I was hoping for."

Pat came into the room and whistled softly when he saw the gun. Going to the breech, he tried out the screw mechanism and smiled sadly at Vincent. "I guess me old beauties are destined for the scrap heap."

"Not yet," Andrew replied. "We're talking more brass here than exists in all of Rus and Roum together. The supply of zinc for brass just isn't there."

"Another reason to push for Nippon. The survey team I sent out there said their territory has a lot of metals we need," Vincent interjected.

Andrew smiled at his engineer. "Subtle, Mr. Ferguson. I'll keep the argument in mind. All right, what else?"

Vincent walked him through the shed, and Andrew marveled at the destructive ingenuity Chuck displayed. It was as if the boy was obsessively compelled to think up as many engines of destruction as possible. He knew Chuck's motive: fear of his own mortality and rage, locked deep within, over the agony that the Merki had inflicted upon his once lovely wife.

Andrew examined the improvements on the rockets that had been so crucial in breaking the final Merki attack and shook his head sympathetically as Chuck reviewed his problems with perfecting a steam-powered Gatling.

"And this thing here—it's got me beat for the moment."

Andrew picked up the model and looked at the cylinder curiously. "What the hell is it?"

"Well, sir, I remember reading in *Scientific American* how Ericsson's monitor was based on a design he once submitted to Napoleon III during the Crimean War. The original design had a built-in infernal machine."

Pat looked at him in confusion. "You mean like the Rebs made? Barrels packed with powder and a percussion fuse?"

"Not exactly. Those kind of infernal machines, or torpedoes, were anchored in place and if a ship hit one it blew up. This idea is different. Ericsson was trying to make one that moved. The weapon was launched out of an underwater tube attached to the bow of your own ship. It would then move at your target, hit it below the waterline, and sink it."

"Devilish," Pat muttered.

"Precisely. I can't remember exactly, but I think the Ericsson design had a vulcanized hose attached to the torpedo. The hose would unwind from a reel as the torpedo moved forward. Jets of air would go from the ship through the hose and blow out the back of the torpedo to power it and steer it. It struck me that if we could put a cylinder of pressurized air inside the torpedo and figure out a way to steer it automatically, the thing could travel on its own, maybe half a mile or more."

"Cost?" Andrew asked.

"We could go to Bullfinch, maybe take something from the Navy Department's budget."

"Cost?"

"Very fine tolerances on this one, sir, a lot of research to be done and testing at sea. I figure thirty or forty thousand at least for development, testing, and fitting our ships out with it."

Andrew shook his head.

"We've got full control of the Inland Sea with our monitors right now. The Cartha ships are falling into disrepair and there's no threat from that quarter. And the cost of building the new naval station on the Great Sea and launching the first monitors here is eating up the rest of the budget. Shelve it for now."

Chuck shook his head in disappointment.

"For the artillery, I'll see if we can shake some money loose at least to get one battery and a couple of thousand rounds of ammunition."

"I'd like to adapt the guns for airship use. A one-and-a-half-inch bore firing a two-pound shell. It'd give our gunner a hell of an advantage in range, sir, and up there range is everything."

"All right on that. Now, anything else?"

"Oh, just the things you already know about, sir. Improvements on the Sharps carbine, a far better design for the trapdoor breech-loading conversion I was thinking about for our Springfield rifles, some other things I was fooling around with concerning railroad engine designs for trapping the steam exhaust and reusing it, and a couple of by-product ideas for the oil we're throwing away after we refine out the kerosene."

"No surprises?"

He stared straight at Ferguson and saw his eyes flicker.

"Well, sir."

"Mr. Ferguson, there's been a couple of rumors floating around. There's no sense in hiding whatever it is you're up to."

"Well, there is one," Chuck finally said, and he led the way out of the workshop onto the landing field for the airships. Chuck walked down the row of hangars and Andrew paused at each of them to look inside. One was empty, the hangar for the airship that had disappeared the week before. As they approached the last hangar in the row, Andrew slowed down when he saw a crew at the far end of the building working on a roof over a recently added extension.

Chuck stopped by the open doors to the building and waited nervously as Andrew approached. The massive doors were wide open and Andrew looked up in awe when he entered the building. The wickerwork frame of a new airship towered above him and stretched the length of the building. Dozens of workers were scurrying over the basketlike framework, and the air was heavy with a pungent scent that made him feel light-headed.

"Damn it, Chuck," Andrew whispered, "you're building the big one, aren't you?"

"Well, sir, we had appropriations for replacements for the ships we lost last year. I just thought I'd sort of throw them all together."

"This is that four-engine design I looked at."

"Yes, sir, it is."

Andrew glared at Ferguson. "You know the spot this puts me in, don't you? Congress will have my hide over this."

"Well, sir, Congress is sort of a thousand miles away at the moment. We could say that we just tried hooking the ships together."

"We had appropriations for eleven airships in our fleet. Now we'll only have six and someone will want to know why."

"Sir. You can see they're starting to hang the skin on it now. It's that new canvas treatment I was telling you about. The smell is from a lacquer we cooked up to make it airtight and help to shrink the fabric onto the frame. It's a whole new design."

"I told you once before," Andrew snapped angrily, "that you're a loose cannon, Mr. Ferguson."

Chuck started to cough again, and Andrew waited patiently for him to recover.

"Sir, you can fire me at any time. I was right during the last war, and frankly, sir, I've got a gut feeling that we're heading into another one. This ship can give us the answer. It'll be ready to fly in a month. I think, sir, that in about four weeks, the day after this ship flies on its first mission, the issue of budgets simply won't matter."

Andrew turned toward Pat, who was grinning.

"No comment from you," Andrew snarled and stalked into the hangar.

Looking up at the airship, he silently cursed Ferguson for being so damned unexpendable and also so damnably right. Politically, he knew this ship would be the last straw for some, another argument that the military was out of control and Andrew was at fault. When the trainload of congressional delegates arrived later today to meet with the Nippon representatives, there was no way in hell that he could hide this thing. That was one of the reasons he had come out early, to see if Chuck had come up with follies that could somehow be concealed until after the elections. This—this was an elephant they couldn't drag out and bury someplace.

But if they stopped work on it, then what? It would just sit in the hangar and rot.

Frustrated, Andrew turned back to Ferguson. "Finish the damn thing. But Mr. Ferguson, as of today, right now, you are fired as chief of ordnance."

Chuck's face fell, and Andrew looked at him coldly until he suddenly doubled over with another spasm of coughing.

Andrew put his hand on Chuck's shoulder. "Come on, son, you're going home with me. I need you elsewhere now."

He saw Emil, Vincent, and Varinia approaching. Varinia broke away and ran up to Chuck's side. Though his face was pale, he forced a smile for her.

"Guess we're going home," he said, and she looked at Emil, who put his arm around Chuck's shoulder and led him away.

As the group left, Andrew turned on Vincent. "You knew he was building this, didn't you?"

"Yes, sir."

"I should can you, too."

"I could say it was outside my department, sir. The air corps answers directly back to headquarters in Rus, sir." Pat shifted uncomfortably, and Andrew fixed him with an unwavering gaze.

"Are all of you in a conspiracy against me? Is that it?"

"Well, sir. We know you're going to run for president next year."

Andrew was so nonplussed he was unable to reply.

"Oh, Kathleen never said anything. Neither has Kal, though I daresay you've told him as well. It's just—we knew you were going to do it. Everyone in the old Thirty-fifth and Forty-fourth has figured on it for some time now."

Andrew turned away and stared back at the ship.

"So we figured we'd just keep it to ourselves, bury it in the books, as they say. If it came up, along with a couple of other things, the blame wouldn't come back on you."

Andrew knew that Ferguson was right. They needed this ship. They needed improved ironclads, another ten corps of infantry, a corps of cavalry, upgrading of seventy-five thousand smoothbores for rifles and rifles to breechloaders. They needed all of that . . . and that was why he was going to run.

Andrew surveyed his two generals and friends.

"Thank you, but I'll take responsibility for this. After all, I'm in command."

"Ah, Colonel, darling," Pat beamed, "you'll make a dandy president—if the Republic is still here to vote for you come next year."

Chapter Two

I am in hell.

It was an unending refrain, played out in a monotone rhythm . . . I am in hell . . .

He raised his head and gazed around. The vast foundry was wrapped in a stygian darkness of fire and acrid smoke, waves of heat washing from the glowing cauldrons. Hunched stick figures, iron puddlers, moved like tormented souls, stirring the liquid fires . . . the ever-present demons standing with arms folded, whips hanging from their belts, ready to lash out if any should falter even for a second.

"Hans!"

Sergeant Major Hans Schuder turned and looked up into the dark, glowing eyes of the foundry overseer—Karga.

"It goes slow. Why?" The overseer's voice rumbled darkly, and once again Hans felt the cold revulsion that he had come to understand their speech and now would reply in kind. Yet another loathsome concession, even the act of speaking. He spared a quick sidelong glance at the iron puddlers; they were hunched over their work, but he knew they were aware . . . terrified that today would be the day they were chosen as "the example." Though Ha'ark had extended his "protection," Karga always found a way to bend the rule, claiming the worker was insubordinate or not longer protected because he failed to do his job.

Hans shifted the quid of tobacco in his cheek, aware that his mouth had suddenly gone dry.

Maybe today is my day, he thought. Why do I still cling to life? he wondered. Am I not now a traitor? I oversee the running of this foundry, the source of the machines that will one day be turned against humans all over this world, and against my own Republic.

The Republic—it seemed now like a distant dream, like a lover of childhood lost; that and Andrew Keane, the boy he had turned into a general. But he pushed that thought aside, for to contemplate that issue was to take the path to the ultimate paradox of his existence, a contemplation that could drive him into final madness.

He studied Karga. It had taken a long time to learn how to interpret the facial expressions of this race properly. To human eyes the features were perpetually set in a visage of rage. But there were subtle yet distinct differences which could be learned if you survived long enough. He could see, though, that today the master was indeed building to an explosive outburst. The features were coarse, leathery, always towering above him, like some ancient predator. Karga's visage was made even more terrifying by the scar from a Merki arrow that had cut his left eye out, leaving the socket a twisted mass of knurled flesh. He could see that the master was in a foul mood, accentuated by the scratch marks that crisscrossed his cheeks. There had been another fight with his mate, or a concubine, and now someone would pay.

"Explain, cattle. Only half the iron needed has been poured today."

Hans nodded in agreement. There was no sense in denying the obvious.

"My master," he began, the mere words grating on what few vestiges of his pride remained, "I told you before, you need to shut down furnaces three through seven for at least two days. The slag in the ovens has to be cleaned out. And the bellows, they're riddled with cracks, we're losing more air than we're blowing in."

Hans nodded toward the array of leather bellows, each one the size of a small house, which were hooked to treadmills, each treadmill standing nearly twenty-five feet high. Inside each mill were dozens of Chin slaves, heads lowered, as they walked endlessly upward on the wooden rungs, their pitiful weight used to turn the drive shafts that powered the bellows.

It was a hellish medieval sight that chilled Hans every time he saw it. Dozens of treadmills, each filled with half a hundred men, women, and children, powered most of the machinery in this nightmare world he now commanded. They walked for sixteen hours a day, with two brief breaks for their daily ration of rice cakes and water. It was the final step in their lives. Few lasted longer than a month before, spent with exhaustion, they collapsed and were dragged out to be hung up like the cattle they were in the slaughter room.

His skilled laborers, those to whom Ha'ark had extended his protection, were dying off as well. After three and a half years, disease, which swept the slave camps regularly, had taken many. Though their rations were better than the ones given to the Chin laborers, they were still barely enough to keep his people alive and working. Suicide was becoming more and more common—the day before, he had lost a skilled Cartha iron master and his entire family, wife and two children found in their bunks with their throats cut, the iron master dangling from a rope beside them. Though Karga was annoyed at the loss of a skilled worker, he was amused by the several hundred pounds of meat thus harvested, which would not be reported but would go directly into his personal stores.

His people lived in the north compound adjacent to the factory. They even had barracks, their food was almost adequate, and they did indeed have one day in seven to rest. As for the Chin laborers living on the south side of the factory, he didn't even want to contemplate the conditions and terrors they were forced to endure.

Three or four steam engines could have humanely replaced all the brute labor on the treadmills, but that was not even worthy of consideration for the Bantag. After all, they held tens of millions of humans under the yoke. A precious steam engine was their new sinew of war and the mere suggestion of such an arrangement would have been met with complete disbelief.

The overseer looked down at him coldly. Long ago he had learned to live without fear. Fear was the blinder, the killer of souls in this nightmare. Whether he was alive or dead within the next minute no longer mattered. He knew that unless he committed a grievous act, he was protected by the word of the Qar Qarth, but there were other ways to torment him. On occasion one of his people would be killed, perhaps for a mistake, often for no reason at all, the death explained away as an accident. The fact that he had wrung a concession of protection from Ha'ark seemed to infuriate Karga even more. Karga was a daily presence to deal with and Ha'ark a distant being who would not question why one lowly cattle was reported dead.

"We have not reached what is expected today. I will not report that we failed." There was a veiled threat in the words.

"Karga, what I tell you is fact."

The language of the Horde rumbled in his throat, and he felt as if each word were an obscenity. Karga stood silent before him, eyes filled with dark contempt, right hand drifting down to rest on the handle of his whip. Hans ignored the gesture. He had seen the whip crack out a woman's eyes and tear strips of flesh from shoulders to buttocks and or wrap around a throat, then be drawn tight in slow strangulation.

Karga's gaze drifted from Hans to the workers lining the edge of the cauldron of molten iron.

"If you kill one of them as an example it will not change fact," Hans said quietly, not letting even a flicker of emotion show through. He knew the work crew was listening, terrified to turn around and thus single themselves out, all of them waiting for a flash of rage, a killing of one, ten, perhaps all of them for no reason other than a foul temper, a slight upset of the stomach, a mating of the night before refused, or just for no reason at all ... for after all, that was the fate of a pet of the Bantag.

"Then we will do another pouring today," Karga finally announced.

"My master. The same problem will still exist tomorrow and the day after."

"Are you telling me no, slave?"

Hans stood silent, looking him straight in the eye. That in itself was a most dangerous gesture. Among the Bantag, to do so was to make a clear indication of equal caste; for a cattle to do it was an act bordering on mutiny. He held the gaze for several seconds, then shifted his eyes away.

"My Master. I present you with fact that cannot be changed. It is the way of iron and machines. You cannot will them to bend like a bow whenever you desire. They must be cleaned, repaired."

"Repaired? Did someone break something?"

Hans could see the puddlers flinch at the master's words. The last time he had become convinced that someone had deliberately broken a tool, half a dozen workers were hurled into the molten pit, which resulted in an even more towering rage when it was pointed out that the six incinerated bodies had contaminated the iron and the pour was now useless ... at that point the entire crew had been annihilated, setting production back even further, until new workers could be trained.

"As you rest your horse, so must you rest the furnace, my master. The same as your harness or bowstring wears and needs repair, so does the furnace."

Hans waited expectantly for a homicidal outbreak and was startled when the master chuckled softly.

"Another pour, then we stop to do what you ask."

Hans breathed an inner sigh of relief, even though the crew had been condemned to a straight twenty four hours of work, a pace that would most likely kill or cripple several of them before the coming of dawn.

Hans bowed low from the waist, keeping his head lowered until the master turned away.

"There are times, cattle, when you are too clever with words," the master snarled. "Someday I shall cut your tongue out and eat it."

Then who will run this for you? Hans thought silently. He knew the pressure the master was under. Iron and steel were needed, tens of thousands of tons of the precious stuff. Overseers who did not meet the demand were removed, and such a disgrace in Bantag society could be met with only one response, suicide.

"If I should ever fall from grace," the master continued, "I will slaughter everyone here, and all whom they hold dear, to be my slaves in the Everlasting Sky."

The threat made Hans shudder, for he knew that in the end it was all but inevitable that the overseer's words would come to pass.

Hans was standing silent, waiting for dismissal, the master looking all the more demonlike, when a worker at the number three furnace behind him, broke open the tap, and a river of molten iron cascaded out onto the pouring floor. Choking clouds of steam and swirling sparks soared upward with a hissing roar.

Karga held him with his gaze, and Hans stood silent, waiting for the barked command of dismissal.

"Go. Return to your quarters."

Hans did not turn away. "Shouldn't I stay here to make sure the work is done to your satisfaction?"

The master chuckled. "They will hate you more if they labor and you sleep. I like that."

"I will need a pass."

Grumbling a curse, Karga fished in the pouch dangling from his belt and pulled out a brass tablet signifying that he was under orders and therefore could leave the foundry.

Hans, bowing low, backed away as the pit master, with an angry curse, turned and stalked off into the shadows. Breathing a sigh of relief, he stood up and looked at the puddlers, who had continued to work throughout the encounter.

"Do you think there'll be a slaughter?"

Hans saw the fear in Gregory's eyes. He clapped the boy on the shoulder.

"It's all right. The bastard can't kill all of us." He tried to force a smile of encouragement. "Hell, if he kills me, you get the job."

A flicker of a grin crossed Gregory's features. "I can live longer without it."

Hans nodded, trying to smile. Though Gregory was still only in his mid-twenties his hair was already thinning and streaked with gray. Like all the prisoners, he had pale, almost translucent features from the overwork and the fear.

"I'd better get off the floor. Try and get an extra watering crew working for those poor devils in the treadmills, and the same for the puddlers. See if you can get to Tamira over at the cookhouse for some extra bread. These poor bastards are ready to pass out."

Even as he spoke, he kept his gaze locked on Karga. A work crew staggered past him, hauling baskets of charcoal. A woman with a small child clinging to the hem of her tattered dress staggered and fell, spilling several pounds of charcoal on the floor.

With an angry roar Karga was on her, his whip cracking. The woman tried to get to her feet and then went back down under the blows.

Karga reached down, picked her up with one hand, and then flung her to the floor again. She lay unconscious, the child screaming with terror.

"Kesus save her," Gregory whispered, "that's Lin's wife and child."

Hans sprinted forward. "Karga, she's exempt!" he snapped. "She's the wife of my food overseer. She is exempt!"

Karga turned with an angry snarl. "Then he is not doing his job properly," he announced with a sardonic laugh. "Otherwise we would not be behind. She deliberately dropped her charcoal to slow down the work. She goes to the pit. If there is one response, it is you, Hans. This is payment to me for the disgrace of not making your people work."

"Karga!"

A muscular black arm came around Hans's throat, pulling him back. Struggling, he looked over his shoulder and saw Ketswana, the foreman of number three furnace, with Gregory at his side.

Hans struggled to break free as Ketswana covered his mouth with his free hand.

"For Perm's sake!" Gregory hissed. "Interfere and he'll take a dozen more. Don't!"

Karga looked toward Hans, his eyes glowing with a fiendish light as the number four furnace cracked open and a torrent of molten iron poured out.

"Get him out of here!" Gregory hissed.

The towering Zulu dragged the kicking Hans toward the number three furnace, his screams of rage muffled as Ketswana held him tight.

He could see Karga throw the woman over his shoulder and start for the door that all who worked in the foundry, prisoner and master, called the Gate ... it led to the slaughter pits outside the factory.

The woman revived and started to scream. But her cries were not for herself ... for Karga was taking her child as well. In that moment all that Hans feared, all that he raged against boiled over. The child was old enough to know what was about to happen, but still she clung to her mother's side, even as her mother screamed and tried to push her away. Karga reached down and scooped up the child.

The sight of the child broke something in Gregory, and he almost stepped forward.

"Don't," Ketswana hissed. "He has laid his hand upon her. She is now for the pit. Nothing will stop him."

For an instant, in the shadows, Hans saw the child look back at him, and in her gaze he almost sensed relief before she was lost to view in the swirling smoke. Yet again he felt the emotion within start to boil over, as if a dam were about to burst.

He struggled for control, not to break, not to let the tears of anguish and pain explode. He stopped fighting against Ketswana's grip and felt the giant behind him loosen his hold.

All around him the laborers had stopped, watching Karga disappear. Then their gaze came back to rest on him. Though they were under his protection, he could sense the accusation, the frustration, the hollow sense of defeat. Two of their own had been dragged away. Even at this moment the blade was being drawn across their throats. Ultimately he could do nothing to protect them. They were all dying, they were already dead, and he could do nothing to save them.

"Damn it!" Hans roared. "Keep working or he'll take more."

Shaking, he looked at Gregory. "Where's Lin?"

"Still in the food warehouse outside the gate."

He knew he should meet him when he finally came in. He should be the one to break the news.

"Post a watcher, tell me when he's back in the camp. I should tell him."

"Let me do it, Hans."

He shook his head. "No, it's my fault. It's my burden now."

I am in hell . . .

He looked up at the Zulu and the dark men of his work crew on the number three furnace. Though he had fought for the Union and had seen the black soldiers of the Army of the Potomac die by the thousands at the Battle of the Crater, still there had been something that had once made him feel uncomfortable in their presence. That discomfort had long since disappeared. The brotherhood of slavery had released him from it. Somewhere south of the Cartha realms there was a black nation who were masters at ironworking. Ketswana, who was the leader of the fifty men and women that the Bantag had brought here, was now his most trusted lieutenant.

"Your rage will get you killed, my friend," Ketswana said softly, the gentleness of his voice a strange incongruity coming from the six-and-a-half-foot giant.

"Thank you," Hans sighed.

He looked past Ketswana at a gang of laborers hauling a cart loaded with freshly cast rails out of the foundry and then back at Ketswana's group, hoisting ore and charcoal into the furnace. In a flash of memory he saw the crews laboring in the foundry at Suzdal—it seemed almost like a dream now. There the laborers had been free men, working with the knowledge that their very survival depended on what they were doing; here it was the postponement of a death that was inevitable.

Why don't we all just simply kill ourselves? he wondered yet again. All we are doing is helping the bastards who are bent on destroying us, and we shall die in agony still. Why do we, why do I cling to living when death would be a release?

"That child, that poor child." Manda, Ketswana's wife, came to her husband's side. He could see the accusation in her eyes. "It's getting worse," she said. "There's no stopping it. It will get worse yet."

He knew what Gregory, his old chief of staff, was thinking. His anger was all too evident. The idea had been presented to him time and again . . . and always he had refused. The risks were simply too great. But now?

"When will they come for your child, Hans?" Manda asked. "Was not Lin's baby like yours?"

Her words cut like a knife into his heart. Suddenly ashamed, he turned away. Was that the restraint? Was that the reason that had compelled him to be cautious? For, after all, though Karga might drag others to the pit, Hans knew in his heart that the bastard would never directly strike at him unless he committed a grievous error. And even then, the case would go to Ha'ark before death would be inflicted.

That is how they bought me, Hans realized with a sense of inner loathing. I have become their instrument. I allow the horror to continue so that Tamira and our precious child will be safe.

He slammed his fists against the side of the furnace until blood trickled from the battered knuckles. He looked back at his friends, fearing that their eyes would be filled with contempt. Instead he saw only compassion, which made his anguish worse.

Lin's child . . . her look will haunt me forever, he

realized. He could remember how six months back he had first held young Andrew, only minutes old, and gazed into the newborn's eyes and seen the mystery of life in them, the eternal spirit. And that same look was in the eyes of the child that knowingly had gone with her mother into the darkness.

"I'm sorry," Hans whispered, his voice thick. "For three and a half years I've tried to keep all of you alive."

He looked back across the furnace, toward the Portal of Death.

"And for what? I was a coward. I can see that now."

Manda stepped up to his side and rested her hand on his shoulder. He was startled at the understanding and gentleness that still existed in the middle of hell.

"I said no because I feared what would happen. To you, to all of you"—he hesitated, wanting to stop the words from flowing—"and to Tamira, and now Andrew."

"It will happen anyhow," Ketswana replied.

Hans nodded.

"Gregory, can you round up the people you told me about?" Hans finally whispered.

A smile creased Gregory's features and he nodded.

"Meet me in my quarters when the shift ends. Tell Karga we need to plan the work schedule and repairs."

The three gathered around him grinned, their eyes suddenly filled with hope.

"Signal the attack!"

Ha'ark Qar Qarth sat back in his chair and observed as the attack went into motion. There were no cheers at first, only the sound of a telegrapher's key clicking behind him. The Bantag warlords, arrayed in a circle a respectful distance behind Ha'ark, looked at each other in silence.

Signal rockets suddenly arced up from the left and right wings of the assault force, which was arrayed in a crescent formation across the open steppe. From the targeted Chin city, on a low plateau a mile away, a flash of light snapped atop a battlement, disappearing in a puff of smoke.

Ha'ark watched intently, counting off the time. A piercing shriek rent the air and the shot screamed past, not a dozen paces to his right. More than one of his Bantag umen commanders blanched and ducked low. Ha'ark laughed.

"Get used to the sound of it."

"My Qarth, it is my right to speak."

Ha'ark turned in his chair and looked back. It was Yugba, commander of the speckled-horse umen.

Ha'ark nodded.

"Sire, good warriors of my clan will die this day."

"The survivors will learn how not to die," Ha'ark snapped back. "Now watch and learn."

More flashes of light rippled along the battlement walls, shot screaming through the air, several of the rounds plowing bloody furrows through the ranks of the third black horse umen, which was mounted and deployed to Ha'ark's right. The commander of the umen stood silent, his eyes straight ahead.

"They're wasting ammunition at this range, but the way you have your formation deployed, the target is far too tempting," Ha'ark said quietly.

He saw, off to his left, the skirmish line of mounted warriors, now deploying across the open field, and he studied them carefully, raising his field glasses to observe the advance.

"Look to your left there. They're keeping their intervals spaced wide enough not to present a target. If a hit is made, only one warrior is lost."

"It lacks power," Yugba replied.

"If you think it lacks power, then send your own

umen in and let us see who takes the center of the city first."

Yugba looked at him cautiously.

"Go ahead and let's see."

Yugba nodded. Mounting his horse, he unsheathed his saber.

"The old ways are still the best for us," he snarled, and he galloped down the line to join his command.

Ha'ark surveyed the other umen commanders. "Any others?"

The rest stood silent. Ha'ark now faced his own circle of four, who stood casually to his left, watching the developing battle with feigned indifference.

Ha'ark smiled. "Any of you care to join the amusements?"

"Why bother?" Jamul, the radio operator from his old unit, replied, making it a point to let his boredom show. "The results will be the same. We trained our warriors; they know what to do."

Ha'ark smiled inwardly. Jamul's words rankled him, but he knew that was Jamul's intent. Show them a different attitude to war.

Ha'ark watched the deployment. The skirmishers were dismounting six hundred yards from the enemy wall, advancing now on foot. A second wave dismounted, advancing fifty strides behind the first, and two more waves spaced themselves at even intervals of fifty paces. Warriors in the front rank opened fire with their rifles—taking careful aim, choosing targets, firing deliberately, reloading their weapons as they advanced, pausing to fire, then advancing again.

A loud cry erupting from the right of the line claimed Ha'ark's attention. Now an entire umen was advancing, warriors riding stirrup to stirrup, the great narga horns sounding the attack, pennants marking the line, the triangle flag of Yugba fluttering above him. The charge thundered forward.

Ha'ark turned to his signaler. "Artillery to advance. Mortars open fire as well."

The signal clicked out along the line, and seconds later the deep, coughing rumble of the mortar batteries opened up. Ha'ark trained his field glasses on the line.

The mortar tubes had already been set and aimed. Crews stood ready, dropping rounds in, the shells lofting upward, slowly enough that they could be seen as flashes of metallic gray streaking heavenward. The weapons were so blasted simple, he could not understand why the Yankees had never thought of them. They were nothing more than iron pipes with a firing pin in the bottom, a small explosive charge in the tail of the round with a percussion cap, and then the shell mounted in the front with another cap to set it off when it hit.

Thirty artillery pieces started forward, the horses pulling them kicking up clods of dirt as they struggled to build up speed. The defenses in the city opened up in dead earnest. A lucky shot caught a caisson, and it disappeared in a thunderclap roar.

All eyes turned toward Ha'ark.

"To be expected," he said quietly, and then he nodded toward Yugba's advancing umen. "I suggest you look to our right for a moment."

The charge was thundering across the steppe, the high, ululating cries of the Bantag host echoing across the field. The cry was picked up by more than one of the umen commanders behind Ha'ark. Some of them drew their scimitars and waved them overhead.

White puffs of smoke erupted along the wall, and seconds later the shots plowed into the line. Horses tumbled down, riders were thrown and then crushed beneath the inexorable wall charging up behind them. The umen commanders were completely carried away by the sight, screaming curses, encouragements, urging the charge forward.

On the left the skirmish line's firepower was increasing. In places the lines were bunched up, and Ha'ark looked significantly at Jamul, who nodded that he was aware of the mistake.

"They still need training," Ha'ark said quietly. As if to add weight to his argument, a shell burst in the middle of a knot of warriors, knocking down more than a dozen of them. The line continued to surge forward. In some places the range was now less than two hundred yards. A scattering of casualties dotted the field, warriors from the rear ranks rushing forward to fill the gaps. The artillery was unlimbering behind them, gunners swinging their weapons around. He trained his field glasses on a crew and watched as they unscrewed the breech, then rammed a shell in, followed by a powder bag.

Primitive, Ha'ark thought, but we don't have the metallurgy skills yet for high-grade steel and brass shell casings except for some lightweight equipment. The gun commander sighted down the barrel, a crew member working the screw to lower the elevation. The commander stepped back and held his hand up as another crew member inserted the primer, then moved to one side.

The gun kicked back, disappearing in a cloud of smoke. Ha'ark swung his field glasses toward the wall and grunted in satisfaction at the explosion, only a few paces from the main gate.

He turned his attention back to the right. The umen, now within a hundred paces of the wall, came to a stop, the riders milling about as they sent volleys of arrows heavenward, darkening the sky. Arrows thundered into the city, some of them flame-tipped, and fires were beginning to erupt. But along the battlement wall the artillery continued the pounding delivering deadly loads of canister that tore bloody paths through the ranks.

A cry of alarm went up from the warriors behind him.

"Yugba's down!" one of them gasped.

Ha'ark trained his glasses on the confusion but could no longer see the triangular blood-red flag.

"Get a rescue team down there with a healer," Ha'ark commanded, and seconds later a horse-drawn cart bounced across the field.

His own artillery on the left was in full play, smothering the gate and walls to either side. Several guns mounted on the battlements were already out of action, one of them lying broken in a pile of rubble. A well-placed shot burst the gates wide open, and Ha'ark looked at Jamul, who grinned with delight.

"I thought the place of a umen commander was forward with his warriors," someone in the crowd behind Ha'ark sniffed.

Ha'ark turned in his chair. "No longer. Let the regiment commanders be the examples. A commander of ten thousand will now lead from the rear, observing the battle, controlling it. What good did Yugba do?"

"He died a Bantag," came the reply.

"He died and the wall in front of him still stands. That was a wasted death. Dying does not equal victory, and victory is what I seek."

Ha'ark turned away with a gesture of contempt and pointed toward the chaos on the right flank. Riders were galloping straight at the wall. Some of them gained the side of the battlement and then leapt on their saddles and attempted to vault up onto the walls. Crossfire from the bastions kept knocking them down. Others were at the eastern gate, axes flashing as they attempted to cut through. Most were able to make only one or two strokes before being swept away by blasts of canister or crushed by rocks thrown from above. Sections of the overhead roofing of logs, designed for protection from plunging flights of arrows, were on fire, but Chin defenders gamely hung on, continuing to fire their cannon and muskets and throwing anything that might crush a Bantag storming beneath them.

"Call them back," someone whispered behind Ha'ark. He turned and looked at the umen commanders.

"What, order a retreat from mere cattle?" he asked sarcastically.

"Call them back, my Qarth. This slaughter is senseless." It was Katu, of the yellow horse umen. Ha'ark could see that Katu fully understood now. As for the others, it was clear that some still did not see.

"In a moment."

Ha'ark faced the battle. On the western side, the entire wall for fifty paces to either side of the now shattered gate was nothing but smoking rubble. Not a single Chin could be seen standing, and the houses behind the wall were in flames. The artillery fire suddenly shifted, pouring in on the flanks of the breech.

The heavy skirmish line stood up and rushed forward in short bursts, warriors in the front stopping to fire, then kneeling to reload as those behind them dashed another dozen paces forward and did the same. The first warriors hit the rubble and scrambled it. Several of them dropped, but the wave continued forward and stormed into the city. From the left flank a column of mounted warriors also rushed forward at the gallop, racing to the shattered wall, dismounting and pouring in. Where the shattered gate had stood, half a hundred warriors with rifles slung on their backs labored to clear a path as the supporting artillery started for the city as well. Along the western crest line facing the city the mortars fell silent.

Ha'ark finally stood up and faced the Bantag umen

commanders, ignoring the debacle that was still under way on the eastern wall.

"Any questions?"

"This was a senseless slaughter," one of them snarled bitterly.

"Yes, it was," Ha'ark replied quietly, "but necessary because of you."

"Because of me?"

"Yes. You. And all like you. For four long seasons I've been telling you that what you call cattle have mastered war and you have not."

"They changed everything, the soulless scum."

"And either you must change or they will plow all our bones into the earth. That is why we must make new weapons and learn how to use them. A third of our army, twenty umens, is now arrayed with guns and artillery, but still you did not understand. Thus this little game today.

"Jamul, what are the estimates on losses?" Ha'ark asked without turning his head.

"I'd say less than two hundred dead and wounded gaining the western gate, it would have been fewer if they hadn't bunched up. At least a thousand on the other flank, and they're just gaining the wall now."

Ha'ark scanned his commanders with an icy stare, challenging a response.

"But the way you did this?" one of them finally offered.

"You mean this exercise?" Ha'ark snapped. "You had to be shown."

"But to deliberately arm cattle, train them, then promise them their lives if they can hold until dark? You just killed and crippled a thousand of our best in this mad show of yours."

"Yugba did," Ha'ark replied calmly. "I did not order him to charge. He did it himself."

"You goaded him, my Qarth."

Ha'ark nodded. "As will our enemy when we face them. Learn that as well!"

Ha'ark pointed at the chaos on the eastern flank.

"Oh, they would have taken the town eventually, but at what cost? What you saw there was exactly the mistake the Tugars and the Merki made. In their arrogance they could not accept the fact that the humans could outthink them."

There was an angry stirring from the assembled commanders.

"I know that it stings," Ha'ark said, his voice dropping. "After all, they are only cattle."

He smiled. "That is undoubtedly what our cousins said, first in their disdain and then in their shock as they lay dying. 'After all, they are only cattle.' We must purge that thought from our minds if we are to win. They are crafty, capable, and in many ways better than we are at this new way of war."

"My Quarth, you are asking us to believe that the world has been turned upon itself, that we now walk in the sky and the earth is above us."

Ha'ark nodded as Vakal, commander of the fourth black horse, spoke. He could sense that Vakal was speaking not in defiance but in confusion.

"We shall set the universe right again," Ha'ark replied calmly. "But your words are true. These humans have set the world, the universe, upon its head. It is our task to set it right again."

"This war will corrupt us," someone in the back of the group hissed. "Let us leave this place. Let us do as Tamuka of the Merki said he would do. We should slaughter all cattle on this world, riding eastward as we have since the beginning. Then when we return to this place in a generation, we can slaughter what is left."

"Madness," Ha'ark snarled. "Do you leave the fanged leopard at your back while you pursue the rabbit at your front? No! You first turn and slay the leopard. You cloak yourself in his pelt, and then, if you wish to lower yourself, you hunt the rabbit."

Ha'ark saw heads nodding reluctantly in agreement.

Damn primitives, he thought to himself. Four long years of this, trying to drum it into them, that they were on the brink· of disaster, annihilation. Even though many had come to accept the guns, still they did not understand the fundamental change in tactics and, beyond that, the profound societal changes that went with it. The day of the mounted charge against a well-positioned enemy was dead. The horse was nothing more than a means of getting to the battle-field. The shock that he would soon deliver would strike even harder the majority of the Horde would go to battle on foot. Keeping six hundred thousand warriors mounted was a logistical nightmare. With the rail line to the sea completed, and his plans for projecting power on the sea, there was no need for his warriors to ride. How that would hurt their pride!

The umen commanders stood silent and he scanned their eyes. Some still gazed upon him as the Redeemer, the one of prophecy sent to return them to their glory. But in the thousands of years on this world their vision of glory had changed. They would charge to it, horses galloping to other worlds. The thought of doing it on steam engines was beyond them. Some had come to waver, his growing net of spies telling him of dark whisperings that he was an impostor. It was time to play upon prophecy again. He nodded to the four companions who stood behind him.

"We came to you from another world as a fulfillment of prophecy. For has it not been chanted that in the time of darkness there will be five, and they will return the Horde unto its former greatness? That we shall stride between worlds and take into our hands all that is rightfully ours?"

He saw that the appeal to the ancient prophecies

still worked as many nodded in agreement. The prophecy was remarkably convenient. It never ceased to amaze him how an ancient chant about five warriors who disappeared but would one day return was one of the key tools in his quest for empire. What fascinated him as well was that fragments of the legend existed in the ancient history of his own world, yet another proof that this was indeed the home from which the race had sprung.

He wondered yet again what might have happened if he had arrived not with five warriors but with only three—or worse yet, alone. Chances were that they would have been riddled with arrows on the spot.

"My lord Qarth."

Ha'ark saw that the healer's cart had returned from the field and that the healer was lying prostrate before him.

"Go on."

"My lord. The commander Yugba is dead. I could not save him."

A low murmur erupted behind him.

The healer was obviously expecting death, but he was also one who had been trained for more than a year to treat wounds on the field. If he could not save Yugba, chances were no one could have.

"You did your best. There is no fault with you. Leave."

The healer looked up at him in amazement.

"No one is to be punished. If I did that to every healer who lost a patient in the war to come, no one would be left. Now go."

Ha'ark turned back to his commanders. "You now can see what has to be done if we are to win."

The group was silent.

He gave a curt nod of dismissal.

"I think they finally are starting to see," Jamul announced, using their native tongue rather than the speech of the Bantag.

"Starting is a long way from fully understanding," Ha'ark replied.

"At least Yugba is out of the way. He was a threat, my friend. He was of the imperial line, and I am willing to bet he was plotting a way to eliminate you."

Ha'ark smiled. "Why do you think I positioned his umen on the right? I knew he would commit rather than let our new army win the day."

He realized it was best not to say more. Later he would go into the city and find the three Chin whom he had armed with breechloading rifles. Their hiding place had been well chosen, and they were to go there if they succeeded in killing Yugba, to wait out the sack of the city. Of course, he would kill them rather than let them escape as promised. One less rival to worry about now.

"You know it will take another season, maybe two, before we are fully ready."

Ha'ark nodded and looked back toward the city, which was now consumed in flames. That was the vexing point of it all. In four years he had wrenched a nation from barbarism to at least the beginnings of a modern state. In the great complex of Chin cities, two days' ride to the east, were factories using hundreds of thousands of laborers. Each week he had a thousand more guns, ten new cannon, another mile of track, and even the first of the new flying machines powered by yet more engines taken from ancient burial mounds. In the dockyards of the Chin city of X'ian, the first of the iron ships was about to be launched. Yet it was all going much too slowly.

What were the Yankees doing? That was the question now. Where were their resources located? And the engines. That was the key. Damnable steam engines. But neither he nor those who had come with him understood how to create an internal combustion engine, let alone how to obtain and refine the oil needed to power it. It would have to be steam, and the Yankees apparently had a far better mastery of how it functioned. The engines built so far for the railroad could barely pull six cars loaded with supplies, yet by all reports from the Merki, the Yankees, three years ago, had machines that could pull a dozen cars. Enough prisoners had been taken who knew something about steam; combined with the knowledge he had, he could at least expect a passable model. The ships he wanted were all underpowered as well. It was the one area in which the Yankees were undoubtedly besting him. Most of all, he feared that the new weapons he was making might be matched by the Yankees, once they learned the secret. His only hope was that when the time came he would have so many weapons ready that he could overwhelm them before they could go into production.

Damn! Damn all of it. The five of them lived daily with machines generations ahead of those the Yankees had—electricity, communication without wire, flight, machine guns, poison gas, even warfare using disease—wonderful things, and yet he could barely avail himself of them. He looked down at the rifle lying in the grass beside him. Even how to make the smokeless powder in the cartridges he brought with him was beyond any of them. Old-fashioned powder was available in abundance now, but all the weapons he wanted, dreamed of, were beyond his grasp. He could make primitive single-shot breechloaders, but it would be a year or more before the cattle under his command were well enough trained to turn out the precision tools necessary to manufacture bolt-action rifles, machine guns, and the shells to feed them.

He could sense as well that the Yankees would move to probe his operations. Already their ships maintained a constant presence at the mouth of the river leading up to X'ian. He had deliberately built the factories nearly four hundred miles back from the coast so that they were safe from attack. That location also gave him access to the limitless labor of the Chin cattle in their fat cities while isolating the source of his strength from attack or from the threat of an escaping prisoner. The railroad made it possible to do this, allowing him to build his forces and then move the supplies where they would be based for the war.

The railroad ... somehow he could sense a weakness there. So far no Yankee flyer had been sighted even approaching the coast. The range was obviously too far from their bases. But suppose they could? They would see the railroad and might follow the track, thus revealing all.

They might very well have been lulled by the message he had sent the year before, which was a mixture of threats and promises. Claiming the land once owned by the Merki but announcing as well that he wanted nothing more, he nevertheless made it clear that any move into what was now their land would be an act of war and would be met in kind.

How long would they fall for that? How long before they came to look and the elaborate secret was finally revealed? Just another year and then it will be too late for them, he thought. We will storm across the sea, land our army, fall upon Roum, and then annihilate what is left. It was time to lull them again, to send another message. And yet there was something else as well. His thoughts turned to the Yankee sergeant whom he had not spoken to in months. Was it there?

Hans scanned those who had gathered in his cramped office and felt a surge of elation mingled with fear. He knew that the precautions they had taken were well thought out: The watcher outside would knock three times on the door as a warning. Watchers were also placed at the four sides of the building, and there were two more watchers at the gate into the compound. The chance of being interrupted on a Bantag guard's random search was nonexistent. It was, however, the prisoners themselves whom he had to fear the most, and as he scanned the men and women crammed into his office he wondered just how well Gregory had judged their character and strength. For in a universe where a bowl of watery soup was the margin between living and dying, the betrayal of another could be purchased with a handful of rice.

Hans looked into their eyes—Ketswana and Manda, Gregory and Alexi, the tragic, drawn features of Lin, and finally Tamira. With a protective gesture she nestled Andrew against her breast and kissed him lightly on the top of his head so that the boy stirred and then with a sigh snuggled into his mother's enveloping warmth. Again there was the surge of feelings. To him, children had always been creatures whom he would make a polite noise over when forced to, but beyond that there was nothing other than the soldier's mentality that they were to be protected. The birth of young Andrew had shattered that illusion forever and explained to him why the murder of Lin's child had pushed him over the edge into this act of madness.

Hans nodded at Alexi, who tapped once on the door. A single tap came in reply ... they were as safe as they could hope to be for the moment.

Hans leaned against the rough log wall and decided that the moment was worth a chew from his precious stash of tobacco. Fishing in his pocket, he pulled out a plug and tried not to see Tamira's reproachful look as he bit down and savored the first bitter jolt.

"Before I go any further I want to clear something

up," Hans began quietly. "We are all dead. The very act of meeting like this condemns all of us to the slaughter pits."

"We're dead anyhow," Ketswana snarled, the language of the Horde sounding a bit frightening in his deep, rumbling voice. "We saw that today. Nothing can protect us, nothing." And he nodded toward Lin Zhu, who sat on the floor in the corner, his eyes red-rimmed with grief. Lin stirred as if he wanted to speak, but then shook his head and covered his face with his hands. Tamira went to sit by him, whispering softly to him even as she hugged Andrew.

Just watching her brought a lump of fear to Hans's throat. She alone was the reason he continued to will himself to live. Though he felt himself a traitor to Andrew, to the Republic, in the end he could not tolerate the thought of what would happen to her if he should someday refuse, or someday no longer be useful to the bastards. But the death of Lin's wife and child had shown him that even he could not protect the two that he loved most.

So ironic. A life devoted to war, to the armies of his two adopted countries, the United States and Rus. Never had there been anyone, until now. He now saw again that expression in her eyes, a look that still could trigger such a surge of emotion in him, even in this hell. For her and Andrew—maybe that's what it all came down to in the end when all other reasons were forgotten.

"If they find out, though"—Hans hesitated, looking at Lin, but then pressed on—"it won't be the quick death of the slaughter pits. It will be the Moon Feast. And it won't be just you, it will be anyone you hold dear." He paused again, knowing it had to be said. "Even to the smallest infant."

He did not need to describe it to them. They had all seen the victims dragged forth for the ritual, slowly roasted over a fire for hours while still alive, then strapped to the table, the tops of their skulls removed and the brains consumed while they were still alive, though the light of life was dying. Being consumed, while the bastards roared with laughter. If it was a family thus condemned, parents would watch their children go, then husbands their wives.

He looked straight into Tamira's eyes. If she shakes her head no, can I still back away? he wondered. She looked down at Andrew, who slept against her breast, and then back at Hans. He sensed that all in the room were watching her.

"I'd rather he die that way than live as cattle," she whispered, her voice filled with bitter resolve.

Hans smiled at his companions. "Then we escape," he announced quietly.

The line had been crossed. He had resisted it for years, out of fear of what would happen and a belief in the mad impossibility of it all. He could feel the rush of emotion, as if he had opened a door and a warm, springlike breeze had suddenly swept into their lives again.

Ketswana stirred, looking at Manda. "We must accept what will happen to those left behind."

"They will be slaughtered," Gregory replied. "If we succeed, the Bantag will kill hundreds, perhaps thousands, in their rage."

"They can't kill all of them," Manda interjected. "They need trained cattle. Some will be killed for vengeance, but not all."

"Explain that to those who are chosen to die. The fact that others will live will mean nothing to them."

"We're dead anyhow," Alexi announced coldly. "The sooner all of us realize that, the better."

"A condemned man doesn't care about the others and will curse any who bring his day of execution closer," Hans replied. "Let me ask all of you this: If you knew that prisoners in the next compound were planning to escape, if you knew that you would be slaughtered in revenge, wouldn't you stop them, or reveal the plan?"

He knew this was the core of his argument against any attempt to escape. It would be impossible to get everyone out, and those left behind would surely die.

"No. I would not say a word to stop them."

Startled, Hans realized it was Tamira who spoke.

"Let's no longer live the illusion," she said quietly. "The death of Lin's wife proved that. Don't you think they are training others to replace us? Don't you think they fear us because we know too much, because they are too dependent on us? If I knew there was hope for someone, anyone, in this nightmare, I'd want them to go."

"Even if Andrew was condemned in punishment?" Ketswana asked cautiously.

"The Buddha will take him to a better world."

Ketswana stood silent and Hans felt a swelling of pride. Tamira's calm gaze, as always, stilled his fear.

He looked at his companions, who each nodded in turn.

"Then we must accept now that we are condemning others to die."

No one replied to his statement for a long moment. Then finally Gregory broke the silence. "It's not just us anymore. We must get word back to the Republic of what is being made there. The Bantag are preparing for a war that could very well destroy the only hope for humanity on this planet. Yes, people will die, but I saw tens of thousands die at Hispania. I ordered some of my closest friends into certain death because it was my duty and their duty so that others would live. That is why we must do it and why we must succeed."

Hans saw the nods of agreement. "Alexi, you're the one who has thought this out. Tell us your plan."

Alexi walked up to the drafting table and brought out from his sweat-stained tunic a tightly folded

sheet of rice paper. As he spread it out, he motioned
for the others to gather around. Even Lin stirred, and
the others parted so their nearsighted friend could
see the map.

"It's death to have such a drawing," Ketswana
said cautiously.

Alexi shook his head and laughed. "That's the least
of my worries at the moment."

"What is it?" Manda asked.

"A map of the camp," Alexi replied. "There are
six barracks buildings in our section, each housing
one hundred people." As he spoke he pointed out
the rows of buildings. "The foundry is just to the
south, here"—he tapped the map with his forefin-
ger—"and the steam engine works are on the other
side of our barracks, to the north of us. The camp
where the Chin laborers live is south of the foundry.

"As you can see, there's a rail yard just on the
other side of the wall on the west side of the compound. Branch lines go to other factories making
guns, to the airship works, and to that new factory
that only Bantag are allowed to enter."

He started to trace out one of the lines. "This is the
one that comes through the gate, into our foundry
compound. It's the track most of you cross over
every day going in and out of the building. My plan
is that we seize one of the trains, run it to the end
of line at the city of X'ian, and from there flee, hope-
fully by boat. I've gone nearly all the way up the
line half a dozen times with new trains. I've never
dared to draw a map, but I've remembered everything. Once we get out by train, I think we can actually make it all the way."

The others all started shaking their heads. Hans
stood silent, looking straight at Alexi.

"Impossible," Hans sighed, his disappointment
showing. Alexi had been the first to approach him
about an escape, before the factory was even half

built, and he had hoped that more thought would have been given to it.

"First, the trains leaving the factory pass through the gate at the entrance. The train has to stop and be checked by those bastards before the gate is opened. Then it goes to a siding to get coal and water before it heads onto the main line."

"And the switches," Lin interjected, surprising everyone by stirring from his grief. "Remember, I am outside the gate every day. There's a Bantag guard at the switch house. He is armed, and I think he has a key that locks the switches. If you do not catch him by surprise the switches will be jammed. But I don't think you'll even get through the gate. It is a counterweighted barrier. They've thought that we might try this and have planned for it. All the guard needs to do is cut the rope to the weight and the gate is locked shut, with us trapped inside. There isn't even enough length of track to build up speed in hopes of smashing the gate down."

Lin shook his head in disgust and turned away from the table.

"Let's hear him out," Hans said quietly. "Go on, Alexi."

"We don't seize the train on the inside. We take it on the outside."

Hans stirred. He had pondered the problem ever since coming to this nightmare. In designing some of the facilities he had tried in one way or another to build in some flaw, some weakness that could perhaps be exploited, but Karga, receiving advice from someone, had always found out the flaws and changed them at the last minute.

"How?"

"We tunnel out to the rail yard."

"Tunnel?"

"Look at the map. From the northwest corner of the factory it's only twenty-five feet to the barrier wall. Once under the wall, we cross under the tracks and bring it up underneath the food warehouse by the main siding where Lin works."

Now Lin examined the map again, with renewed interest. "I don't know," he said quietly.

"Just listen," Alexi said excitedly. "It's less than two hundred feet, as opposed to four hundred feet from any of the barracks. You know the Bantag worry about tunnels; they're always looking under the barracks because they figure that's where we'd dig. But I'm telling you we can dig one right under their noses, from inside the factory."

He nodded at Gregory.

"I guess this is where I come in," Gregory announced, standing up. "When Alexi first suggested that I find a place in the foundry to dig a tunnel, I thought he was insane. But I kept my eyes open and finally hit on the spot."

His gaze locked on Ketswana.

"I never told you this before, my friend, but it's right behind your furnace, number three, in the charcoal pile."

Ketswana laughed. "We're in the northwest corner, so where else could it be?"

"The two corner furnaces are furthest away from the two entry gates in the middle of the building. I've already checked and I know the guard posts there cannot clearly see number three, even when all the furnaces are cold. When we've got pours going and the building fills with smoke, number three might as well be on the other side of the world."

"What about roving guards, especially Karga?" Lin asked.

"I've been watching them for months now. The heat in the back of the buildings tends to keep them away. They usually stop a good thirty yards short. For those who do come closer, we'll set up a watch system."

"Are you talking about digging in the open?" Hans asked.

"This is the ingenious part of Gregory's plan," Alexi chimed in. "Next time number three is shut down to be cleaned and recharged with ore and charcoal, we quickly cut through the floor in the charcoal pile alongside number three furnace."

Alexi pointed out the place on the map.

"We pull up the flagstones, keep others working around them, shoveling charcoal, and they dig down. Once they're a few feet in, we can build up a wall of charcoal around them to conceal the work. By the time the shift is over, they should be seven or eight feet down. I've designed a lid that we can then place over the hole, with two men down inside."

"What about air?" Hans asked. "How will they breathe?"

Alexi smiled and pulled out another slip of paper.

"I thought of that." He rolled the paper out. "By a small bellows. We run a pipe up through the tunnel, out through a hole in the lid, and hide it in the charcoal pile. We have one man work the bellows to pump the bad air up the pipe. A second pipe, which also starts in the charcoal pit, feeds fresh air in to replace the bad air pumped out."

"Petersburg. The Crater," Hans whispered.

Alexi looked puzzled.

"I'll tell you about it sometime. Something of the same idea that we used in our war on Earth. All right, you've got the air taken care of. What about getting rid of the dirt? And lumber for shoring up the tunnel?"

"We bag the dirt, hoist it up, and throw it into the furnace or scatter it on the floor. Shoring—I don't think we'll need much. The soil underneath is clay, but to be on the safe side we should shore as we go under the building foundation and tracks. We can steal the lumber from the barracks and smuggle it in. Or a treadmill breaks and we repair it, but some of the broken parts wind up hidden in the charcoal pit."

"And the breakout?" Hans asked. "How do we pull that off?"

"On the night of the next double Moon Feast." Even as he said the words, Hans felt a shiver of dread. Those who in some way had antagonized a Bantag guard might think that the issue had passed, until the afternoon of the feast, when they, and their loved ones, were suddenly tied up and led away. Karga often made a game of it, casually threatening whoever got in his way, laughing at the terror on their faces.

"That's only thirty days from now," Ketswana said.

"Precisely," Gregory replied. "Ketswana, since it is your furnace we're going to be digging from, I think you should be head of security for this operation."

Hans smiled at the suggestion. Ketswana had the trust of most everyone in the factory. He also had an uncanny skill at spotting traitors in the ranks and those occasional new arrivals who turned out to be loyal pets, placed in the factory to learn of anything unusual going on.

"Such a secret will be impossible to keep for long," Ketswana said, automatically falling into his new job. "Someone will slip. Once the word gets out, it will be impossible to control. There'll be panic, people demanding to be taken, threatening that if they're not, they'll tell, or simply they'll tell anyhow, to spare themselves or gain a moment's favor with the master."

Hans nodded slowly in agreement. "The date is the Moon Feast, then," he interjected. "Besides, the bastards start celebrating early that day. Most of them will be drunk by sundown."

Alexi smiled and nodded. "I already have the parts

for the bellows. We can start tomorrow when we begin the next load for the furnace."

"Keeping the secret, though," Ketswana said. "There's no way that this secret will ever be kept."

"Only the work crews and those in planning will know right now," Alexi replied. "That will keep the number down to thirty at most. The night of the breakout we'll try and pull out as many as we can."

"How many?" Ketswana asked.

Alexi hesitated. "There's just under seven hundred in our compound. I think we can get three to four hundred out before the guards realize what's happening."

"Are you mad?" Ketswana snapped. "There'll be a panic. A mob will form at the tunnel entrance, clamoring to get in."

"Most won't know until the moment we tell them," Alexi relied.

"But sooner or later they will find out. By all the gods, there'll be madness, for all will know that if they're left behind they'll be slaughtered in vengeance."

Hans extended his hand for silence. The very issue Ketswana had raised was the reason he had buried a dream of escape for so long.

"We can't save everyone," Hans said quietly. "All we can hope is to save some. Ketswana, it will be your job to prevent the panic until we've seized the train and are ready to flee."

"Seizing the train," Tamira mused. "I've heard much about the tunnel, but nothing of what we will do once it is finished."

Hans smiled at the criticism. It was a point he had forgotten in the momentary excitement.

Alexi responded. "Lin, this is the part that you will have to arrange. The tunnel will come up under the food warehouse."

"Why there?"

"Because it's the closest building outside the compound. We can hide everyone there until the moment comes to rush a train. On the day of the breakout you must make sure that the corner of the building closest to the factory has a cleared floor space. As soon as you close the warehouse our diggers will break through."

"Usually there's at least one Bantag guard prowling about, though. Sometimes he goes into the building, if only to steal food."

Gregory nodded. "That's why I'll go through first. It will be the most dangerous moment. If need be I'll kill him before he can spread the alarm. Once that's secured we can start bringing people up. The warehouse will provide us with food for the journey as well."

"Again, though," Ketswana interjected, "why so many? If you think we can save everyone, it's a fool's dream. The guards are in the foundry day and night. At some point they will notice people gathering around the entry hole."

"It will be your job to work out a schedule and a means of concealing it," Hans replied. "If we're going to try this, I don't want just a handful to have their chance."

"Seizing the train is only the first step," Alexi added. "Chances are, we'll have to fight our way out, and the more people we have, the better the chance of making it all the way. I've got a list drawn up of who we need and the priority in which they get out."

"Not in writing?" Ketswana asked, his voice filled with concern.

"No, of course not. Those who work on the tunnel and their families. Those who work in the warehouse that we tunnel into. The yard crews and workers on the train should go first."

"Some of these people have children, young ones," Manda said.

"I've thought about that," Alexi replied. "The children have to go, of course. For the very young ones, we'll bribe a guard for some opium to make them sleep so they don't make any noise."

"That could be dangerous for them," Tamira said. Then realizing all that was being implied, she smiled and nodded her head.

"We wait until the daily trainload of rails has gone out and the engine is loaded with wood and water. Then we rush it. I don't like the fact that it's open flatcars, but at least we're sure it will be there and ready to go. If there should happen to be another train in the yard, preferably with boxcars, we'll take that one instead. Just before we make the rush, Gregory will lead several men to the switch house, kill the guard, and get the keys for the switches. The telegrapher works in there as well. I'll make sure he's one of us. He'll order any trains on the track ahead onto sidings, and he should know the next day's schedule as well. We then cut the wire, rush the engine, and head out. With luck we can stay ahead of the news of our escape."

"And once at X'ian, then what?" Hans asked.

"I've been told that at X'ian there's a navigable river all the way down to the sea and freedom. I think this has to be true because I've seen loads of what looks like ship's armor and several very large guns being moved westward on the line."

"When was the last time you actually rode a train that far?" Lin asked.

"I've never been there," Alexi replied. "They only let me run the train back in the early days when the line was still being built. Since then all engineers are Bantag, though occasionally they'll still have human firemen working in the tender, but we don't know where they're kept."

"So how can you be sure?"

"I can't," Alexi replied. "But I do know that's

where the rail line goes. It fits a logical pattern. We time our arrival into the town at dark. By that time we should have caught at least one train loaded with guns."

"A big if," Hans interjected.

"A good chance, though. There's at least one or two boxcar loads going up there every day or two. I overheard a couple of guards talking about it several months back, that there's several training camps for their new army along the rail line."

"You mean we're going right through training areas?" Hans asked.

"No alternative," Gregory replied. "But if we can seize some weapons it will give us a fighting chance once we get into X'ian."

"You're talking about turning our people into combat troops in a single day, Gregory."

"Well, sir, I figure that over the next month you can teach Ketswana and his workers how to use a gun. That way they'll have something of a head start."

Hans could not refrain from laughing at the thought of secretly drilling with imaginary weapons right under the noses of the guards.

"Alexi and I were in the army, and at least four of the Cartha laborers were in their army during the war against us. It's a start, and desperation can be one hell of a reason for learning quick."

"Assuming we get the guns in the first place," Hans replied, trying to hide his sarcasm.

"Something like that, sir. If we're very lucky we might not even have to fight," Alexi continued. "I think it's a fair assumption that the train must come up close to a dockyard. We swarm out, surprising the bastards, seize a boat, and then get the hell down the river and out to sea."

"And what about the pursuit?"

Alexi grinned.

"We smash everything on the way. Burn bridges, tear up track, cut telegraph lines. We'll sow chaos all the way up the line. At each place we arrive they'll know nothing. If we can bluff our way through, well and good. If not, we fight, try to trigger rebellion with the people who are slaves there, and move on. I'd like to think that in X'ian we might even get thousands of people rioting."

Hans sat quietly, trying to absorb all that was being offered. Part of him wanted to believe that this mad dream was indeed possible, that in a month they might be free, heading back to Rus, to safety, to living. Yet another part of him whispered that it was a fool's dream. So much could go awry. He had heard the words "assume," and "hope for" too many times in the plan presented to him.

He saw that the others were caught up in their own mad dreams, the mere telling of it convincing them that it was real. Yet, he thought, if any single link in the chain of events breaks, it will all fall apart. The tunnel is discovered, a panic breaks out on the night of the escape, the train breaks down, the switches jam, we run across armed Bantag troops while we have no weapons, word gets out ahead of us—any of a million random events could destroy even the best of plans.

"What about the flyers?" Lin asked quietly.

"What about them?" Alexi replied.

"First. If only we could seize them, there would be our escape."

"A dream," Alexi replied. "They're kept half a dozen leagues away, back toward the main encampments of the Horde. We don't know anyone there, we don't even know exactly how to get to them, let alone how to fly them. Even if we did, each flyer can carry, at best, only half a dozen humans. Hundreds would be abandoned."

"But in all your plans of escape," Lin continued,

"I haven't heard your plan for how to deal with them. We can cut the talking wire, that I see, and once we are clear of this cursed place those ahead of us will know nothing. But all they need to do is send a flyer up. If it gets ahead of us with word of our escape, they'll just have to tear up fifty yards of track, smash a switch, or burn a bridge, and we'll be trapped."

Alexi nodded and Hans watched him closely, waiting for an answer. "Pray to Kesus that the winds favor us and slow the flyers down."

"And that's your plan for them?" Hans replied coldly. "Rely on prayer?"

Alexi looked around the room and then finally nodded.

"We'll all have to pray that it's not just the winds that favor us," Hans said quietly.

He scanned the group, wondering yet again. He knew that if he said no, they would listen. It rested with him. He could see the youthful enthusiasm in Gregory, believing that all things were possible, and it conjured up a memory. Andrew would say yes, but I would urge caution, urge him to think about it some more. And yet what alternative was there here? Can I lead them, knowing it's pure madness even to try? That's what they want—and it's the one thing I can still do.

Getting to the train will be the first step. Then it will be fighting all the way up the line for hundreds of miles. That's something they tried to skip over. Hell, they gave Andrew's men the first Congressional Medals of Honor for stealing that train in Marietta, Georgia, and trying to smash the line north to Chattanooga. They also caught and hung Andrews and half a dozen of his men. Hanging would be preferable to what the Bantag will do to any they catch trying to escape. Even the Moon Feast would be a blessed relief.

He looked at Tamira again, Andrew still asleep in her lap. At least they won't take them alive, he thought quietly. She smiled that bewitching, childlike smile of hers that could still make his heart constrict. Yet again he sensed that somehow she could read his mind, knew that he was contemplating her death, and knew as well that it would be a final act of love.

He suddenly realized that he had been lost in thought and that his companions were waiting.

"Each of you, get your teams organized. Gregory, you oversee digging and concealment; Ketswana and Manda, security. Alexi, intelligence on the outside. Lin, your role comes in when we get ready to break out. The building has to be ready and rations for four hundred people for a week prepared. Ketswana, I want you to know if a Bantag or anyone who is not in on the secret gets within a hundred paces of the mine. Watches are to be kept on any person we don't trust completely. Alexi, train schedules. We have to pull in the telegrapher and the dispatchers."

He saw the childlike delight in their eyes, as if a stern and elderly schoolmaster had suddenly announced a holiday.

"For weapons, it's going to be picks, shovels, and whatever knives and sharp tools we can steal from the kitchen when the time comes."

He took a deep breath.

"Assume from this moment on that we are all dead. Even if we succeed with the tunnel, getting out and taking a train are improbable at best. It's hundreds of miles to the end of the line, and again, the odds are against us. If word gets ahead of us for any reason, we're dead. Once at the end of the line we'll have to seize a boat; we don't even know if one will be there. We're not even sure of the size of the garrison there, the defenses, or how to get past them. And if we do get a boat, then what? Even if we get to the open sea, it's at least five hundred miles to republic territory.

"If possible, we'll need to recruit people who have experience with boats, anyone who has worked on the rail gangs or traveled on the line, and especially anyone who has lived or worked in X'ian."

He turned to Ketswana. "We will have to fight terror with terror. Once a person is approached, he cannot back out or refuse. If he refuses, he will soon realize that as soon as we make our break, chances are he will die anyway. In that situation he is bound to denounce us."

He hesitated. "Anyone who refuses must be killed. Is that clear?"

Ketswana nodded slowly in agreement.

"Everyone we recruit must understand as well that if we are denounced, somehow, some way, if any survive they will track the traitor down and kill him, even if he is moved to the furthest reaches of the Bantag realms. Ketswana, I want you to select two or three people that no one will ever know about, not even me. If we break out, they go with us. But if we fail, they will be the seekers of vengeance."

"It has already been done," Ketswana replied with a chilling grin.

Hans carefully studied the towering Zulu and his wife. There was such cold determination in the man's eyes that Hans felt a sense of awe. He realized that Ketswana would kill without a second's hesitation if any of them were ever threatened.

"Are you ready to start digging tomorrow?"

"As soon as we begin loading the furnace," Gregory replied.

"Then let's do it. Now get out of here. We've been together too long already."

He could not recall the last time he had felt such joy in those around him. One by one they slipped out of the room until finally he was alone with Tamira.

"Will it truly work?" she asked.

"Of course it will."

And, as always, he knew she could tell when he lied.

Leaning back from his desk, Andrew listened as Kathleen opened the door downstairs.

"Mr. President. What a surprise. Won't you come in?"

Andrew put down his pen and rubbed his eyes.

"Andrew, we have company."

The voice echoed up the stairs, and standing up, he looked down at the pile of reports. For once he almost wished he could stay with the paperwork of running an army. He scanned the room, filled now with the memorabilia that Kathleen had so proudly put on display. She had wanted to hang the original painting by Rublev, the most popular Rus artist, of Andrew surrounded by his staff at the Battle of Hispania, but Andrew had preferred instead a simple portrait of himself, Katherine, their daughter, Madison, and the boys, Abraham and Hans. His shot-torn guidon rested in the corner, and a display case against the wall opposite his desk held half a dozen books on the wars and the latest release by Gates Publishing, *A History of the Thirty-fifth Maine and Forty-fourth New York*. His most treasured possessions of all, his Congressional Medal of Honor and papers of commission to the rank of colonel signed by Abraham Lincoln, were framed next to his desk.

Lincoln. How his thoughts so often drifted to him, wondering where he was now, and what he was doing. Was he a lawyer again back in Springfield or, and the thought was troubling, was he still alive? He thought of Kal, waiting downstairs. Lincoln was Kal's model for how a president should look, and though the effect was near to comical—the short, stocky peasant wearing a long black broadcloth coat, a top hat, and even a beard—the effect was nevertheless touching.

"Andrew?"

"Coming."

He brushed a few flecks of lint off his vest, wondering for a second if he should struggle into his jacket. But no, this was an unofficial call, in the privacy of his home. He descended the steps, pausing at the top one to look into the boys' room. Both were fast asleep, and he smiled. Thank God they had been born after the war. The scars of it were somehow imprinted on Madison, even though she had barely been two when it ended. Perhaps it was the universal fear consuming the world around her that had lingered, but even now she would sometimes awake in the middle of the night, crying that the "bogey merki man" was coming to eat her. He listened for a moment and heard a peaceful sigh from her room, then continued down the stairs. As he stepped into the parlor he saw Kal waiting, his back turned, studying the painting that he had refused to hang in his office but that wound up over the fireplace mantel instead.

"It's embarrassing, that painting," Andrew said casually.

President Kal turned with a smile, and stepping forward, he extended his left hand, which Andrew grasped warmly.

"Storm coming on," Kal said with a smile, and for an instant Andrew wondered what he was alluding to. "Funny, when one's coming I can actually feel my lost arm tingle. Does yours bother you like that?"

Kal nodded at his empty right sleeve, and then at Andrew's empty left one.

"At times. It's been ten years since I lost it, and funny, even now, I'll suddenly try to grab something with it."

Kal looked back at the painting. "That Rublev is a wonder. An icon painter who found even bigger business painting heroes. I like this one the most. You look so calm there, your confidence radiating out to all who served with you on that field."

"I was scared to death," Andrew replied softly, "and you know it."

He smiled at the memory of the only time he had ever been dressed down by Kal. It was in the days after the disaster along the Potomac ... Hans, where I lost Hans. He had lost all hope of ever retrieving the situation until Kal had met him and forced him to continue.

"We were all petrified," Kal replied, still gazing at the painting. "And you pulled us through."

"Tea?"

Kathleen came into the room bearing a simple wooden tray and a steaming pot of tea.

"I see only two cups here," Kal said. "Get one for yourself."

"No, I suspect there's political talk coming on. I've got to prepare my lecture for tomorrow's class."

"Doctor Keane, your students will not suffer for want of a preparation I suspect you've already made. Please join us?"

Kathleen smiled. "Who can refuse a presidential order?" And she left the room, returning a moment later with a third mug. Pouring the tea out for her guest, she motioned him over to the chair by the fireplace. Kal settled down with a sigh, putting his mug on a side table so that he could extend his hand toward the fire.

"Chilly out for this late in the year."

Andrew nodded, saying nothing, sensing that Kal was nervous.

Kal finally looked up. "My friend, we must talk."

"I know."

"Let's talk budget first. This latest bit regarding the airship is beyond belief. How could you allow it to happen?"

"You might not believe this, Kal, but I didn't know until the day before yesterday. I'll take responsibility for it, but those under me kept it concealed so it wouldn't reflect on me."

"That damn son-in-law of mine. Did he know?"

Andrew nodded.

Kal sighed and sat back in his chair.

"I fully disagree with the method, but don't come down too hard on him. He did what he thought was right."

"And what are you going to do, Andrew?"

"I've filed unsatisfactory reports on everyone involved. Ferguson will be docked pay and has been placed on inactive status."

"But you're putting him on inactive status anyway because of his health."

"Kal, what are you suggesting I do? Fire all of them?"

Kal took a sip of his tea and looked at the painting again.

"We can't do that," he said softly. "Fire Pat, Vincent, and Lord knows how many others. According to the law we should. But we won't."

Andrew breathed an inner sigh of relief. If Kal had pushed on that point, the way he knew several in Congress undoubtedly wanted, he would have offered his own resignation and taken the blame squarely on himself.

"We'll play the game that it was an administrative mistake."

Kal sighed again, and his gaze drifted toward the fire.

"Your Lincoln, I wonder if he ever wished that he could simply walk out the door of the White House and go back to his home and close the door."

"Most likely every day, Kal," Kathleen interjected.

Kal smiled sadly. "I never thought I'd long for the days when I was an ignorant peasant, living off the scraps of my boyar Ivor's table. If I could forget the fear of the Tugars, it would almost seem to me that I was happier then."

"Your children, your grandchildren are happier now," Andrew replied. "We might not be, but that is our sacrifice so that they can sleep soundly and without fear."

Kal stared at his old friend, as if wanting to push on but not sure how to do it.

"You want to talk about this rumor of my running for president."

Kal nodded. "Why?"

"You think it's a personal attack on you, is that it?"

"We've been friends ever since the day I was first shown into your tent, a frightened peasant, sent to figure out if you were a demon or not."

Andrew chuckled at the memory.

"You and your comrades raised me from ignorance, and for that I shall be forever grateful."

"But ..." Andrew prompted.

"But I am in complete disagreement with you now, old friend."

"As it should be," Andrew replied.

Kal looked at him quizzically.

"Isn't that what the Republic is all about? Disagreeing and then settling our disagreements in public debate."

"A fine sentiment, my friend. But this is different. It is a fundamental argument about the direction the Republic must take."

"It is always that way," Andrew said forcefully. "Every generation views its issues as so earth-shattering in their significance that neither side can, at the start, broker a compromise, but usually that is the end result."

"What about your Civil War?"

Andrew nodded sadly. "It could have been negotiated, if cooler minds had prevailed. Lincoln all but begged in his first inaugural for both sides to come to the table to talk. We did not, and half a million died as a result."

"And our argument?"

"Kal, we see the world in two different lights. Rus is the world you know, it is the land you were born to, love, fought and sacrificed for, and someday shall be buried in, honored as the first president of the Republic. Your thoughts shall always be of Rus first."

"I sense a rebuke in that."

"Not at all, my friend. It is miraculous how you engineered the signing of the Second Constitution, uniting us with Roum, in spite of the misgivings of Congress. I think that as governor of Rus under the new Constitution you will be exemplary."

"But not as president of the Republic?"

Andrew looked his friend straight in the eye and finally shook his head.

Kal reddened. "And you believe your vision is more clear."

"I think so, Kal. Plus, I think I can win."

"And drag us into another war in the process."

"That is what divides us, Kal, the issue of war."

"You believe it is inevitable. I do not," Kal replied heatedly. "We won our fight against the Tugars and the Merki, and heaven knows the bloody price we paid. Half the population of Rus was annihilated."

Kal's voice grew flat. "There are times I wish that you had followed the counsel of Cromwell, taken your ship and fled before the Tugars arrived. You could have returned after they passed, and we would have lost but one in ten of our number. Then we would have had twenty years to prepare for the conflict."

Andrew leaned forward in his chair. "The past cannot be changed. And remember, Mr. President, it was you who incited the rebellion against the boyars, forcing us into staying. If you had stayed your hand, your wish, no matter how wrong, would have come to pass. If there's a fault there, it is yours.

"And remember this too, Kal," Andrew snapped. "Pat and I came to this forsaken place with more than five hundred men under our command. Fewer than half of them are left. I lost a lot of good boys dragging you and Rus out of slavery."

"Andrew."

Kathleen stood up and moved between them, refilling Kal's mug.

"Both of you just settle down for a moment," she snapped. "You cannot undo what was done, and damn it all, there is no fault. Half of Rus is dead and the Lord knows I held the hand of enough of them as they died, Kal. Half the boys of the Thirty-fifth and Forty-fourth are gone and I held more than one of them as well. So stop arguing about what was and think about what will be."

Both men looked up at her and slowly settled back into their chairs. As she filled Andrew's mug, she gave him an angry look of reproach. He bristled slightly, and she stood before him, unmoving, until his features finally relaxed and he nodded imperceptibly, signaling that he had his temper under control.

"We both lost," Andrew finally said. "But their children will not have to make the fight and sacrifice that they made."

"I don't want to lose what's left," Kal replied. "We've poured our strength and wealth into running the railroad a thousand miles beyond Roum, without a single cent of return. We are putting ourselves out on a limb. It might even provoke a response from the Hordes."

"So we're to leave the people out there to the mercy of the likes of Tamuka?"

"Don't try to back me into the corner of being without compassion," Kal snapped back angrily. "What can we do? At best, we can now field an army of two hundred thousand. A quarter of them are already tied down guarding the frontier to the west, southwest, and along the Roum narrows between the Inland Sea and the Great Sea. And that front is slowly bleeding us, five hundred dead this year alone. If a war should trigger with the Bantag, all the progress of the last three years will be sacrificed. And what in the end—another hundred thousand dead?

"Let us take our breather now, Andrew. Take two, three, even five years to build for ourselves. Then let us drive the railroad westward, and ten years hence, if there is to be a final showdown with the Hordes, let it be thousands of miles to the west."

Andrew shook his head.

"That will condemn half the world to the revenge of the Hordes. In those ten, fifteen years, they will sweep around the world, but this time they will slaughter everyone, Kal, everyone. And they will build and prepare as well. The war our children will have to fight will be ten times worse."

"They'll have no factories like ours," Kal replied. "They will face our modern weapons with their bows or old smoothbores. The progress we can make in the next ten years will give us even greater superiority."

"Can we be so sure?" Andrew said softly.

"What I can be sure of is that if we provoke another war, we will not survive. The miracle at Hispania will not be repeated twice."

"And suppose it is the Bantag who come looking for us?" Andrew questioned.

"A defensive war. The fortification line between the Inland Sea and the Great Sea."

"It still exists only on paper. We have a string of strong points, but they'll be cut off in the first hours of a campaign and left in the rear to rot. We need ten thousand laborers on that line for six months to make it worth anything."

Kal nodded and extended his hand. "I know, I

know. And if I ask for it, Congress will scream bloody murder. Ten thousand laborers are needed back here already. Those ten thousand could break a hundred thousand acres of virgin land, bring it under cultivation, and guarantee a food surplus, or better roads, or millions of board feet of lumber instead."

"If we don't prepare, there won't be anything left to defend," Andrew replied. "At least run the rail line on to Nippon. That's nearly four million more people, an additional ten to fifteen corps once we train and arm them."

"And the political ramifications in Congress?" Kal replied. "They'll outnumber both us and the Rus."

"Ah, so now we get to the bottom of it all," Andrew replied sharply. "Better to let them die than become voters."

Kal stood up angrily.

"That was out of line, Andrew," Kathleen snapped

Andrew looked sharply at Kathleen and then back at Kal. He saw the anger and also the hurt in Kal's eyes.

"That was uncalled for," Andrew said softly. "I apologize."

Kal nodded, unable to reply.

"Kal, we're going to run against each other. I think it comes down to that. Besides, it's what a Republic is supposed to be about. We have two different visions of how to arrive at the same place—security for our people."

"That means you will have to resign your commission," Kal replied.

Andrew nodded sadly. The thought was a depressing one. He had been in uniform for more than a decade. To hang up his uniform after such long service was in many ways a frightening concept. The salary that Kathleen drew as assistant director of medical services for the armies, would help them to get by, but the daily routine that stretched back to a drill field in Augusta, Maine, in the summer of 1862 was a hard tradition to leave behind.

"When will you announce?" Kal asked.

"I was thinking after the congressional elections in November."

"I was hoping you would agree to that," Kal replied.

"Until then, I will observe the Constitution, sir. You are my commander in chief and I will obey all orders without protest."

"Who should replace you?"

"I was thinking your son-in-law."

"Vincent? Good heavens, he's only twenty-seven years old."

"And has the respect of every fighting man in both Rus and Roum. Don't worry, Pat will be his number two and will keep a steady hand on him."

"Won't some people think I'm playing family politics?"

Andrew smiled. "He's the best for the job, Kal. Trust me on that."

"All right, I'll consider that."

"Kal, there is one request I do have now."

"And that is?"

"The airship. It should be ready within the month. Let it go into Bantag territory."

Kal looked at him in surprise and then shook his head. "You remember the message from their Qar Qarth. Leave them alone and they'll leave us alone."

"Then explain why we've lost five hundred boys out on the frontier."

"Border skirmishing is bound to happen with a race we've been at war with. But actually flying into their territory is different."

"It could settle some issues once and for all, Kal. Either we'll find something out there confirming the rumors or there'll be nothing but open steppe. Sir, I pray it's the latter, but if it's the former, it might very well make the difference between our living and dying."

"Congress would have my head over this."

Andrew fixed him with his gaze. "Sir, you are the president."

A flicker of anger crossed Kal's features.

"We could do it at ten thousand feet," Andrew said hurriedly. "If there's nothing there, they might not even notice it. And frankly, sir, even if they do notice it and protest—well, the hell with them. Besides, it would take weeks, perhaps months, for word of the mission to get back, at which point we could simply call it a bloody lie."

As he spoke, he was watching Kathleen, wondering what her reaction would be to his encouraging the president to be untruthful.

"Do you really believe there's something out there?"

"Yes, sir, I do, and if there is, the earlier we're warned about it, the better."

Kal stood up slowly and put on his hat. "Damn it all, then do it. One flight only, and no one is to know, especially in Congress, or the Home First Party will be down our throats."

Opening the door himself, he walked out and disappeared into the fog.

"I hope that you're right and I'm wrong, my friend," Andrew sighed.

Chapter Three

"Okay, do it."

Hans could not help but look back nervously over his shoulder. From where he was standing the row of treadmills was not visible, concealed by a support wall for the furnace. The corner was dark, the darkness enhanced by the towering piles of charcoal and the black walls and ceiling, which were covered in a heavy layer of ground-in dust. Number three was stone-cold, the crew inside it clearing out the last of the ash and slag. The air was choking, his eyes watering. It was the perfect setting for what they were starting. The spotters deployed across the factory floor were giving the all-clear. Only three Bantag were in the building at the moment, all of them down by the main entrance, watching a crew loading iron rails onto a train.

Hans flinched as the pick hit the floor with a high-pitched snap and bits of mortar sprayed in every direction. Ketswana's work crew, loading up wicker baskets of charcoal, worked with boisterous energy, shouting, scraping shovels to scoop charcoal, but they could not completely cover the sound of the pick being swung by a Cartha laborer.

Hans moved away, trying to act casual, whispering to the charcoal haulers not to work so energetically; otherwise their diligence itself might draw attention. The crew inside the furnace was working at a furious pace, slamming picks and shovels, and as Hans stepped away he let out a sigh of relief. From thirty paces away, the sound of the pick digging into the factory floor was indistinguishable from the usual cacophony echoing in the vast brick-walled building.

A spotter standing nearby suddenly pulled a dirty strip of cloth out of his tunic and wiped his face— the danger signal. Hans looked up and saw one of the Bantag guards casually strolling toward them, looming like a demon out of the smoky gloom.

Damn. It was Uktar. The Bantag was stupid beyond belief and thus, in a way, dangerous. If he suspected that a cattle was somehow smarter than he, the thought would move him to torment or kill the source of the offense. He also had the unnerving habit of simply stopping and staring at a work gang, sometimes for an hour or more before moving on. By that time the gang would be all but ready to collapse from working at a frenzied pace under his baleful eye. If he stopped by the charcoal pile and delayed the cutting, they might not get through and set up before the cleaning out of the furnace and reloading was finished. It would mean a delay of at least a week, and something told him that with the threat of the Moon Feast, if any who knew about the plan were selected, they would spill the information to try and save themselves.

Uktar slowly came to a stop and turned to watch the crew on number four getting set for a pour. It was less than thirty yards away. Hans swallowed hard and nodded as Gregory came up to his side.

"Signal to resume."

Gregory looked at him wide-eyed. "He might hear."

"We just cover the noise. If we stop every time one of them is anywhere near, we'll never get it done. It's a madhouse of noise in here. The dumb bastard will never know the difference."

Hans tried to sound casual, but his stomach was balled up in a tight knot.

Gregory nodded to the watcher, who put his handkerchief back into his tunic.

"Don't signal again unless he's damn near on top of you," Hans whispered as he passed the watcher and then continued on his way.

Hans slowly walked the length of the factory floor, making his features a mirror of indifference. He paused to watch a crew loading the last of a batch of iron rails onto a flatcar, the crew gasping for breath, pushing the heavy wooden-wheeled handcarts back into the factory.

Karga stood by the open door, his hands resting on his hips, as his human scribe read off a production report. Finished, the scribe stood with head bowed, waiting nervously. Karga barked out a command and the scribe scurried away. Hans too started to turn away.

"Come here!"

Hans saw Karga coming toward him. He lowered his head and waited.

"You are to go outside the gate."

Surprised, Hans looked up.

Karga extended his hand. He was holding a medallion of pure gold dangling from a heavy rope chain of silver. It was a summons from the Qar Qarth. Any who wore the medallion, human or Bantag, were safe from molestation whether they were called from the next yurt or half a world away.

"Appear outside the gate. A guide is waiting."

Don't think ... his mind was all but screaming the thought ... don't think about it.

Bowing low, he backed away from Karga. He knew the overseer was curious, wondering why Hans was being summoned. He might fear that Hans would reveal something that he, Karga, would prefer to keep hidden.

"We will speak when you return," Karga growled as Hans turned away. The threat was clear. Say the wrong thing and someone will pay, perhaps someone dear.

Hans walked along the outside of the building, looking at the flatcars and locomotive out of the corner of his eye. It was strictly forbidden for any human, other than those few cattle who worked the trains, to examine any of the equipment. To dare to set foot on one was punishable by instant death. He walked slowly, trying to take in details. The engine had a curiously alien look to it—heavy, overbuilt, lacking the graceful lines engineered in Ferguson's designs. There was not a single item of ornamentation on it, except for horsetail standards mounted to either side of the cowcatcher and a rack of polished human skulls arrayed across the front. Alexi was standing in the engine cab. Hans gave him a subtle nod and moved on.

He approached the entry gate, slowed, and extended his arms wide, holding up the Imperial summons. A Bantag guard casually swung his rifle around, pointing it at Hans, and motioned for him to step forward. A second guard wordlessly snatched the summons from Hans's grasp and examined it, a look of surprise crossing his features. He finally nodded to a guard in the watchtower next to the gate, and the guard unsnapped a heavy stone counterweight, which swung the gate open. It was a simple device, Hans realized, but quite cunning. If there was a disturbance, the guard merely had to cut the rope holding the counterweight and the gate was thus held firmly in place. A dozen men could not hope to raise it. The same device was used on the gate for the train. Given the short length of track inside the compound, it was impossible to build up sufficient speed to crash the locomotive through.

For the first time in months, Hans stepped through

the gate, passing beyond the heavy log walls that surrounded the compound. It was an amazing feeling, and for the briefest of moments he felt free. It seemed as if a different sun shone on this side of the wall—cleaner, brighter. He moved as slowly as he dared, limping slightly from the wound he had picked up at Cold Harbor, which had been made worse by the round of canister that cut into nearly the same spot at the Potomac. To his right, the food warehouse by the rail siding was a bustle of activity, a labor crew working to unload bags of rice. Lin stood to one side, sheaf of paper in hand, meticulously checking off each bag. If the count should be off by even one, the Bantag would assume that a theft had occurred. Punishment could range from withholding rations for a day to execution. Lin was extremely careful in his count . . . yet his attention to detail had not spared his wife and child. Hans could see the drawn features. His quiet sobs had echoed in the barracks the entire night.

A human dressed in the scarlet livery of the Qar Qarth was waiting, and to Hans's delight the messenger was mounted and holding the bridle to a second horse.

"You're late." The man spoke in the language of the Horde, his tone nervous.

"I just received the summons," Hans announced as he swung into the saddle. He saw Lin looking at him and he gave a subdued wave, trying to indicate there was nothing to fear. Following the lead of the messenger, Hans nudged his mount into a slow canter.

"Do you know why I've been summoned?"

The messenger looked at him with haughty disdain.

Hans smiled. "Look, cattle. You might report every word we say. Hell, I might report every word you say. We might even lie about what was said. I just asked a simple question."

"The Qar Qarth wishes to speak with you."

"About what?"

The messenger looked away.

Hans shook his head. "You know, we're the same race, the same side, and look at you. You're terrified of me, afraid that with one wrong word on your part, your precious position will be lost."

He spat the words out, while the messenger rode on in silence. Curbing his anger, he realized that an opportunity was being lost, and he diverted his attention to the sights around him. The rail yard was to his right as they rode northward away from the factory. Half a dozen trains were parked, several with boilers lit. He saw a dozen flatcars loaded with breech-loading artillery. The muzzles of several of the guns were powder-stained, as if they had been recently fired, and one of the caissons was scored from shrapnel. Curious. They'd obviously been in a fight recently. Where?

He tried to examine the details, troubled by the fact that the Bantag were now turning out such weapons. The Rebs had some during the war, and he knew Ferguson had developed plans for breechloaders. Were they making them yet? A new sight caught his eye ... an armored train with an iron-sheathed car forward of the engine, an artillery barrel protruding from the forward gun port. The engine, as well as the two cars behind it, were covered in iron.

What caught his attention next were two trains, each with two flatcars. The cargo was covered with heavy tarpaulins. His damned escort was leading him away, but he desperately wanted to swing by for a closer look. Something about the bulk and shape was troubling. There seemed to be the glint of an artillery barrel poking out from one of the tarps. Bantag guards were posted around each of the trains, and even from a hundred yards away he knew they were watching him, poised to move if he should deviate from his path or even slow down for a second.

What the hell were they? Half a year back, some of the crews from the steam engine works had been taken away, never to return. There were rumors of a new factory on the far side of the Bantag camps, built in a narrow valley from which no human, once sent there, ever emerged.

His escort was gazing straight ahead. He wanted to ask but knew it was useless.

"Damn it," Hans snarled, "don't you have anything to say?"

"If you want to live, don't ask," he whispered. "Don't even think about it, especially around him."

As they crested a small hill, Hans looked back over his shoulder. The nightmare factory filled the low ground below, dark smoke belching from its chimneys. The hills beyond were scarred by the open-pit mining for iron ore, thousands of antlike figures moving in endless procession up and down the slopes. The sight of such mass labor back in Suzdal had always filled him with hope. There was the feeling in the air that what he was looking at was free men laboring to maintain that precious freedom. Here it was the endless torment of hell. His gaze swept down the valley to the west, following the train track as it dropped down into the steppes beyond. Three hundred fifty miles to freedom, he thought wistfully.

"Schuder!"

Startled, Hans turned. It was Ha'ark, sitting alone, waiting for him.

Clear your thoughts, the escort had warned him, clear your thoughts! Hans bowed low from the saddle, struggling to purge all that he had been thinking of. As he looked back up, he saw Ha'ark's gaze boring into him.

Ha'ark nodded to the escort and the man withdrew, his eyes piercing Hans as if he did not even exist.

"I wanted to speak with you, Schuder. It has been long since we last talked."

"I am at your command," Hans replied quietly.

"You sound obedient, Schuder," Ha'ark chuckled softly. "Is that because you are broken or is it because you are hiding something else behind your groveling words?"

"I want to live," Hans said, his tone flat.

"You were thinking about what lies up that rail track, were you not?"

"Yes." He knew there was no sense in denying it.

"You were considering just how far it was to freedom."

Hans nodded, saying nothing, engaged in the effort of forcing away any thought that might be dangerous.

"Which means you are not broken, not reconciled to your fate."

"Would you ever be broken, reconciled to captivity, to working, to helping your enemies?"

Ha'ark laughed. "I would not be captured."

"I once thought the same thing. It's hard to effect that, though, when you're knocked unconscious and wake up in chains."

"You divert the intention of what I wish to speak of," Ha'ark snapped. "If you are not reconciled, then that means you might still be dangerous to me."

"If you go and look at the factory I helped to create," Hans said, a bitter irony creeping into his voice, "you will see nearly two hundred tons of iron a day being poured. Steam engines are being produced, cars for your trains, the trip-hammers for rail, it is as you order. The state of our minds, whether we love you or hate you, cannot alter that fact."

"But it can still make you dangerous."

Don't think . . .

"There are rumors that you are planning a revolution, or perhaps an escape."

"Absurd," Hans replied calmly, looking straight into Ha'ark's eyes. "Escape how? And to where? And as for a revolution? You have a full umen guarding us, armed with rifles and artillery. What would we fight with? Our fists?"

Ha'ark nodded. "Still, it has been suggested that we separate you. Your women, your children should be moved to another camp. There they will act as assurance of your continued loyalty."

Hans remained silent for a long moment. Almost casually, he pulled out his plug of tobacco and bit off a chew. As had become a habit, he offered the plug to Ha'ark, and the Qar Qarth took what was left.

"Order that, and we will commit suicide," Hans finally replied.

"An empty threat. Go ahead. We can now replace you with others who have been trained."

"If you don't need us, and if you have come to fear us in some way, then why not kill us all? Is it because you still need us?"

Ha'ark smiled. "Yes, we can still use you."

"All we have left is the ones we love. It is the threat of harm to them that keeps us to our tasks."

"Such as yourself."

Hans nodded. "Separate us and there is nothing left to live for in this world. If you do this thing, I can assure you we will die. Then go ahead and replace us, but I can promise you as well that your iron production will be cut in half for weeks, perhaps months."

"Then this rumor."

"Who told you that? Or are you just guessing?"

"It doesn't matter who. I just thought to ask."

Hans leaned over and spat on the ground, Ha'ark following suit.

"You know something, human. I think on another world, in a different world, you and I might have been friends. I admire your courage. There is not another human on this world who would dare to address me as you do. To a point, I like that."

Hans was silent, struggling to keep his thoughts clear, not to let his guard down in this ostensible moment of friendship.

"Are all your soldiers such as you?"

"Most. Our army is made up of free men. When a man is free and must defend that freedom with his life, it does something to him. He learns to control his fear, he knows the sacrifice will be worth it. That, like it or not, he's the one that's been called and it's his duty."

"Your Keane. I suspect he learned that from you."

"It was already there. All I taught him was how to lead in battle and the tactics of fighting. The character was there before I ever met him."

"Yet you made him tougher."

Hans smiled. "When you go against him, you'll see just how tough he can be. If you want another opinion, ask any Merki."

Ha'ark laughed and shook his head. "I heard about the council that was held between the Merki Qar Qarth and Tartang, the Qarth of the Bantag, before the start of the war."

"The one you murdered?"

Ha'ark leaned over, fixing Hans with his gaze.

"He was a fool. He should have offered alliance with the Merki and not tried to use the war to his own advantage, thinking of stealing some cattle and horses while the Merki sacrificed themselves for our race. If it had not been for him, the issue would have already been decided."

"And I would not be here now," Hans said.

Ha'ark nodded. "Human, though I might find something in you that I like when we speak alone, know that we are mortal enemies. That is as fixed as the stars overhead. You saw what is beginning here.

The type of war you unleashed upon this world can have but one conclusion. Either you shall outproduce us and win or we shall outproduce you and win. That is the harshest lesson my people still must learn. In the end, valor is nothing. Whoever has the heavier armor shielding, the heavier artillery, the swifter airships—that is the race that will win."

"Courage still counts," Hans said quietly. "Always has, always will."

"What is courage against a bullet? This new age upon this world is still young. The places where these new weapons are made are everything in the balance of victory here, and two thousand miles away in your Rus and Roum. One sharp campaign that destroys the ability of the other to produce new weapons, and the balance will forever be on the side of the victor. You can run no further than the end of your rails. The Merki didn't quite grasp that. I have studied the story of your retreat from Suzdal to Hispania. Masterful, but fragile. All based upon one rail line."

Hans nodded, neither agreeing nor disagreeing.

"You are guarded around me today, Schuder."

"Why shouldn't I be? You are discussing the annihilation of my people."

"We can still talk, though."

"You talk with me to gain insight, information, which you will use against my friends."

"Ah, but there is something about our conversations that intrigues you as well. An insight into who we are."

Hans nodded. "I know you view your people here as barbarians. I daresay there's more in common with us, the Yankees, than with them. Why not come over to our side?"

Ha'ark laughed. "Better to rule in hell than serve in heaven."

Startled, Hans looked at Ha'ark. He had heard the

line before. His first commanding officer out in Texas used to say it all the time.

"You got that from one of us, didn't you?"

Ha'ark smiled. "No. From one of our own epic ballads, when Gorm is cast down into damnation. Curious."

Ha'ark's features seemed to soften for a moment.

"You were a student before all this, weren't you?" Hans asked.

Ha'ark nodded. "I wanted nothing to do with the war, the one back home. A little problem I had with the daughter of—what would you call it?—a judge, forced me into enlisting and I was sent to join the shock assault troops in the war against the Imperial Traitor."

His features hardened. "I learned much there, much I never imagined, much that has served me well here. My student's knowledge was childishness, but it has served its purpose. To know how to manipulate these primitives, to give me a model to rule. The other four in my battle group who came here with me. Two are gutter sweepings, but the type needed to create my new army. The other two are like me, students before the war and by chance both of them carried enough arcane knowledge to help us arm this world."

Ha'ark smiled. "Like your own Ferguson."

Hans felt an icy chill. Chuck Ferguson, the genius behind the industrialization of the Republic, was perhaps, after Andrew, the most important man alive on this world. If the Bantag knew who he was, that meant he was vulnerable.

"Yes, if I can find him, he will most certainly be dead. We don't need him. My two companions carry within them far more knowledge than he.

"Does he know how to make a lifting surface, a wing, for his aerosteamers? What about turbine engines? Blast furnaces? Oh, we already have one of those working, and soon we will convert the factory you run. What about cold-core casting for guns and atomics, or wireless telegraphs? Do you know any of it?"

Hans tried to register the words, to store them away as he continued to chew and to stare at Ha'ark, not allowing any thoughts to cross his mind.

"Are you plotting an escape?"

The question caught him off guard as he struggled to absorb what Ha'ark had just said, an errant thought whispering to him that if he could carry this information back to Chuck, somehow the boy might be able to figure out what Ha'ark was referring to.

Hans shook his head.

Ha'ark stared at him, and for a moment Hans felt as if his mind were being peeled back, that in some devilish way Ha'ark was looking within it.

He raised his gaze, staring straight into Ha'ark's eyes.

"If even one person attempts to escape, I will annihilate everyone in that factory of yours."

"I understand that."

"I just wanted you to know. Make sure everyone knows. You will be responsible for making the announcement."

"Of course, my Qarth."

Ha'ark fished in his pocket and pulled out a heavy packet filled with chewing tobacco.

"You've got me taken with the habit, so I thought to keep you better supplied."

Hans took the pouch and could not help but nod his thanks.

"You realize, Schuder, that as long as you stay loyal, you, your wife, and your child will be protected. Your child will grow, have children of his own, and be safe in my circle."

"I understand that."

"But? There is something burning inside you."

"Yesterday, the wife and child of one of the assistants that I am responsible for were murdered by Karga."

He found himself regretting that he had even said it. Ha'ark was a distant presence, Karga was constant and could make daily existence a torment.

"Did she do something wrong?"

"She tripped and fell, dropping some charcoal. But it was more than that. Karga was angry that we had to shut down production on several furnaces to clean them out."

Ha'ark smiled.

"These people of mine live by terror," Ha'ark replied. "They know no other way."

"And it is the way you rule them?"

"A little more subtle, perhaps, but it is there."

"You extended protection to myself and my workers."

"They would not be sent to the pits or the Moon Feast without cause. But I sense cause here."

"A few pounds of charcoal are worth a human life?"

"Yes," Ha'ark snapped back angrily. "Karga is the overseer. If production is not met, he will pay. If he must pay, then your people will pay. That is the way of this world. That is how Karga understands his world, and you must adjust or die. Be more concerned for yourself, Schuder, you and your wife and child. I give them direct protection and that will last as long as you serve. Harden yourself to the others and you will live longer."

Ha'ark gave a curt nod of dismissal and turned his mount away.

Hans watched him go, still guarding his thoughts.

"For your own good, if my suspicions that you are considering a rash move are true, consider the idea no longer," Ha'ark shouted, not even bothering to look back.

Hans's escort was waiting for him. He reined his horse about and fell in alongside, starting the long ride back down the hill. Showers of sparks bellowed up from smokestacks, and a train carrying the tarp-covered objects lurched forward. A long gang of Chin laborers dragging limestone blocks and looking like laborers on the pharaoh's pyramids, staggered beneath the lash as they dragged their burdens away from the rail yard. Hans rode on in silence, keeping his mind clear, wondering if Ha'ark could somehow probe within him even when he was not present.

"He knows."

Startled, Hans looked at his escort.

"He is not sure what, but he does know something. Consider this to be a warning."

"Of what?" Hans asked innocently.

"His mind reaches far."

"Then why are you talking?"

"I know where it reaches, but it is not here, not inside me or you. His thoughts are already elsewhere."

Hans looked back over his shoulder and saw that Ha'ark had stopped and was staring at him. He felt a cold shudder, as if an arrow of ice had plunged into his soul.

Riding through the encampment, Ha'ark let his thoughts wander. Somehow there is something not covered. I could start the war now and most likely win if the blow is hard enough and swift enough, but it is still better to wait. Yet what is this sense of warning?

"Did you learn anything?"

Jamul rode up beside him.

"He is crafty. Of course he would thirst for freedom. I could sense it as he looked at the rails heading west, that freedom was somewhere over the horizon."

"You can't blame him for that. He is useful because

he is strong. His workers are disciplined, they listen to him, they outproduce any of the other factories."

"That strength is dangerous."

"Of course it is. You walk a fine balance here, my friend. It would be better if we could simply kill all these humans and have our own people do the work. Then we would be far more secure. Instead, they idle their days away."

Ha'ark laughed.

"Easier to teach our horses to talk. It is hard enough to get some of them even to stand as guards for the factories, to drive the workers inside of them. The only ones that fit that task are of the lowest caste."

"Basing all of this on slavery I think will hurt us."

"Are you growing soft?"

"No, just looking at it with a cold eye. It is always the humans who have the special skills. We seem to be trapped. The work that is essential is done by humans, but because it is done by humans it is viewed as beneath the dignity of our own people."

"When the war is finished, then we can worry about your philosophy, Jamul. We are not that numerous. We can field sixty umens from our own forces, eventually forty more from other Hordes. If we could work some miracle like you wish, to have our people work in the factories as well, that number would be cut in half. Slaughter all the humans, and it would be one tenth. Perhaps someday, but not now."

They reined in beside Ha'ark's yurt and dismounted. Taking a cup of fermented mare's milk from one of his concubines, he strode into the yurt. At the scent of roasting meat he realized how empty his stomach felt.

"This is all rather amusing," Ha'ark announced, speaking in his old tongue. "Here we live beyond our wildest imaginings, here we have limitless power."

"As long as we win," Jamul replied.

Ha'ark nodded at one of his guards standing by the entryway.

A moment later a human was brought in. He stood with head bowed, but Ha'ark could sense the terror.

"You have done nothing wrong. Your suspicions may very well be right."

Dale Hinsen raised his head and gave Ha'ark a sidelong glance.

"Did you kill him, then, my Qar Qarth?"

"No. He is useful to me yet."

He could sense the flash of disappointment. There must be some deep hatred there. Good.

"Use your spies, keep a watch on all the factories. If you can find proof, he and anyone involved with him dies."

"Yes, my Qar Qarth."

"But it must be definite proof, not your plotting, for if it is that, it will be you who dies instead."

"Never, my Qar Qarth."

Ha'ark gave a curt wave of dismissal, and Hinsen withdrew.

"More sniveling than most," Jamul said, his disdain showing.

"But amusing."

"I do not understand this game you play."

"Hans is Keane, the teacher who shaped Keane. By watching him, I learn about my opponent. An advantage, since my opponent knows nothing yet of me. Can he keep his thoughts hidden? If so, that will tell me much. Perhaps he is innocent, and my own fears and the whining of my chief of spies has fed my imagination. If so, then I know something more as well—that Hans can indeed be broken. I am curious too just to see how it ends. Thus why ruin the diversion that can teach me much?"

"And your true thoughts on this?"

Ha'ark smiled.

"He will try to escape, and when he does I will perform the final act. I will give his child and woman to the feast and let him live long enough to watch. That should teach me something about his Yankee character as well."

"Karga's coming back!"

The shouted warning echoed down from the entryway above, and Gregory felt as if his heart had turned to ice. They were five days into the tunnel and, according to the morning's measurements, seven feet beyond the camp wall. He looked at his assistant, who was stretched out behind him, and nodded for him to douse all but one of the lamps. With the approach of the Bantag guard the pump would have to be shut down, and within minutes the air would grow fetid. Putting out the lamps would give them a little more time.

Something he had never admitted was his fear of being in a confined place. The reassuring blasts of fresh air coming from the end of the wooden air pipe now stilled and the terror again took hold. The smell of the damp clay assailed him, conjuring with it thoughts of the grave. He tried to stare at the lamp flickering before him, focusing his thoughts.

"I'm going home, going home," he chanted it softly to himself.

Home . . . and yet there was anguish in the thought. I was most likely listed as dead, more than four years ago. My wife? Would she have . . . ? The night before he had left for his new command on the southern frontier she had told him they were expecting. The child would be nearly four now. What would she say? Funny, it was always a little girl in his mind—laughing, squealing, running to him with open arms.

He was glad for the darkness as the tears came. Is she now calling someone else Daddy? He couldn't blame Sonya if she did. After all, I'm dead. But if I come home and she's remarried, then what?

Married. He could so easily imagine it, being with her, the passion before they had even gone to her parents. Was she sharing that now with someone else? He forced it away. Think of anything else, anything. There was always that young Chin girl in the next barracks, the one with the curious green eyes. No, I made a vow.

A burst of cool air sputtered out of the leather pipe by his face. He looked over his shoulder and saw Vasga, one of his Cartha diggers, in the shadows.

"You all right?" Vasga asked.

"Sure, fine."

Vasga looked at him intently and Gregory, embarrassed, realized that the tears might have streaked the dirt on his face. Mumbling a curse, he returned to his diggings.

"How was the hearing today?"

Stifling the oaths that were about to explode, Andrew tossed the leather dispatch case on the chair next to the door. Madison, Abraham, and Hans enveloped him, the boys going for the knees, Hans now able to crawl up to his father, and Madison flinging her arms around his waist.

"A nightmare—and your day?"

Andrew settled down on the sofa in the parlor, picking up little Hans and trying to listen intently as Madison told about the terrible adventures her dolly had endured playing in the backyard.

Andrew looked up gratefully as Kathleen appeared bearing a cup of tea. Nadia, their Rus nanny, peeked through the door, and the exhausted look in Andrew's eyes was signal enough for her to intervene and take the children out into the kitchen.

"So give me some good news," Andrew said.

"Emil's really onto something with this Simes theory of his,"

Andrew shook his head questioningly.

"That's what he's calling the microorganisms that cause disease. They're named after his mentor, Simmelweiss."

"A strange honor."

"Oh, for a doctor I think it's rather nice. He thinks he might have a treatment for rabies. That little girl I told you about, the one that was bitten by the rabid cat. She's recovering. If this works, he might be onto a cure for a whole host of diseases. Typhoid and consumption are next on his list. You'll read all about it tomorrow in *Gates's Weekly.*"

Andrew tried to listen to her. Emil had certainly cut typhoid in the army camps to a fraction of what he remembered back on Earth by posting strict orders on camp sanitation and sources of water. A cure for it would be even better, but the frustration of a senatorial hearing had simply left him drained.

"Go on," she said. "The standard formula for conversation is that I say something and you reply. Then you say something and I reply."

He saw her playful smile, and yet again he thanked God that he had found her, someone who was willing to endure the weeks and months when he was gone, the tension, the long silences, the locking away in his office, sometimes till dawn.

"Sorry, it's just they're so damn shortsighted."

Kathleen looked to the kitchen door to make sure the children had not heard him.

"Well, their dad's a solider, they might as well get used to it."

"He's also a college professor, and they shouldn't get used to it."

He shook his head and smiled. "Sorry."

"Go on, then."

"The stink over the airship. Couple of the senators

are calling for a full investigation. They know they can't get Ferguson since I've officially put him on permanent sick leave, but they're after Hawthorne and Pat."

"What do they want?"

"To have them cashiered from the service for misappropriation of funds. Part of the fuel is that Vincent is the president's son-in-law, and it's a way of getting at Kal. But, by God, Kathleen, those are my two best officers. We lose them and we cripple the army. It's not like I have deep pockets, with a ready supply of well-trained personnel waiting to move up. We lost damn near half our officers corps in the war. We've got a lot youngsters who are good regimental and brigade commanders, but the type of thinking needed on the corps and army level takes years to develop."

"Vincent got it without the training."

"He's a rarity. A Sheridan type, born with it."

"So what did you say?"

"I indicated that if the issue were pressed I'd refuse."

Kathleen shook her head. "You can't do that. Remember, you're always the one saying the army has to answer to the civilian government. I fully agree with what those two fools did, but it was wrong anyway."

"I know that. I'm not saying I'd refuse directly. Rather, I'd resign."

"And?"

"Well, there was a lot of hemming and hawing. Damn near every senator is a veteran, several of them front line combat as enlisted men. They're behind me, but more than one, several of them from the old group of boyar retainers and royalty in Roum, see a chance here possibly to reassert their power. We got rid of the Hordes, and as far as they're concerned it's time to set things back right and let them take over. They had power. They lost it but still haven't accepted the fact that there's been a real revolution."

"What happens next?"

"They wanted a committee appointed immediately to call in Hawthorne and Pat and put them on the grill. Marcus, God bless him, managed to get it delayed by several weeks."

"So you're betting on the first flight to prove something."

Andrew nodded and, standing up, went over to the mantel, and looked up at the painting of Hispania.

"Funny, if we find nothing, they'll really have us. If we do find something, it'll be forgotten and the Union Party will scream that the Home First Party tied the army's hands and has now left us open."

He shook his head. "A paradox here. If we win we lose and if we lose we win. I sense we'll find something, but I pray to God we don't."

"And if we don't?"

"I resign. Maybe that will shield Pat, though I suspect Vincent might very well go because of his father. It'll be drummed around as an issue in the next election and the Union Party will go along with even bigger budget cuts to try and stay in power."

"Too bad Hans wasn't here. He'd have sniffed out this little plot of Ferguson's, found a way around it, and no one ever would have known."

Kathleen stood up, put her arm around Andrew's waist, and looked up at the painting.

"Your nose is too big."

"What?"

"In the painting. Your nose is too big and he gave you shoulders like Pat's."

Andrew laughed. He had always been self-conscious about his slender frame, and though the painting embarrassed him, he did secretly like the more heroic build the artist had given him.

"No wonder Lincoln aged so much in four years," Andrew said. "Here we were, fighting a war for survival, and there was more than one in the Senate and the Congress who didn't give a good damn about anything other than his own power and what he could wring from it while our boys died by the tens of thousands. I do wonder at times if the Republic will actually survive."

"Lincoln most likely wondered that every night," she said, holding him close.

Chapter Four

The knock on the door caused him to look up with a start. It was followed by two more knocks, and he felt the pressure in his chest relax.

"Come."

The door opened, and Ketswana, followed by Manda, slipped into the room.

Hans looked at Alexi and Gregory and saw the tension drain out of their faces.

"You're late," Hans said.

"Karga and two of his scum were poking around the furnace. I felt I should stay. I thought my heart would stop when he paused at the charcoal pile and started poking it with a stick."

"Do you think he was onto something?" Gregory asked.

"No, but I was afraid one of my crew might give something away or, worst yet, that the diggers would hear the rapping and misinterpret it. Remember, three taps means it's all clear to bring up the dirt. Every second I expected the hatch to open."

Hans said, "We change that tonight."

Gregory nodded.

"Anything else, Ketswana?"

"I think we might have a problem. A new puddler was assigned to my furnace today. I don't trust him. I asked around, and no one seems to know him. He says he was an ironworker in one of the Chin cities before the Bantag came."

"Then why wasn't he swept up when they first got here?" Hans asked.

"My thinking as well. He knows what to do, but he just doesn't seem to quite know what to do, if you understand me. Little things, but they make me think he was quickly shown how to do his job by someone and then sent in here."

"Anything else?"

"One of my men told me that after a couple of hours he started to talk. The usual chatter, what bastards the Bantag are, questions about food and such, but then came the real one. He said he'd give anything to escape."

"That could be the talk of anyone," Hans interjected, "but go on."

"It was the way he said it. At least that's what my man told me. He said he'd gladly work on any scheme to get out, no matter how dangerous."

"Watch him," Hans replied sharply.

Talk of escape was the dream of nearly every slave, but to talk about it openly was a quick way of being sent to the pit. The man was either a fool or a spy.

"What troubles me, though, is that he is so clumsy," Manda interjected. "Perhaps he was told to be clumsy, to make himself obvious."

"Your thinking being . . . ?"

"So that we might not notice the real spy, believing we've already found one. There might be someone else, who will stay quiet, never say a word, just watch and listen while this fool speaks loudly."

Hans nodded in agreement. There was always a steady flow of new workers being brought in to the factory to replace the dead. To inquire about them directly might be dangerous. He thought about the layout of the factory. Number two furnace was in the southwest corner of the building and number four was on the north wall, thirty yards from number three. Gregory had chosen his spot well. No one could see directly into the charcoal pile, even from the treadmills, but they might notice the traffic, the workers occasionally going behind the furnace and not reappearing for hours, or the crew assigned to hauling the dirt, which was dumped into number three or scattered on the floor and then covered with charcoal or ore.

The problem was compounded by the fact that except for half a dozen others, the only people who knew about the tunnel were the workers assigned to Ketswana's furnace. There was only one watcher on number four and one on number two. They couldn't be there day and night.

"They know something is up," Hans said. "I sensed that from Ha'ark. Now I'm certain of it. Keep an eye on this bastard."

"We could kill him without any trouble," Ketswana replied with a smile.

Hans thought about that for a moment and then shook his head. "There's a slight chance he might be just a fool, but I doubt that. If we do kill him, it will set off a warning that there's something we want hidden and it might be at number three. My gut instinct tells me they don't suspect a tunnel inside the foundry; otherwise they would have torn it apart.

"I want you to assign three people to this man. Befriend him, always have someone by his side. Whenever the dirt crew or a new digger is going down, make sure he's diverted."

"We need to find out just how much they suspect," Ketswana interjected. "I'll see what we can do on that."

"Just be careful."

"What about setting off a false rumor," said Alexi, "that there's a tunnel somewhere in the barracks, or that there's a plan to seize a locomotive from inside the steam engine works?"

Hans shook his head. "First off, whoever said it to someone we suspect, that man's as good as dead. They take him in and torture him to death. Second, any type of rumor will only arouse them even further to find something. We have to go as we are."

Hans looked at Ketswana, who nodded in agreement. "What about the schedules, Alexi?"

"I met with the telegrapher early this evening. He's scared to death, and I sense he wants to back away, but I think he knows what will happen if he does. He says the schedule's usually light on the night of a Moon Feast and the track all the way to X'ian more often than not has only half a dozen trains on it during the night."

"Will he crack?"

"I hated to do it, but I told him that if he does we'll find his two children even if we can't get at him and that we'll denounce him as being in on the plan from the start if we're taken."

"What about his switchman?"

"He says he'll go along with it when the time comes."

"Fine. How's the tunnel?"

"Six days should have it done. That'll give us an extra day if we run into a problem. We're under the tracks. It's scary when a heavy train passes over and everything starts to shake. Thank Perm it's clay rather than sand."

Two knocks, followed by two more, suddenly interrupted them.

Hans waited. Ten seconds later there were two more knocks. The few papers they had out were instantly rolled up. Ketswana, grabbing the papers, reached up under Hans's desk and slipped them into a narrow slit carved in the back of the desk leg. Alexi, trying not to move too fast, went out the door into the main barracks and casually walked toward the back door while Tamira quickly uncovered the small pot of precious tea and filled five cups. Seconds later the door was flung open and Karga, bending low to clear the sill, stepped in.

"Working late?"

Hans looked up as if surprised. "We were going over the work shift to fill in for the sick."

Karga stood silent, his hand resting on the butt of his whip. "Tea?"

"Remember, I do receive a special ration by order of the Qar Qarth. I try to share it."

"Why are you working now? It is late." The voice had a cool edge to it, typical of Karga, Hans had realized, just before an explosion of temper.

"Because if I don't and we fall behind, you will kill someone as an example, that's why. There's disease in this camp, even worse in the Chin camp, but our production schedule doesn't change, so I have to figure out who will work longer hours."

Karga looked down at the scattering of papers on Hans's desk that were filled with names. He knew Karga couldn't read Rus, let alone English. Karga picked the papers up.

"I'll take these."

"If you do that, I'll have no way of rearranging the schedule of workers for tomorrow."

"Then someone will die. It is that simple," Karga replied, and slamming the door, he disappeared.

Hans felt a momentary fright, wondering if somehow a list of who was in on the conspiracy, or a plan, might have inadvertently gotten mixed in with the other paperwork. Then the other thought hit him: Only one other person in all the Bantag realm could read English.

*   *   *

"How does she look to you?" Vincent Hawthorne asked, stepping into the hangar and looking up with awe at the vast bulk of the new airship floating above him.

"Frightening, just plain frightening," Jack Petracci replied softly. "I never dreamed of actually flying something this big."

"We've come a long way from that first flight you and I took together back in Suzdal," Vincent said.

Jack walked slowly down the length of the hangar, gingerly stepping over the vulcanized canvas hoses that snaked out of the building and out to the gas generators on the downwind side of the hangar. They'd been loading the ship with hydrogen for more than a day, and only within the last hour had it gained positive buoyancy. The job was a dangerous one. Lead-lined vats mounted on railroad cars were backed into the edge of the field, filled with zinc shavings and sealed, then sulfuric acid was piped in. The resulting chemical reaction released hydrogen, which flowed through the hoses attached to the top of the car and into the shed. The slightest mistake and someone could be burned to death by the acid. A single spark, a wisp of hydrogen, and the entire shed and everyone in it would go up. The rail tracks were made of wood capped with rubber to avoid any sparks, and the locomotive that backed the equipment in was moved all the way back to the rail yard so that no errant sparks might drift into the work area.

Feyodor, Jack's engineer, came into the shed. "Four engines at last! Something I've always dreamed of."

"At least I don't have to worry about you bungling," Jack shot back. "You can screw up an engine in flight and we still might get back."

"I worry how you're going to handle the power."

"Let me worry about that. You just worry about keeping them running."

"If you don't like the work I do, get another engineer. I'd be glad to stay on the ground for a while."

"Any time you want to turn coward is fine with me," Jack snapped. "It's a volunteer outfit, remember. You can resign right now."

Vincent, shaking his head with amusement, left the shed. The two had been arguing ever since they first flew together, and yet when it came time to go up, they always went as a team. He knew it was a way for them to hide their fears, and looking at the flyer hovering above him, he could understand why. A single explosive shot or flaming arrow would end it for them. They had already been shot down once and crashed two other ships. By rights they should have been dead years ago.

Waving his hands and shouting, Jack came out of the hangar. "If I don't kill him on the ground, I swear I'll crash a ship just to get rid of him," he snarled, stalking off across the field.

Vincent turned to see Feyodor coming toward him, laughing softly.

"What was that all about?"

"I told him he'll never be able to handle the ship." Feyodor smiled. "Anyhow, no one else is crazy enough to try, especially for the type of thing we're going to do with it."

Vincent looked sharply at the engineer.

"Oh, no one told me, but I'd be a fool not to figure it out. We're going south, then crossing the sea to find out what them filthy buggers are up to."

Vincent looked around cautiously, then turned back to Feyodor. "Don't even discuss your assumptions," he snapped.

"General Hawthorne, you can yell all you want, but I know what it is we're up to. I'm not dumb enough to talk, and besides, I'm the only engineer he'll fly with."

Vincent wanted to launch into a solid dressing-down, but the sparkle in Feyodor's eyes stopped him. The pilots and engineers of the air corps were somehow beyond him and his ability to establish discipline. The standard line, "Go ahead, I'll live longer if you lock me up," had been repeated countless times at discipline hearings.

There was something else as well. He could not help but admire someone who did fly. On his own dress uniform were the wings of a pilot, pinned over his right breast in honor of the flight he had taken in a balloon on the desperate night he had floated out of Suzdal to blow the dam above the city, thus destroying the Tugar Horde storming into the lower part of the city. That one flight was enough to last a lifetime, and he sensed that the members of the air corps knew they could stretch the limits with him and get away with it.

Feyodor surveyed the airship with pride. "Heavens, she's a beauty. *Flying Cloud,* same name as my first ship. Why, she's so modern we even have a hole in the floor so we can go on the heads of them damn Bantags."

"How soon will she be ready?" Vincent asked.

"First I want to run the engines up on the ground. Then take them apart to check everything. We should wait a day as well. There's bound to be leaks. We'll hang some weight on her till she sinks, then take the weight off. Following morning we check again and see how much lift we've lost, but the crew that made her are good workers. I think she'll check out fine.

"Maybe tomorrow afternoon we'll do a short hop up and around for an hour. Then we check everything again. Another cruise, this one for three or four hours into the wind and back at high speed so we can calculate our air speed. Then we do the same thing again, check the engines, weigh her for gas loss. I'd say seven or eight days, we'll be ready to sail if the weather's good."

Vincent thought about the telegram in his pocket, informing him that Andrew was coming back out in seven days. The reason was obvious, if something went wrong Andrew wanted to be present to shoulder the blame.

"Can't get it up sooner?" Vincent asked.

"Well, sir, we could, but this is the only ship like her that we've got. Lose her, and it'll be months, if ever, before we have another."

"Just see what you can do. I'd like you up earlier if possible."

"Why, sir?"

"Let's just call it personal, that's all."

Muttering a silent curse, Dale Hinsen shuffled through the papers on his desk. He knew Karga was waiting for the right answer, and for a moment he was tempted simply to pull out a sheet or two, say they were plans for escape, and have Hans denounced.

It would be amusing to do it that way, an innocent list of names the evidence that sends his old sergeant to the pits. But it would be his word against Hans's—would Ha'ark believe him? Something told him that if there were a confrontation, Ha'ark would sense the truth in Hans's words and the lie in his own. It might mean I would go to the pits instead.

He looked up at Karga. "There's nothing here. These are work lists, production records, checkoffs of who is sick and who is doing extra work."

"The sick should be disposed off," Karga growled. "This allowing others to do their work is weakness."

It did strike Dale to be an unusual show of compassion for the Bantag. Hans had argued early on that the production quota was fixed and how it was arrived at should be immaterial, rather than demanding that every single person be on the floor. Ha'ark had been sold on the logic that it was senseless to slaughter a trained worker merely because he or she could not work for a few days. What he had perhaps not realized was that it built a deeper unity in the camp; rather than dividing people against themselves, it made their survival a collective effort.

"And our spies?" Karga asked.

"I made all the promises you authorized. Freedom from the factories, placement in the protected circle of the Qar Qarth, and the right to live wherever they desired within the empire. I have ten in the foundry, five in the steam engine works, another five in the cannon foundry, five in the rifle works, and another dozen scattered in the other establishments. We are well covered."

"But this is nothing," Karga snapped, pointing at the work sheets.

Dale picked up the pile of papers and started to shuffle slowly through them. Red lines were drawn through those who had died. Check marks with the letters "c.b." must indicate confined to bed, and "l.w.," he reasoned must mean light work.

He continued to look through the papers while Karga paced back and forth. He knew that Karga hated him, hated him because he carried the official protection of the Qar Qarth and because as the head of security for all the camps, he had access to knowledge that the overseer preferred to keep to himself.

He looked down the lists for each of the twelve furnaces. Number six had half its crew down, two of them dying within the last week from galloping consumption. He continued down the list and stopped at number three. Six men were listed as being on light work or confined to bed. Something triggered his memory, and reaching into his desk he pulled out the reports from the previous week. Again there were the same six, and the week before that as well.

He knew Karga, like most Bantag, found it difficult to differentiate between individual humans. Looking down from a height of seven to eight feet at prisoners who were dressed in rags, emaciated, filthy, and foul-smelling, they usually couldn't tell them apart. All they bothered with was the daily check of numbers and as long as the living and dead counted each day matched up, they were satisfied.

Number three, mostly the black men. Hinsen wrinkled his nose with disdain. He had cared little for them back on Earth. After all, they were the ones who had caused that war that he was drafted into. Let them free their own asses. And now here they were again.

Could there be something going on here? It was most likely innocent enough, but then again, the same six for so long while all the others stayed healthy. And something else now struck him as well. By the very nature of the way the foundry was organized, the men and women who worked there worked as a unit, roughly thirty to each furnace or trip-hammer. If something was indeed being plotted, it would most likely be done within that group, for no secret could be kept for long in such a unit, and beyond that, the friendships and bonds that were formed would compel them to do it together.

Yet again he wondered how an escape would be planned and executed. There were, as far as he could see, only three ways out. Either they seize a train as it is going through a gate, they somehow jam a gate and charge it, or they dig out under the wall. If they were going to charge the gate or seize an engine it would mean a large number of them going at once, and yet again the work crew would have to be the unit.

A tunnel? He had suggested that the barracks be

built with raised floors to preclude such an effort. The foundry itself? He had never set foot in the building. Even Ha'ark had agreed that it was too risky for him ever to go into the camp, first because his identity needed to be kept secret, and second, if he was recognized, someone might simply want to trade a life for a life. It would be just like Hans to order such a thing, he realized.

But the foundry or any of the factories—could they be digging out right under our noses? He thought about it and then let the thought drop. Impossible. Each of the factories had a clear caste system, the trained workers and the Chin slave labor. All the Chin were told that if they saw something wrong and reported it, they would be set free to go back home. The system had worked well. Nowhere in any of the buildings was there a place where the Chin did not wander about.

So where else if it is a tunnel? The cookhouses were the only buildings built directly on the ground—perhaps there. He made a mental note for the spies in each of the cooking areas to be doubly alert. There was one other place—the latrines and bathhouses. He had some vague memory of a story about Reb prisoners getting out through a latrine pit, but could you get thirty or forty out that way? Possible.

The only thing left, he realized, was to get more information. Perhaps it was time for more-direct methods.

Hans looked over his shoulder and saw that no one was nearby. The trip-hammers up at the east end of the building were thundering away, making it possible to talk.

"We're sloping up now," Gregory whispered. "Three days should have us there."

"Are you sure on the measurements?"

That was increasingly his greatest anxiety, that the tunnel would pop up outside of the warehouse, or worse yet, under one of the tracks.

"Before we even approached you on it, Alexi paced it off a dozen times. The tough part was making a compass and having him sight the angle in correctly without being spotted. Once we got the angle in we were on our way."

"Gregory, if we're more than a couple of feet off, we are dead."

"Don't worry. Remember, I was in staff school. I still remember the stuff drilled into us on geometry. And Alexi worked for railroad construction. It's on the mark."

He looked sideways at Gregory, wondering just how confident the young officer really was.

"I wonder what it'll be like back home," Gregory said wistfully. "Four years is a long time."

"You'll be a hero."

A sad smile flickered across his features, "I wonder. I lost my command; all except Alexi are dead. Will they even remember me?"

Hans said nothing. For four years Gregory had slept in the barracks right next to the small room allotted to Tamira and himself. The walls were paper-thin and he could hear the dreams, the nightmares.

"She'll still be waiting."

"Do you think so?"

"Of course she will, son. Your daughter's most likely heard endless stories about you. She'll know you on sight."

Gregory sadly shook his head. "My wife, she was so young, only seventeen when we were married during the retreat from Suzdal. After that, we had less than a year. I can't expect her to spend her life as a widow."

He smiled wistfully. "She was so beautiful with

her golden hair that always seemed to fall over her eyes when she let her braids down. I remember . . ."

His voice trailed off into silence, and he looked away for a moment.

"It's just, well, it's just that I came to accept it all. I was dead, she was living and would go on living. Now I'm coming back and suddenly the memories are so alive again. So real, I can see her, imagine her."

He looked at Hans, then said brokenly, "Imagine her now with someone else."

"Don't torture yourself, son," Hans replied. He had always been so awkward when it came to talking of such things. Tamira and simply trying to stay alive here, and coaxing others to stay alive, had opened up something inside him, and he could sense the anguish.

"I know soldiers' wives. If the body's brought back, or a trusted friend says that they saw you dead, maybe then, after the grief subsides, maybe then they'll find someone else. But even then, it can take years. You're different. The unit simply disappeared. I guess Andrew would have sent out patrols, they might have found where the battle was fought, they might have found evidence."

He didn't add the rest. There would be no graves or rotting corpses lying on the steppe. All that would be found would be the blackened and cracked bones from the feast.

"You're missing. You told me yourself there were rumors that the Merki and Bantag were starting to take prisoners. That's what she'll think and believe. And besides, there'll be something in her heart telling her you're still alive. Believe me, I've seen it."

"I talk to her every night," Gregory said. Hans didn't reply, for in the silence of the night, he had heard the whispered conversation, the murmuring of others in the barracks, praying to their God or gods, crying, talking to loved ones, dreaming that they were home, that home and living were still possible.

"See, right there. Don't you think she feels that? Haven't you felt her talking to you? Telling you about your daughter?"

Gregory nodded. "At first, all the time. But now she seems so distant. I can barely remember what she looks like, except for her eyes, peeking out from under her hair, the scent she use to wear."

"All of it will come back," Hans replied, putting his hand on Gregory's shoulder. "And besides, I want a front row seat when you go up on stage again to do *Henry V*."

Gregory, forcing back the tears, tried to smile. "We few, we happy few, we band of brothers . . ."

Having walked down the length of the factory to the east end where the trip-hammers and rollers were, where the newly poured iron was shaped into rails, the two turned and started back. Hans suddenly stiffened.

"Something's up," he announced softly.

Karga was already on the floor, followed by half a dozen guards. Stepping out into the center of the factory floor, they turned and started down the row of furnaces. At each of them Karga slowed for a second and pointed a finger, then a worker was pulled out by one of the guards.

Hans quickened his pace. He could see one of the watchers on number four pull out a handkerchief and wipe her face, passing the signal up to Ketswana. The gesture seemed to be enough to draw Karga's attention, and he pointed the woman out. A guard grabbed her.

Are they onto us? Hans wondered. He steeled himself, walking deliberately. Though he had concluded long ago that Karga did not have the ability to sense thoughts, still his natural caution had conditioned him to be wary.

Karga was already down by number three, watching the crew. He casually pointed at one of the men, and guards quickly dragged him out.

"Is there a problem?" Hans asked. As Karga turned, he bowed low.

"Perhaps."

Hans slowly straightened up and saw the wolflike grin. "Can I be of service to solve this problem?"

Karga shook his head.

"I thought it would be of interest to speak to these people," and he casually gestured with the butt of his whip toward the terrified group that had been gathered up. "Then they are being sent to another factory."

Hans spared them a quick glance. The woman stood with eyes lowered, jaw firmly set. She was the wife of one of his Cartha watchers on number four.

Ketswana started to come over, but a subtle wave of the hand caused him to stop. Karga, seeing the gesture, looked curiously at Ketswana.

"Perhaps he should come as well."

"He is the captain of the furnace. If he is away, production might fall off."

Karga stood for a moment as if considering something. "His man here should be enough for now."

"And may I ask where they are going? They are protected."

Karga threw back his head and laughed. "Oh, they won't die, be certain of that."

Karga's gaze now shifted to Gregory. "I do think, though, that you can spare your young assistant."

"Without him I cannot work," Hans shot back.

"He is a good assistant?"

"I couldn't ask for better."

"Then maybe it is time he was given more responsibility somewhere else."

Hans struggled to remain calm. He knew that once the people selected left the compound they would never return. Occasionally, skilled workers were pulled out to become the leaders of new groups of slaves elsewhere.

"If that is your wish. But I ask this of you. I have too many responsibilities to train another one. Leave him with me," he paused for a moment as if calculating something. "Leave him till two weeks after the next moon. That will give him time to train a replacement."

Karga stood silent as if considering. "Two weeks after the moon?"

"That would be adequate."

Without another word he flicked his whip toward the prisoners and stalked away, the guards pushing them along. He could hear Gregory breathe a sigh of relief.

"Zumal." The voice speaking the single word was choked with grief.

Hans saw Ketswana standing behind him, fists clenched tight. From the corner of his eye he also saw the new man assigned to the crew, watching them as he continued to work.

Hans quickly turned his back.

"My cousin. We were raised together when my mother died."

"Hide it," Hans whispered. "Hide it. We're being watched."

"That bastard back there, he must have told them to pick Zumal."

"They usually can't tell one of us from the other," Hans said quickly, not adding that Zumal was easily distinguishable by the pink scar on the side of his face where he had been splashed with molten iron. "Hide it. Now get back to work."

Ketswana watched the retreating form of Karga. "With my own hands I'll choke the life out of him," he hissed.

"Don't let it show." And as he spoke Hans casually

turned to look over the remaining crew. The new man quickly turned his head away.

"And don't touch that spy," Hans whispered. "If you do that, you're dead as well."

Grabbing Gregory by the shoulder, he walked off.

"Thanks. I thought he had me."

"Maybe the time I asked for will throw him off," Hans replied.

As the group turned to go out the gate, he saw the woman look back for a moment.

"God help you," he whispered softly.

The screams from the next room frightened him. The suffering of others had never troubled him, but the thought that there might come a day when he would be screaming like that filled him with horror. The screams were cut short with an awful choking noise, as if someone were drowning.

The door into the questioning room was flung open, and Karga came out.

"Nothing, damn it! Nothing," he snarled. "Twelve of them, a day wasted, and nothing matches."

"What did this one say?"

He tried not to notice as a Bantag guard dragged the woman out of the room feetfirst. She was battered almost beyond recognition, and finally her throat was cut. The blood still dripped from the wound. Hinsen swallowed hard and looked at Karga.

"They were protected, you know," he said weakly.

"They died by accident," Karga snarled. "As you will too if something happens and Ha'ark finds out."

"Did she say anything?"

"Nothing that mattered."

Dale could see the trickle of saliva running down Karga's face. The woman must have spat on him, thus triggering the burst of rage.

He heard the body of the woman bouncing down

the steps, and he saw one of his spies, the one from the number three furnace, watching, wide-eyed.

"You sent for me," the man said, his voice quavering as he looked first at the body and then at Karga.

"Is there anything to report?"

The man stood silent.

"Anything?" Karga roared.

"I think they suspect me. The big one, the leader. He stared at me. I could see it."

"He stared at you?" Hinsen snapped. "And that's all?"

"Yes."

"If they can't do better than that, I'll send all your people to the pits," Karga roared.

Dale looked at him, frightened. If his spies were wiped out, then what of him?

"Try something else first."

"And that is?"

"Change the work crews. Mix them up, assign them to different furnaces. That should break up the groups, set them off balance. The crews on the outside, change them completely. If they have any hope, they must have some of the outside workers."

"I can't do that," Karga snapped. "Who will take their places? No one else is trained."

"Then take half of them and throw them inside for several days. It might make somebody panic, afraid they'll be left behind, and they'll talk."

He paused for a moment. "And take Hans."

"I can't do that. He speaks directly to Ha'ark."

"I don't mean kill him. Move him to another factory. Say you have a problem in the new foundry, and he is needed there to fix it. Even if it is only for a moon. Surely my lord the Qar Qarth will not object to that. You can leave Gregory in charge. Say as well that it is done to prove that Gregory will be capable of running a new factory once Hans is returned."

Karga nodded thoughtfully. "Once he is away it

will be easy enough. We can arrange for an accident or two. One of my people bumps into Gregory when he is near an open vat. That takes care of two. If there are leaders in this, it is those two."

A flicker of a smile lightened Karga's features. "Fine. On the day of the Moon Feast. We'll take Hans and a dozen others. Even though they are protected, his being taken on that day might lead them to think the protection is broken. It could cause someone to talk."

Karga looked intently at Hinsen. "If something does go wrong. If there is an escape, everyone dies. Do you understand me? Everyone—the workers, your spies, and I'll make sure you go as well."

Laughing softly, he stalked out of the room.

Terrified, Dale watched him leave. His spy still waited outside, wide-eyed with fear.

"Close that damn door and get back to your job," he screamed.

"Two days," Tamira whispered. "Do you really believe we'll make it?"

"Of course we will."

They spoke in the softest of whispers, as they had learned to do in the years together in captivity. Andrew, who was sleep on the other side of Tamira, stirred and whimpered. She rolled over to look at him, whispering a soft song in words Hans did not understand but that he knew were a lullaby.

He listened to her, all thoughts stilled for the moment, as if the song were for him as well. He felt as if he were floating, drifting in a peaceful world, imagining that come dawn he would awake, open the door of a cabin, and look out upon fir-clad hills and a sparkling lake. Funny, he had been to Maine only once. The army had assigned him from a regular infantry unit to help the Thirty-fifth form up, and he spent a month in Augusta as the recruits came in. It was the first time he had talked with Andrew. They took their company of raw recruits out on a daylong march. Leaving the city, they headed north and stopped at midday at a small village. Andrew had picked the spot well, an open field on the side of a hill, looking down on a long, sparkling lake. He could still remember it—Snow Pond, Andrew called it. They had sat there, talking about the war, Andrew so new to it, asking childlike questions. The spot had haunted him ever since . . . the summer breeze, crystal-white clouds drifting overhead, the waters of the lake catching the sunlight so that they sparkled like gold. He had even thought back then that when the war was over, Snow Pond would be a place he would return to.

The lullaby ended and Tamira snuggled back into his arms, sighing. The dream settled around him, young Andrew playing in the high grass, laughing, a breeze rippling the surface of the water . . .

Two light knocks on the door brought him upright. "Come."

He saw the shadow of Ketswana looming above him, and for a frightened instant he thought it was a Bantag.

"Hans, there's a problem."

It was Gregory, stepping out from behind Ketswana.

Tamira was awake, holding him.

"They find it?"

"Not yet, but they're onto us."

Wide awake now, he stood up, pulling on his trousers, motioning for Tamira to still Andrew, who had started to cry softly.

He went to his desk and sat down.

"They're going to shift workers around, starting tomorrow," Gregory said. "Mix up the crews. It'll mean the men from Ketswana's furnace will be pulled away, and new ones, people we haven't let on to yet, will be on number three."

"Are we done digging?"

"I think we're under the warehouse. One of my diggers reported he could hear them moving things around above him."

"We can scatter the remaining dirt on the tunnel floor. That should solve that."

"There's more, though. The outside workers, half of them are being pulled in to work in the factory. We might lose our telegrapher, Lin, and his people in the warehouse."

"How do you know this?"

Gregory looked at Ketswana. "Tell him."

"The one we thought was a spy, the one with the twisted grin. He told me."

Hans whistled softly. "Go on."

"He came up to me in the barracks just after the shift changed. He spilled everything, said he was a spy for Hinsen placed to find out if there were any plans for an escape. He was so frightened he was crying."

"What did you say?"

Ketswana laughed softly. "I told him he was a madman. Then I said I would tell the guards of his confession, and that's when he truly became frightened. He started talking and couldn't stop."

Ketswana's voice suddenly tightened. "He told me about the twelve who were taken away. They were all tortured to death."

Ketswana stood silent for a moment, struggling to control his rage.

"Did any of them talk?"

"No." And there was a fierce note of pride in his voice.

"Go on, tell him the rest," Gregory interrupted, his voice sharp.

"The morning of the Moon Feast, they're taking fifty people."

"For the feast?"

"I don't know. The spy said he heard Hinsen and Karga talking. They'll take fifty." He fell silent again.

Gregory finally stirred. "I'm one of them and so is Alexi."

Hans leaned back in his chair. "Is this man telling the truth? Because if he isn't, and he was sent to you with this tale and you don't report him, you're dead."

"He was so frightened he was shaking," Ketswana replied. "He begged to be taken along. He said if there is an escape, everyone else dies, including all the spies."

"Did he give the names of who they are?"

"First he claimed he didn't know. Then I told him again that I'd denounce him, so he talked. It was the ones we suspected."

"You didn't promise anything, did you?"

Ketswana laughed softly. "I had to do something. He was so frightened I was afraid he might run back to Hinsen. I told him there was nothing but since he was honest with me, he was under my protection. But if anything ever happened to me, he would drown in a pit of molten iron, for someone would surely get him."

Hans nodded. "It could be an elaborate trap. No one heard you talk."

"No. I even sent Manda away when he came into the barracks, and everyone else in there left."

"Fine."

He closed his eyes for a moment.

"There's nothing we can do about the workers' being shifted or losing our outside contacts. We have to let that happen."

He looked at Gregory. Damn it all. Everything had

been planned on the basis of getting out the night of the Moon Feast when every one of the bastards, and even most of the guards, would be drunk. The schedule as well could be counted on to be light, with few trains on the tracks. Usually they loaded up the day's pouring, moved the train out of the compound, and then let it sit there for the night.

"We have to go tomorrow night," Tamira said, coming over to join Hans, the baby in her arms. "We're not leaving Gregory or Alexi behind, and the fifty others, some of them will undoubtably be Ketswana's people. We go tomorrow."

Hans looked at her, then at Gregory. "We go tomorrow night."

Gregory shifted uncomfortably. Ketswana looked at him as if to still any protest, and he finally nodded, lowering his head.

"Can you have the tunnel ready by dark tomorrow?"

"If Lin's in the warehouse I'm certain of it."

"And if not?"

"We'll just have to cut through whatever's above us, but we'll do it."

"Fine, then," Hans whispered. "It's tomorrow."

The two smiled and Hans motioned for them to leave. As the door closed, he looked at Tamira. "It's a terrible risk. All the plans were based on the Moon Feast. We might get out there and find half a dozen trains blocking us further up the line, some of them loaded with troops."

"You can't wait, though," she said quietly. "We can't leave Gregory behind."

"I'd stay myself if it came to that," Hans sighed.

"Do you think he suspected?" Gregory whispered as they sat down on his bunk.

"I just hated lying to him," Ketswana replied.

"Look, it was the only way we could convince him

to move it up. If we had barged in there announcing that they were going to take him and it was time to break, he'd have fought like hell."

"The schedules, though. It's going to be tough."

"Of course it'll be tough. Damn, do you honestly think we're really going to make it? Maybe we've cut our chances from one in fifty to one in a hundred. So big deal."

Ketswana looked at him and smiled.

"And another thing," Gregory said. "I want to make a promise with you."

"Go on."

"No matter what happens, we make sure the three of them get out. It'd be just like Hans to suddenly turn and stay behind to buy time. He did that to me once before, at the Potomac. The last train was pulling out, he could have gone on it, rightfully claiming that he was going back to organize the next line of defense."

Gregory looked away for a moment.

"Kesus, it was hell. Rain, fog. We knew the bastards were closing in. But not one person panicked as that train lurched off, leaving the rest of us to walk. He turned to me and then ordered me aboard. I refused, but he shouted at me to get on the train, that I was needed to organize the bringing up of a relief."

Gregory sighed and shook his head.

"I got on the train. I'd like to think I did it because I was ordered to, but there was a voice inside telling me Hans Schuder had just given me my life. The train started to pick up speed and I looked back. He was standing there, cradling his Sharps carbine in his arms, chewing on a plug. And then he shouted, 'Marry that girl.' The night and the fog closed around and he was gone. I knew then what he had given me."

Gregory looked around the barracks.

"I got my extra year of life, my marriage, my child. I never would have had it. I would have died on the Potomac."

"The promise," Ketswana whispered.

"We give him his life, no matter what the cost."

Chapter Five

Hans swept his gaze around the room. "As soon as it's dark we go."

One after another, he saw the nods of approval except from Alexi and Lin.

As predicted, both had been pulled from their jobs that morning. Lin was now in the kitchen and Alexi was moved off the train.

"I don't know what we'll find in the warehouse tonight," Lin said. "Yesterday I made sure the back half was cleared, but there must be a train unloading today. It could be stacked in the wrong place."

"Then we cut through it."

"The schedules," Alexi said sharply. "What the hell is going on? We lost our telegrapher. He's been moved to another station. I don't even know the new one. And damn it all, it's the middle of the afternoon and we've yet to see a train come in to pick up the rails. No train here now means there might not be one at all, or it could be late. If that happens, there's no guarantee of a train outside tonight."

"There's a train outside nearly all the time," Lin replied. "Maybe once every couple of weeks the rail yard's cleared."

"And suppose that happens tonight? And why do we need to move it up in the first place?"

Hans gave Gregory a sharp look, afraid that he might reveal the real reason. If something did go wrong, he did not want Gregory to shoulder the blame. Gregory lowered his eyes.

"Let's just say we have every reason to believe they're closing in on us," Hans replied calmly. "I've made the decision. We go tonight. I fear that if we don't, some—maybe all—of us will be taken away tomorrow."

"Are you certain?"

"As certain as I can be. I've weighed the risks. Look, they went to the trouble this morning of scrambling the work force. There must be a reason for it. Tomorrow, for all we know, they could lead a group off, and if they do that, someone might tell."

He looked straight at Alexi, who finally gave a nod of agreement.

"As for the train. If we get out there, and find nothing, then we're going to close the hole back up, and wait it out until one shows."

"All right, but I tell you I'll be praying nonstop until I feel a hot firebox in front of me."

"You'll have one tonight," Hans replied. "The plan goes as we laid it out. The problem is that Ketswana's work team has been shifted around. When we open the tunnel up, Ketswana, the people by the furnace have to be told. Get to the ones you know first. Gregory, see if you can mark some of them out as well. Remember, anyone who refuses to go must either be kept quiet"—he hesitated for a moment—"or silenced."

Ketswana nodded.

"Ketswana, once they start moving out, go out on the floor. I think you might be able to pull some of your own men and women back. If a guard asks, tell him you just want to borrow them for a moment since there's a problem with the furnace that they understand. Keep them close to you then.

"Next, we start moving out people in the barracks. Our building goes first, then the captains we've selected in the other barracks start sending them out. All barracks go equally. The guards shouldn't notice anything unusual if there're only four people leaving one building every six minutes rather than one building dumping out and then the next. We'll have a diversion team working with the guards at the gate. One of the trip-hammers is going to break; that should draw them over. As they slip in by groups of four, they should pick up charcoal or ore baskets, scoop up a load and take it down. Four go in, one goes back with the baskets stacked inside each other, then four more come in and we keep it moving."

"They're bound to notice at some point," Gregory interjected.

Hans nodded. This was the part he dreaded, the one link in the plan that, no matter how often he contemplated it, made the end still look dark.

"There's just over six hundred and thirty people in the compound. I want to get them all out, but I don't see how they can. Those too sick to get up on their own two feet have to be left behind. That's at least fifty at the moment. We have fifty people with children. They go."

He looked at Manda, who nodded.

"We have the opium drops. Heaven help us, I'm not sure on the dose, but the child is to be drugged once inside the tunnel. I'd like to think we can clear the barracks out completely before the guards change in the middle of the night and do their walk-through. If the alarm is given, everyone in the barracks is to make a run for the building, then we barricade the doors into the factory. With luck they'll think it's a riot, not an escape. We might be able to hold the door long enough for another fifty, maybe even a hundred, to get out."

"It's going to be chaos around the tunnel," Alexi said.

"I know. Ketswana, that's why I want you to get

as many of your people near you as possible. You must hold them back. I'll be with you throughout."

What he left unsolved was the question of how the last of Ketswana's team was to get down into the tunnel, especially if there were a panicked mob.

"Let's just hope we can get everyone in the barracks out. When it becomes evident that too many people are missing on the floor, we kill the guards and then try and get the last ones out."

"What about the Chin?" asked Tamira.

Hans looked at Lin and shook his head. "There's a thousand of them in the treadmills. There's no way we can save them too. I'm sorry."

Lin nodded sadly in agreement.

He could sense the tension throughout the compound, and his gut instinct, which had kept him alive through a dozen campaigns and a hundred or more skirmishes going back nearly thirty years, told him it was time to get out.

"It's two hours till dark. We start then," Hans announced.

"How you feeling, laddie?"

Jack Petracci, chief pilot of the Republic's air corps, looked wanly at Pat. "The usual, ready to throw up."

Pat laughed and slapped Petracci on the shoulder. "Hero of the Merki War, holder of the Congressional Medal, and him afraid."

"You dumb mick, you think it's so easy, why don't you come up on the test flight then?"

Pat gazed wide-eyed at the airship hanging at the mooring mast and shook his head.

"Go up in that?" He laughed softly and shook his head. "Madness."

"So shut the hell up," Jack snapped.

Pat put an affectionate arm around Jack's shoulder and whispered, "I think I'd pee meself."

Jack swallowed hard, trying to ignore Pat as he

started to ramble on about the old days with the Forty-fourth New York Light Artillery.

How did I get myself into this? Jack wondered. If only I'd kept my mouth shut about helping old Professor Wiggins and his Traveling Aerial Circus back on Earth before the war, I never would have been drafted as the Republic's first balloonist. But then again, would we be here now? He knew that in war there are any number of critical moments, when the actions of a single person can decide the fate of a nation. Dozens of his comrades had had those moments, and most of them were now dead.

And me? He was seen by many as one of the great heroes of the war. *Gates's Illustrated Weekly* had run three front-page etchings of him, the new lithograph series *Heroes of the Great Wars*, had two drawings of him in action, and as far as his love life went—well, that at least was a reason to smile.

Andrew had given him something of a free hand in designing the uniform of the air corps, and Ferguson's wife had come up with a design that made him and his comrades stand out. Trousers and jacket were sky blue, with white piping on the sides of the pants, around the wrists, and down the front of the nine-button blouse. The army slouch cap had been abandoned for a leather helmet and goggles pushed up onto the forehead. What he really liked, though, was his flying coat, a fleece-lined leather jacket with a high collar to ward off the chill that was found at ten thousand feet. He knew the uniform was the envy of the services, and wherever he went there was always an unending stream of young men begging to join the elite corps of forty trained pilots and engineers.

At the moment, he would trade it all for a safe berth on the ground, even down in the belly of a monitor on patrol in the Inland Sea.

"I think we're ready to cast off," he whispered, swallowing hard.

"Don't you think you should be a little less adventurous on this first trip?" Pat asked.

Jack shook his head.

"We've had three shakedown runs. She flies well enough. We built her for the long runs; it's time we did one. The weather's perfect, wind out of the west, northwest at fifteen knots, might be higher aloft, and we've got her headed southeast. I'll go up to six or seven thousand, level out, and throttle her back to half setting. I'm willing to bet it's blowing at thirty to forty knots up there. If so, I figure that by early morning tomorrow we should be fetching up on the east coast near where we want to look."

"Good luck, lad."

Jack nodded a silent reply, and slipping out of Pat's grip he started toward the airship *Flying Cloud*. He walked slowly down its four-hundred-foot length, carefully studying its lines. So much about this ship was new. The wicker framework was built out of the bamboo-like trees growing along the eastern shore of the Inland Sea, which when soaked could be bent to nearly any shape but when kiln-dried had a strength like iron with only a fraction of the weight. Silk had been abandoned in favor of the far more plentiful lightweight canvas, which was treated with a glue distilled from oil that shrank the canvas in place and made it airtight as well.

Reaching the stern of the ship, he carefully studied the rudder and elevators, and the cables that ran from them to the cockpit. On the last test flight the cables had stretched to the point that his engineer had to disconnect them from the control stick and then winch them in tighter, an operation that was safe to undertake in calm air over friendly territory but could spell disaster in a high wind in enemy airspace. Turnbolts had been spliced into the lines, and he could only hope they would solve the problem.

He started forward again, nodding at the ground

crews holding the castoff lines, and finally stopped at the ladder leading up to the cockpit, which hovered a dozen feet overhead.

Feyodor saluted at his approach. "She's a fine ship and it'll be a fair evening, sir."

"Oh, shut the hell up," Jack snapped angrily. "You know I can't stand your eagerness for this thing."

"Ah, Colonel, and if you didn't fly, how many fair ladies of Rus and Roum would be opening their bedroom doors to you?"

"Enough. You, you're so ugly, though, it's the only way you'd ever stand a chance."

"True, true. And thus my argument is proved."

The comment diverted Jack for just a moment. What was her name? Livia? Now there was a moment to treasure.

"Full load of fuel, capped off. All engines warmed up, all controls checked. Full ammunition load for both guns. Camera is mounted. We're ready to go, sir." Feyodor finished the checklist and waited expectantly for a reply.

"Our top gunner?"

"Here, sir."

Jack saw the diminutive gunner assigned to the new top position.

"Sergeant Stefan Zharoff reporting, sir." The gunner saluted eagerly as Jack eyed him up and down.

"How old are you, boy?"

"Eighteen, sir."

He couldn't weigh more than a hundred pounds, Jack thought, and that was for weight on this world, not even on Earth. He vaguely remembered interviewing him along with the dozen other candidates selected for the newly created position. It was the eager, toothy grin and freckles he remembered the most. The thought of having the gunner's assignment all but made Jack's stomach turn over. He would spend most of the trip on top of the airship in a lonely turret manning one of the new breech-loading two-pound guns. His job, as well, was to actually get out and if need be attempt to patch any holes, while holding on to the web of light silk ropes wrapped around the outside of the ship.

Stefan was looking up eagerly at the ship, his eyes burning with excitement.

"All right then, boy. Up you go."

"Aye, sir!"

For some reason, naval phrases had crept into the air service, something Jack couldn't quite figure out but had come to tolerate.

Stefan scrambled up the rope, the ship above them dropping ever so slightly as it bore the additional weight.

"All right, Feyodor, you next."

"Good luck, laddie."

Jack looked angrily at Pat, knowing that Pat understood the superstition among flyers that one never wished another luck before a flight. Jack was just about to climb aboard when he saw Hawthorne approaching.

Smiling, Hawthorne took his hand. "Thanks for getting her off early," he said. "Andrew will be furious, but I'll just argue you had a fair wind and took it."

Pat chuckled and shook his head. "The supplies on the *Petersburg*, did they arrive yet?"

"We just got the message an hour ago, they're in and waiting for you."

"Maybe we won't need them, but if we run into trouble it's three hundred miles closer."

Giving a curt salute to Pat and then Hawthorne, he scrambled up the ladder, his stomach twitching when the ship bobbed down several feet and then bucked slightly as the evening breeze pushed broadside against it, causing it to turn slowly like a vast weather vane.

Jack climbed in through the bottom hatch of the cabin and pulled it shut. Crouching low, he went forward to sit down in the captain's chair. He strapped the leather seat belt in place and then unbuckled the restraining straps on the brass elevator and rudder control. He eased the stick back and forth, then up and down, looking over his shoulder through the open rear port to check that the controls were functioning correctly.

"All engines ready," Feyodor announced.

Jack studied the two engines mounted forty feet forward of the cab, their ten-foot propeller blades slowly turning over, and then he checked aft for the two engines mounted forty feet astern.

"Stefan, are you ready?"

The boy, sitting on the floor behind Yuri, grinned, "Aye, aye, sir!"

Jack shook his head in disgust.

"Ready to cast off."

Jack slid the left side window open, stuck his head out, and looked down at his ground crew chief. He held a clenched fist up and then snapped off a salute. The chief saluted in reply and then extended his arms, holding red pennants in either hand. He waved both of the pennants, signaling for the port and starboard crews to cast off.

"Full up helm!" Jack announced as he pulled the stick into his stomach. "One half throttle, all engines."

"One half throttle, all engines!" Feyodor shouted. Jack watched the duplicate engine controls directly in front of him as the four brass levers to the four fuel tanks clicked open. Several seconds later the propellers began to spin faster, blurring, and he felt the first slight surge of power as the nose of the ship began to edge upward. Easing in rudder, he pointed the ship straight into the flicker of a breeze coming out of the west, northwest.

"All engines running smooth, temperatures within range," Feyodor announced.

That little piece of technical engineering still amazed him. Somehow Ferguson had figured out a way to run some hot air back from the four caloric engines into gauges set into the cab, figuring out as well how much heat would be lost in transit. The gauges weren't as accurate as those set on the engines and Feyodor would still have to leave the cab on a regular basis to go out on the catwalk to check and, if necessary, repair the engines in flight.

The nose of the ship continued to pitch upward, and Jack leveled out the climb at forty-five degrees, checking to make sure the tail didn't drag. He saw the ground dropping away rapidly, and Pat raised a flask of vodka in salute.

The ship surged up slightly, and he felt his stomach drop and then flutter, beads of sweat breaking out on his face. He cranked open the forward windows to let the backwash from the engines swirl in. Using more left rudder, he swung the ship around to a southerly heading. The course would take him down southeast, across the Great Sea.

The ship surged yet again, buffeted by a shift in the wind. Unable to hold back any longer, he stuck his head out the side window and vomited. As he gasped for breath, he saw Pat waving from the ground, obviously laughing, holding up his flask and then taking a drink.

"Wish I'd hit you, you bastard," he groaned. He wiped the sweat from his face and set *Flying Cloud* on course, trying to block out his fears of all that could go wrong.

Dale Hinsen gazed intently at the terrified worker who stood trembling before him.

"And you say the escape is ready to go?"

"Yes, Gakka."

"How will they do it?"

"I don't know, Gakka. Just that there is an escape planned for tonight. The black men, I heard two of the black men speak while I was relieving myself behind the charcoal pile. They did not know I was there."

Dale smiled inwardly at the honorific normally used when speaking to one of the Horde.

"You know the Moon Feast is tomorrow. If you are lying to me I promise that you will be delivered not to the table of the Qarth but to that of Karga."

The Chin worker trembled. The barbarities that Karga performed went far beyond the slow death by fire.

"Who is the leader of this?"

The worker hesitated.

"Who?"

"The Yankee."

"Schuder?"

The worker looked at him, confused.

"The one man said, 'The Yankee has given the order.' That's all I know, Gakka."

Hinsen smiled. A decade-long dream of vengeance was finally at hand.

"If this is true, you'll be removed from the treadmill. If not . . ." He left the sentence unfinished as he motioned for the worker to withdraw.

Hinsen carefully considered his options. He could not just send a message to Karga. If he did that, and the rumor was false, he would pay. If the rumor was true, Karga would take the credit for unmasking the plot and leave him out. Nor could he go to Ha'ark, especially if the report should prove to be false.

The one alternative was to go to the factory. The freedom that he enjoyed allowed him to do that, but his mere presence would arouse comment. If some sort of escape were being planned, his arrival could tip Hans off, and again he would have nothing. No, it was best to wait, wait until dark. There would be time enough then to act.

Ha'ark stirred, breaking away from the sleeping embrace of his concubine. It was nearly time for the setting of the sun, and he sat up. But there was something else, something in his dreams, a troubled warning, a vague uneasiness. As he dressed, the warning continued to float in his mind.

"Pull the hatch."

Gregory glanced at the watcher standing by the side of the furnace, who nodded reassuringly. The one guard was still alone, halfway down the length of the foundry.

Ketswana stood silent beside him, his eyes bright with tension. One of the diggers set the crowbar into the corner of the flagstone cover and pried the rock up. Hands from down in the tunnel reached up, pushing the flagstone back, and Gregory knelt down.

"Everything secure?"

"We're ready to cut the last couple of feet."

Gregory took a deep breath. "All right, then."

He nodded at Lin to follow, and they scrambled down the ladder. Crawling on hands and knees, Gregory led the way, warning Lin not to brush against any of the supports. When he reached the inclined shaft leading up to the warehouse, he came up behind a digger who was looking back down the tunnel, illuminated by the flickering light of a lamp strapped to his forehead.

"How far?"

"Only a foot or two. You could hear them up there earlier. I think they just left for the day."

Gregory looked back at Lin's face, barely visible behind him. "We're going to punch through. As soon as we're in, you get yourself up there, and if anyone's inside you better start talking real quick. If one of them panics, it's all over."

Gregory looked up at the digger and said, "Go ahead."

He winced as the man reached up and with powerful jabs hacked his way through the clay. Anyone inside the warehouse would have to be deaf not to hear the noise. He could imagine cutting through only to find himself staring into the face of a Bantag. The digger continued to cut, a rain of clay cascading down. The man paused occasionally to scoop the loose earth back with his bare hands, grunting to move forward another couple of inches and then cutting again.

"Through the clay. Sand now." And even as he announced the change, a cascade of sand tumbled into Gregory's eyes, blinding him, followed a few seconds later by something different, small hard pellets that rained down with a dry, rustling sound.

"Rice," Lin whispered. "It's rice."

Gregory opened his eyes and looked up. The digger was reaching up, tearing at the strawlike fabric of a rice bag, the precious granules flooding down on them like a river.

"How many bags were in there?" Gregory hissed.

"Nearly a thousand, but on the far side of the warehouse. I made sure this side was cleared."

If they've moved the pile we're doomed, Gregory thought.

Cursing, the digger reached up and tore at the bag. Gregory wanted to tell him to be cautious but knew that was ridiculous. This was the moment he had dreaded since the start of it all, the fear that their calculations were off and that they would come up outside the warehouse or that someone would be inside the warehouse when they broke through. The digger, swearing incessantly, tore into the next bag, and another river of rice poured down into the tunnel. Gregory scooped it up as the cascade all but buried the man struggling above him and tried to push it back down the slope. The irony suddenly struck him that he was cursing at a supply of food that would have moved him to tears of joy under any other circumstances.

The flow of rice continued as the digger cut into yet another bag and then another. There was no way to tell how much time passed, but Gregory sensed that they were already behind schedule and that their intricate timetable was falling apart. He could well imagine the tension back in the foundry as the first escapees moved into position in the charcoal pile but then were forced to wait.

"I think I'm through!"

Gregory felt a cool burst of fresh air. The digger struggled upward and suddenly his feet disappeared. Seconds later a hand reached back through and Gregory grasped it. Pulled up through the hole, he breathed a sigh of relief. He saw that they had come out on the side of a pile of rice bags that must have been laid down during the day. If the tunnel had emerged only a few feet more to the right they would have come up in the middle and been trapped for hours. Lin popped up out of the hole, muttering a soft curse, and Gregory held up his hand for silence . . . someone was opening the warehouse door.

Crouching low, he waited, feeling for the knife blade strapped to his right leg. The digger squatted beside him, his hands wrapped around the handle of his shovel.

The door slid open.

"Jakgarth, jakgarth?"

It was a Bantag guard.

Gregory waited. The guard stood silhouetted in the doorway, holding a lantern and peering into the building. Gregory saw the glint of a barrel in his right hand . . . a double-barreled shotgun.

He waited, praying. The guard stood silent, his head cocked, as if listening. Suddenly a trickle of rice slithered out of a cut bag, pouring down into the tunnel.

"Jakgarth!"

The guard stepped into the warehouse, and the distinctive click of a gun being cocked echoed through the cavernous building.

Gregory waited, slipping the blade out of its scabbard. The lantern cast flickering shadows against the walls. Gregory looked over at the digger, who was coiled like a spring. The guard continued to advance, moving slowly, raising and lowering the lantern. Stopping now less than ten feet away.

Why doesn't he see us? Gregory wondered.

He took another step and stopped.

"Baktu!" The word was a drawn-out hiss.

Gregory sprang up over the bags of rice, leaping straight at him, blade raised high. Startled, the guard stepped back, trying to swing his shotgun around, dropping the lantern.

Gregory slammed into his chest, the blade scraping against the Bantag's leather jerkin, the guard grunting in surprise. Gregory fell to one side and tried desperately to scramble back to his feet. The shotgun continued to swing around, and even in the shadows Gregory knew the barrel was poised only inches from his head. He tried to spring back up with his blade, but he knew the race was lost.

A dull thump resounded in the warehouse, followed an instant later by a gasp of pain. The Bantag staggered to one side, his head snapping forward. Another blow resounded, and something warm and sticky splashed onto Gregory's face as the Bantag sagged to his knees, the shotgun clattering to the floor beside him.

The digger stood behind the Bantag, his shovel blade flashing in the dim light as it cut a deadly arc, slamming into the Bantag's neck and severing his head, which tumbled to the ground by Gregory's side. The body kicked spasmodically as it slowly crumpled into the sacks of rice.

Gregory staggered to his feet, his knees like jelly. Trembling, he examined the Bantag, and then, with a rising sense of panic, he realized the door was open. He scooped up the shotgun. The weight of the gun, the feel of the oiled barrel in his hand, filled him with sudden elation.

Training the weapon on the door, he saw that the digger was grinning at him. Gregory nodded his thanks and then motioned toward the door. "Close it."

"Wait," Lin hissed. "There's always a guard wandering outside through the yard. Someone might notice him missing."

Damn! "Pass the word to start them through," he said to the digger. "I'm going outside."

Gregory reached down, and fumbling with the chin strap, he tore the helmet off the guard's head and then worked the cape loose from the body. He donned the helmet and cape and started for the door.

"What the hell are you doing?" Lin asked.

"Playing guard."

"You're two feet too short. They'll spot you in a minute."

"Got any other suggestions?" Gregory hissed. "You're even shorter. Now help me close the door!"

Pulling the cloak tight around his shoulders Gregory stepped out onto the warehouse platform and looked around.

Damn! . . . the train wasn't there! Lin started to tug the door behind him.

"Wait!"

Trying to look casual and avoid tripping over the cape, which dragged on the ground, he walked slowly down the length of the platform. At the end of it he paused, listened for a moment, and then drew a deep breath. He peeked around the edge of the building toward the rail yard. A lone train with five boxcars stood on a siding. He studied it intently. The engine was cold. He felt as if his heart would burst. All this effort for nothing. There was no way they could pull back now, cover up the hole, and wait for tomorrow night—not with a decapitated guard in the warehouse. When the watch shifted in the middle of the night, his absence would be noticed and the search would be on.

He walked slowly back to the door, and from the corner of his eye he saw a guard on the watchtower overlooking the entryway into the foundry. The guard was looking straight at him.

Gregory slowly held his shotgun up as if saluting. The bastard's got to be blind if he doesn't figure it out, Gregory thought, even as he reached the door and started to slide it shut.

The guard raised his gun and then turned away.

Breathing a silent prayer of thanks to Kesus, Gregory left the door open by a crack.

"Listen carefully, Lin. The nearest train's a hundred yards away on the siding and the engine's cold. Send word back to Hans, tell him we need Alexi up here now. Tell him we've got four hours at best before the guards change and they find out."

Cursing silently, Hans crumpled up the dirty scrap of paper that had been passed back through the tunnel and then turned to Alexi.

"You've got one train out there with a cold engine. Get to work."

Alexi swore vehemently.

"This would be the night the train gets in late. They won't be done loading till near dawn."

"We can't wait till then. Gregory just killed a guard. Once they change guards at midnight, they'll know. We go with the engine out there."

Motioning to his fireman, Alexi disappeared into the tunnel.

Hans stuck the scrap of paper into his pocket and started down the length of the foundry. Karga was nowhere in sight, and the spotter motioned toward the main door out the barracks compound.

Damn. Now what?

He slowed to watch as four more escapees from his barracks casually came into the foundry, bearing sacks of charcoal, and walked toward number three. He looked over at the treadmill walkers. One of them was looking straight back at him, and he wondered if anyone in the mills had caught on yet that there was a steady stream of people coming in but no one going out.

With his heart in his throat, Hans stepped out of the building and onto the loading platform, where a work crew was shoveling charcoal into wicker baskets. Four more escapees came from around the side of the pile, grabbed the baskets, and started into the warehouse.

He slowed as he approached a waterboy and stopped for a drink from the boy's bucket.

"Karga?" he whispered.

"Passed here twenty minutes ago."

Hans nodded and casually continued on, walking around the train and out toward the number one barracks. A watcher by the door nodded, then jerked his head toward the gate.

"Karga left ten minutes ago."

Why would he leave the factory? Hans wondered.

"The other guards?"

"At their usual posts."

No plan ever survives first contact with the enemy. How many times had he told Andrew that? Easy enough to say when there was an officer to deal with the headaches, come to a conclusion, and give the orders.

Hans stepped into the barracks. The floor was crowded with escapees, all of them waiting expectantly.

Hans looked over at Tamira. He would have given his life at this moment for her to be already through the tunnel. He knew as well that no one would have objected if she had gone first, but his own sense of pride and his understanding of what had to be done prevented him. She would be the last to leave the barracks. He squatted by her side and looked into her eyes. He could sense the fear that was about to explode, but she forced a smile.

Reaching out, he let his fingers brush across Andrew's cheek. "He's asleep?"

"I gave him the draught a half hour ago."

Hans looked anxiously at the child in her arms. He could only hope that they had guessed right on the number of drops of opiate. Once into the tunnel she was going to have to crawl the length of it while pushing Andrew ahead of her. If he should cry at any time, either in the foundry or in the warehouse, everything was lost.

"We'll be going soon," he whispered.

She grabbed hold of his hand and squeezed it fiercely. "This all started because of me, didn't it?" she whispered.

Hans smiled. There was no sense in lying. "Our son will be free," he whispered back. "That's why."

She nodded, tears clouding her eyes, and finally let go.

"Ketswana will bring word when we can get the rest of you out."

A muffled cry from a child struggling not to take

the opium greeted his words. He stood silent for a moment, sensing the panic that was about to erupt.

"Remember, neither Tamira nor I gets out until the rest of you do."

He headed back to the door.

"Now!"

The door slid open just long enough for three men to slip out and then slammed shut again. They looked at him, wide-eyed with fear.

"Don't worry, it's all right," Gregory whispered.

"Hell, I thought we'd just run into the world's shortest Bantag."

Gregory grinned, glad to hear a familiar Rus voice again.

"Walk in front of me. Try and hunch over a bit so we don't look quite the same height. The train's in the main yard."

The three set off, Gregory waiting several seconds before following. From the corner of his eye he studied the watchtower and saw that the lone guard was still looking inward, not having bothered with a second glance in his direction.

Rounding the side of the building, he breathed a sigh of relief as they set out through the shadows of the rail yard. The three reached the engine and scrambled up into the open cab. Alexi pulled the firebox door open, and Gregory winced at the metallic grating sound.

"Thank Kesus, there's still a bit of a fire in there," Alexi announced. "She's not stone-cold."

"How long to get up steam?"

Alexi stood up and in the darkness peered intently at the gauges. "Water's still warm." He said. "Good supply of wood in the tender."

Gregory almost wanted to weep with relief. He hadn't even thought of the wood until now.

"Hour at the most. Problem is, we're bound to

draw attention. Smoke from the stack, and once she starts cooking up, steam will be venting off. Where's the nearest guards?"

Gregory looked up and down the track. The nearest structure was the control and dispatch building, barely visible in the starlight, a hundred fifty yards away. The light from a dim lantern was reflected in the window.

"Must be at least one up there," he whispered.

Alexi looked out from the cab. "They're bound to hear it.

Gregory nodded.

A desperate plan started to form. He quickly outlined it to Alexi, who shook his head.

"We need the train schedules, it's the only way."

"I think you're insane. At least let me get started here first. That way, if you fail, some of us still might get out."

"Thanks for the confidence."

Alexi sighed, extending his hands. "Go ahead, then, you damn fool."

Without waiting for a reply he turned and crawled through the firebox door into the boiler, whispering for his two helpers to start passing wood in.

As Gregory rounded the corner on his way back to the warehouse, he saw that the guard at the tower was looking in his direction. Again, he raised his shotgun in acknowledgment. The guard did not reply for several seconds, as if coming to a decision, and then finally waved in reply and slowly turned away. As Gregory walked along the platform, he saw the Bantag turn and look at him again.

He must be suspicious, Gregory realized. After all, how many five-and-a-half-foot Bantag are there? He tried to walk casually past the warehouse door, slowed, then came to a stop. One of the weaknesses of their plan was already obvious. The sounds coming from inside the warehouse as it filled with escapees could not be contained—muffled whispers, the dull thud of something dropping, a badly concealed cough. Each noise sounded to him like a thunderclap.

In the next few minutes the guard turned around several times to look at Gregory and then back to the factory compound. Gregory slowly paced back and forth, the minutes seemingly dragging into an eternity. Every couple of minutes the guard peered at him again. He ignored the glances, trying to act as if he were numb with boredom, his head lowered, his feet shuffling. He'd have to make his move on the dispatch hut soon, but it was best to hold off as long as possible. He drifted to the end of the warehouse and checked the locomotive. It was starting to build up steam, sparks spiraling out of the stack as the heat from the fire increased the draft. Pops and hisses, like the sound of a teakettle heating up, echoed in the yard. He looked back again at the guard, who apparently had settled down. Gregory eased back toward the door.

"Lin?"

There was a moment's pause. "What is it?"

"How many so far?"

"Just over a hundred and fifty."

It was way too slow.

How much longer do we have? He walked back around the warehouse and saw a fiery glow flickering as the firebox door popped open.

The sound of heavy footsteps echoed. To his right he saw a column of half a hundred Bantag guards come around the corner of the compound wall, moving quickly. He felt as if his heart would stop.

He waited for the column to turn toward him, but it continued straight past, running toward the main gate. He stepped back into the shadows, watching intently. In the middle of the crowd he saw a lone human. Though he had never laid eyes on him before, he sensed who it was and spat out the name like a curse.

"Hinsen."

Hans looked around the foundry floor. They had put more than two hundred into the tunnel so far, and nearly everyone was out of his own barracks. At the nearest treadmill, he saw, the pace had slowed. Several of those inside stared straight at Hans and then at the new crew of charcoal bearers walking past. They must have figured it out by now, Hans realized.

Hans walked away, moving up the floor in the opposite direction from number three.

"Hans!"

It was Ketswana.

"Gregory just passed a message back. Fifty armed guards at the gate. Hinsen's with them."

"Who?"

"Hinsen. Gregory just sent the message back up through the tunnel."

"Hinsen." In all the time here he had never actually seen the traitor. Why, why of all nights would he come here tonight?

The realization was like an icy hand clutching his heart.

"They know."

Hans tried to absorb the information. At least once every couple of weeks the Bantags pulled a surprise search during the night, looking for hidden food, weapons, any excuse to haul someone away to the pits. He wanted to believe that was the case tonight. But even if it was, they would soon discover that several of the barracks were half empty.

They had to know that something was up. Someone must have talked, most likely directly to Hinsen. Otherwise he would not be here for the kill.

Hans looked around at the factory floor. "The other guards?"

"At their usual posts."

"Get ready to kill all of them. Get ready as well to send the signal for a mass break to the other barracks."

"It's going to trigger a panic."

"I know."

He mentally tried to count off how much time had elapsed since the train crew had gone through. An hour perhaps, maybe an hour and fifteen minutes. Was that enough time to get up steam? All he could do was hope.

"Once we get our people in, slide the doors shut and wedge them. That should buy us a little time."

"What about the breakout?"

"If we're lucky, the bastards will focus here. Let's pray that Gregory keeps his head and waits as long as possible to rush the train. Now go."

He watched Ketswana turn to leave. He desperately wanted to ask for the one favor, just the one favor, but knew that he couldn't.

Ketswana looked back. "Manda's with Tamira. I'm going to get her now."

Hans felt his knees go to jelly and he nodded his thanks.

Sick at heart, he turned and waited by the door. When the rush broke into the foundry there would be a panic and somehow the door would have to be shut when the Bantag finally closed in. He waited anxiously, knowing that Ketswana might not get to her in time. And then what? He watched the entry gate and waited.

"If you are wrong," Karga snarled, "I'll personally see to it that your skin is flayed from your body while you are still alive."

Hinsen, struggling to control his fear, forced a

smile. "The information is good, and I am surprised that you were not aware of it."

As he spoke he looked toward the first captain of the guard. He knew that if he was right, the first captain would undoubtedly back him up, thus ensuring Karga's fall so that he could ascend to command.

"Has there been anything?" Karga snapped at the gate captain.

"No, sire. The cattle labor. A few more than usual seem to be going into the foundry. They must be calling in extra workers to finish a pour."

Karga hesitated and then looked back at the guards Hinsen had rousted out. If he dismissed them now and it later turned out that a breakout was attempted, he would pay with his head. If there were no breakout, he would simply look diligent in his work and he could later find some means to take care of Hinsen.

"Open the gate. We're going in."

"Lin."

He waited a moment, the seconds dragging by with painful slowness until there came the muffled reply.

"Something's going wrong in the camp. Keep the door cracked open. If you see them moving toward the warehouse, start the breakout. Do you understand?"

"Where are you going?"

"Just wait here."

Gregory slipped away from the door and headed back to the locomotive. He heard a whispered hiss of warning at his approach and saw Alexi's anxious face suddenly peering out from the cab.

"How goes it?"

"We're almost up to steam now."

"Start pouring it on. Something's gone wrong in the camp. We need steam now!"

"I can't work miracles, Gregory."

"Well, you'd better conjure one up damn quick," Gregory snapped. Even as he moved toward the dispatch building he saw a long rectangle of light suddenly appear as the door was flung open. A Bantag guard stood silhouetted in the light, watching the rising commotion by the gate.

Moving quickly, Gregory walked straight at him. Lowering his shotgun, he put it under his cape, holding it firmly with his right hand while fumbling to bundle up folds of the cape over the front of the barrel. The guard stepped out of the one-room shack, looking toward the gate and then toward Gregory again.

"*Vuth ka Zagha?*"

He knew he was being asked a question. He continued to advance, shaking his head emphatically.

"*Vuth ka Zagha?*"

There was a rising urgency to the voice. Gregory broke into a slow trot, coming straight at the guard, who now seemed to tower above him. The Bantag looked down at him as he approached, and then suddenly there was a dawning recognition . . . that he was indeed looking down at someone of human height.

Gregory leapt forward, jamming the barrel of the shotgun up into the Bantag's stomach. Throwing his full weight behind the blow, he pulled the trigger.

The blast of the shotgun, though muffled by the layers of the cape and the Bantag's body, still stunned him. The impact knocked the Bantag back into the room, and Gregory fell in on top of him. He kicked backward, struggling to pull the shotgun free from the smoldering cape. Two humans were in the room, clawing their way into the opposite corners. A low, gurgling moan came from the Bantag, who started to kick spasmodically. Gregory came to his feet and looked down at him. He closed his eyes and smashed the butt of the gun down on the Bantag's face. With grim satisfaction he felt the skull cave in. A muffled cry escaped one of the humans, and Gregory brought his gun back up.

"A sound from either of you and you're both dead."

They were wide-eyed with terror.

"Listen to me. We're escaping. There's hundreds of us. Decide now. Either you help us or—" He raised his gun, pointing it first at one, then at the other.

One of the two looked straight at Gregory and then down at the dead guard. A smile creased his round features, and leaning forward, he spat on the Bantag's corpse. The other just stood there, trembling with fear.

"Which one of you handles the switches?"

The one who spat nodded and pointed at himself.

"Good. You have your keys?"

The switchman knelt down in the pool of blood spreading out from the Bantag and tore a bunch of keys off his belt. "Now I do."

"We're firing up a locomotive. I want a clear line out to the main track heading west."

"You can't," the other one gasped.

Gregory raised his shotgun again.

"No, no. I don't mean it that way. There's an inbound train coming. It's due in fifteen minutes."

"Kesus damn all," Gregory snapped angrily. "Do you have the dispatch schedule?"

The telegrapher nodded toward his desk and Gregory examined the sheets of paper. They were in Chin. Again he cursed.

"Like it or not, both of you are coming with us."

The telegrapher's companion was still grinning. "Once you killed that bastard, what choice do we have anyhow?"

Gregory carefully studied the switchman and sensed he could be trusted to keep his head. He saw that the Bantag was armed with a crude revolving pistol. Now he pulled it loose from the creature's grip, then he tossed the gun to the switchman.

"Don't use it unless you have to."

The switchman looked down at the gun in his hands and then back up at Gregory, a childlike delight in his eyes.

A shot echoed outside. Struggling to control his panic, Gregory stepped out the still open door and looked toward the camp. The column was pouring in. No one, as yet, was coming in their direction. Somehow, in all the confusion, no one had heard his gun go off.

"Just be ready," Gregory announced, and with his cape still smoldering he started back to the warehouse.

"Run, damn it! Run!" Hans roared.

From out of the shadows of the camp compound, he saw the crowd racing toward the door. He felt a moment of pure fear. Tamira was nowhere in sight. Then he saw Ketswana, Manda by his side carrying Andrew, herding Tamira in front of them. They burst through the door as a rattling volley of rifle fire swept the compound, dropping half a dozen.

"How close?" Hans shouted as Ketswana came up to his side.

"By the gate!"

A minute at most, Hans calculated. He watched the crowd still surging in. He'd give them thirty more seconds. He started to count slowly.

He reached thirty, and still there were a couple of hundred out in the area between the factory and the barracks, many of them recoiling from the rifle fire sweeping the open area.

"Close it!"

As Ketswana and his men leaned into the door, he

heard shrieks from those still outside, and the surge forward was renewed.

"Keep closing it!" Hans barked, filled with loathing at what he was condemning those outside to, but knowing that if there were a panicked pileup by the door, it would never be closed and the Bantag would easily get into the factory.

The door creaked shut, the last few struggling to get through. One woman was halfway through when the door started to squeeze her. Hans leapt forward and grabbed her by the arm, pulling her on in. Wailing, she started to turn back, but he held her. Hands were still reaching through even as the door continued to close, and Hans turned away, sickened, still holding the woman as Ketswana's men struggled to push the hands back out. Rifle shots reverberated out in the compound. A bullet cut through the opening, hitting one of Ketswana's men, who collapsed with a shriek. He could hear rifle shots striking the iron-shod door and then the beating of rifle butts on it.

The door slid into place, and the cries outside were cut off.

"Wedge the door!" Ketswana cried, and his men struggled with a section of rail, heaving it into place. Half a dozen men pushed through the crowd, dragging a cart loaded with iron ore. A dozen more gathered around the cart and tipped it up and over. A steady patter of rifle shots thundered against the door from the other side, the heavy oak boards, backed with iron, absorbing the blows.

Hans stepped back and surveyed the factory. A struggle was going on in the corner of the number eight furnace. A rifle shot snapped out, and then there was a wild, howling cry as the mob of workers fell on the guard and dragged him down. He saw the guard being picked up. It was Uktar. Roaring with insane glee, the mob bore him over to a bubbling cauldron of molten iron and hurled him in. Hans saw that Ketswana was directing the shutting of the door into the Chin compound. As the door slammed, workers started to pile rails up against it.

Hans shouldered his way through the crowd to Ketswana's side. "The doors should hold until they bring up a cannon. We've got maybe fifteen minutes to get these people through the tunnel."

"And what about the rest?"

There were at least two hundred workers on the factory floor. When the reality of what was happening finally sank in, it would create a mad panic to get to the tunnel. The workers in the treadmills were now adding their voices to the growing confusion, screaming to be released.

Hans struggled to block out their cries of agony. Long ago he had realized that he could not save everyone, but as he saw them now, he felt that his heart would have to turn to stone if he were to survive this night.

"Ketswana. Set up a line of your men. There might be a rush on the tunnel. I'll try and feed as many through as possible until they break in. Then you and your men make a run for it!"

Hans hesitated for a second, fixing Ketswana with a stare. "Don't pull the hero out here. By God, I need you and your men on that train!"

Ketswana smiled, and it suddenly occurred to Hans that he had never seen the towering Zulu smile before. "The same for you, my friend. Just make sure Manda gets out!"

Hans reached up to slap his friend on the shoulder.

He saw Tamira and Manda and raced over to them. "Let's go!"

He half dragged them toward number three. Only a handful of workers on the floor knew exactly where the tunnel was, but at the sight of Hans running past, they started to follow, by ones and twos, and then the mob surged forward. Struggling to keep ahead of them, Hans reached the side of the charcoal pile, the cordon of Ketswana's men letting him through.

God forgive me, he thought, but she deserves this, I deserve it. He pushed Tamira toward the tunnel entrance. She grabbed Andrew from Manda's grasp. She started forward, then hesitated.

"For Andrew," Hans shouted. "Now go!"

She sprang forward, grabbing him fiercely around the waist.

"No time now," he whispered softly. "I'll be along shortly."

She kissed him on the cheek and broke away, stepping down into the tunnel. One of the diggers handed Andrew down after her.

"Manda, go with her."

She hesitated as well.

"Damn it, woman. Go!"

Head lowered, as if ashamed to be so chosen, she followed Tamira down the tunnel. Hans watched her go, and for the first time in years he found himself whispering a silent prayer.

The mob was pressing in, trying to squeeze around the furnace. He picked up a crowbar and held it up.

"One at a time, damn it!" he roared.

The panic subsided as all turned to look at him.

Scanning the crowd, he pointed at a young boy of fourteen or fifteen and motioned to the hole. The boy bolted forward and went down. He counted to ten and then pointed at a Chin woman, and then at what looked to be a Cartha. Screams echoed from the far end of the factory, growing louder as he slowly counted people off, but to his amazement, the panic close around him subsided. He felt perversely like the angel of life, choosing who would live and who would not. Finally he started picking Ketswana's men. He had to make sure that as many as possible got out. They would serve as a disciplined corps of fighters.

"You next!" And even as he spoke, an explosion echoed through the factory.

"There must be a way out of there!" Hinsen shouted, trying to be heard above the growing clamor of Bantag guards preparing to storm the factory.

Karga glared at him. "You said there was an escape planned. They must have been preparing to steal the train. But now they've fled into the building."

"No, damn it! Hans wouldn't be that stupid."

"They are in there. We will kill them!"

A gun crew pushed through the crowd, dragging a muzzle-loading fieldpiece. They swung it around to point at the door. The gun was already loaded. The gun commander whipped his linstock over his head till the slow match on the end glowed brightly and then he brought it down. With a thundercrack the gun kicked back, and part of the door a dozen yards away crashed in from the blow. The crew leapt forward to reload.

Hinsen turned and walked the length of the building, making sure that his Bantag guards flanked him. At the front of the train he stopped by the locomotive. The cab was empty, the flame within the firebox nothing but a dim flicker. This was not the way. If they tried to storm the gate, they'd need a train once they got out. This train was almost cold.

It had to be outside. There had to be a train outside! But how to get to it? Suddenly, it all became clear. Angrily he turned to one of his guards.

"Get me out of here now!" he shouted. "I need to get outside the gate!"

*   *   *

Hardly believing that their luck still held, Gregory watched as a second column of Bantag guards rushed the gate to the Chin compound and stormed in. No one had yet approached him, but to be on the safe side he stayed in the shadows by the side of the warehouse. The report of a cannon reverberated, a flash of light beyond the compound walls flaring like a lightning bolt. Muffled cries echoed from within the warehouse. If the noise outside should ever die down for a moment, Gregory knew that the sounds would most definitely carry to the gate.

Trying to stay in the shadows, he worked his way back up to the door and slipped it open. As he stepped into the darkness, he remembered to pull his helmet off in order to avoid triggering a panic. His sudden appearance from outside nevertheless caused some to draw back with cries of fear.

"Damn it, shut the hell up!" he hissed.

As his eyes grew accustomed to the darkness within he saw that the room was filling up quickly.

"Now listen!" he snarled, trying to gauge his voice so he could be heard, while at the same time keeping it low enough that it would not be noticed at the gate.

"When I give the word to run, don't stop. As you come out the door, turn and run to your left around the building. You'll see the train. There're five boxcars. Get into them and then stay the hell out of the way."

"Lin!"

Lin stepped forward.

"Guards are swarming all over the gate. They know something's up."

"I know. Word just came through the tunnel."

"One of two things is going to happen, then. They'll find the tunnel and the alarm will be on. Or they'll finally come over here. We wait as long as possible for those still inside. When they start to move in this direction ..." He hesitated for a moment. "I need some of your people to rush the guards."

The cannon fired again, eliciting muffled cries from within the warehouse. Gregory waited for the voices to subside. He drew a deep breath as he said the words, knowing what he was asking.

Lin smiled. "I planned on it from the beginning. Maybe we can get some guns!"

Gregory slapped Lin on the shoulder and returned to the door. He struggled with the fear that was tearing him apart. If someone had told him at that moment that he seemed to be a pillar of strength, he would have laughed hysterically. His mind kept racing, wondering if he was making the right decisions, wondering if he was going to get caught, wondering what he would find if he ever got home.

He tried to control his thoughts and watched the gate to the compound, which was wide open. Twenty more guards came rushing down the wall and poured in. He breathed a sigh of relief and then saw a knot of guards struggling to get out. They stopped for a moment and to his amazement Gregory recognized Hinsen. Hinsen paused, looking back and forth frantically.

Gregory held his breath. "Come on, you bastard, this way, come this way and you're dead."

Hinsen seemed to look straight at the warehouse for a moment, then turning to his left he started to walk along the compound wall, stopping at the section adjacent to the factory. In the distance a train whistle sounded, and for a second Gregory wondered if Alexi was giving a signal. The whistle sounded again. It was the incoming train the switch-master had told him about. He could only hope that the man was out there to route the train through the yard and then throw the switches back.

The cannon fired again, and from within the compound a deep throaty roar erupted.

"They're inside!"

The panicked scream was drowned out by a volley of rifle fire. The high, ululating shrieks of the Bantag storming into the building were instantly counterpointed by the hysterical wails of those still waiting to get into the tunnel. The crowd surged forward, and Hans held the crowbar up high.

"Damn it! Don't panic! Don't panic!" He grabbed hold of one of the diggers and pushed him toward the tunnel, the digger pausing for a second to reach back to the crowd and pull a Chin girl through. Hans let her pass.

Rifle fire echoed in the factory, a bullet whining over his head smacking into the brick wall behind him. He could sense that he was about to lose control, that the crowd would press forward in a final mad struggle for life. He tried to see past the surging crowd and caught a glimpse of a line of Bantag riflemen, relentlessly pushing down the length of the factory, driving a terrified mob before them.

In that instant he knew clearly a truth that had been with him from the moment he had started this desperate plan—there was no way that he was ever going to get out. No matter what they did, in the final moments there would be an all-out panic to reach the tunnel, and he would have to die trying to hold them back.

The crowd surged forward again, shrieking, pleading. Someone went down, others tripped over the first one, and then it all exploded out of control. Hans raised the crowbar but did not have the heart to strike as they pushed him aside, tearing at each other to get into the tomblike hole that led to life.

Slammed up against the wall, he gasped for air, raising his hands to his face to protect his eyes when a flurry of bullets slammed into the wall on either side of him. From around the side of the furnace came a Bantag, his rifle cast aside. He waded through the press, his saber rising and falling. Another Bantag appeared, raising his rifle, and it seemed as if their eyes locked. The Bantag, howling with the frenzy of battle, pointed the rifle straight at Hans.

The Bantag let out a shriek of agony, his gun somersaulting in the air as he fell, and Ketswana was there, pulling a saber out of the Bantag's back. He struck again, nearly decapitating the second warrior. He shoved his way through the crowd, his men crowding around him. He pushed on through the press, roaring a wild chant.

Reaching the tunnel entrance he turned, brandishing his saber. The mob gave way for a second. Ketswana reached out, grabbed one of his men, and bodily threw him into the entrance, then shoved a second one after him. He looked around, still shouting, and then he grabbed hold of Hans.

"Go!"

"You first!"

"Damn your eyes, go!"

Hans tried to fight back, but the giant's meaty hands were wrapped around his collar. Lifting him in the air, Ketswana dropped him. Hans half fell into the tunnel, landing on top of the man who was still on the ladder below him. He wanted to scramble back out, but Ketswana towered above him.

"Go!" he insisted. "You're slowing us down!" The warrior stood like a pillar above him.

"Damn it, come with me. We still need you!"

"Die here? Like hell. Go! I'll follow."

Hans paused for a second, then scrambled down the ladder. Crouching low at the bottom, he got down on his hands and knees and prepared to crawl through. Several of the lamps had been knocked down, so the tunnel was wrapped in darkness. The pumper was gone, and the air was fetid, choking. He scrambled along, bumping into the man ahead of him. The pace was maddening—crawling for a dozen feet, then stopping for as many seconds, then crawling again. Someone bumped into him from behind and cursed in an unknown tongue. His eyes started to water from the stale air, and he began to feel lightheaded. The sounds of the conflict back in the factory became faint, and suddenly he felt the tunnel begin to slope upward. For a second he thought he heard a train whistle, and in a moment of fear he thought the train was already pulling out. An instant later gunshots echoed up ahead.

Dale Hinsen watched as the train clattered past and turned onto a siding. He saw the switchman throw the switch back after the train had passed. He watched the train thoughtfully as it slowly clicked down the track, passing a lone engine sitting in the middle of the yard, steam venting from it.

A single train out here. He looked back at the factory again. There was no way through the factory wall and then from there over the compound wall.

A tunnel. It had to be a tunnel!

Hinsen looked around wildly, his attention focusing on the train again.

That had to be it! A tunnel and take the train. But where . . . a foul curse escaped him when he realized that the food warehouse was directly between where he stood and the only train that could take Hans and his scum to freedom.

"They're in the warehouse!" Hinsen roared. "In the warehouse!"

His guards stared at him, confused.

"Damn it all! They dug a tunnel straight into there!" He pointed at the building. "Stop them!"

One of the guards looked down at Hinsen, confused by the fact that a cattle would dare to give him orders.

Hinsen started forward but then stopped. "Go on!"

Another of the guards finally stepped forward. Hinsen watched intently. The door to the warehouse began to open, and the advancing guard slowed down.

At a flash of light in the doorway, the guard spun around, clutching his shoulder. Then the door slid wide open, and an explosion of humanity burst out of it.

"Hinsen! You bastard!" Someone was running toward him.

Hinsen backed up, not sure what he was seeing . . . it was wearing a Bantag helmet but swearing at him in Rus. The figure slowed, raised its hand. Hinsen dived to the ground as the revolver cracked again. The bullet that grazed his shoulder knocked him backward. A flurry of shots rang out. Curling up in a ball, clutching his injured shoulder, Hinsen saw his three remaining guards firing back. A dozen men came charging out of the mob that now poured through the door. Several of them dropped, but the group pressed on, leaping at Hinsen's guards.

Kicking backward, he struggled to escape the melee.

"Hinsen!"

He looked up at a man wearing a Bantag cape, but what caught and held his attention was the gun pointing straight at his head. Even as Hinsen shrieked, he saw the finger squeeze the trigger . . . and the hammer slammed down on an empty chamber.

Another volley of shots echoed behind Hinsen, and several of the men who had overwhelmed his guards went down.

"I'll see you in hell!" Gregory screamed, and he ran.

The line of men started to pull back, several of them clumsily working the heavy breeches of the Bantag rifles captured in the rush. Hinsen looked back over his shoulder and saw a swarm of Bantag guards pouring through the factory gate.

One of the guards ran toward him and Hinsen extended his hands, smiling with relief.

The guard raised his saber. A realization suddenly dawned. "I'm one of you!" Hinsen shrieked. "I'm one of you!" even as the blade descended with enough force to cut a man in two.

"Move it! Move it!"

Hans stood by the tunnel exit, pulling the last es-capees out, shoving them toward the door. Two of Ketswana's men came through, there was no one for a moment, and then a curly black head appeared. Hans reached down and pulled Ketswana up through the hole.

"No one behind me," Ketswana gasped.

Hans could see the horror in the man's eyes. A stream of blood poured from a wound that had laid open his scalp and nearly severed his left ear.

The two ran for the door together. As they cleared the warehouse, Hans saw a line of Bantag skirmish-ers deploying out from the gate, rifle fire flashing, a bullet whipping so close to his face that he felt the wind of its passage. The Bantag began to press for-ward. Breaking into a run, Hans sprinted toward the train, which was inching along, thundering puffs of smoke erupting from its stack. Swarming around the sides of the train, dozens were still struggling to get on board. A man running beside Hans, carrying a Bantag rifle, staggered and fell, the back of his head gone. Hans reached down, snatched up the rifle and a bandoleer of ammunition clutched in the dead man's hands, and kept going.

Its wheels spinning, the train was slowly picking up speed.

"Hans!"

He saw Gregory standing in the wood tender, holding a rifle. Hans slowed his pace and waited for the engine to go past, hot steam swirling around his legs. A hand reached out from the cab, and grabbing hold, he felt his legs go out from under him. He threw his rifle up into the cab and then struggled to gain a hold with his other hand. He finally kicked his way to a foothold and scrambled up into the cab. Gasping for breath, he crawled over to the open firebox and saw that Ketswana had leapt up behind him.

Hans struggled up, then dodged to one side as one of the firemen staggered backward and then crumpled against the side of the cab, blood pouring from his chest.

Hans jumped into the tender and worked the breech open on the rifle, then slammed a round in. Bantag were swarming the side of the train, slashing into those still struggling to get on board. Hans pointed straight down and fired a shot into a warrior's face from less than ten feet away. He went down. Out of the crowd someone scooped up the Bantag's gun and started to run alongside the cab. He threw the gun up into the tender even as a bullet cut him down.

Hans looked back at the crowd still pressing around the train, sickened by the panic and horror. He slammed another shot into the breech and dropped a Bantag who was scrambling to climb into one of the open boxcars.

The sound of the track rumbling beneath him changed as the train lurched through the first switch. Hans saw two men running on the opposite side of the cab, and Ketswana reached down to pull them in.

"Hans!" Gregory was by his side, pointing up, struggling to work the breech on his rifle.

Standing atop the cab was a Bantag waving a scimitar. Hans raised his rifle, squeezed ... the gun was empty.

With a wild shriek the Bantag leapt down. Going down on one knee, Hans braced the butt of his rifle on the floor of the cab and impaled the Bantag on the bayonet. The creature continued to shriek even as Hans shoved him to one side. The surviving fireman turned on the Bantag with a wild shout and smashed him with a log.

The train continued to gain speed as it roared through the second switch and out onto the main line. Several dozen were still running alongside. Sickened, Hans watched as one by one they either were cut down by Bantag rifle fire or collapsed by the side of the track, unable to keep up.

Another line of Bantag guards came running out from the west side of the compound, racing for the track, four of them carrying a section of rail.

"Gregory!"

He pointed at the four, realizing they were trying to get ahead of the engine to throw the rail across the track. Gregory leaned over the side of the tender, took aim and fired. The four continued forward.

Hans slid another round into the breech of his rifle and closed it. The weapon, designed for a Bantag nearly eight feet tall, was unwieldy for him. The train swayed and lurched as it thundered down the tracks. He found his target, lost it, and then swung back on it again. The lead warrior of the four was no longer visible, blocked by the engine. He shifted to the last of the four and squeezed the trigger. The Bantag spun around, going down, still holding on to the rail. The other three struggled to pull free even as the engine thundered past.

Hans suddenly recognized the one in front ... Karga.

"Karga, you son of a bitch!" Hans roared, standing

up triumphantly. Karga looked up, screaming with rage as Hans offered a universal salute of contempt.

Despite the rifle shots snapping around him, the joy of the moment overwhelmed him. Karga finally disappeared from view as the train rounded a sharp curve. All the time they continued to gain speed, and Hans stood atop the pile of wood in the tender, still unbelieving, as the wind, thick with the smell of wood smoke, eddied around him. They roared up a low rise, and he could look back and see the factory compound, now nearly a mile away. Several of the barracks were on fire. He knew what horror was unfolding back there, and again the wave of guilt tore into his soul. Before the night was over, those left behind would be dead.

"We were all dead anyhow."

It was Ketswana.

"I know, but still."

"We were all dead anyhow!" Ketswana snapped angrily, and Hans could sense that the words were seeking comfort for both of them.

A strange sound suddenly came to his ears, the sound of laughter, of crying, but the crying was different. It was hysterical release.

Hans looked at Gregory. "Tamira, the baby, Manda? Did they make it?"

Gregory collapsed against the side of the tender, panting hard. "I'm not sure. I saw them go through the door ..." His words trailed off.

Hans knelt by his side, wondering if the boy had been hit.

Gregory forced a smile. "Never been so scared," he whispered. "Not even at Hispania. Out there alone, every second figuring they'd see us ..." His voice broke again.

"Lin's dead. Rest of his men, dead. They charged the bastards bare-handed. I told them to and they did."

Hans nodded, knowing the guilt, remembering the panic around the tunnel. He looked at Ketswana, wondering what horrors he had endured in the last seconds before going down the tunnel.

Gregory smiled. "One good thing, though," he whispered.

"What's that?"

"Hinsen. I saw Hinsen die. Cut down by a Bantag. It was wonderful."

Hans nodded, trying to take the information in, realizing that at the moment, at this particular moment, even that news would not bring any joy.

The train slowed and Hans looked up with a start. "What's wrong?"

"Got to cut the telegraph line!" Alexi announced. "Only takes a minute."

As the train slid to a stop, Hans leapt down from the cab and worked his way down the length of boxcars, shouting for everyone to stay inside. At the next to last car he felt as if his heart was about to burst ... Tamira was looking down at him, Andrew in her arms.

His knees suddenly shaking, Hans went close and reached up to take her hand.

"Andrew?" he whispered.

"Still asleep."

Hans saw Manda by her side, and Ketswana let out a whoop of joy as she leapt down from the car into his arms.

"In the car," Manda said, "it's loaded with guns and bullets!"

Hans spoke to Ketswana. "Pull a couple of men out of each car, get them into the tender, and we'll show them how to load and fire with the guns we have back there. Then we'll send them back to the cars, and they can teach everyone else. By damn, if they do corner us now, there's going to be one hell of a fight!"

The whistle shrieked, signaling that the telegrapher had cut the lines. A shuddering lurch ran through the train. Hans looked at Tamira again.

"Try and rest," he said, even as he reached up to kiss her. He gave her a reassuring smile. "Our son will be free," he said softly, and he ran back to the cab and climbed inside.

"Nothing will stop us now," Alexi roared.

Hans stood silent, watching the smoke swirling out of the stack. Gregory came to his side.

"The wind's in the right direction for us, but I wish it was stronger," Gregory whispered. "If they can get a flyer up, it might get ahead of us."

Hans nodded as he fumbled in his pocket for the plug of tobacco that Ha'ark had given him only the day before.

He bit down on the tobacco and offered it to Gregory, who tentatively took it and bit down. The boy started to chew and gagged, but he continued chewing nevertheless.

Ha'ark. There was no way the bastard could let them escape. If they ever got back to the Republic, the news they carried regarding the buildup, the new weapons, would destroy his plans. Beyond that, if he did not bring back the bodies of those who escaped and impale them on public view, the millions of prisoners of the Bantag might find hope to resist.

Hans pulled the precious map of the rail line out of his pocket. Forty miles to the next main station. A spur ran from there up into the mountains to the south, where limestone was mined for flux. They'd have to resupply their wood and water as well. There would also be a garrison. He saw that Gregory was already pulling a circle of men around him to teach them how to load and aim the rifles. Two hours to turn out an infantry . . . madness. But then again, the whole thing was madness. Leaning over the side of the tender, he spat out a stream of tobacco juice and again the question loomed—What would Ha'ark do now?

"How many trains do we have?" Ha'ark snapped, dismounting at the edge of the rail yard. Pulling his rifle out of its scabbard, he started off at a run toward the factory.

The Bantag yardmaster ran alongside him to keep up.

"Five, my Qarth, dispersed at other sites, but we can have them here before morning."

Jamul galloped up and dismounted to join him.

"Get the warriors of our First Umen loaded aboard as quickly as possible."

Jamul shook his head. "They're encamped half an hour's run from the rail line. Just to get the message to them and get them formed, down to the tracks, and loaded will take nearly till dawn."

Ha'ark swore vehemently.

"There's the guards units. We can get at least two or three companies of them in a matter of minutes."

Ha'ark grabbed Jamul by the shoulder.

"I'm going ahead right now. You get as many of the First Umen on trains as possible and follow me."

"Shouldn't I go first? It is not your place."

"I'm going."

He walked toward a group of guards who were on their knees.

"Karga, where is Karga?"

"My Qarth."

Ha'ark saw Karga prostrate on the ground before him. "Up, damn you."

The crack of a cannon echoed from within the factory.

"How did they escape?"

Karga nervously told him of the tunnel and the breakout.

"Did I not send you word that I suspected this?"

"Yes my Qarth."

"And?"

"We searched the entire compound from one end to the other. We questioned dozens of cattle. Nothing was revealed."

"Obviously you did not question or search hard enough," Ha'ark snarled.

Karga lowered his head and then fell to his knees. With a ritual flourish he drew his scimitar and held it before him, the point of the blade touching his body just below the sternum.

"Your command, my Qarth."

Ha'ark looked down at him, simmering with rage. It would be simple enough to order him to fall on his sword.

Another cannon report echoed.

"What is going on in there?" Ha'ark demanded.

"The cattle, my Qarth. They are rioting."

"How many dead?"

"Hundreds by now."

Ha'ark realized they should all be killed. Word of this should never be allowed to seep out to all the other cattle laboring in the mines, factories, and cities now under their control. But we'll lose our main supply of rail, he thought. What we have in there are the best-trained animals on this world, the ones we traded from the Merki.

Ha'ark stood silent for a moment, listening to the screams coming from the other side of the wall. A ball of fire erupted heavenward from the factory roof.

"Kill them all," he said quietly. "All of them."

He looked around at the guards behind Karga.

"All of them!" he roared.

They saluted and ran back toward the factory.

"We have enough cattle trained in other factories now. We should have killed these people anyhow. They thought they had a place to run to, the Chin don't."

To Karga he said, "You're coming with me."

Karga's face showed his surprise.

"I will not give Schuder the pleasure of thinking you dead. I want him to see you one more time. You're coming with me."

He could see the flicker of relief on Karga's face. But what he had planned for him, and for Schuder, would soon cause this one to wish that he had been allowed to die.

A train emerged from the smoke behind him, its bell tolling, and came to a stop. Warriors from one of the guard companies raced out of their barracks on the far side of the rail yard and began to clamber aboard the flatcars. Ha'ark climbed up to the engine.

This was nothing but a hunt for escaped cattle, an ignominious task. But there was something else now, something he could not quite explain. It was Schuder. Somehow the human had succeed in besting him. He had kept his thoughts hidden, he had succeeded where no one had dreamed possible. He carried with him, as well, knowledge of all that was planned. Worst of all, Ha'ark sensed that Schuder carried knowledge of him. He had to see this done himself.

He looked down and saw Jamul.

"Take command here in my absence," he instructed Jamul. "Finish the job in the factory. Send someone out to look for the break in the telegraph line, get it repaired, and see if you can get a signal further up the line to block them. Also, get a flyer up to try and get ahead of them. Once we do that, they're trapped. When you've loaded as many as possible from the First Umen, come forward."

Jamul bowed low in salute and left. Ha'ark watched him go, probing, wondering. It wasn't quite safe for Ha'ark to go like this. There was the loss of face for what had happened. Some of the other Qarths would surely take secret delight in that. Jamul was loyal; he was too stupid not to be. But there were always the old clan Qarths. Could they take advantage of this? Possibly, but such an act would be madness, to split their ranks. Wisdom told him he should stay. But that was impossible now. It had become all too personal and the thought that consumed him was the dream of looking into Hans's eyes as he ripped his heart out and devoured it.

Chapter Six

Hans watched Alexi nervously.

"The switch to the main line is open," Alexi reported. "If I remember correctly there's a water tower just beyond the station and a woodlot beside it."

Hans leaned out of the cab. The station seemed quiet. He could see a light shining in the single log hut next to the track. In the dim glow cast by the Great Wheel overhead he thought he could see a dozen yurts, but nothing stirred around them. With luck they might even get in and out without the alarm being sounded.

Alexi gave three short blasts on the whistle, and his firemen eased off on the throttle and pulled down on the brake.

"Keep your steam up," Hans instructed him. "Be ready to get us the hell out of here if there's a reception waiting."

He turned to the men Gregory had been training. "If we stop here, you men get back into the cars. Break out the guns and ammunition. Start showing the others how to use them. Sooner or later we're going to have to fight, and I want every man and woman on this train to be able to shoot. Each of you will be responsible for leading the people in your car. If we have to fight, Alexi will give one long blast on the whistle. Get out and then follow me."

The men nodded eagerly in reply.

"There's the water tank," Alexi announced.

Hans looked at Ketswana and Gregory. "No shooting unless we have to. If there's a Bantag in the hut, try to kill him quickly and quietly."

Ketswana grinned, raising the scimitar. The engine drifted past the station. A quick glance in the window showed a single human inside, looking up. Ketswana jumped from the train, followed by Gregory. The two leapt onto the platform and made for the door. Hans leaned out to watch. Ketswana flung the door open and stormed inside. The train continued to glide forward and Hans stepped down, rifle in hand. Ketswana was already back out the door, grinning.

"One of them, he'll never wake up from his sleep."

Gregory came out, dragging a man behind him. "Do you know who we are?" Hans asked him in Bantag.

The man looked at him goggle-eyed, then turned his gaze toward Ketswana, who stood to one side, his scimitar dripping with blood.

"If you want to go with us, you can, but be quick about it."

Hans headed to the woodlot, where a crew of a dozen men were already at work, hurling logs up into the tender while Alexi and the fireman struggled to swing the spout from the water tank around to the intake pipe.

"Hans!" Gregory ran up to him. "We've got a problem. There's a train due from the west here in about an hour, the telegrapher just told me."

Damn.

"Did they have any warning at all here?"

"He said they knew the wire was dead, but figured it was just a break in the line. The guard was asleep, like Ketswana said."

"Any garrison?"

"A couple of hundred," and he nodded toward

the yurts lined up along a low ridge a hundred yards to the south.

"Hans." Ketswana called him over.

Ketswana held up his hand. "Listen."

Hans came to a stop at the end of the train and looked back to the east. The only sound that he heard was the whirring of the night in the high grass.

"There," Ketswana whispered.

Hans cocked his head but still heard nothing.

"It's a train," Gregory hissed. "Can't you hear it?"

Hans shook his head.

"There," Ketswana said again and pointed. Hans peered down the track, and suddenly he saw it, a low cloud of smoke hanging on the horizon, just visible in the starlight, briefly illuminated by a flash of red.

"How far?" Gregory asked.

"Three miles, maybe four," Hans sighed.

We knew we'd be pursued, he thought. But to come on so damn quick!

"We've got five, maybe seven minutes at most. Gregory, tell Alexi to hurry it up. Look in the cabin and around the woodlot for tools. Try to smash a hole in the water tank. Ketswana, get that switchman back here, throw the switch onto the spur line and then jam it."

The two sprinted off. Hans started back down the length of the train, pausing at the next to last car. Tamira stood there waiting for him.

"Andrew?"

"Just fine," she whispered, and in the shadows he could see that she was holding him.

"Is there any food or water in there?"

"I was hoping we could get water here."

Hans shook his head and explained what was happening.

Anxiously she looked out the open door. This time he could hear the whistle, a low, mournful sound in the distance. A hammering erupted from the track behind him, and he winced at the sound. Why the Bantag encampment on the ridge wasn't astir was beyond him.

"We're leaving in a minute," Hans announced. He reached up quickly to touch her side and then ran back to the front. Alexi was on top of the engine, holding the water spout over the intake pipe.

"What about the train up ahead?" the engineer asked.

"We can't stay here!" He pulled out his map and examined it intently. "There's a siding twenty miles up the line."

"He'll be past there before we make it," Gregory announced, coming up to join Hans.

"We can't stay here," Hans snarled. "Unless that bastard behind us is a complete fool, he'll come in here slow, expecting us to throw the switch. They must have armed warriors on that train, and we've yet to get our people ready to fight. We run for the siding and just hope to get there first."

The insistent whistle of the train behind him now echoed clearly, and Hans could see the engine light and its reflection shimmering off the rails.

The crew in the woodlot worked furiously, the logs slamming against the iron side of the tender.

"Yakazk?"

Startled, Hans saw a Bantag coming toward them out of the shadows.

Hans unslung his rifle and leveled it. The Bantag stopped, wide-eyed, and started to turn around.

His finger edged against the trigger, then stopped. A shot would stir them all to instant action. One of them yelling and hollering might be dismissed as a drunk, gaining them crucial seconds.

The Bantag continued to back up, his expression terrified.

Hans grinned at him, taking pleasure in seeing the fear in his eyes.

"I'm letting you live, you bastard," Hans snapped. "Now go tell your friends about it."

With a wild scream the Bantag turned and started to run.

Not sparing him a second thought, Hans said to Alexi, "Let's get the hell out of here! Signal Ketswana!"

Alexi leapt down into the cab, the wood crew still working with a frenzy as the engineer gave three short blasts on the whistle, then slammed the throttle in, setting the wheels to spinning.

Hans looked back anxiously. The approaching engine couldn't be more than half a mile away. Suddenly he remembered the telegraph line and started to curse himself until he saw someone sliding down the nearest pole. Gregory had obviously detailed someone off.

The train lurched forward with a shudder, and Ketswana came racing down the platform. "We threw the switch, and bent part of the mechanism!"

Hans climbed up onto the engine, Ketswana following. A rifle shot snapped past. Now Hans could see Bantag pouring out of the yurts at the camp. More shots echoed, and from the boxcar behind him a scream erupted.

Bantag came boiling down the hill, but as the train pulled out, half a dozen shots from the boxcars dropped several of them.

"Pour it on, Alexi!" Hans shouted. "Everything we've got."

"You know, if we don't get there first, we could very well have a head-on."

"What the hell?" Hans snarled. "There's worse ways of going!"

Ha'ark leaned out of the cab and saw the sparks showering up from the retreating engine, less than a quarter mile away. His train lurched to a stop and he hopped down, while several of his guards raced forward. He walked over to the switch with one of the engineers.

"How long to fix this?"

The engineer looked at him wide-eyed.

"How long?"

"Shortly, my Qarth. Shortly. But we should get water and wood. It's more than eighty miles to the next supplies."

Ha'ark uttered a curse and strode over to the station and watched as several cattle were driven up the side of the water tower to raise the spout so the precious liquid would not drain away.

In the cabin he saw the headless body of a warrior sprawled on the floor.

Damn fool, asleep, most likely.

Guards ran past him in the darkness, not even aware of who he was. Ten minutes, more like fifteen, before they could get under way again. Too much lead time and they'll be able to stop and smash a switch or tear up a rail.

He grabbed one of the guards running by. "Rails, do you have any extra rails, tools, spikes here?"

The guard pointed off into the shadows. "On the other side of the spur."

"Damn it all, load some of that equipment on one of the cars."

The guard hesitated.

"My Qarth, the switch is fixed," the engineer shouted.

The guard looked at Ha'ark, wide-eyed, and started to bow low.

"Damn it, just get to work!" Ha'ark roared. "I want a work crew that knows how to repair track going with us—cattle or warrior, I don't care."

The guard saluted and ran off as Ha'ark, still cursing, watched the escaping train recede into the distance.

"Land ahead," Feyodor announced.

Mumbling a curse, Jack sat up and rubbed his eyes. A loud snoring rumbled above him in the upper berth. When he kicked the sagging hammock swaying just over his head, the snoring stopped.

"What time is it?"

"About an hour before dawn." Feyodor nodded toward the eastern horizon.

"Lord, we made time!" Jack said. "It must be forty, fifty knots blowing up here. We're going to have to duck low for the run back."

Stefan sat up, rubbing his eyes.

"Sleep all right?" Feyodor asked. He offered a mug of steaming tea.

"Wonderful! The air up here's so clean," Stefan said enthusiastically.

"Oh, shut up," Jack growled, wrapping his hands around the mug to cut the chill. He gazed down at the tea, the question trying to form, and then finally back up at Feyodor.

"I went forward and set a kettle on the engine," Feyodor said, anticipating the question.

Jack looked out at the catwalk and shook his head. "And suppose you'd fallen? Here we'd have drifted for hours, you damn fool, before we woke up and knew you were gone."

"Look, do you want the tea or not? At least it's something hot."

Jack sipped the scalding brew, pleased that Feyodor had thought to bring along some honey to sweeten it.

"There's land ahead."

Jack crouched down and went forward. In the early light of dawn he could clearly see a low range of hills, the mist drifting through the passes and valleys. The moment transcended all his fears. The darker shadows of tree-clad mountains to the north swept out like long fingers across the steppe. To his right the indigo blue surface of the Great Sea was capped with long rollers, kicked up by the strengthening northwesterly breeze. He knew he was gazing upon land that no free man had ever before set eyes on.

Jack settled down in his chair, taking another long sip of tea, and nodding his thanks as Feyodor handed him a buttered biscuit and a slab of cold salt pork. He chewed meditatively on the tough meat, blocking out the exuberant chatter of Stefan and Feyodor in the aft section.

He cocked his ears for each of the engines, slowly throttling them up and then back down to cruise setting. The wind gauge read just under thirty miles an hour, but with the breeze almost astern he estimated they were doing seventy or more.

A mile below, he saw a scattering of yurts and the upturned faces of Bantag looking at the strange apparition. The air was so crystal clear that he felt he could almost see the details of their faces, their openmouthed astonishment. Stretching his arm out the window, he waved and then made a rude gesture.

"Do you think we passed it during the night?" Feyodor asked.

Jack unfolded the map drawn by the naval survey that had scouted the eastern coast. For several minutes he carefully scanned up and down the coast and then examined the map again.

"I think we're about thirty miles north. That small bay that curves up into the mountains. On the map here."

He pointed at the map and then over to his left. Feyodor craned his neck to look and finally nodded in agreement.

"Let's drop her down, get out of this wind." He

pointed *Flying Cloud*'s nose down at a twenty-degree angle and went into a dive, while turning to the southwest. The wind continued to push them away from the coast and he eased in more throttle, turning into a west-by-southwest heading. Finally they started to gain and as the ship dropped below five thousand feet the wind appeared to abate so that he could finally steer southwest to maintain a southerly course.

As dawn continued to spread, the sky to the east glowed red and he could see a broad estuary coming down to the sea. A spread of white sails stood out clearly as they drew closer, running close-hauled several miles off the coast.

"Steam sloop *Vicksburg*," Feyodor reported, raising his telescope to sight the ship.

Jack nodded and examined the toylike ship when Feyodor passed the telescope over. It was one of the picketboats patrolling this, the outer edge of enemy territory, yet another extension of an undeclared conflict. Half a dozen settlements of what he guessed to be descendants of the Chinese dotted the eastern shore of the sea. Bantags garrisoned them, and picketboats like the *Vicksburg* cruised by on occasion to take a look. Bullfinch was calling for more aggressive action, cutting out raids, even arming the locals and triggering a rebellion, but Congress and the president kept overruling him. What was up the estuary was unknown, for any approach up the river was blocked by a dozen galleys based on the inner side of the bay. Today that would change.

"Stefan, time to get topside," Jack instructed. "We're in the badlands now. Keep a sharp watch. We don't know if they have any flyers, but we'd better be on the safe side."

"Aye, sir!"

Jack shook his head as the boy eagerly buttoned up his leather flight jacket, stuffed half a loaf of bread into one pocket, and tucked a flask of water in the other. Pulling his helmet on, he strapped goggles over his eyes. He opened the aft door and, reaching out, grabbed hold of the rope ladder. Hanging nearly upside down, he scrambled up the side of the ship, the wind whipping his jacket and trousers. He soon disappeared over the side.

"The boy's a natural-born pilot," Feyodor said admiringly.

"He's insane," Jack grumbled in reply, his stomach knotting up at the mere thought of hanging on the side of the ship.

A high, piercing whistle sounded next to Jack and he uncapped the speaking tube. "I'm in place, sir. It's beautiful up here," Stefan cried.

"Are you strapped in? If we start maneuvering I'm not going to have time to warn you."

"Aye, aye, sir!"

Jack shook his head again, recapped the speaking tube, and looked back to the front.

"That estuary runs southeast. I'm going to take her back up a bit. How's our fuel?"

"We're fine. Just over three quarters."

"The run back, though," Jack replied. He searched the ground below for any sign of smoke, and caught sight of a plume rising from a row of buildings near a long shed, which he suspected was for the galleys.

"Seems to be backing around to westerly down there, maybe five, ten miles an hour."

He checked his fuel gauges again. He wanted to keep a good reserve. Maybe go in for an hour or so, then come about.

Settling back in his chair, he finished his breakfast, occasionally raising his field glasses to study a detail or point out sights for Feyodor to sketch or note in the logbook. The disk of the sun broke the eastern horizon, and long shadows raced out across the steppe.

"There must be a sizable town further up this river," Feyodor said, breaking the silence of the last hour, which had been interrupted only by occasional comments from Jack to note a village or some other sight that might be significant.

Jack nodded in agreement. Dozens of boats dotted the river, and the airship had passed what looked to be two construction yards, one with a bargelike ship more than two hundred feet long sitting on the ways. A dozen more galleys were beached along by a small cove as well, and he could clearly see a throng of several thousand humans in a walled enclosure, their dark forms surging back and forth, faces turned upward at his passage.

A flash memory struck him of the burial of Jubadi and the horrific slaughter pit he had witnessed.

"I'd love to swoop down there with a load of guns, and let those poor bastards break out," Jack whispered.

Feyodor didn't reply, field glasses trained forward. "I think that's a town up ahead." Lowering the glasses, he picked up the telescope and extended it, bracing the end of the tube on the forward railing of the window.

"Take a look," Feyodor said, passing the telescope over to Jack. It took him several seconds to focus it. Then the image snapped clear, and he whistled softly as he scanned back and forth.

"I think we'd better get a photograph of this," he said.

After a few minutes he put the telescope down and picked up his field glasses again for a broader view. He examined a shipyard for several minutes and to his horror finally realized that there were more than a dozen vessels with iron siding on the ways, black pipes sticking up through the decks. The town spread out along the riverfront, and he could clearly see gangs of laborers working in the yards. An

earthen fortress dominated the yard and what looked
to be artillery was mounted to fire on the river.

Feyodor unsnapped the hatch to the first camera.
Sighting down, he flipped the shutter open, counted
to ten, and closed it. The image would be blurry, but
it should still be decipherable.

He shifted his gaze for a moment to look down-
stream again. The river swung at this point in a loop
to the south before turning north again, so that what
appeared to be another earthen fortress abutting a
village that guarded the approach was in fact further
away. If any ships were going to run up the river,
they'd have to pass the lower fortress first.

He studied the fortress for several seconds, and
then something caught his eye—a plume of smoke
rising just beyond it. Thinking vaguely that something was not quite registering, he shifted his gaze
away.

Then realization suddenly dawned, and he
grabbed the telescope and swung it back and forth,
finding the smoke for an instant, losing it, then finding it again.

"Merciful god, they've got trains."

Feyodor stood up and leaned forward with his
field glasses trained on the ground.

The rhythmic puffs of smoke moved slowly beyond the ridgeline. Jack inched his telescope forward
from the direction of the advancing smoke and then
saw the rails, cutting through the ridge. A side track
ran toward the fortress town, the other branch ran
straight on into the city, which was now almost directly below.

"Off to the east of the town, Jack. It looks like
hangars for airships!"

Jack tore his attention away from the rail line and
looked where Feyodor was pointing. Six long, narrow buildings were arranged like spokes around a

vast open field. Even as he watched, the nose of an airship emerged from one of the hangars.

"We're going to have company," Jack announced.

Now he looked back toward the ridge and finally saw it . . . an engine was cresting the cut, a string of half a dozen flatcars behind it, each one bearing a large boxlike structure covered with tarps.

"Should we come about?" Feyodor asked.

"I want a photograph of the train."

"Are we coming about, then?"

Feyodor was right. What they had already discovered would shake the hell out of Andrew and, better yet, out of Congress and the president as well. He continued to study the engine. It was bearing some sort of cargo in toward the port. It had to be something manufactured—otherwise, why the effort to cover it with canvas? He saw no evidence of factories or any facilities for making iron plate or engines or foundries for cannon or ammunition. If the bastards took the trouble to lay track, it had to lead to something important.

Judging from the plume of smoke from the locomotive the wind was backing around more to the west. Still a quartering headwind for the return.

"I want to see where this track leads," Jack announced.

Feyodor looked at him and shook his head. "Keep an eye on that ship coming out. By the time he gains altitude we'll be well ahead, but as we come about, he might be a problem."

Jack reached over to the speaking tube and blew through it so the whistle on the other end sounded.

"Stefan. There's a ship coming up. If they have one, there might be more. Keep a sharp watch now!"

"I hope we get into a fight, sir!"

Muttering a curse, Jack set the ship over onto a more easterly head, aiming for what he could now see must be a railroad cut through a ridgeline twenty miles away.

"There's the other train!"

Hans climbed halfway out of the cab to look forward and saw a smudge of smoke hovering on the track directly ahead, visible now in the early-morning light.

"Is he past the switchoff?"

"How the hell should I know?" Alexi shouted, the tension of the chase beginning to tell.

Hans saw that the other engine was slowly gaining and was now only a couple of miles behind them.

"If they've gone through the switch we're in for it!"

"I think I see the switch signal!" the fireman shouted, leaning out from the other side of the cab. "The other engine's yet to pass it."

Hans looked down at his rifle and fumbled nervously at the bandoleer of ammunition slung over his shoulder. Scrambling up to the back of the tender, he looked through the hole chopped into the boxcar.

"Get ready back there. Remember, one long blast means come out fighting. Pass the word back."

Someone waved from the inside. Hans shook his head. If only he had a company or two of his troops from the Rus army, or better yet from the old Thirty-fifth, he'd be tempted just to slam on the brakes and let the bastards chasing them come in for a fight. He would almost welcome one as a release from the tension. He knew he could at least count on the two hundred people in the cars to fight, but there would be no discipline, and he doubted if one in ten of them could hit a Bantag even if the muzzle of the gun were pressed into his stomach.

"The other train's slowing!" Alexi announced, and he held the whistle down, giving repeated blasts.

"Can you signal him to clear the way?"

"That's what I'm doing."

Alexi stared at the crude steam gauge.

"They're still on the main line. They're throwing the switch!" the fireman shouted.

Alexi looked at Hans, who let go a string of oaths.

"I've got to ease off on the throttle," said Alexi. "They might not be clear at the other end of the switchoff."

Hans leaned out to see down the track. The engine was still closing. There was no way of telling how many warriors were behind him. At one point, a dozen miles back, the track had curved enough that he thought he saw at least four or five cars behind the engine by the light of the crescent moon. If so, there might be upwards of two hundred Bantag in pursuit. It would be a massacre.

"Just get us through the damn switch. Don't set off a signal unless there's warriors on that train. If it's just a freight we kill the crew, open the throttle, and send it back against the bastards behind us!"

Alexi nodded. Hans signaled Ketswana and Gregory. "Get ready!'

Alexi continued to ease back on the throttle, edging in the brakes. A Bantag and two humans stood by the switch, the Bantag obviously furious. The train turned onto the side, and as it did so Hans leaned out of the cab, aimed his rifle, and shot the Bantag before he even had time to react.

The two humans looked up at him in disbelief, and one of them lit out in blind panic onto the open steppe. The engine shifted back as it started to run parallel to the main line and two more shots rang out. Gregory and Ketswana had dropped the other Bantag in the cab. Hans held his breath as he scanned the boxcars, expecting at any second for them to burst open and a stream of warriors to pour out . . . but nothing happened. Alexi had guessed right—the train was too long to fit onto the siding. The ten cars stretched past the second switch leading back onto the main line.

Alexi edged the engine forward and then gave a final pull on the brake as the last of the cars cleared the switch.

"Let's go!" Hans roared. Leaping down from the cab, he motioned for Gregory to run down and throw the switch, while the switchman from the yard handled the one to turn them back onto the main line once the rest of the train was cleared.

Hans stepped up into the cab of the train and found the human operators gaping at him. "If you want to live, get the hell off this train!" he roared in Bantag. The two continued to look at him, then down at the dead warrior at their feet, then back at him.

Leaning out the cab again, he could see that the train pursuing them was slowing to a stop several hundred yards away, the troops pouring off either side. Seconds later, a bullet cracked past.

Gregory stood up from the switch and waved the all clear. Hans pushed the throttle forward, and the wheels beneath him started to spin.

He leapt down from the cab. The two operators were still standing aboard their train, staring at them. He raised his gun and pointed.

"Off! Now!"

The two looked at each other and then jumped from the opposite side.

The train started forward, wheels still spinning, then finally gripping so that the train shuddered and lurched.

As soon as the last of the cars cleared the switch, the switchman threw his weight into it and easing the track over. Bullets were now cracking past, a plume of dirt kicking up by Hans's feet. He leapt back up into the cab as the engine started forward and saw the telegrapher looking up at the pole. A young boy who had been sent up the pole to cut the line was now hanging over the crosstree, blood pouring out of his chest. He reached up feebly with his knife, cut the line, and then slumped over.

Hans looked away, watching as Gregory and Ketswana raced up beside the train and jumped back into the cab.

"Let's hope that wrecks the bastard!" Ketswana roared, hanging on to the side of the cab and leaning out to watch the show, in spite of the bullets zinging past.

"How far to the next stop?" Gregory shouted.

"Junction forty miles ahead and we're nearly halfway there," Alexi replied, not adding that the map showed a Bantag encampment, a bridge, and a rail yard. If there was a place that could stop them cold, it would be there.

"Back it up!" Ha'ark roared.

The human engineer looked at him disbelievingly.

"Let it come down to us, back up before it and match its speed."

The engineer pulled back on the throttle, throwing the engine into reverse. The train coming toward them was picking up speed and Ha'ark leaned out of the cab, watching intently. He found it perverse that part of him was actually enjoying this pursuit. It reminded him of a legendary chase back in the early age of steam, two hundred years ago during the Wars of Succession on his home world when Cagar'du, the True Heir, escaped from prison and was pursued by rail for five days until finally cornered and killed in single combat by his rival, the founder of the Lektha Dynasty.

The human engineer allowed the engine to draw closer, until with a barely perceptible bump the two engines touched while going backward down the track. Unable to contain himself, Ha'ark swung out of the cab, ignoring the shouts of protest from the company commander. Easing down the side of the engine, he hesitated for an instant and then leapt across to the other engine. He worked his way down to the cab and climbed aboard, snapped the throttle down and then pulled in the brake. Sparks showered out beneath him and his own train started to pull away. The train finally came to a stop and Ha'ark, grinning, leaned back in the cab, waiting for his warriors to run up to his side. He could see the looks of admiration in their eyes.

Good, let it add to the legend a bit.

"My Qarth. Look!"

Ha'ark leaned out of the cab and looked where one of his soldiers was pointing.

Skimming low over the ground, just clearing a low rise behind them, two flyers came into view.

Ha'ark watched them, admiring their lines, the sleek, rigid-frame bodies . . . and the wing-lifting surfaces that extended to a span of nearly a hundred feet.

To his eyes they were tragically primitive. It would be generations before there would be any hope of lifting the barbarians he ruled to piston aircraft, let alone jets, but it was a start. He saw the superstitious dread on the faces of many of his warriors as they gazed heavenward, some of them making the sign to ward off evil . . . and more than one of them looked sidelong at him in awe, for after all, had not the Redeemer created this wonder to cast down the evil spirits that possessed the cattle?

"Run this train back up to the siding, push as many cars as possible onto the siding, and disconnect them. This was sent by the ancestors to aid us."

The company commander looked at him, not understanding.

"You'll see."

* * *

"Jack, shouldn't we be turning back soon?"

Jack ignored Feyodor's plea, though he did check the fuel supply and then returned his attention to the ground below. By the way the shadows of the newly forming cumulus clouds were drifting across the steppe it appeared that the wind had backed around a bit more to southwest by west, perhaps even due southwest. If so, luck was on his side. It would mean a wind abeam to crab into, but at least they wouldn't be running into a straight headwind going back.

"Fifteen more minutes. We've seen nothing but some sidings, a few spur tracks running up into the hills southward, most likely for lumber or ore. But no factory."

"How's the pursuit astern?"

Feyodor got out of his seat and scurried the length of the cabin to see the view out the rear window.

"Way back there, a good fifteen miles or more. They just don't have the speed."

Jack chuckled. He could well imagine the consternation of the damn Bantag right now, a four-engine airship cruising their skies with impunity. It was the only source of comfort at the moment. They had covered at least a hundred fifty miles of track, and as he looked to the far horizon it seemed to go on forever. Just how the hell did the bastards do it in four years? A locomotive had been captured during the Cartha War and the Merki had a chance to study the steam engine on board the *Ogunquit* before it went down. But a train line? Did the Merki capture some railroad personnel with the old Third Corps and trade them off to the Bantag? And why build it at all, if not for the renewal of a war against the Republic?

There was all that the technology implied as well. It was obvious that a telegraph line was strung along the side of the track, which meant they had galvanic batteries and instant communication. They had at least rudimentary precision tooling, some form of industrialization to make the hundreds of miles of rail, steam engines for trains and ships. What was more troubling, though, was the realization that they had somehow adopted the thinking of industrialization. The Merki were able to mimic it to the extent needed to acquire artillery and muskets, but that was the limit of it. Somehow, something had come into the Bantag Horde and changed part of their thinking, at least as far as the concepts of a modern war were concerned. It was evident from what he had seen from the air that the human population below was enslaved, and according to what Andrew had told him, the Chin population was almost beyond counting, perhaps in the tens of millions or more. That meant almost limitless labor to turn out the tools of war for their Bantag masters.

On the horizon he saw a plume of smoke. Then he saw two more behind it. Three trains coming up the line at once. Perhaps there was something interesting on board.

"All right, Feyodor, let's use the camera to get these three trains together. Then we'll come about and head for home."

"We've got to stop for water and wood!" Alexi shouted. "If we don't, we'll be out of steam in another five miles, ten at most!"

Hans leaned out of the cab to check the rear. The engine behind them was gaining fast. For the first ten miles out from the last siding, the chase had not reappeared, and he had wondered if somehow the engine they had sent back indeed managed to wreck the pursuers. It was clear now what their strategy was: to keep running the train behind them, and he suspected that if they slowed down, the engine would just keep coming and ram them, while the second train, several miles further behind, would finish off what was left.

"We're going to have to seize the rail yard, switch the chase train off onto a siding, then put up a fight till we've loaded up on water and wood."

He could see the junction straight ahead less than a mile away. No troops were deployed out, so he knew that the telegraph line had yet to be repaired. What was curious, though, was that the flyers, which had both managed to surge ahead of him, had banked off southward about fifteen minutes ago and disappeared into the growing bank of cumulus clouds overhead. The strange shape of the airship, had been startling, but there was no time to worry about that now.

"Everyone knows what to do!" Hans shouted. He looked at Gregory and Ketswana, who nodded grimly.

"Get ready, then!"

"Slow her down," Ha'ark announced.

The human engineer looked over at him with relief. Sparks flew as the engineer applied the brake and the speed dropped off. Ha'ark looked at the half dozen guards who had boarded the engine at the insistence of their company commander.

The speed diminished to not much more than a slow run.

"Jump!"

"My Qarth, you can't," one of them protested. "Let me have the honor!"

"Idiot, I'll be along. Now jump!"

The guards looked at each other until finally one of them went over the side, followed an instant later by the other five. The two humans tumbled out after them.

Ha'ark released the brake and then slammed the throttle forward. An instant later he jumped off the side of the cab, rolling head over heels in the high grass. Coming to his feet, he watched as the train surged straight ahead, racing at the escaping train, and he grinned with delight.

"Hit the whistle!"

Alexi gave one long blast, and the boxcar doors slid open, the escapees pouring out.

Hans nodded to Gregory and Ketswana, who leapt off the cab to take command of the ragged battle line. Ketswana's group swarmed across the rail yard while Gregory's formed a skirmish line covering the bridge.

The rail yard to his left erupted in pandemonium. Hundreds of slaves scattered in every direction, Bantag, most of them armed only with scimitars, stood in openmouthed amazement at the screaming, berserk mob charging toward them.

"It's going to cost lives for this water and fuel!" Hans shouted.

Alexi nodded as Hans leapt from the cab and led the switchman and four of Ketswana's men back down the track.

The pursuing engine was coming on fast, as he had expected it would, and reaching the switch leading into the rail yard he helped the switchman slide the track over. They had barely locked it in place when the engine came roaring through and went careening into the yard.

Hans watched incredulously as part of the attacking party led by Ketswana jumped out of the way. The engine, still gathering speed, roared on, straight into a row of boxcars. With a resounding crash, the runaway locomotive lifted the first boxcar off the rails, tossing it aside like a broken toy, and then smashed into the second. The engine rose up like a dying beast and then fell over on its left side, the second boxcar flipping over in front of it, the third jackknifing off the track in the opposite direction. A hiss of steam erupted as the engine plowed into the ground, sparks showering, plumes of dirty smoke boiling out. A ragged cheer went up at the spectacle . . . and then was drowned out by a thunderclap explosion when the first boxcar detonated.

Hans hit the ground, the shock of the explosion knocking the breath out of him. Like a string of firecrackers, the other six cars detonated, one after the other. Hans watched, horrified, as some of his people, caught in the explosion, were tossed into the air like broken dolls, their screams of anguish sounding thin and distant as tons of powder in the cars continued to erupt.

Debris soared heavenward and then cascaded back to the ground, a broken train wheel corkscrewed through the air, tearing up the earth to his right, bouncing back upward, then finally coming to rest thirty yards down the track.

In shock, Hans looked back at his train. Burning debris had rained down on the cars, and several people were already scrambling onto the roofs to kick the embers off. Standing in the doorway to the next to last car was Tamira, with Andrew in her arms, shrieking in terror.

Hans looked numbly back up the track. The second engine was still coming on. In another minute it would be upon him, loaded with an organized enemy force ready to fight.

"What in hell?"

Jack leaned forward in the cab as the string of explosions raced down the track.

"What is going on down there?" Feyodor cried. "Are they crazy?"

"We're going down," Jack announced even as he pushed the helm forward.

"What for?"

"To see what's happening. Look at that. A bunch of people poured out of that first train. It looks like they're shooting."

Jack's heart started to race. Was it some sort of war? Was it possible that there were human armies here fighting the Bantag? He had to find out.

Dropping through four thousand feet, he saw the struggle below laid out before him like a panorama. Around the first engine he could see a crew of humans loading wood frantically, and taking on water from a tank. A wavy line of humans were pulling back around the wrecked train, some of them firing guns, while from a Bantag encampment hundreds of warriors poured out like ants stirred from a nest. Further to the west he could see another engine slowing down and Bantag leaping off of flatcars.

What the hell was going on? And then a thought started to form. Like Andrew's Raid. Were these people trying to escape? But to where? And who the hell were they?

The whistle in the speaking tube to topside shrieked, causing Jack's heart to skip. He pulled the plug.

"What is it?"

"Two flyers above us! Coming out of the sun and fast!"

He felt a thump, the blast of the topside gun thundering through the speaking tube.

"Feyodor. Clear the aft gun! Full throttle!"

Feyodor bounded out of his seat, and racing aft he pulled the levers that opened the back end of the cabin so that the two-pounder would have a clear field of fire. He heard Stefan's gun thump again. He should pull the hell out now, but he still had to find out what was going on.

"Hang on!"

With throttles wide open, he dived for the ground.

"Gregory, keep up your fire! Keep it up!"

Hans paced the length of the ragged volley line he had thrown up at a right angle to the track. The other engine was stopped less than a hundred yards away, on the far side of the bridge over the shallow stream. Bantag warriors were pressing out to either flank. Half a dozen men and women on the line were already down. A bullet clanged against the rail next to Hans's feet and ricocheted off with a howl, plucking at his trousers.

He pulled out his plug of tobacco and bit off a chew, feeling a strange exultation . . . he was on the firing line again . . . it was Antietam, Gettysburg, Wilderness, the Ford. It was good to be alive, if only for this moment, this one last chance to strike back.

Raising his rifle, he drew careful aim on a Bantag and squeezed off. The warrior spun around, then fell.

Behind him the switchman and his crew were hammering on the switch lever, trying to bend it out of shape while half a dozen men struggled to pry part of the track up with their rifles.

"A flyer!"

At that moment Hans felt as if his heart would burst. A flyer, larger than any he had ever seen, was diving down out of the clouds. Emblazoned across its bow was . . . the flag of the Republic.

Tears filled his eyes at the sight of her, and stepping back from the volley line he threw his arms wide, waving with wild abandon. Then he saw the other two flyers diving down on the ship from astern.

A hole burst through the bottom of the ship a dozen feet forward of the cab, splinters showering out. Jack ignored the hit.

"How low you taking us?" Feyodor screamed.

"We'll level off at a thousand."

"That's rifle range!"

"Shut up, damn it, and start shooting."

"At what? It's madness down there."

"Anything big! But don't hit the lead engine! That's ours."

Jack finally eased back on the stick and then he saw one man standing behind a ragged crowd fighting by the bridge just east of the station.

In the sea of dark-colored clothes this one stood out clear with sky-blue trousers and a navy-blue jacket. The upturned face had a gray beard, and the arms were waving excitedly.

"Jesus Christ in heaven," Jack whispered, his voice coking.

A pane of glass forward shattered, showering him with shards.

"It's Schuder!" Jack screamed. "My God, it's Schuder!"

"What?"

"Feyodor, it's Hans Schuder down there!"

Jack continued to press the ship down, diving straight in. Feyodor came up behind him, looking forward.

"Get back to your gun! No—get me a message streamer!"

Jack finally pulled back on the helm, and the ship's nose started to rise. Leveling out at less than five hundred feet, he raced over the train. He leaned out of the cab, waving, and screaming, then pressed on down the track.

Recovering his senses, he shuddered as half a dozen bullets smashed through the cab and wooden splinters blew in every direction. On his left he could see the shadow of his ship, and then, above it, he saw two more shadows.

"They're closing in!"

He could barely hear Stefan's voice over the howling of the engines running at full throttle.

A shot screamed past, arcing from above, slamming into the ground, and detonating.

Explosive shells. Damn, if one goes off on this ship, that's it.

He pulled back hard on the helm, causing the ship to pitch up, and then he saw the other ship take a sharp turn to his left.

"Feyodor, do you see that?" Jack shouted. "Get 'em!"

Startled, he realized that the two ships had ... wings on them like a bird's.

He had a sudden recollection of speculating with Ferguson that wings added to a ship could give it additional lift, enabling it to cut back on the use of hydrogen gas and diminish the bulky drag. Now the first enemy ship was in a banking turn, it wings fully exposed. The turn seemed tighter than what he could do. He sensed that even though he had four engines to the enemy ship's single engine, the Bantag could match or maybe even exceed his speed. Jack pushed the helm hard to the right so that the stern gun would bear, all the time studying the enemy ship.

Feyodor fired and a hole burst in the enemy wing. The ship continued to turn and then lined up. A flash of light ignited.

Feyodor let out a cry as the shot snapped just aft of their ship.

"Got him!" The scream came from topside.

Jack checked their shadows and saw one of them falling in on itself. Seconds later a stream of fire plummeted past on his right, the wings collapsing in on the body of the ship. He caught a glimpse of two Bantag tangled in the burning wreckage just before it impacted. He experienced a moment of regret, for he felt some sort of kinship with anyone mad enough to fly, even if he was of the Horde.

"See the second one!" Stefan called, and a second later a thump ran through the ship, followed straightaway by yet another shot from Feyodor. As before, a hole appeared in the wing, this one detonating on impact so that six feet of wing sheared off. The ship lurched, the side that had lost the wing dropping down, so that for an instant it looked as though the ship would roll. Then it recovered and turned sharply away.

"Feyodor. Two things quickly! We're going straight back over. Try to get a couple of shots into the engine that's chasing them."

"Then what?"

He hesitated for a second. He was tempted to hover and run a line down to Hans to get him out. But he knew that would be futile. The old bastard had stirred something up, and there was no way he would abandon it.

"Second thing. That message streamer. Get it to me now!"

"They got one!"

Hans followed his man's pointing finger. A Bantag flyer engulfed in flames plummeted from the heavens, crashing half a mile away. A ragged cheer went up from his fighters. The sight of something going wrong for the hated enemy gave them a momentary boost in morale. The bodies were piling up at either side of the track and he could see he was losing three, even four, to every one of the Bantag.

"Gregory, you've got to hold. I'm going forward!"

"Tell them to hurry up, damn it. This isn't the First Suzdal here. They're not even militia. We're about to get overrun."

Hans made his way down the length of track and, to his horror, saw Tamira standing upright in the boxcar, Andrew screaming on the floor at her feet, while she scooped up handfuls of ammunition and passed them out the door. Splinters of wood showered around her as bullets hit the car. Hans slung his rifle over his shoulder and swept her into his arms. He grabbed Andrew with his free hand, quickly turning his back to shield the child as another shower of splinters rained down around him.

To hell with worrying about what others would think. He ran the length of the train, then stopped behind the tender and pushed her down.

"Damn it, woman, just stay down!"

"The flyer—it was your friends?" she cried.

"Just stay down!"

A chain gang of twenty men and women were heaving logs off a woodpile while others carrying wooden buckets were running alongside the train, lifting them into the cars. Hans suddenly realized that no one had had a drop of water since the escape. He grabbed a bucket from one of the runners, took a deep gulp, and carried it over to Tamira.

"Bring it into the cab with you when we pull out. You're riding up here."

"I can't do that, Hans."

He forced a smile, shook his head, and turned away.

Up forward he saw Ketswana's line starting to draw back, a surge of Bantag waving scimitars rushing toward them. Arrows arced up over the burning wreckage to their left, plunging down into the workers. Even as he watched, one of them fell. He noticed that half a dozen on the woodpile seemed to be local slaves who had fallen in with them.

"Alexi?"

"Two minutes! We need a full tender."

"Where's that damn telegrapher?"

The man came bursting out of the station even as he called, dragging what Hans guessed was one of his comrades.

"Train just pulled out of here half an hour ago heading west," the telegrapher shouted. "We should be able to follow it up the line."

He nodded to the young Chin telegrapher standing

next to him, and even as he did so the boy crumpled, his head exploding from a bullet.

Hans saw that Gregory's line was beginning to break under the pressure. Some of the Bantag were almost across the bridge and firing from less than fifty yards.

"Alexi, we've got to get out now," Hans roared. The wood crew sprinted toward the train and threw the last logs up into the tender. Hans flung the telegrapher toward the tender and then reached between the boxcar and the tender to pull Tamira and Andrew up, putting himself between her and the hail of bullets sweeping the siding. He pushed her up into the cab and watched until she ducked down into the woodpile. As he reached the cab, a thumping roar echoed from above, and he saw the flyer racing by less than a hundred yards overhead. He saw someone leaning out of the cab . . . it had to be Petracci.

From Petracci's hand, a streamer of red cloth trailed out and fluttered down. Hans offered a salute, Petracci saluted in return, and then the ship headed into a steep, spiraling climb, its tail gun firing at the engine behind them. He tried to follow the red streamer as it plummeted but lost it in a coil of smoke drifting overhead.

Ketswana and his unit came into view down the side of the track, dragging their wounded, and Hans barely noticed that the train's wheels were spinning, Alexi holding the whistle down. He watched intently as Gregory led his survivors toward the train. They finally broke and raced to the cars, the pursuing Bantag howling in a frenzy, charging up out of the river-bed and across the bridge.

Hans trotted alongside the tender and finally leapt back aboard. Bantag swarmed down toward the track, waving scimitars, some of them slowing to fire arrows. One of them gained the tender and leapt up the steps, his blade held high. Ketswana, who had reached the tender just ahead of the pursuit, turned and drove his bayonet into the Bantag's midsection. The warrior fell back with a scream, and Ketswana loosed a triumphant shout.

The last of the Bantag were left behind, and then, to Hans's amazement, he saw that hundreds of slaves lined either side of the track. Some of them started to run, and hands reached out from the boxcars to pull them up.

"Slow down a bit," Hans shouted. "We lost nearly a third of our people back there. Slow down!"

Alexi eased up on the throttle, and with that more than a hundred slaves broke loose and sprinted toward the train, crying to be taken aboard. A screaming howl overhead startled Hans, who saw that a cannon back in the rail yard had apparently been manhandled off a flatcar by a Bantag crew. The shot soared out into the steppe and detonated half a mile away.

"Pour it back on!"

Hans watched as the enemy gun crew bent to their work. To his horror the gun appeared to be a breechloader. One of the crew was turning a screw mounted to one side, and he could see that the barrel was being lowered.

The crew stepped back. Another flash. A geyser of earth erupted less than thirty yards away.

The crew leapt forward, shifting the trail, another round slammed in. Hans leaned out of the cab to look forward. The track dipped down into a tree-covered hollow a quarter mile further on.

"Pour it on! Pour it on!"

The gun disappeared in a puff of smoke, and a second later the last car on the train exploded. A shudder ran through the train, and for a horrifying moment Hans thought they had derailed. Smoke billowed from the stricken car.

"Pour it on!"

Hans stood impotent. Rifle shots erupted from the other cars, and to his amazement he saw one of the gunners drop, hit by a remarkable shot from more than six hundred yards away from a lurching train. The gun fired again, the shot so close over the tender that he could feel the blast from its passage.

The train finally hit the edge of the hollow and started down, the rail yard disappearing from view. As they thundered across a bridge, a parting shell detonated in the trees behind them.

Hans sagged against the side of the tender. He looked at the water bucket Tamira had lugged aboard. It was already empty. Nearly a day since they had eaten, as well, and at the thought of it he realized just how light-headed he was feeling.

"Sir? Sir?"

Hans looked back to see Gregory standing atop the boxcar behind them, blood trickling down his left arm.

"What happened back there?"

"Slaughterhouse, Sergeant. Lost half my people holding them back. Just about everyone that got into the last car was torn apart when the shell hit."

The train was already out of the hollow, and to his amazement the distant gun fired yet again, the shell dropping nearly parallel to the train a hundred yards to one side.

"Two miles or more," he whispered. "They got range on our Parrott guns."

The last car was still trailing smoke, and Hans silently cursed himself. They should have stopped on the last bridge, disconnected the car, and left it there. It might very well have set the bridge on fire.

"And there's this," Gregory shouted. He passed a bundle to Ketswana, who scrambled up to the back of the tender and then passed it on. "Fell from the airship. One of the women ran back and picked it up." He hesitated. "She died getting it back to the train, so it better be worth it. I think it's a message."

Hans took the weighted container, noticing that the sides of it were streaked with blood. He tore open the small leather dispatch case tied to the red streamer and a lead weight fell out. Inside there was a note. He pulled it out and unfolded it.

> Sgt. Schuder! Thank God. Take fort, below town at river. Rail spur leads to it just before last city on river. Big town death trap for you. Hold out! Will send help! Petracci.

With shaking hands he examined the rough map Jack had sketched, and then he pulled out his own map and compared the two.

Unbelieving, he shook his head. He felt a hand slip around his waist and saw Tamira standing on tiptoe to see the note.

"Your friends? The Yankees?"

Hans nodded, unable to speak, and at his acknowledgment a shout of triumph erupted from Ketswana and the news swept the length of the train like wildfire, as if rescue were already at hand.

On his own map there was no indication of a fort, only a spur that simply went off into the unknown. They had had no real plan before this, only the thought that they would somehow make it to the docks, seize a boat, and escape. Now there was hope.

All sorts of dreams formed in that second. He saw the airship receding to the west and felt a wave of guilt at his wish that he could be on that ship, that Jack had swept down to pick up Tamira, Andrew, and himself. He looked at Ketswana, Alexi, Gregory, and all the others, who were shouting excitedly, slapping each other on the back.

But what help? The note did not say they were waiting for him. Ha'ark had taunted him that the

Republic was asleep. Just what could Andrew do for him now? It must be a thousand miles for Jack to get back, and as he watched the ship climbing higher he saw two more flyers on the far western horizon, climbing as well, as if to intercept. Could Jack even get back? And then what? Even if we took the fort, all of the Bantag strength would be upon us. How the hell could help reach us then?

"We're going to make it!" Alexi shouted, holding down the whistle in long, repeated blasts.

Hans looked at them, unable to speak, wondering if it was all a dream.

Ha'ark strode angrily through the wreckage of the rail yard, turning with a snarl as Karga approached.

"My Qarth, the new engine will have steam up shortly, and they're almost done repairing the switch."

Ha'ark simply stared at Karga, who silently withdrew. Cursing, he looked at the burning wreckage and then at his own train. Smoke still poured out of the hole that the shot from the enemy airship had torn in the engine.

One of his precious airships was a burning wreck, the other one had landed near his train and the crew was now struggling to repair the wing.

"Damn!"

Slamming a fist into the palm of his hand, he stalked back toward the switch, slowing to watch the half-dozen humans, armed with sledgehammers, who were trying to bend the switch lever and track back into place. What infuriated him even more was the burning wreckage in the rail yard. He hated mistakes, especially when they were his own. He had thought the chase engine could ram through before they could divert it.

Schuder was proving to be a tougher foe than he had imagined him to be. Even now, trying to probe his thoughts, he caught a fleeting glimpse of hope, mingled with sadness, and then nothing.

A train whistle sounded from the yard, and he saw the first engine starting to back up, pushing half a dozen flatcars already loaded with warriors, nearly double the number he had had before. The human laborers stepped back from the switch and a Bantag yard worker threw it. The engine backed through and across the bridge. A second whistle now sounded, and up the spur line the next train he had summoned appeared. There was only one car in front of the engine, an armored car. He watched approvingly as the train clicked through the switch and drifted to a stop in front of the troop train.

Ha'ark said to the Bantag yardmaster, "There's at least five troop trains behind us. Clear the damaged engine from the line and move them forward. They've most likely cut the telegraph wire further up the line toward X'ian. I won't have time to stop and fix it. Send someone behind us with a handcart to try and find it. Signal up to X'ian about what's happened here."

The yardmaster saluted nervously.

Ha'ark looked over at the human workers, who stood huddled in a knot. "How many of them escaped?"

"More than a hundred, we believe."

Ha'ark nodded. "Kill all the rest," he barked. "No one who saw this is to survive."

He scrambled up into the armored car, nodding in reply to the crew's salutes. He strode forward, easing past the breech-loading cannon, which pointed directly forward through an open port.

"Let's go!"

Chapter Seven

"There's the train," Alexi announced as they crested a low rise and slid to a stop. The telegrapher jumped out and started to climb the nearest pole to cut the line again.

Hans could see it, less than a mile ahead, moving slowly up to the next crest of hills. He climbed to the top of the wood tender and looked behind them. Studying the horizon intently, he thought he could detect a plume of smoke and then a second one. They were starting to catch up but were still a good eight to ten miles back.

He looked ahead down the hill again, shading his eyes from the slanting afternoon sun. There were three open flatcars on the next train, two of them covered with tarps and the third—filled with Bantag troops.

The engine was struggling to crest the rise, and even at this distance he could see that it was somewhat smaller than the others.

Damn. It was still twenty miles to the next switchoff, which would have a woodlot and a water tank. Without this slow mover in front of them they could barrel on through, resupply, and perhaps get farther ahead. The telegrapher slid down the pole and ran to the next one, coiling the wire as he went. At the next pole he cut the line again. Unless the enemy were carrying two hundred feet of spare wire, they would have no way to reconnect, though they could still run a signal forward. It was maddening that Hans had to stop every ten miles or so to cut the line, but if he didn't they would face a deadly reception somewhere ahead.

The telegrapher ran back to the train, dragging the coil of wire, and Alexi started forward again. Hans continued to study the last flatcar. It looked like at least twenty-five Bantag were on board. There was no sense in getting boxed in. They'd have to seize the train ahead.

Hans outlined his plan as Alexi throttled the train up, and minutes later Gregory returned from the nearest boxcar with a dozen men and women carrying their rifles. The train ahead was lost to view for moment as they climbed the next ridge, and then it reappeared, less than half a mile away now.

"Bring us up fast, Alexi!"

With repeated blasts on the whistle, they raced forward, the range rapidly closing to less than a hundred yards. Hans looked around the cab and tender to make sure that everyone was down except Alexi. From the fireman's side of the engine Hans saw that most of the warriors huddled on the flatcar were watching their approach. To his dismay, they were armed with rifles. The Bantag engineer was facing them and waving a fist angrily.

"Can you get him to stop?"

Alexi shook his head. "Maybe. Rather strange, though. It's not like we can then go around him."

"Keep blowing the whistle."

The stalemate continued for several minutes, the engine ahead rumbling slowly on. Finally the Bantag engineer threw up his hands in exasperation and motioned for the human engineer to pull the throttle back. The engine ahead slowed and Alexi eased up as well until the two trains were moving at barely a walk.

"Get ready," Hans snapped.

He watched as the Bantag engineer leapt off his train and strode toward them, swearing vehemently, the warriors on the flatcar standing up, some of them laughing.

"Now!"

Hans jumped from the cab, and the others piled out to either side. He ran straight past the Bantag engineer, not even bothering to slow down, and came around the front of the train. Leveling his rifle, he took careful aim and dropped one of the warriors on the flatcar. The others looked at him, dumbfounded. Flipping the breech open, he slammed another cartridge in, snapped it shut, cocked the hammer, aimed, and fired, dropping another. Another rifle cracked by his side. It was Gregory, cursing madly as he worked his breech open.

A flurry of shots now erupted. The Bantag finally recovered their wits and scrambled for their rifles. Half a dozen jumped off the car, drawing their scimitars, and charged, two of them straight at Hans. He dropped one at less than ten paces and then he crouched down and raised his bayonet. The remaining Bantag leapt to one side, his blade slicing down. Hans raised his rifle to parry the blow, which landed with such force that it numbed his hands and made sparks fly from the barrel of his rifle. The Bantag recovered, and raised his blade again. Hans came in low, his bayonet thrusting up to catch his opponent in the throat.

He staggered back as the Bantag fell.

The battle was already over, the dead lying heaped around the tracks. Ketswana was at his side, kneeling by one of his men who had been shot in the chest. Hans saw half a dozen more down, two of them clutching at wounds. Ketswana drew a knife and put his other hand over his comrade's eyes. Hans turned and walked away.

"Alexi!"

"Here." The engineer came forward from the train.

Hans stepped away from the track and looked back. The plumes of smoke were closer now, maybe only five or six miles, ten to fifteen minutes at most.

"Are you going to run our train back at him and take the new one?" Alexi asked.

Hans shook his head. "We'd be trading a faster train for a slower one. He'd most likely pull the same trick as last time. Reverse, match speed, then catch it. Once he did that, he could run us down."

"What about cutting a rail in front of our train?" Alexi proposed. "We back our engine up, run it forward, derail it. That would block them."

Hans thought for a moment, then shook his head. "That'd still mean packing two hundred or more people onto three flat cars. There's another camp to get through yet. If they see us coming that way, it might get them stirred up, and again, we'd be trading a faster engine for a slower one."

Alexi nodded his head and cursed. "Try to tear up a rail behind us, then. I'll give you five minutes. I'm going forward to run the next train. Maybe we can reverse them at the next switchoff."

Alexi saluted and returned to his train. Hans could not help but grin. Some of the old military rituals were surfacing. It felt good to be saluted again.

He sprinted down the track toward the engine they had just captured. The human operators were cowering in the cab, one of Gregory's men standing with rifle aimed at them. Hans ignored them and examined the engine.

"Do you know who we are?" Hans snapped in Bantag.

The two shook their heads in unison, both of them trembling with fear.

"We've started a war against the Bantag. I'm a soldier of the Republic."

At the mention of the word "Republic" the two

began to talk excitedly, one of them pointing at his own chest and then at his comrade's.

"Cartha," he announced emphatically.

Yet another prisoner sold by the Merki to help build the Bantag war machine.

"Take us," the fireman stuttered, obviously still terrified by what he had seen—cattle slaughtering Bantag. Hans slapped him on the shoulder and then jumped off the cab and started back to his train.

"Hans!" Gregory was on the first flatcar, tearing the tarp back. "In the name of Perm, look at this!"

Hans scrambled onto the car and stood, slack-jawed in amazement.

"What is it?" Gregory asked.

Hans shook his head. Lifting the tarp, he moved to the front. The entire thing was covered in iron plate, the sheets bolted together. At the front there was an opening more than big enough to stick his head through, and he peered inside. All was darkness within. There was the smell of grease and coal.

"They're getting closer!"

Hans pulled his head out and stepped back. Ketswana was by the side of the car.

Hans nodded. "Gregory, get a dozen of your people up to this train with me. Ketswana, you're still on the second train. Let's get going."

The pursuing trains were now less than two miles away. Hans saw a flash of light.

He stood silently, watching Gregory and his unit sprint up and pile into the tender. Alexi leaned out from his cab and waved. Hans motioned to the Cartha engineer, who gave two short blasts and then eased the throttle in. Hans was still silently counting when he finally heard it, the scream of a shell coming in. A detonation erupted a hundred yards behind the second train.

He stepped up into the cab as they started to crawl forward.

"Alexi said they bent a section of track. With luck the bastards might run up on it and derail," Gregory said.

"I doubt it," Hans said quietly.

Hans looked back at the tarp-covered load behind him. There was a gun in it. Whatever it was, it would be worth taking in spite of the extra weight.

Another shot screamed past, but he did not even bother to turn around as they continued to race westward.

His hand shaking, Andrew put the telegram down on the desk and looked up at Pat, who stood before him, loudly blowing his nose.

Hans ... alive! Emotion swept him like a torrent, and he lowered his head. The door behind him burst open.

"Is it true?" Emil cried.

" 'Tis true," Pat replied, still choked with emotion. "Petracci just landed at the defensive line air base. Lord knows how he did it in the dark."

"So what is this? A damn wake?" Emil laughed, slapping Andrew on the shoulder.

"You damn Irishman, give me that flask," Emil demanded. Uncorking it, he held it aloft. "For Hans, God bless 'im."

Emil tilted his head back for a long gulp and then passed the flask to Andrew, who smiled and took a drink himself.

"I never did believe him dead," Andrew said.

The door opened, and an orderly entered, holding a long sheet of paper.

"Latest report from Petracci," he announced excitedly.

Andrew grabbed the sheet and started to read, Pat and Emil crowding around to look over his shoulder.

Sighing, Andrew took off his glasses and leaned

back in his chair. Thoughts of Hans fled for the moment.

So it was war, as he had always feared. They had trains and flyers of a new design, were building what looked to be ironclads, had troops with rifles. It was a mobilization undreamed of, and he silently cursed all the mistakes he had allowed to happen over the last four years. If only we had pushed forward more aggressively, had put more effort into improving airships, had built up the fleet of the Great Sea and pushed patrols up the river.

"See that copies of this are immediately sent to the president," Andrew snapped to the orderly.

"He'll shit," Pat said with a sad chuckle.

Andrew glared at Pat. "He's the president, damn it. Remember, we're on the same side."

"But, Andrew."

Andrew held up his hand. "The differences are buried as of right now. We're already at war again, and remember, damn it, we answer to the president, not the other way around."

The room fell silent. Sighing, Andrew stood up and went to the window. The shock would have been a bitter blow to start with, but that could wait. Now there was Hans.

He felt numb, as if a ghost he had almost managed to finally bury had come back. And I did not find you, my friend. I did not look hard enough. A wave of shame coursed through him, that he had allowed himself to believe what the Merki said and ignored the instinct that told him somehow Hans had survived. How can I face him after that? he wondered.

"Andrew, this looks bad," Pat finally said.

Andrew turned. "Escaping by train, still two hundred miles from the river. Then this fort Jack mentions. Seize that and hope we can get up river?"

Pat shook his head and put the telegram down.

"We get him out. I don't care what it takes, we get him out."

"But how?" Emil interjected.

Andrew walked back over to the desk and picked up the two telegrams, studying them intently. Then he went to the door and pulled it open.

"Get the latest deployment reports from Bullfinch, and ratings for all ships in the Second Fleet," he shouted, sending two of his staffers in the next room scurrying.

He sat down and waited in silence, drumming the table with his fingers. A minute later an orderly burst into the room, bearing the daily reports and a leather-bound reference book listing all the ships of the navy and their designs.

Andrew looked at Pat.

"*Vicksburg* is the only one on station. Wooden-sided steam and wind-powered sloop."

He shook his head. "It'd be torn apart in the river by the rams."

"*Petersburg* might do it if we can locate her."

"Are you going to try and run the river?" Emil asked.

"What else can we do? It's the only way to get them out."

"Talk about a provocation for war," Pat sighed. "It'd be a violation of the president's orders. He'd have Congress down his throat."

"I'll worry about that later."

He tore through the ratings book, pausing for a second on the *Vicksburg.* Four guns, fifty-pound rifles, wooden-sided. He shook his head and kept going to find the *Petersburg,* the one ironclad now deployed. It carried one of the hundred-pound Parrott guns forward and eight broadside five-inch rifles. Displacing only six feet, the side-wheeler carried two inches of armor backed with oak.

He closed his eyes. The ship was still on shakedown with Bullfinch on board. They weren't even sure where it was at the moment; its orders were to cruise southward but to remain out of sight of land. The *Franklin* was the one other possibility, a four-gun propeller-driven ship based on the original designs used in the Cartha War. But that was still docked for final fitting out. Even if it could sail this instant, at best speed it would take at least two and a half days just to get to the mouth of the river, and it drew nearly ten feet.

There were half a dozen light sloops, good for patrolling but useless for running up the river against resistance.

He sat in silence, listening to the clock ticking in the corner. From the next room he could hear the telegrapher sending the repeat of the dispatch to Kal. It was impossible to imagine that Kal would not approve the operation to bring their friend out. But there was always Congress. Running the river would be an open act of war, and he could well imagine that some in that chamber would want to debate the issue. Kal could order the rescue attempt in any case, but he might very well want to consult the leaders and Marcus before proceeding. Time—it would be a waste of precious time.

The telegraph fell silent for a moment. A series of rapid clicks suddenly came back, a short reply, and then another message started. Andrew half listened, still wrapped in thought as an orderly came in bearing a fresh report. Andrew scanned it while Pat watched him intently.

"It's direct from Petracci. Says repairs on his ship should be completed by dawn. He wants clearance to fly back to check on Hans's progress."

"Permission granted," Andrew replied.

He stirred and asked Pat, "How many airships are based here at the moment?"

"Three operational."

"Get a pilot and engineer out to the field right now. I want one of them up as soon as possible."

"At night? We don't have any boys that are all that good at night flying, Andrew. Hell, they get killed just about the time they finally start getting the hang of it."

"I want one up"—he looked at the clock—"by eleven, ready to make a run."

"Whatever for?" Emil asked.

As he started to explain, Andrew almost wanted to laugh at the astonishment on his friend's faces.

Cursing soundly, Ha'ark paced the siding as his straining warriors struggled to push the engine off the track. He should have expected this. The only alternative to pushing the engine off now was to wait until dawn and thereby lose the chase altogether. The bent track at the place where Hans had obviously captured a second train had delayed them long enough for Hans to gain the next yard. There they had moved their own train forward, backed the captured locomotive around through a switchoff, then run it back through the switch, which had been set only halfway back, so that the engine derailed.

That had given them an hour's lead and now this. Without a strong headlight Ha'ark's train had moved along at barely a crawl. Three times they had stopped in time where a rail had been bent, but this trap was more cunning. All the spikes were pulled from two sections of rail and both the armored car and the engine had derailed when the track shifted.

Fuming, he looked back up the line. In the darkness he could see the smoke from nearly a dozen stacks. Jamul had pulled together a dozen trains carrying four regiments of his best infantry and two batteries of breechloaders. Schuder had but one of two alternatives when this chase finally ran down. Go into the city and try to seize a boat, or go to the citadel guarding the approach. Either one was a death trap. Unless the citadel commander was a total fool, Schuder would never gain entry, and even if he did, they would be upon him and would storm the place. If he did seize a boat, word would reach the citadel long before he got there and they would be smashed.

Ha'ark's only hope was that the kill would be delayed long enough that he would have the glory of it.

Jack stood shaking his head as *Yankee Clipper* touched down at the edge of the open field, landing far enough away to avoid *Flying Cloud* if the wind should suddenly shift. Andrew Lawrence Keane climbed out of the engineer's seat on unsteady legs and walked toward Jack, saluting the swarm of soldiers who stood in wonder even as they struggled to grab the mooring lines.

"Sir, begging your pardon, sir, but just what the hell are you trying to do?" Jack asked. "I could have been up an hour ago except for your order to wait."

"I'm going with you."

"Sorry, sir, but I don't think so."

Andrew looked down at Petracci, who still stood at attention. "Would you care to repeat that, Colonel?"

"Sir, as commander of the air corps I respectfully decline to take you with me."

"You know I could relieve you for insubordination," Andrew snapped.

A flicker of a smile crossed Jack's features, as if dismissal would almost be a relief.

"Then who would fly back out there, sir?" he finally replied.

Andrew stared straight at him, his gaze not wavering.

"Sir?"

Andrew turned to a young second lieutenant who

was standing stiffly behind him, obviously nervous about interrupting the argument.

"What the hell do you want?" Andrew snapped.

"Sir. A telegram from the president, sir."

Andrew grabbed the sheet of paper, and the lieutenant hastily retreated.

Andrew. Full support of anything you order to save Hans, even if it means war. House and Senate leaders agree. It is the least we can do for someone who helped to make us free.

Kal

P.S. I've ordered Petracci not to let you fly.

Andrew turned back to Jack. "So you already knew this."

"Yes, sir. Sorry, sir." He hesitated for a second. "But even without the order, I'd still refuse, sir. You're too valuable to risk up there. Can I show you something, sir?"

Andrew nodded and followed Jack to *Flying Cloud*. Jack walked along the bottom of the airship, which was hovering a dozen feet off the ground, more than a hundred men straining at the ropes to hold her in place.

"Look at the cabin, sir. I counted ten bullet holes. We took three artillery rounds through the ship, if any of them had exploded, that would have been it. One of the engines had to be shut down coming back, and Feyodor won't vouch for the repair job. I'm not going to risk you up there."

"But it's all right for me to send you up in it?"

"Sort of what I got drafted to do on this mad world," Jack said quietly. "I don't like it, but I'm stuck with it. The same as you, sir."

Andrew nodded and looked up at the cabin again.

"Tell me about Hans, everything you saw."

As Jack recounted his experiences, Andrew stood quiet, his head bowed. He could imagine all of it, Hans looking up as the ship soared over, chewing a plug. How he had ever managed to escape, from wherever it was they had held him, was something he sensed only Hans could have done. And what had they done to him, he wondered? What horrors had he endured these years, believing himself lost, most likely forgotten?

He finally looked up when Jack finished, and stepping closer, he put his hand on Petracci's shoulder. "What do you think his chances are?"

"Honestly, sir?"

Andrew nodded.

"A snowball's chance in hell, sir. I'm not even sure if he retrieved the message. Going back up the line I had to dodge three more flyers. If he runs the train into that city, he won't stand a chance. The end of the line by the dockyard is packed with Bantag. There's a huge fort next to the docks. Even if they seize a boat, it'll get cut to ribbons by the artillery.

"I swung over the fort that I told him to go to for a second look. Just in case he does what I suggested. Kind of modern in its look—earthen walls, four heavy guns covering the river, two the land approach, a couple of light carriage-mounted fieldpieces. The fort is built against a village of them Chinese folks. The village has a brick wall, which looks to be filled in front with earth."

"Defenders?"

"Looked like a garrison there of about seventy or eighty."

"And Hans's strength?"

"I counted maybe a hundred fifty, two hundred with him at most. I think that fort's the only place they can go, but then what? I bet there'll be a umen or more ready to swarm over him. He's got no place to run, sir. The whole thing is madness. I guess the old man just decided to destroy what he could, go out in a blaze of glory, and we just sort of stumbled onto it."

"Are you saying we shouldn't try anything, then?"

Jack shook his head. "Hell, sir. I'd give my right"—he stumbled, lowering his gaze—"excuse me, sir."

"That's all right. Go on."

"Well, you know, sir. I just don't know what we can do."

"We need to find *Petersburg* and order it to run the river. Do you think they could do it?"

"I'm not sure, sir. There's galleys in there, and I saw another bastion above five miles up the river from the bay and then one about ten miles before the fort I told Hans to take. Hard to tell what kind of guns, but they looked pretty big. Besides that, we're not even sure where *Petersburg* is."

"That's part of what I want you to do. You're going to take *Flying Cloud* straight back to that fort, and we'll see if Hans made it that far. The ship I came here on will take the western coast, then cut across. With luck we might spot Bullfinch. I want the other airships down here as well."

"Sir, there's no hangar here yet. If any of them ships get dinged up or need an overhaul or anything like a breeze more than twenty miles an hour kicks up, we'll lose them for certain. I've darn near used up all the supplies here as is, gassing up and patching the holes."

"Before I left I ordered the airships to move down here at first light and to sweep the ocean looking for *Petersburg*. We've got to find Bullfinch and his ship and order them in. That's our only hope. If it means losing a airship or two, then we'll take that risk."

Jack nodded in agreement.

"Sir?"

It was Feyodor. As Andrew turned to face him, he

came to attention, and, grinning, snapped off a salute. Stefan, who was standing beside him, just stood gaping until Feyodor nudged him, and then he clumsily saluted as well.

"So this is the lad who dropped two flyers?" Andrew asked.

"Actually only one for sure, sir. I think Feyodor got the other, but we didn't see it burn."

"I plan to see some more of your shooting, son."

Jack started to utter a protest, but Andrew's look cut him off.

"That's my oldest friend out there," he said softly, "and you've just told me he probably doesn't stand a chance. By God, without him, I never would have been anything but a scared lieutenant and most likely would have finished the war that way. He made me. He made this Republic, and if he's going to die today I want him to know that I'm with him, that I did everything possible to try and repay all that I owe him."

Andrew felt a sense of shame when he realized that he was on the verge of losing control, his voice quavering. He was embarrassed that he was near to begging one of his subordinates.

"He's like my father, in some ways more than my father," Andrew whispered. "I want to see him, if only to say the good-bye I never had a chance to say before."

Jack stood silent, stunned. "Sir?"

"What?"

"You won't do anything rash? I mean like try to join him?"

The thought had crossed his mind, but there was Kathleen, the children, the Republic.

"No, I couldn't. He wouldn't want that, either."

"Aboard my ship I'm in command, sir. Will you agree to that?"

"Of course."

Jack fished in his pocket, pulled out the telegram, and motioned to the young lieutenant who had brought it to him. The lieutenant approached and again nervously saluted Andrew, then Jack.

"Son, there's something wrong with this message from the president. I think whoever wrote it down got it confused."

The lieutenant started to open his mouth to say something, but then he looked over at Andrew.

"Same with mine, lieutenant. Send an inquiry back to the White House, tell them to repeat both messages."

"But, sir?"

"Just do it!"

"Sir." The confused young officer started to withdraw.

"And son," Jack added, "take your time."

Wishing more than anything that he had a set of field glasses, Hans slipped back down from the low crest and said to Gregory, "Your eyes are better than mine, son. Tell me what you saw."

"It looks like the track goes right into the town, sir. Bastions to either side. Think I saw a couple of them devils up there, but the gate's closed."

Hans nodded. Had they been warned somehow? Shortly before dusk a flyer had passed over them. Did they suspect? Or had Ha'ark managed to get ahead of their cuts in the telegraph line and send a message through?

No, if he had, there would have been a reception waiting at the last siding, five miles back up the line.

Now what? Ram the gate? Chances were it was barred with iron, and besides, even if they did break through, it would most likely smash up the train, derailing it and leaving a gap for the bastards to storm through.

Turning back toward the east, he shaded his eyes

against the sunrise. He couldn't see any pursuit coming up the line. Turning to look north, he gazed down the broad open valley that led to X'ian. Though he wasn't sure, he thought he could see an earthen fort in the middle of the town, down by the river. He could only hope that Jack had guessed right. He turned back to the bastion in front of him.

"No sense in wasting time. Let's go. Keep everyone in the cars. We'll see what happens."

Gregory saluted and started back down the track, Hans following slowly behind, struggling against exhaustion and hunger. Approaching the engine, he wearily climbed into the cab and nodded to Alexi.

"Go slow, give a couple of blasts now and then. But stop as close as possible to the gate if they don't open it."

Alexi nodded and eased the throttle in. The train slowly started over the rise, and the fort came into view, a mile away. A heavy morning mist hung on the fields, the ground fog swirling as they passed.

Everyone except the fireman had been sent out of the cab, back to the cars. Hans looked over at the dead Bantag whom they had hauled aboard at the last station. They had propped him up against the side of the cab on a stack of wood, his head lowered to conceal the fact that most of his face had been shot off.

Alexi gave two short blasts of the whistle, followed a moment later by two more, and then started the bell tolling. He could see a guard stirring in the watchtower by the gate, leaning over the side as if to shout to somebody below.

Alexi gave two more sets of two and Hans watched intently, silently praying. Several Bantag on the left bastion guarding the approach scrambled to the top of the earthen embankment to look down on the train. He could see the barrel of an artillery piece poking out of an embrasure, the gun aimed straight at the track.

One shot into the train, that's all it would take. The gate was less than a hundred yards away.

"Ease it off," Hans growled. "Keep ringing the bell."

The train slowed to not much faster than a walk and inched onto a wooden drawbridge that crossed the dry moat. The defenses were laid out well, the moat sloping down to at least ten feet, and then a sheer climb up, the approaches into the moat covered with rows of sharpened stakes.

One of the Bantag on the bastion shouted a question.

Hans gestured at the dead warrior sitting inside the cab, then raised his hand and threw his head back in the universal gesture for drinking. The warrior on the bastion laughed.

Suddenly, to his absolute amazement, the gate swung open.

"Ease us in," Hans whispered.

As they crossed the outer works, Hans carefully scanned the grounds. Several dozen yurts were lined up on either side of the track in the open area between the outer wall and the low brick wall of the inner town. Bantag were idling about. The sight of them standing in a fortress seemed a bizarre incongruity. As mounted warriors they were incomparable; he could almost sense their boredom and bewilderment as garrison troops.

The train drifted through the middle of the parade ground, then turned sharply to come up close against the town wall, which he assumed marked the quarter occupied by Chin who had lived here before the Bantag had come to stay. A loading dock ran down the side of the track, with ramps leading off it. Chin laborers were already forming on the siding. If they got off at the dock, the laborers would undoubtedly panic and get in the way.

"Stop the train."

Alexi nodded and pulled the throttle back, venting steam.

"Now!"

Alexi let go with a long blast. Picking up his rifle, Hans leapt from the cab. The doors to the four boxcars were flung open. The people inside poured out, screaming their defiance. To Hans's amazement they actually held back, following Gregory's shouted orders to form a rough line. The Bantag out in the encampment area stood in shocked amazement, not sure at first what they were seeing. Some of them finally turned and started to run, others came forward, shouting, still not sure what was happening.

There was the reassuring sound of rifles being raised and then lowered.

"Fire!"

A disjointed, ragged volley swept down the line. Half a dozen Bantag out in the field tumbled. Hans shook his head. Damn poor performance for rifles at this range, but it still amazed him that they could do it at all. A steady crackle of fire erupted up and down the line. Bantag scattered in every direction. Hans turned and saw the gang of Chin laborers beginning to scatter, many of them running back through the gate into their town. He sprinted toward them.

"We're killing the Bantag!" Hans roared. "Help us and be free! We're from the Republic!"

Most of the Chin continued to run, but he saw several of them slow down, stop, look at him.

"Tell your friends. We're from the Republic. Kill the Bantag and we'll set you free."

A bullet snapped past him, dropping a Chin who was running back through the gate. Hans turned, raised his rifle, and took careful aim at a Bantag standing on a bastion to his left. The Bantag crumpled and fell. As he ejected the shell, he saw the men he had been shouting at looking at him in open-mouthed astonishment. They turned and ran back into the town.

The last of his people were out of the train and firing across the field. He leaned against the side of the engine and started to fire methodically, dropping three more Bantag in as many shots. The shots were picking up from the other side, and though uncoordinated, it was beginning to take its toll, the far more experienced riflemen of the other side unable to miss across the hundred yards of open field.

Hans strode along behind the line, shouting instructions, pausing to help one of the diggers reload, peering through the smoke, and nervously looking about for Tamira.

"Gregory! Ketswana!" he called.

A blast erupted from one of the bastions, the canister round sweeping through the line to Hans's left. It knocked more than a dozen to the ground and shredded the side of the rail car.

"Ketswana, bastion left of the gate. Gregory, to the right!" The two saluted.

"Cease fire!" Hans roared. Another canister round, this one from their flank, swept down the line, most of it hitting the ground in front of them.

"Charge!" Hans leapt forward, waving his rifle, and started for the left bastion. A ragged cheer erupted, and they all followed. The few Bantag still standing in the courtyard and around the yurts backed up, some of them turning and running. The sight of their hated tormentors running from them drove the charge forward with a mad enthusiasm. Hans reached the earthen ramp leading up to the bastion and then dove to one side. A second later, a round of canister, fired from a light field gun positioned at the top of the ramp, swept down, knocking over the first wave of the charge. Regaining his feet, he started up the slope, not bothering to look back to see if anyone was following. The gun crew was fumbling with the breech, swinging it open. Hans shot one of the loaders who was running up with another round. The four gunners gathered at the back of the gun saw him coming. One of them drew a revolver, leveled it, and then was knocked backward as the charge swarmed up the ramp. Within seconds the gun crew was finished. Hans quickly saw that there was still nothing out in the fields beyond the fort except for a few mounted Bantag, who were several hundred yards away and merely looking curiously in their direction. A wooden-plank walkway ran along the wall to the first bastion on the north side of the fort, and he saw half a dozen Bantag running about, one of them leveling a rifle and firing.

"Gregory, keep moving!" Hans shouted.

With a wild cry Gregory started along the bastion wall. Hans grabbed several of the diggers, and motioned them to help him with the gun. Swinging it around, he aimed it into the back of a bastion on the southern wall where more than a dozen Bantag were pouring fire into Ketswana's people as they stormed past them into the other bastion flanking the gate.

Hans picked up the canister round from the fallen load and slammed it into the gun barrel. He ran back to the limber chest and pulled out one of the silken bags he saw sticking out of wood trays. He slammed the bag into the gun behind the round, closed the breech, and then tightened the elevation screw. Motioning for his newfound gunners to bring the gun to bear, he fumbled through a leather pouch on the body that he assumed was the gun captain and found a fresh friction primer. He hooked the lanyard into the primer, inserted it into a small hole on the top of the breech, and sighted down the barrel.

His intended targets, noticing him at last, turned

their fire his way, and a rifle bullet dropped one of his men.

"Stand clear!"

The two surviving crew members jumped back, and Hans jerked the lanyard. The gun recoiled, and through the smoke he could see the canister round tearing through the Bantag. Ketswana's charge, which had already seized the southeast bastion, went forward down the length of the wall.

The rifle fire started to die down. Breathing heavily, Hans leaned against the bastion, trying to collect his thoughts.

He could hear screams still coming from the town. He grabbed his two gunners and headed across the parade ground. Bodies of the dead and wounded, Bantag and human, lay everywhere. He looked up at the walls where his two storming parties were wiping out the last of the defenders and saw that his numbers must have been cut by at least a third. Even with the additional hands taken in the fight at the depot, they were probably down to fewer than a hundred forty, maybe a hundred seventy at most. Again he felt a surge of relief at the sight of Tamira, who, along with half a dozen women and children, were helping to tend to the wounded. She forced a smile when she saw him.

He slowed as he approached the open gate into the city. A mob of Chin were coming toward him, shouting unintelligibly, gesticulating, screaming, waving picks, shovels, hoes. He started to back up as they spilled out into the parade ground, ready to run for Tamira and drag her back to the bastion.

The mob slowed down and half a dozen of them approached Hans, dragging something behind them. The ones up front parted, and to his amazement he saw that they were dragging a Bantag warrior, the clothes half torn from his body, blood pouring out of dozens of wounds. They flung him down, and Hans saw that he was still alive, kicking feebly.

The Bantag looked up at Hans. "Kill me," he groaned. In spite of his hatred Hans felt a surge of pity. No soldier should have to die this way, he thought, amazed that such a feeling could still be elicited after all that he had endured.

The howling mob danced around the warrior, some of them raining blows upon him, and then they fell upon him. Hans turned away, wishing the Bantag would stop screaming.

An old man came out of the crowd to Hans, his head bobbing, and spoke in a singsong voice.

Hans shook his head, not understanding a word. "Do you speak Bantag?" Hans finally asked.

"Curse speech," the old man replied, startled to hear the words coming from a human.

"We now the Republic?" the old man asked.

Hans saw the glimmer of hope in his eyes. So the legend had reached even here, in spite of all that the Bantag attempted to do to stop the spread of the word.

Hans looked back at his depleted ranks.

"How many live here?" he asked. "Men, women who can fight?"

"Near a thousand in the town. Those that can fight? All but the old ones and children. Seven hundred."

Hans nodded.

"Why? Your army is coming now. We are free, aren't we?"

Hans looked him straight in the eye. "You're going to free yourselves. You're the army now."

Handing his field glasses back to one of his staff, Ha'ark stood silent. He could see them lining the walls, waiting for him. Troops were piling out of the trains behind him, forming into ranks; the artillery crews were pulling their guns off the flatcars and pushing them slowly up the slope.

From out of X'ian he could see a large formation coming up at the double to reinforce the attack.

Half a umen would be available for the attack by later that day. The flyer that had hovered over the city for nearly an hour had reported that the town had risen and the garrison was dead. What would they have—five hundred, maybe seven hundred at most? And they were slaves, more likely to kill themselves trying to load a cannon than actually capable of inflicting harm.

"A Yankee flyer."

Raising his glasses, he saw the airship coming down out of the scattering of cumulus clouds, and the sight of the airship decided him.

"Let them see their comrades die," Ha'ark announced. "Start the attack."

"My Qarth."

It was Jamul. "My Qarth, we have no heavy artillery yet to breech the gate. Even five mortars well placed could make it a death trap in there, but we have none yet. Most of these warriors are little better than garrison troops and guards. Shouldn't we wait until the first regiment of the Chuktar Umen arrives?"

"Every minute we give them is a chance for Schuder to show those cattle how to work the guns and prepare. Let's finish this now so we can go home. And let the Yankee flyer see the slaughter and report it. Start the attack."

Hans nervously paced the wall. At last he had found a pair of field glasses in the yurt of the fortress commander, and now he trained them across the open ground.

"If we had five companies of the old First Suzdal,

we'd hold this place till Doomsday," Gregory proclaimed.

Hans grunted a noncommittal reply. Five hours to train this rabble how to fight using modern weapons, he thought, shaking his head ruefully. The heavy muzzle-loading guns had each been prepared with double shots of canister; once they had been fired he wouldn't even bother to reload them. As for the lighter breechloaders, a crew had been detailed off in each of the bastions. Gregory and Ketswana would handle the guns in the bastions facing east. Alexi would take the one on the first bastion facing south. As for the other three bastions, he could only hope that the men from his digging crew had at least comprehended enough of the crash course to remember to swab the bore after each shot so they didn't blow themselves up.

As for the Chin, to his surprise many of them understood the rifles issued to them from the stockpile seized in the fort and taken from the train. Many had surreptitiously watched the Bantag drilling with the weapons, and some even claimed to be able to handle the artillery, so most of the artillery crews serving on the bastions were Chin.

He consulted the rough sketch he had made of the fort and the town, trying to mentally calculate what would unfold. The west wall was part of the old town, and from the commanding bluffs it looked straight down on the river below. The Bantag had banked earth up over the brick wall and mounted two heavy muzzle-loading guns, positioned to fire on any ship attempting to come up the river. For the moment he doubted that an attack would swing in from that direction, since the plunging fire from above would be murderous and the only way to gain the wall was by scaling it with ladders.

The bluff that the town rested on curved back to the east, running most of the length of the north wall.

Four more guns were pointed in that direction, trained on the river and the approaches to the city. An attack from that direction would either spill off the bluff or be funneled up against the eastern bastion. A protected bastion at the point where the new fort had been added on in front of the town jutted out, offering an infilading fire the length of the moat. It would be a killing ground if the enemy tried to gain access.

It was the south and east walls that he knew were the weak points. The ground on the south wall sloped gently for most of two hundred yards, except for the last fifty yards, which dropped steeply away to the river flats below. As on the west and north walls of the town, the brick wall had been banked over with earth, the sides covered with entanglements of sharpened stakes, but it was nevertheless an open front. Through his field glasses he could see Bantag gunners manhandling their pieces up along the next ridgeline, which was slightly higher than the position of his forces. The bastards would be able to rain fire down on them.

The eastern approach was much the same, though the ground was rougher, intersected by several gullies and streambeds that would slow an attack. The railroad embankment coming up toward the gate was a natural avenue of attack, but wide open to fire along its entire length. He had thought about smashing the drawbridge but decided instead to pull it up rather than create wreckage that could be used by the attacking force as cover.

He could see them deploying out along the ridge, forming into assault lines, their battle standards held aloft. The sight gave him a cold chill. The standards were blood-red and from a distance reminded him of Reb battle flags. He felt almost nostalgic. At least against the Rebs, the fight was an honorable one and if overwhelmed, surrender was still a possibility. He looked down the line at his "army." He could see the fear on their faces, especially the Chin, whom he suspected would never have joined in if they had known the truth. But they were committed now, knowing what would happen if the Bantag should ever break through.

But he also sensed that in spite of their fear they would die gamely.

A plume of smoke erupted from the ridge, followed within seconds by a dozen more. The first shots screamed overhead, one detonating in midair over the parade ground, another striking the northeast bastion, where a geyser of dirt spurted up. He could see more than one of his troops waver and look around fearfully, but none backed away.

The bombardment continued for several minutes. Hans silently counted the intervals, wondering what Pat would say about artillery that could fire three times a minute and hit targets over a mile away.

Several rounds detonated in the parade ground, and another exploded at the parapet on the number one bastion of the north wall. He paced back and forth deliberately, making a studied effort to ignore the bombardment, pausing to slap one man on the shoulder or share an off-color joke with another, knowing that his men were watching him, gauging his reaction, and, he hoped, drawing strength from it.

"Here they come!"

A line of skirmishers deployed out from the ridge facing the eastern wall. He raised his glasses to study them. This was no Merki attack of massed lines, as he had faced back on the Potomac. They were at good intervals, spaced six yards or so apart, moving deliberately. After fifty yards a second line started out, and after another fifty the third line moved forward.

They know what they're doing, he realized grimly. No massed targets, close to range, then start laying down fire. Against trained infantry, he would not have given it a second thought. His men would have hunkered down, laughed, and started picking off targets. The lines continued forward, well spaced, until finally they were ten deep, spread back for more than five hundred yards.

Hans strode to the southeast bastion. "Gregory."

"Sir?"

"I want deliberately aimed fire with that light gun. Go to it."

Grinning with delight, Gregory turned to his crew, shouting and pantomiming orders. Hans moved over to the northeast bastion, ducking a well-aimed round that skimmed overhead. At Ketswana's gun, he sighted down the barrel, stepped back, and handed the lanyard to his friend, who grabbed hold and, with a resounding battle cry, fired.

Ha'ark stood silent, watching as the first round detonated behind the first rank of attackers, dropping two of them. A second later a gun on the southeast bastion fired as well, but the round fell short.

Behind him the next line of attackers came up out of the ditch and started forward at a walk. His heart swelled at the sight of them. They seemed like something out of the legends of the Usurper Wars, when attackers marched into battle, flags held high.

Though he fervently wished for modern weapons, true aircraft with bombs that could shatter the entire fort in seconds, or even just a single machine gun to sweep the battlements, he still felt a certain contentment with it all. Five years ago the barbarians he ruled would have charged on horse against the walls, waving their swords and spears, shooting arrows. Now they were going forward like soldiers, rifles at the ready. Even though they were not of his elite umens, still they were of his creation.

"They're not counter battery firing," Jamul observed.

"Waste of effort for them," Ha'ark replied. "He doesn't have any trained cattle up there who can work the larger guns with accuracy. I wonder if he even has the heavy guns loaded at all. Best to concentrate what he can against the infantry."

A line of smoke erupted from the front of his line, and he raised his field glasses to study them. The front line had stopped a bit short. He would have preferred to see them a hundred yards closer—after all, it was terrified cattle they were facing—but the first volley, even at five hundred yards, should startle them. The smoke would help to obscure the advance as well. He was pleased to see that training was finally overcoming their damnable pride. Some of the warriors were lying down, or at least sitting, taking careful aim. The second line advanced through them and continued forward. Moving another fifty yards, they stopped and opened fire. The third line now passed through the second, advancing another fifty yards to engage, so that within a couple of minutes there were five lines of infantry, spaced out across two hundred fifty yards, pouring fire at the fort. The remaining lines had stopped at six hundred yards and waited now for the order to close once a weakness began to show.

"That's it, lay the gun on the wall." Hans reached around the trembling Chin woman, notching the rear sight up another level. Standing behind her, he pressed the gun in against her shoulder. Then he guided her finger up to the trigger and stepped back.

The woman staggered from the recoil but then grinned at him with delight. Cursing soundly in English, he smiled and continued down the line. A steady hum of bullets whistled overhead, occasional spurts of earth kicked up along the bastion wall, but so far he was surprised at how few casualties they had taken. It made him wonder just how much training their opponents really had in marksmanship.

The methodical nature of the attack was at least giving him time to get his own people familiar with how to load the guns and shoot them—not that they were hitting much. Through the eddies of smoke he saw only a couple of score fallen.

Another line came bursting forward, sprinting to less than two hundred yards, and he grinned.

"Now, watch!" he shouted, shouldering his way up to the wall and drawing the attention of a dozen or more defenders. Resting his rifle on the battlement wall, he took careful aim and a Bantag went down, shrieking, holding his stomach. He quickly reloaded, hitting a second one in the chest, then reloaded and fired again, spinning another around to the ground.

Exclamations at his prowess were cut short when one of his own tumbled off the battlement, the top of her head gone. Hans saw that it was the girl he had been trying to teach only minutes before.

"Start killing the bastards!" Hans roared. "Kill them!"

He stalked away to the southeast bastion, which was drawing most of the attention of the artillery. They were zeroing in, earth geysering over Gregory and his crew as they sent back sprays of canister into the advancing line, unable to miss with the range down to two hundred yards.

"The crew's getting the hang of it!" Gregory shouted above the explosions.

Hans peered up over the wall, then ducked as a shot screamed in and dirt sprayed over him. He saw that a heavy skirmish line was swinging out along the southern wall, so Alexi finally had some targets as well. Rifle fire erupted down the length of the wall, and he saw several Bantag drop with the first rounds.

"We could take this all day," Gregory announced.

"It won't be long now. He'll realize we're not panicking without a really hard push. Get ready for a charge. And remember, don't fire the heavy gun till I give the word!"

Even as he shouted out the command, he heard the distant braying of nargas, the traditional war trumpet of the Hordes. An angry cry went up from the field, and through the smoke he saw the lines begin to rush forward.

The charging lines compressed as they hit the entanglements and rows of sharpened stakes forward of the moat. Rifle fire redoubled along the wall as the range closed to the point that even the most inexperienced found they could now hit the targets. Hans walked along the line, stopping to slap down the rear sights of his troops, which many of them forgot to lower as the range dropped. Bantag warriors, some armed with axes, began to slash their way through, cutting paths in toward the moat. A column of troops attempted to charge down the railroad embankment and from there leap into the moat, but a blast of canister from Gregory's gun swept them back.

Hans paced up and down the line, shouting encouragement, stepping over the bodies of the dead and dying, sensing the desperation around him, and also the exhilaration of slaves who were finally striking back at their hated masters.

"Artillery!"

At the shout, Hans looked up to where one of Ketswana's men was pointing and saw two horse-drawn guns advancing toward them along either side of the railroad embankment. The gunners swung their weapons around at less than four hundred yards and started to unlimber. Hans ran down to Gregory's bastion and saw that he had already perceived the threat and was bringing his fieldpiece to bear. A loader was fumbling through the limber chest, but Hans shouldered him aside and pulled out a round of shrapnel. He was relieved to see that the fuses were percussion; otherwise there would have been even more confusion and wasted time trying to teach a loader how to cut and insert timed fuses. Hans passed the shell over to the loader, who ran it to Gregory.

Even as Gregory stepped back from the gun, lanyard held taut, the first Bantag gun fired, the shell impacting on the gate. Gregory's gun answered, and the round hit the embankment twenty yards in front of one of the guns. The two guns started a methodical drumming against the gate, a dozen rounds shrieking in, until Gregory finally dismounted one of the pieces. Another gun was up in less than a minute, dragged forward by one of the horse teams that had been sent back from the first two guns.

Hans ran down from the bastion and standing to one side examined the gate. Another round hit and sent a spray of splinters and metal shards into the courtyard. He darted up for a quick look and found himself facing a swarm of Bantag who, screaming wildly, were surging out of the moat, axes raised high to chop their way through the tottering barrier.

"Can you bring us any lower!" Andrew shouted.

"Sir, there must be five thousand of them bastards down there with rifles than can shoot half a mile, and a dozen artillery pieces to boot. Besides that, we got those two ships to deal with." Even as Jack shouted back at him, the two-pounder behind Andrew fired, and Feyodor screamed a curse as he burned his hands pulling the hot breech open to extract the shell casing.

The airship rode a thousand feet above the river, now less than a mile away from the fort. A swarm of antlike creatures could be seen moving in on it from the east and north sides. Over his shoulder Andrew saw another Bantag flyer moving to intersect them from above. Though he would not have admitted it, he was petrified. Every surge of the ship from eddies of wind convinced him that it was coming apart. He had long ago separated himself from his breakfast and, for that matter, from what was left of any meal he'd had in the last day.

Perhaps Kal and Jack had been right. He felt like a useless spectator, someone who served only to get in the way.

"I'm taking one swing over the fort, sir, then we're getting the hell out! There's gonna be four airships on us in a couple of minutes if we stay here!"

Andrew wanted to argue, but one look from Jack told him it was useless to try. He read one last time the hastily penciled note before sealing it into a message pouch and handing it to Feyodor, who turned away from his gun and attached a red streamer and whistle to it.

With engines howling, Jack guided *Flying Cloud* straight toward the fort. Clearing the west wall, he pulled the stick in to his stomach and the ship reared up.

Andrew struggled to hang on, pulling himself up into Feyodor's chair, and then leaned out. The fort was obscured by smoke, and to his horror he saw a storming party swarming up out of the moat. In desperation he looked at the chaos below, trying to see through the fog of battle, hoping that somewhere he would see the blue uniform of his old comrade.

"Message away!"

He saw the red streamer swirl down toward the parade ground and then disappear.

A loud explosion detonated at nearly the same instant, and a thunderous shudder ran through the ship.

"We're hit!"

Andrew turned back and saw the number three engine dangling, its propeller gyrating as the engine swung off its mount. The propeller sliced into the bottom of the ship and shattered amid an explosion of splinters. Sparks snapped out of the engine as bits of torn cloth wrapped around it.

"Cut the fuel!" Feyodor screamed. "Cut the fuel!" He pulled open the back hatch, scrambled out onto the catwalk, and started aft, climbing down as the ship continued to soar heavenward.

"We're getting out!" Jack roared. "Hang on!"

A bullet tore through the cab, shattering the window next to Andrew, and a shard of glass sliced his cheek open.

He saw that Feyodor got to the damaged engine and reached up over it to the copper fuel line. As he bent it up, the fuel ran down his arms. A flicker of flame ran across the dangling engine, and for an instant Andrew thought that it would jump to Feyodor.

Pulling out a knife, Feyodor started to hack at the one support beam that still held the engine.

"Coming around," Jack announced.

Andrew wanted to shout that Feyodor was dangling out in space, struggling to kick the engine free, but he thought better than to interfere.

"Damn it, sir. Man that damn gun back there. We got another one closing in!"

Andrew climbed out of the seat and slid down the cabin to the two-pounder. The nose of the ship was dropping as he grabbed a shell out of the rack, shoved it in, closed the breech, and clumsily swung the gun around. He tried to line up on one of the airships, but *Flying Cloud* continued to drop out of its spiraling turn and the enemy ship disappeared from view. Frustrated, he looked down and saw that the swarm was building up around the gate. He lowered the gun, wrapped his finger around the trigger, and fired. The recoil knocked the wind out of him, and for a moment he thought he might have broken a rib.

He opened the hot breech to eject the shell casing, which hit his leg and burned his trousers. He kicked it away and started to reload. Another shudder ran through the ship, and he looked up to see Feyodor dangling in space, the engine tumbling away. The sudden loss of several hundred pounds of weight caused *Flying Cloud* to surge up, and Andrew watched wide-eyed as Feyodor struggled to hang on. Finally Feyodor swung his legs back onto the catwalk and let go of the shattered engine spars. He collapsed onto the wooden framework and started to crawl back to safety.

Andrew shifted his attention back to the fort. Twin tongues of flame erupted on either side of the gate, and the host swarming in around the broken gate were swept down as if a giant's hand had crushed them.

"Double canister at ten yards!" Andrew roared. "Leave it to Hans!"

The attack at the gate wavered and then broke, streaming back across the moat.

Feyodor swung back in through what was left of the aft cabin door, reeking of coal oil. Gasping, he fell onto the deck.

"Damn you, next time let me know when you're going to dive!" he cried, crawling toward Jack, his eyes filled with rage and lingering terror.

"What the hell was I supposed to do? Come aft and ask your permission?"

"You bastard, I'll be damned if I ever fly with you again. That engine got blown clean by an artillery round. I told you before to stay higher."

The two continued to argue as Jack piloted the ship back out over the river. From overhead Andrew could hear the thump of Stefan's gun, and the scream of a shell from one of the pursing flyers streaking past them in reply.

He swung his own gun around as they cleared the

fort, hoping to give a parting shot. For a moment the smoke in the parade ground cleared, and in the center of the field he saw a lone figure, looking into the sky. Leaning out over the gun, Andrew extended his hand.

"Hans!"

For an instant he thought he saw his friend snap off a salute, and then the smoke closed around him and he was lost to view.

"That crazy fool," Hans muttered, watching as *Flying Cloud* set a northwesterly course and headed up into the clouds. He held the message streamer in his hands. It would be just like Andrew to do something like this, the damn fool. And him a colonel.

"Didn't I teach you better than to risk yourself without good reason?" Hans mumbled.

He unfolded the message.

> I'm aboard *Flying Cloud*. Hans, my old friend, forgive me for not finding you. You must hold out. Ships dispatched and will come upriver to get you tomorrow. Hold Out!
>
> > God Bless You, My Friend,
> > Andrew

Hans stared at the message and then back at the ship. Forgive what? Smiling, he shook his head. It would be just like Andrew to blame himself for something he couldn't control too.

Hans handed Gregory the message, even though it was written in English.

"From Keane?"

Hans nodded, suddenly unable to speak.

"They've pulled back, sir. Keeping a skirmish line about six hundred yards out and moving some of the artillery around to face the gate. I got some of my people swabbing out the big gun, figure we'd take a crack at some long-range shooting with it."

Hans nodded his approval.

"More than a hundred casualties, sir. Most of them dead from head wounds, but by Kesus, we tore them up out there."

"See if you can rustle up some food, find that old Chin fella who looks like their leader. Christ, we haven't eaten in nearly two days."

Hans walked slowly over to the shattered remains of the gate and peered out through one of the cracked timbers.

"I don't think they'll come on again today. But he'll tear this whole eastern wall of the fort apart with artillery and smash the gate down proper. I want everyone under shelter except for the artillery crews and those people you think are halfway good with rifles. I want the rest inside the bricked section of the town or in the bombproofs under the bastions. Get them busy fortifying the town and also piling up earth onto this gate. Next time they'll come on in column and rush straight at us, none of the fancy footwork. I want a fallback position so we can tear them apart when they do."

"We're going to make it, aren't we?" Gregory asked eagerly. "The colonel will get us out."

"That's what he dreams of," Hans said softly, pulling Gregory back from the gate as an artillery round shrieked in and detonated on the other side.

Chapter Eight

"I told you not to ride with me, sir."

Andrew nodded. He felt as if he had aged ten years in as many hours. He also felt clumsy, not only because of his one hand but also because of the trembling in his legs. He slowly swung out of the cab and worked his way down the rope ladder to the ground. He watched as Jack, then Feyodor, came down after him, followed at last by Stefan. Of the four, only Stefan seemed pleased with the adventure, eager to boast of his latest kill.

"She'll be out of action for at least a day," Jack told them. "I'd prefer to try and run her back up north to hangar her. She's riddled with holes, and we have to put in a whole new mount before installing an engine. That means draining the hydrogen out of the number four cell."

Andrew stepped out from under the ship, looking up at the shadow looming overhead.

"Well, Colonel, darlin', so how was the flying?"

To his surprise, Andrew saw Pat walking toward him. "Did they find *Petersburg*?"

Pat grinned. "She's on her way."

"And how the hell did you get here? Don't tell me you flew!"

Pat shook his head and laughed. "Not on your precious life. I took a train down to the end of the line and then placed me solid arse on a solid horse and rode."

"That's eighty miles by horseback."

"Tell me about it," Pat groaned. "And with piles, no less."

"You should have let Emil treat them when he wanted to."

"That butcher got me under the knife once, and then I was unconscious. He won't talk me under it again, especially not to go poking around back there."

"What's the latest report?"

"One of the airships found *Petersburg* couple hours before noon. She's running full steam for the river. *Franklin* heaved off as well, along with two sloops. Bullfinch sent back a message that he'd sail through hell to get there."

"How far out is he?"

"That's the bad news. He won't reach the mouth of the river much before noon."

Andrew shook his head.

"And there's worse to it. They'd been shaking her down real hard. The bunkers are low. He says he might just be able to get up the river, but as for getting back down . . ." Pat shrugged his shoulders.

"And *Franklin*?"

"Two and a half days at full steam will bring him to the river."

"Too late. I saw them throw back what I think was the first attack. But it was only an opening move. I could see reinforcements coming out of the city and what looked like several more trains coming up from the east, thirty or so miles away. He was facing four or five thousand."

"How many does he have?"

"I guess around seven hundred, maybe a thousand."

"Jesus pity," Pat sighed. "Bullfinch thinks he can pull off maybe two or three hundred at most. If he can't take all of them, Hans won't leave. You know that."

"Well, if there's anyone still left, that might be all they have. I expect by dawn tomorrow, though, they'll have maybe a umen or more up there, with heavy support. I saw a number of light field guns, but if there's heavy equipment in the fort, they must have siege artillery they can bring up by rail. He'll get hit at dawn, and now you're telling me we won't be there much before dark tomorrow?"

Pat nodded sadly.

As they walked over to a clapboard shed that served as a telegraph station and headquarters for the temporary airfield, Andrew told Pat about their flight back.

"Petracci should be locked away in an asylum for going up in those damn things. We were losing air all the way back. One of the cells was completely drained of hydrogen. And their damn flyers chased us a hundred miles out to sea. Fortunately we didn't see any of their new design that Jack reported."

"We lost one of the flyers today," Pat interjected. "He's at least four hours overdue now."

"Damn."

"And the president. He's howlin' mad, he is."

"Now what?"

"You, you damn fool. He's threatened to pull your shoulder straps over this trick."

It took a second for Andrew to realize what he was talking about.

"He's that mad?"

"Andrew, you directly disobeyed an order from the president. What do you expect?"

"And if the roles were reversed, I wonder what he would have done?"

"Exactly what I telegraphed back," Pat said with a chuckle.

"And?"

"No reply to that one."

"What about getting Hans out?"

"Andrew, there's times I think this Republic just might survive. Congress voted unanimously to support any and all operations to get Hans out, even if it means war."

"Unanimously?"

Pat smiled. "Well, there were a couple, but you got to remember a lot of them fellas with their fancy titles were part of the old army. I heard that Senator Vasili Greckoff pulled a revolver out of his pocket, proudly announced that Sergeant Major Hans Schuder had once personally kicked him in the ass when he was a private with the Second Suzdal, and then said he'd shoot any son of a bitch who was too cowardly to get Hans back."

Andrew shook his head and laughed, even though he knew he should be outraged over a display of weapons on the Senate floor.

"What did Marcus do?"

"Laughed and said he'd take a sword to any man that tried to stop Vasili. So it was unanimous. Folks all over Suzdal are going wild at the report. Father Casmir is calling for a holy vigil, he is, continuous prayers until Hans is saved."

"But the threat of another war."

"Hell, I guess everyone's scared, but they're not showing it right now. That will come later. They're all caught up in Hans. General thinking is that he laid his life on the line to help set them free and now it's time to pay back. Hans was the martyr of the last war. Remember that crazy monk came out of the north and said he saw him in a vision and that he should be a saint."

Andrew couldn't help but laugh at the thought of it. Not being a Catholic, and having once carried a bit of a suspicion of all things connected with popery, he had found the Orthodox bent of the Rus difficult to fathom. He had heard about some icon painter in Murom who had turned out some images of Hans in classic icon style, wearing a halo. Murom had lost two regiments when Hans and the Third Corps were cut off, so he was something of a cult figure there. He could well imagine the reception if they ever did get him out.

"Well, with him alive, I do wonder what that monk's saying now," Pat continued.

Pat led Andrew to the back room of the shack, where he collapsed into a chair.

"You wouldn't happen to have anything on you?" Andrew asked.

Pat uncorked a flask and handed it to him. He took a quick gulp.

"So what do you think the chances are?" Pat asked.

Andrew lowered his head, trying to shake out the last vestiges of fear that still clung to him. It was funny—he had overcome his fear of gunfire, but there was something about that moment with Feyodor hanging in midair and bullets pounding the cabin that froze him. Perhaps it was the thought of falling and burning, wrapped in the shreds of the ship as it plummeted to the ground in flames.

"Are you all right?"

"Just overcome with it all, Pat. I mean, we left him out there at the Potomac and thought him dead."

"Remember, Andrew, I was the one that couldn't get through to him and pull him out when the Merki broke through. It was me more than you on that score."

Andrew shook his head. "I'm not blaming you, never have. You saw his standard go down, saw the square overwhelmed by the Merki charge. We thought him dead."

He hesitated for a moment.

"And yet I never quite believed it, never quite felt

it in my bones. You said the same thing. Now I know what Emil meant when he said that most people feel that way when they lose someone close but never see the body, never have proof positive that it's finished.

"There were those rumors after the war, the people escaping to us from the Merki and the Bantag, saying they had seen someone dressed in Yankee uniform."

"Hinsen, the bastard."

"No, Pat, we talked about that before. There were some prisoners taken after Hispania. We kind of figured that out, but we didn't go after them. We wrote them off as dead. And losing Gregory and that unit against the Bantag. We should have pressed the issue then. Instead it was called a border skirmish, and the men were assumed to be dead."

"And how could we have gone after them?" Pat asked. "The Merki, the Bantag are still mounted. We ain't, except for one division of cavalry. And even if we did get close, then what? They'd have cut their throats. Besides that, there was never anything positive—a name, a unit number—just rumors."

"But there was always Hans in the back of my mind, Pat. He was always there. None of this we created here would ever have happened without him."

Pat looked at Andrew as if to protest, but the expression on his face cut him short.

"He made me. If I did anything here, it was through him. I owed him more than what I gave back. That has haunted me for five long years. That's why I had to fly out there. Because if we don't get him out, I wanted him to know that."

"Do you think we'll get him?"

"I don't know. I just don't know," Andrew whispered. "This operation is on a shoestring."

"And when hasn't it been?"

"This time, though, is different. Usually we absorbed the attacks, concentrating our strength to meet them. Now we're flinging ourselves forward into the unknown. We have two sketchy air reconnaissance flights, and that's it. We don't have time to concentrate, to scout it out, to prepare. It's like we're throwing a spear and just hoping the point will find the one tiny hole in the armor. It indicates something even broader to me after these next couple of days are over."

"What's that?"

"This one will be different. Before, always before, we managed to get our target clear. We defined who our opponent was, figured out his weakness, and then tried at every turn to use that to our advantage. Our biggest advantages in the other wars were steam and factories. In the Tugar War we were able to build weapons that could match theirs and then force them to fight us on the ground of our choosing. In the Cartha War we built the armored gunboats, took control of the sea, and cut them off. In the last one, we used rail strategically. We could outrun them when we had to, concentrate where we had to, and then force them to come to us.

"I fear this one is different."

"How?"

"There's someone on the other side now who thinks like us and organizes like us."

"That bastard Hinsen?"

"I don't think he counts anymore. What little knowledge he had the Merki used. He couldn't have shown them how to build railroads and breech-loading artillery, how to organize industry to support and create those things. There's some mystery out there."

"The Redeemer?"

Andrew nodded.

"He must have come through a Tunnel. That's the only way it could have happened."

"So old Muzta was right, then."

Muzta—what a world that Tugar has seen, Andrew thought as he took anther sip of vodka. Ten years ago he was master of the Northern Horde of Tugars. The Horde that had bested twice their number in the legendary war against the Merki a generation before our coming. Now he lives on the fringes, in some ways even tacitly allied with the cattle he once despised.

"To have accomplished in four years the transformation of the Bantag into an industrial power is as revolutionary as what we did. More so, in a way. We were driven by terror. For them, it is not an issue of whether they will live to see tomorrow. Twenty years from now it might come to that, but to get them to stop migrating, to build things, to adopt so many of our ways—it is almost beyond belief.

"And that, Pat, is what frightens me. If he could accomplish that, what else is he doing out there? We've had two flights over their territory, both of them focused on Hans. Where does that rail line lead and what might we discover at the end of it? If they could do that in five years, what might they accomplish in ten?"

"We have to stop them now. That's all there is to it."

"That's the point," Andrew replied. "We are shifting into another kind of war."

"War is war, Andrew. You face your enemy, you kill him or he kills you, until one side or the other quits."

"That's not the point of it, Pat. There's a tremendous difference here. In all the other wars we fought here, we were defending something. We were defending the right to live. It was that simple. Nothing complex, no higher ideals like our war back on Earth with concepts like Union. We used the word 'freedom' but ultimately it was simply for life."

"I always thought the two were one and the same," Pat said quietly.

Andrew looked at Pat in surprise. Once again the facade of the brawling Irishman had given way to something else, profound in its simplicity.

Andrew smiled and handed his comrade the flask.

"I stand corrected on that point," Andrew finally said. "But there is the issue of defending ourselves to stay alive and projecting a war forward into the heart of an enemy's territory to ensure the same thing. Our people clearly saw what they were fighting for. The enemy was at the gates. If they broke in, we were all going to die."

"It will be the same thing this time," Pat replied.

"If they get to our gates, we're finished. There'll be no last-minute miracles. If they get that far, we'll be overwhelmed. I can see this so clearly now, Pat. It's a different war for a different age. We must project it forward. Skirmishing for position out on the steppes is meaningless. If we dig in defensively we'll eventually be destroyed. The Tugars and the Merki carried their war machine on their hip and beneath them. It was based on the horse. As long as there was grass, as long as there were bits of steel for blades, feathers for arrows, that's all they needed to threaten us with. We built factories and smashed them. This Redeemer is doing the same."

"So we smash his factories."

"That's the difference now," Andrew replied. "It's not going to be just killing Bantag, and heaven knows, they can field sixty umens. We can't just defeat them, we're going to have to field an army, build a navy and an air corps. We going to have to project ourselves forward in an offensive war. Tear up their tracks, blockade or smash their ports, advance a thousand miles if need be to search out their last factory and destroy it. And even then, if enough of them escape, they can ride five thousand miles away, and by the time we get there we'll find more factories and trains and armies waiting for us. In the last war they had tactical mobility with the horse, but we had strategic mobility with rails. Now they're matching that and still have the tactical mobility we don't have yet.

"And I tell you this, Pat. I fear this Redeemer. I fear the knowledge he must have. I sense that he comes from a world that is ahead of us. Jack told me about the two airships with wings. Ferguson was only musing on that possibility, and they already have it. It means that this one might very well have other ideas beyond Ferguson, beyond all of us. We saw how a rifled musket, muzzle-loading cannon, and finally that rocket barrage shattered the Merki. What if they have some new weapon we don't have? What if the weapon is so advanced it renders everything we have obsolete on the first day of battle? That is the core issue in a military sense. They could smash us in the field, and before we have time to build a counter they are into our heartland and we'll never recover."

"There's always what ifs in a war, Andrew. Them flying machines. Remember, it was the Merki who first put engines on them."

"But we were already on the edge of that one."

"If you worry yourself about this, you'll go mad with it all."

"It's my job to worry about it. And it's not just the military side of it, Pat. I wonder how our Republic will react to a war like this. If that Redeemer has any sense, he'll try to divide us. He'll claim that we invaded first. He'll see what we have, then try for peace, and I do wonder if the Republic has the stomach to prosecute a war that in the long term is essential for survival but in the short term might not seem to be worth the expense in lives and treasure. The war to save the Union damn near tore our own country apart. If it hadn't been for Lincoln I think it would have."

"Andrew, you're thinking way too far ahead here. Let's just worry about Hans tonight."

Andrew nodded wearily. "I better get some sleep. I'm going back up tomorrow."

"Like hell you are," Pat snapped angrily. "Or are you forgetting that you're commander of the armies, but it's me, Pat O'Donald, who's in direct control of this front and if anyone should be going, it's me."

Andrew fixed him with a determined gaze. "It's not a military issue for me now, Pat. It's friendship, the same way I know you would throw everything aside if it was me out there or would go yourself if I weren't here."

Pat smiled and shook his head.

"If they can get *Flying Cloud* patched up enough by tomorrow morning I want to be taken out to the *Petersburg*. I'm going up that river to meet him," Andrew said.

"Sir, could you come here a moment?"

Hans turned away from a group of Chin men and women whom he was trying to instruct in how to aim a rifle.

Alexi and Gregory stood behind him.

"Now what?"

"A couple of minutes, sir. We want to show you something."

Hans nodded wearily and followed them across the parade ground, barely looking up as a shell screamed overhead and detonated somewhere beyond the north wall.

"Sir, Alexi here's been looking at that machine we have on the flatcars we took from the second train."

"I told you not to waste your time on that. We've got less than eight hours to get ready."

"I'm sorry, sir," Alexi interjected. "I just couldn't

keep away from it. I want to show you what I found."

As they approached the flatcar, several Chin women joined them, carrying lanterns. The tarps had been pulled back and the dark bulk of the machine loomed above them.

Alexi scrambled up onto the flatcar and Hans followed, silently cursing his knees. At the back of the car Alexi took a lantern from one of the women and held it aloft.

"That's a steam engine in the forward car." Then he held the lantern up high and pointed to the back car. "And you can see the gun in the back car."

"So? It's some sort of armored gun back there."

"Sir. These two halves fit together. Look at the bolt holes on either side. And you see those three shafts on the front and the two on the back?"

He led Hans around to the back of the second car and pulled back the rest of the tarp to reveal a dark pile of iron wheels more than six feet across.

"Wheels, sir. The wheels fit on the shafts. They had to take them off because they project out too far from the side of the flatcar to transport it."

"So?"

"Sir. This is an armored land cruiser. Bolt the two halves together, put the wheels on, and off it goes."

"What? The damn thing's part of an armored train or something. We should have dumped it off rather than hauling it along in the first place. I just thought we could use the gun."

"Sir, Alexi thinks he can put it together," Gregory said.

Hans shook his head. There simply wasn't time to fool with it now.

"I've figured it out," Alexi said hurriedly. "It's actually an interesting design. We jack the two parts up. They only have to come up about half a foot. We build up the ground on either side of the cars by a foot or so. We can tear up some lumber from the siding. Take the wheels off the back of the car, roll them forward, and slide them onto the axles. Power up the steam engine, back it up until it's against the gun half of the cruiser. Bolt them together and we're ready to fight!''

Hans looked at him, still not convinced. ''And you think you can drive this thing?''

''Damn right! I can drive it, sir. The engine's almost identical to the one on the locomotive, only smaller. We put a gun crew inside. There's a wheel up front that's used to steer and half a dozen firing ports on either side of her. In one of the crates inside there's some real beauties, heavy one-inch rifles and ammunition in there for the cannon as well. It's brilliant.''

The way he said the word ''brilliant'' troubled Hans. If they're making these things, what else were they preparing?

''How many do you need?''

''Give me fifty workers and I'll have it ready by dawn.''

Hans stared at him intently. Alexi could be of far more use training the Chin in how to work a fieldpiece or fire rifles. But if he could actually do it, the damn thing might come in handy. He finally gave a barely perceptible nod and walked off into the darkness.

''The night is long, my Qarth.''

Ha'ark nodded and motioned Jamul to sit in the other camp chair by the fire.

Jamul settled into the chair and looked up at the Great Wheel.

''A long way from home,'' he sighed.

''Wonder if home is even in that galaxy overhead,'' Ha'ark replied.

''Do you miss it?''

Ha'ark chuckled. ''Home. What was home? We

were two drafted soldiers, caught in a war not of our making. We should have died in that ambush. Even if we had lived, that bastard sergeant would have had us killed by now."

"I don't mean that."

Ha'ark snorted with disdain. "What we were? Not of the upper caste. Students before the war—and if we had lived? Then what? You saw the mangled veterans of the last war, forgotten, disdained because they had fought on the losing side. I'm glad we're here."

"I'm not."

Ha'ark looked at him.

Jamul lowered his head. "This slaughter sickens me."

Ha'ark laughed. "Life is war, war is life."

"Easy enough for you to say, oh, Redeemer."

Ha'ark bristled at the sarcasm in his voice.

Jamul looked at him. "After all, you are the Redeemer. But the question is, do you really believe it?"

Ha'ark stood and looked down at him.

Jamul smiled. "Remember, I knew you as Ha'ark, a scared recruit, the same as I. Do you really believe what you've become to these primitives?"

"And why not? If the prophecy fits, wear it. We came to this world for a reason and have found it."

Ha'ark nodded toward the encampment spread out in the valley below.

"These are the illustrious ancestors of legend. It was from here that our race sprang while here there was the descent into barbarism. We have come to return them to their rightful place."

"Their destiny, as you call it?" Jamul replied. "You want to unleash them on other worlds?"

"The humans we face. All that I learned and could sense from Schuder. If once we can defeat them here and marshal our forces, in ten, fifteen years we'd be ready to cross to their world, once we've learned the secret of the Tunnel of Light and how to use it."

Jamul did not reply, his gaze fixed upon the fire.

"I cannot accept that we must defeat the humans," he finally said. "Too much has been done by our 'illustrious ancestors,' as you call them, to make it otherwise. But I am weary of it all."

He looked at Ha'ark. "And you, my friend. What have you become? What amazes me is that you actually believe all this. You believe you are the Redeemer."

"There is no alternative but to believe. And is there complaint from you? You are one of the companions."

"Oh, thank you for that."

Ha'ark bristled. "On the day we came here I saw the terror in your eyes. Remember it was I who killed our stupid commander, not you. It was I who remembered enough of the old language to ensure our survival, the overthrow of the last Qar Qarth, the life of luxury you now lead. I do not hear you complain about the concubines, the wealth, even the choice food."

He nodded toward the human limb roasting on a spit over the fire.

"That, at least, has come to trouble me," Jamul replied. "If they have souls, which I am coming to believe, then it is sacrilege to use them as we do."

"It's either that or we die, you and I die," Ha'ark snapped back. "It has been the way of this world for thousands of years. I have asked much in the changing of them. To ask that as well is to go too far."

"It makes them an implacable foe. If we faced such horror we would fight to the death as well."

"They didn't fight until the Yankees came. That proves something to me right there."

"Hans—does he have a soul?"

Ha'ark looked across the open fields to the fort.

Do you? Ha'ark wondered. You've deceived me, you've defeated me throughout this chase. You've been a worthy foe. There was something in the human he even admired, the inability to submit.

"That's not the question now," Ha'ark finally replied. "We must destroy them tomorrow. We must not just destroy them, we must wipe their memory from the face of this world. We've taught our people that the Yankees and the cattle who follow them are possessed by demons, and therefore are foes worthy to fight. We must unleash their hatred and fear. And the Yankees now know of us. Their flyers have at least seen what we are doing. Therefore the war begins."

He studied Jamul carefully.

"I need you and the others to fight this war. There are so many things still to be made, to be improved upon. It will be years, perhaps a generation or more, before we can train the primitives we rule to think as we do, to make machines, to create and control so much of what we left behind from our world. Do you understand that?"

Jamul nodded slowly.

A flurry of rifle fire erupted from the fort, and he looked up to see the pinpoints of light flashing along the parapet and return fire coming from the field.

"Damn it all," said Ha'ark. "If only we could drive our warriors to fight at night. One storming column and we'd be over the parapet and this would be finished. We'll lose twice, three times as many trying to take it in the daylight."

"They're not trained for it anyhow," Jamul replied.

"Neither are the cattle."

"It's going to be carnage out there tomorrow."

"A good blooding for them. Let them taste real action rather than the shams we've been staging."

He surveyed the encampment. Two regiments of his elite umens had come up during the night, along with a battery of thirty-pound guns. The other units could launch the first assaults, a fitting punishment for panicking before the gate and running. And then let them see what well-trained troops could do.

He looked back up at the Wheel and smiled.

"We have indeed come a long way," he whispered.

"Hans?"

Stirring from a dreamless, exhausted sleep, he saw her by his side, sitting up, looking down at him.

"What?" He wanted to tell her to sleep, that the hours till dawn were precious, but then he saw the glimmer of a tear, caught in the reflection of the starlight streaming in through the window.

"Will we live?"

"Of course, Tamira."

She tried to force a smile. "I keep thinking, if it wasn't for me, this never would have happened."

There was no sense in denying the truth of that now. But then again, if it wasn't for her, he would have been dead years ago. It was always to protect her that he had restrained himself from some final act of madness that would have resulted in his death. It was because of her, and especially because of Andrew, that he had agreed to try the escape.

"All those who died," she whispered. "And now, tomorrow, all the people of this town who will die as well."

"We were doomed anyhow. At least we regained our honor, our pride."

"And is that what Andrew will one day die for? If he lives through tomorrow, will he one day be killed anyway?"

He wanted to say no, but he couldn't. How many wars have been fought, he wondered, with those who did the bleeding, the dying, promising themselves that they suffered thus so their children would never know such horror?

"At least we're giving him the chance to live, to be a man, to be free. That's the best we can hope for."

He knew the words were small comfort, but he had never lied to her. He could not bring himself to do it, not with her golden eyes gazing into his soul.

He reached up and brushed the hair off her forehead, and she lay back down, snuggling against him. Why does she love me so? he wondered. I'm an old man, past fifty. She could have had so many others, and yet she chose me.

"I'll always love you," she whispered. "I never knew anyone to be so gentle and yet so strong."

He looked at her and again brushed the lock of unruly hair from her forehead.

"Go to sleep," he whispered.

"I can't."

"And?"

Smiling, she gently wrapped her arms around his shoulders and pulled him closer.

"Cast off all lines!"

Andrew felt his stomach knot as the ship began to climb. He closed his eyes, cursing this madness that had seized him and now compelled him to go up in an airship again. In the darkness he could just make out Jack's profile to his left. Behind him he saw Feyodor hunched down in the small aft compartment of the ship. They had argued vehemently over that, Andrew insisting that he sit on the floor and Feyodor arguing just as fiercely that he'd be damned before he'd let his commander sit on the floor. It was Jack who finally settled it, with the statement that he was captain of the ship and Andrew was to have the chair.

"You might as well settle back and get some sleep, sir," Jack said, interrupting Andrew's thoughts. "Six hours till we get there."

"And what about you? You had less than four hours' sleep in the last day and a half."

"What the hell, sir. There's only so many hours. Considering how long I expect to live, I might as well stay awake for most of them."

"I hate dragging you back out like this."

"Let's just hope *Flying Cloud* can stand it We've got only three engines now and we're leaking badly. Lose one more and we're in trouble, especially with the wind picking up again from the west. It'll help us get down there, sir, but I ain't too sure about getting her back."

"Well, let's hope this is the last run."

"Do me a favor, sir. Don't put it quite that way," Jack said quietly, and Andrew saw him nervously finger the miniature icon dangling from a cord around his neck. "You make it sound like we're not coming back."

"The way you fly, it's a wonder we ever get back," Feyodor interjected.

Andrew leaned back in the chair, pulling a blanket up around his shoulders, and gradually his thoughts drifted away while Jack and Feyodor continued the argument that had been running for years.

"Sir?"

Hans looked over at Gregory, who was pointing at the railroad embankment and a small triangle of white cloth held aloft by a mounted Bantag.

"Flag of truce?" Gregory asked.

Hans raised his field glasses to study the warrior. Then he saw anther rider approaching from behind the rise. It was Ha'ark.

The flag bearer galloped forward and Gregory shouted the command to hold fire. The rider slowed as he approached the moat. It was Karga!

"The Qar Qarth wishes to speak with Schuder."

Hans looked down at him in surprise, not replying.

"Let me just shoot the bastard," Gregory snarled, and a chorus of angry taunts erupted along the wall.

Hans remained silent for a moment, and then a smile creased his features. "Oh, why the hell not? It'll buy us a little more time."

"You're not going out there, are you?"

Hans leaned over the battlement and cupped his hands. "He can meet me halfway. I'll use your horse."

Karga hesitated for a moment, then dismounted.

"Damn it, Hans. He'll get you out there and then spring the attack. You'll be trapped on the outside."

"Maybe, but I doubt it. The bastard's curious about something. And like I said, it'll buy time."

He looked back at Alexi, working feverishly on his contraption.

On his way down the side of the bastion, he motioned for Ketswana and several of his men to follow. He crawled through the wreckage of the gate and slid down the other side, Ketswana following.

"Get some sort of ladder rigged up for when I come back. I don't want to have to crawl up out of the moat, and I might have to move fast."

"Be careful."

Hans patted the revolver tucked into his belt and smiled. Then he slid down the side of the moat, scrambled up the other side, and cautiously approached Karga.

"So your holy one wants to talk and sent his pet to fetch me."

Karga, his features contorted with rage, said nothing, merely extended the reins.

"For what it's worth," Hans said, "there's a hundred rifles aimed at you. Anything happens to me, and you go straight to your ancestors."

"It would be worth it to see you dead."

Hans laughed. "I'll tell you something, though. My friends will find your body, gouge out your eyes, cut off your tongue, and cut off something else as well, so you'll be a blind, dumb eunuch in the next world."

Karga struggled to suppress his rage and fear. "I'll eat your heart for that."

"Stand on line, then. Your false redeemer gets his first chance at that. But I'll tell you what you can eat," and as he finished the description he spurred the mount around and galloped across the field, laughing.

Most of the Bantag dead and wounded had been recovered during the night, but he could see trails of blood and parts of bodies where canister had torn into their ranks. Ha'ark came forward at a canter and Hans slowed his mount, forcing him to come closer. Ha'ark finally stopped fifty yards away.

"So, Hans Schuder, shall we argue about who shall come the last steps?"

"We could. Remember, I've been a sergeant for twenty years, I can shout in hell and still be heard in heaven."

Ha'ark nudged his mount forward and Hans, smiling, did the same.

"I want to offer you terms," Ha'ark said.

Hans continued to smile. "Free passage out of this hellhole is the only terms I'll consider."

"So you expect rescue? Impossible."

"And why not? But we could just simply stay here for a while instead, maybe stir up a rebellion or two."

"I have five regiments ready to assault. If you throw those back, I'll have a full umen by the end of the day, and if need be two umens after that. You know it is useless. You've made an excellent campaign. It has provided good training for my troops. I am impressed, but it is ended."

"Then finish it."

"A waste. I'll lose some good warriors, though the

training will be helpful for those who live. I'm offering you and those who escaped with you life."

"As what? Slaves? We'd rather be dead."

Ha'ark stared at him intently and Hans could almost sense a moment of regret. Ha'ark reached into his pocket and Hans stood ready to draw his revolver. Ha'ark slowly withdrew his hand and offered a plug of tobacco.

"Thanks. I've run kind of short, what with all the excitement," Hans said. Tearing off a chew, he held out the rest to Ha'ark.

"Keep it. I'll get it back later."

Hans shook his head.

"We can still call this war off," Hans said. "You know the terms. All humans to be set free. You live where you want. It's that simple."

"And again, no. Your race outnumbers us by ten, maybe a hundred to each of us. How long would it last?"

"Try."

Ha'ark shook his head. "The offer I made is final. Your lives, you return with us. Your wife and child, I give my blood pledge they will never be harmed. Your child will live, Hans, grow, have children of his own, and my pledge will be extended to them as well."

"I'd rather he be dead," Hans said softly, "than to live as a slave."

He could sense some final understanding within his opponent, a smile flickering over Ha'ark's features.

"You'll be worthy opponents, I can see that. There will be glory in this war."

Hans leaned over and spat. "The hell with glory. The fight is for survival and you will lose."

"Even if I do, you'll never live to see it."

"We'll see."

"Then there's nothing more to discuss."

"We could talk about the weather," Hans said dryly.

"And give you more time?" Ha'ark shook his head and started to rein his horse around. Then paused. "By the way, no help is coming. The airship you saw yesterday was destroyed. It went down in flames."

At Hans's expression, Ha'ark smiled. "Ah. So you didn't know?"

"The hell with you," Hans snarled.

Ha'ark studied him intently. "There was someone on that flyer. Wasn't there? Keane, perhaps? The bodies were burned to ashes, but I shall send my men to examine the remains and find the skull of the one with only one arm. It will make an excellent feasting cup."

"I'll see you in hell," Hans cried, furious that he had finally lost control.

"Good-bye, Sergeant," Ha'ark said calmly. He held Hans's gaze for another moment, as if regretting the final parting, and then he reined his horse about, dug in his spurs and galloped off.

Hans struggled with the desire to pull out his revolver and shoot the bastard, but in spite of what had been said, the honor of a truce still held sway. Hans turned his own mount as well and started back across the field at a gallop, expecting for them to open fire any second. Reaching the moat, he reined in hard, dismounted, and threw the reins to Karga.

"So he told you?" Karga said with a laugh.

"Get the hell out of here, you lowborn son of a bitch," Hans growled, "before I order you blown apart."

Hans started to slide down into the moat.

"Hans! Cattle scum!"

He turned to see a revolver in Karga's hand, and in that instant a volley erupted from the wall. Dozens of bullets blasted Karga. A shout of joy issued from the fort as the hated overseer was torn apart.

Hans grinned. It was a gift from Ha'ark, he realized. Karga could not have reacted any other way. The humiliation of being taunted from the wall by his former prisoners would have goaded him into it. It was a fitting punishment as well. Hans looked back and saw a lone rider watching in the distance. Ha'ark held up his hand, and Hans returned the gesture.

At that instant the Bantag artillery opened fire. Hans reached the bottom of the moat and scrambled up the other side. The first rounds came screaming in and detonated on the earthen wall to his right.

Ketswana extended his hand, pushing Hans forward and up through the narrow hole in the gate, then scrambling in behind him to slide down into the dirt piled up on the other side. Ducking low, Hans covered his head as a shower of splinters exploded from the gate.

"What did he say?" Ketswana asked, brushing the dirt from Hans's uniform as they ran into the bombproof under the northeast bastion.

Hans struggled to control his features. It must have been a lie. Yet he had seen the damage to the airship as it headed back up into the clouds. Damn it all, Andrew, why did you risk yourself like that? It would be like Ha'ark to say such a thing, if only to unnerve him. But now the doubt was there, the fear that help would never come, and worse, that all he had pinned his hopes on for the survival of the Republic was destroyed as well.

"Hans?"

Ketswana was looking at him anxiously.

"Nothing. The bastard said nothing at all."

Chapter Nine

"Ease off helm, steady now! Steady, damn you!"

Admiral Bullfinch stood on the bridge, cursing under his breath, as the flyer hovered thirty feet above him, matching the speed of his own ship. Having to turn into the wind was wasting valuable time, taking him back from the direction he had been steaming, just under eleven knots.

"Mr. Ivanovich, get a couple of men, hustle below, and bring up half a dozen tins of coal oil. They might want some fuel."

The midshipman saluted and dashed below while Bullfinch resumed watching the airship. *Petersburg* had not been designed with this type of docking in mind. The twin smokestacks projecting up amidships were twenty-five feet above the waterline. If the airship even brushed against them, a disaster might result.

A line snaked out from the airship cabin, and to his astonishment he saw someone extend his legs over the side and then slip out of the cab, dangling with the rope wrapped around his waist. The figure started to descend.

"Mr. Andreovich!" Bullfinch roared. "Pipers and marine detachment topside!"

With a sigh of relief Andrew finally felt his feet touch the deck and two deckhands helped him untie the bowline wrapped around his waist. Bullfinch rushed forward from the bridge, marines and pipers following, fumbling into position to present arms. The pipers started to trill a salute.

"Fine, Mr. Bullfinch, enough of that now," Andrew said, quickly saluting the colors and returning Bullfinch's salute. "Do you have any coal oil on board?"

"About thirty gallons. They're bringing it up now, sir." Even as he spoke Ivanovich appeared topside lugging two of the five gallon tins, two of the crew followed, dragging four more. A deckhand tied three tins to the line, and they were hoisted aloft. A minute later the rope came down, three more tins were tied on, and before they were even halfway up, Petracci had already put his helm over and was heading back to the southeast. Bullfinch shouted for the helmsman to put *Petersburg* back on her heading and motioned for Andrew to follow him aft.

"You should sight land within the half hour," Andrew told him. "Jack said heading south, southeast, half a point south, will put you straight for the entry to the bay."

Bullfinch nodded, and when they reached the open topside bridge he checked the compass, altered the course slightly, and passed the word for his orderly to bring tea and hardtack.

"I'd almost venture to say, sir, that I'm surprised you dropped in like this," Bullfinch finally said, handing the cup of tea to Andrew.

"Surprised myself. I swore yesterday I'd never ride in that damn thing again, but it was the only way to get there."

"Do you have any kind of chart of the river, sir?"

Andrew fished in his pocket and pulled out a folded piece of paper. Bullfinch studied it and shook his head.

"No indication of channels, depth, navigational hazards?"

"Just what we think are the fortresses sketched in there at the entryway to the bay and the mouth of the river, then along those bluffs about ten miles below where we're heading."

"And *Franklin*?"

"Coming up at full steam, but it won't arrive off here until sometime early in the morning two days from now."

"Well, with luck we should be in and back out by then. Just as long as she meets us—our bunkers will be empty by then."

Andrew sipped the tea, trying to calm his nerves from the ride out.

"So Hans is really alive then, sir?"

"As of yesterday," Andrew said quietly.

"How many are we trying to get out?"

"Seven hundred to a thousand."

Bullfinch looked at him, incredulous. "Sir, we haven't the room."

"Make room. Put them in the coal bunkers, engine rooms, I don't care how, but make the room. We are leaving no one behind."

"Land ho!"

Andrew saw the lookout on the narrow walkway between the smokestacks pointing directly forward.

"This time no one gets left behind."

Blood streaming into his eyes, Hans peeked over the side of the parapet, ducking instinctively when a rifle bullet cracked up a puff of dirt inches from his cheek. He slid back down, lying back against the bastion wall. A Chin woman, crawling low, came to his side, demanding to look at the bayonet gash that had cut a jagged line from his forehead across his cheek. The Bantag who had delivered the blow lay dead by his side.

She said something unintelligible. He tried to wave her off, but she insistently pushed him back and began to wrap a bandage around his head.

Ketswana crawled up. "Building up again along

the south wall. Looks like they're shifting a regiment."

"They'll try another rush on the gate, then throw the second punch straight over the south wall."

The Chin woman finished and pantomimed that he should go back into the town and lie down. He smiled and waved her away. Shaking her head, she continued to crawl down the battlement.

"Make sure all wounded are pulled back into the town. We can't stand another rush like the last one. Let's hit them hard as they come across, but when I give the word we break and fall back."

Ketswana, mimicking the salutes he had seen Gregory and Alexi give, crawled back to his bastion.

"Gregory?"

"Here, sir."

Hans saw him standing upright next to the thirty-pound gun, supervising the reloading with canister.

"We're going to pull back when the next charge hits."

The air seemed to be alive with artillery rounds screaming in from the batteries setting up an infilading fire to sweep the walls. The Bantag guns had found their range. Few shots were skimming clear over the fort now; most were either impacting on the wall, dropping in to sweep the parade ground, or striking inside the northern wall, making that position all but untenable. Why the Bantag didn't have mortars was a mystery, but he was thankful. A dozen of those weapons zeroed in on the fort would have been insurmountable.

Hans looked back toward the gate in the brick wall. Alexi was waiting, barely visible in the smoke from the fires that were consuming the town.

A narga sounded from across the field, and Hans stuck his head up over the battlement to look. A line of infantry stood up and rushed forward, staying low. The skirmishers who were deployed across the field, using the bodies of the fallen for cover, redoubled their fire. Smoke obscured the field, and he could sense, more than actually see, a column of assault troops moving to the right of the railroad embankment. The skirmishers stood up, joining the advancing line, moving closer, pausing for a moment to fire, reloading as they dodged back and forth. Running low along the battered walkway over the gate, Hans dashed into the southeast bastion. He had guessed right. A second column of nearly a thousand Bantag was charging at the double straight toward the bastion, anchoring the middle of the line just forward of the brick wall.

He kept shifting his gaze back and forth, judging the distance as the two columns continued to close. A steady patter of rifle fire from his defenders tore into the columns, dropping dozens of Bantag, but still the columns moved forward. It was obvious that they were fresh troops and well disciplined. He raised his hand as the signal for the heavy guns to get ready to fire.

Ha'ark snarled angrily as he watched the charge go in. This was costing too much, far too much. Nearly half of his five regiments of elite troops were dead or wounded, the survivors broken, incredulous that cattle should offer such fanatical resistance.

Bursts of canister swept down from the two bastions guarding the gate and at that instant the flanking column from the south leapt forward at the run, shifting its angle of attack.

"Get my horse," Ha'ark shouted. "Let's finish this thing."

Hans slowed as he approached the open gate, urging the last defenders into the town. He could see that some of the wounded had been left on the wall . . . he hoped that death would come swiftly for them.

A dark head appeared atop the southeast bastion, followed seconds later by dozens more and a red flag coming up and over. A flurry of rifle fire erupted, bullets smacking the brick wall on either side of him. Along the wall above him, the new reserve line was waiting, fortunately still holding fire.

The last of the survivors staggered through the gate as scores of Bantag swarmed down into the parade ground and raced to sweep either side of the fortress wall. He stepped back through the gate and into the narrow street of the town, holding his hand up to block the intense heat from the fires. He continued to wait, letting the numbers build, listening to the fire from the south bastion anchored on the brick wall, which swept the approaches up to the town.

A steady stream of bullets was penetrating the still opened gate, and he could hear the triumphal shouts of the Bantag rushing forward.

He turned and pounded the butt of his rifle against the iron-sided monster beside him.

"Now, Alexi!"

A plume of smoke billowed up from the ironplated smokestack, and he heard the rushing of steam. The machine remained still and Hans waited, tense with fear. He could hear the drive wheel turning inside and then the sound of the leather drive belts being engaged. The machine seemed to groan from the strain, great gouts of smoke thumping out, and then ever so slowly it lurched forward, its heavy iron wheels crunching on the graveled street. The pilot in the forward section of the iron monster turned the front wheels as the machine inched down the street, almost imperceptibly picking up speed. The machine swung ponderously around as it approached the gate. Hans stepped behind it, feeling the heat that radiated from the boiler at the rear. It slowly straightened, its smokestack barely clearing the arched en-

tryway, and at that moment he heard the triumphant
screams of the Bantag die away.

"Now. On the wall! Now!"

A ragged volley erupted from overhead as more
than a hundred defenders stood up and delivered at
close range. At nearly the same instant the ten-pound
gun in the forward half of the land cruiser let loose
with its deadly load of canister, sweeping the parade
ground. The machine slowly clinked out from the
gate, moving at top speed, which was not much better than a slow walk. The breech-loading gun fired
again. The first of the two side ports was now exposed, and the gunners within joined in with their
one-pounders, firing their oversized shotgun loads
into the Bantag who had been rushing down along
the inside walls of the fort.

Still behind the land cruiser, Hans could imagine
the panic breaking out in the parade ground at the
sight of the mechanical monster lurching toward
them. Turning, the enemy forces ran for the smashed
gate, exactly what he had hoped for. The compressed
mass was torn to shreds by two more blasts of canister. The few survivors still on the parade ground who
were not caught in the melee around the gate
streamed up over the north and south walls, only to
be swept by fire from the central bastions jutting out
from the brick wall.

He could hear the hollow sound of bullets clanging
against the land cruiser, almost like the sound of hail
drumming on a tin roof. Alexi guided the machine
into the center of the parade ground so that all four
of the gunners manning the one-pounders arrayed
two to each side had clear fields of fire on the insides
of the bastions, while the ten-pounder fired a final
blast of canister through the gate.

Hans, who had stopped inside the shadow of the
gate into the town, shook his head in wonder. He
saw a porthole on the back of the machine open.

Alexi grinned through it, waved, then slammed it shut.

Bantag riflemen continued to hold the outside slope of the east wall, but everywhere else the attack had been stopped cold.

"So now what are you going to do?" Hans laughed.

Standing against the outside wall, Ha'ark could not help but feel admiration. No one had told him that the second train they had taken was carrying a land cruiser, and somehow they had figured out how to bolt it together and use it. Typical of these damn humans, he thought. Adaptable in a crisis. He wondered if an equal number of his own race, caught in such a situation, would be able to think and act as creatively.

He could see his staff standing around him, their heads bowed, waiting for his explosion of rage.

"To be expected," Ha'ark finally announced. "This is not an exercise like those we practice on the Chin cities. This is real, and he did the unexpected."

"Shall we renew the assault?" Jamul asked quietly.

Ha'ark angrily shook his head. "We might carry it by a massed rush but it's a hundred yards across that parade ground, then to the bottom of a wall that has to be scaled. If we try flanking assaults they'll be funneled in and swept by artillery before they even reach the outside walls. Masterful. By pulling back and holding the center of the fort, he has left us no way of bringing artillery up to smash our way through. He got his forces out in time, so he must have three, maybe four hundred rifles."

"Our nearest land cruisers?"

"They just finished loading two of them in X'ian," Jamul replied. "It will be hours, though, before they're brought up, unloaded, and reassembled. Another report came in as well. The telegraph line to the coast is down. The last report was of a flyer and then smoke, most likely from an approaching ship, on the horizon."

"They'll try and run a ship up," Ha'ark replied. "Can we send anything down?"

Jamul shook his head. "None of our iron ships is ready yet."

"Send down anything that can float. They might not have any iron ships. Also, I want a report from a flyer."

"We've heard nothing. Three flyers are coming up, but they will not be here until just before sunset."

Ha'ark said nothing. Though they had learned to build the machines of war, he could see the glaring weakness of logistical inflexibility. The system was too rigid, unable to adapt to rapid changes. They had yet to master the art of organizing, and as a result precious equipment was scattered in all the wrong places, rather than concentrated where it was needed. Another valuable lesson, he thought, showing us more things that we will have to change. He looked back at the moat and then up at the railroad drawbridge.

"I want the following done immediately. First, find several large tarps and bring them up here. Second, locate the nearest armored train and order it forward immediately. Finally, the flyers are to be diverted here."

He smiled.

"This shall be an interesting challenge."

"Prepare to repel boarders!"

Andrew pulled out his revolver and clumsily checked the load. His head was ringing from the explosive roar of the guns and the sensation that he was trapped inside a kettledrum with giants pounding on the outside. Another shot struck the ship, on the port side just forward of the number two gun.

The oak beam backing cracked, sending splinters spraying across the deck.

"Don't these people ever give up?" Bullfinch snarled, looking out the forward gun port as another galley swung about in front of them, oar blades flashing in the afternoon sunlight. The ram sprinted forward, coming straight at them. Bullfinch stepped away from the gun.

"Clear!"

Andrew backed away from the gun, and Bullfinch gave a curt nod.

The gun recoiled and in the swirling smoke Andrew felt as if Bullfinch, with his black eye patch and the devilish grin lighting his features, looked like a pirate of old. Moving back behind the gun, Andrew saw a geyser of water subsiding, the bow of the ram shattered by the blow of the hundred-pound rifled bolt. He could hear the screams of the human rowers as the galley skidded off course and its bow went down. *Petersburg* plowed forward, smashing into the galley, pushing it under. Surviving Bantag jumped free of the wreckage, some of them gaining the bow of *Petersburg*. One of them crouched, rifle raised, aiming at the port. Bullfinch pulled out his revolver, fired, and the Bantag crumpled.

Bullfinch could hear fighting topside as the marine contingent, exposed on the deck, fired down on boarders who had scrambled up on the starboard side from a galley that had managed to swing alongside for an instant before a shot from one of the five-inch guns smashed it.

Another kettledrum boom ran through the ship and Andrew struggled to keep his balance. Bullfinch looked up and then started back down the gun deck with Andrew behind him. A head appeared in the hatchway leading below.

"Another hit on the waterline, sir. Couple more cracks. We're still taking water."

"Can the pumps handle it?"

"We might have to break out auxiliary hand pumps, sir."

"I can't spare anyone now, but pass the word if it gets any worse."

"Aye, sir."

Bullfinch continued down the length of the gun deck, the scrambled up the ladder to the armored bridge. Andrew followed, ducking low to fit into the cramped quarters now occupied by the helmsman, the first officer, the assistant engineer, and a midshipman rapidly sketching in details on a map.

"Sir, one of the shots breached the armor around the port side paddle wheel," the first officer said. "Several staves are broken. I suggest dropping the speed a bit on the starboard wheel to balance it. Otherwise we'll be wasting fuel by having to counter it with the helm."

Bullfinch looked at his first officer and reluctantly gave the word.

"But she feels shaky, sir," the engineer continued.

"What do you mean, 'shaky'?"

"Just that. I'd like to shut her down and check to see if the drive shaft was bent at all or cracked by the blow. The frame for the wheel might even be going."

Bullfinch looked at Andrew, and then shook his head.

"Sir, if the wheel seizes up, or the frame lets go, you'll only be running on one engine and any turn to starboard will be damn near impossible."

"We've got to get there before dark," Andrew snapped. "I promised him that."

"Sir, the promise won't matter if we lose a wheel," the engineer pressed.

"Son, you're doing your job by telling me that. But once it's dark we'll have to crawl up this river and that will mean we won't get there till dawn. They might hold out till the end of the day, but I doubt if they'll make it through a second night."

The engineer stood silent and then nodded his head.

Andrew peered through the narrow view port. Another shot came screaming past, this one from behind, impact on the far shore. One galley was left blocking the river, but apparently the sight of what had happened to the rest of the fleet caused it to put its tiller over and race for shore. Out on the deck the last of the Bantag were down, and marines, crouching low, were running back to the deck hatches, with their wounded.

"Those Bantag got guts," Bullfinch said, "sending guns against an ironclad. I thought for sure we'd see at least one armored ship."

"Maybe they didn't have a model to work off of. Besides, it takes time to build a fleet from scratch, and the junks and galleys the Chin use can't be built up the way we did with the Roum transports."

"Well, one thing's for certain," Bullfinch replied. "If we don't get our asses up there and out right quick, they'll think of something. I thought for sure they'd have a chain someplace at one of the narrows. I wouldn't be surprised if they try to sink a galley in the channel or maybe even shift some of those torpedo mines we dodged."

Andrew looked over at the first officer, who was supervising a midshipman sketching a rough chart of their passage. Several dozen X's marked spots where torpedo mines had been spotted.

"The river must be down a couple of feet with this dry spell, and I'd guess the current's sluggish," Bullfinch continued. "Otherwise those bastards wouldn't have been bobbing on the surface."

He ordered the helmsman to swing closer in toward the starboard bank.

"I think we're rounding that big loop here," Bullfinch said as the turn in the river began to straighten out from an easterly heading to a run almost due north.

"If so, we're ten miles out," Andrew replied. "Just under an hour and a half."

He walked to the other side of the armored bridge, squeezing past the first officer and midshipman. The sun was setting, its rays slanting in through the port.

"Just hang on," he whispered. "Hang on."

"What the hell are they doing?" Gregory asked, daring to peer over the side of the wall.

The tarp had been dropped over the shattered gate minutes before. Hans was glad that Alexi had ventured only one shot at it with a canister round. It had shredded in parts, but a second one had been dropped behind that one. With the limited rounds left in the land cruiser it would be wasted unless a clear target showed. A steady patter of rifle fire caused the tarp to jerk and billow. At least Alexi had backed the cruiser off from facing the gate directly, so if they were moving a heavy gun up, it would have to be pushed through before it could be brought to bear.

Two flyers had been seen to touch down nearly an hour ago, but neither had ventured up over the fort. The sniping between the two walls continued, and there was a slow but steady stream of casualties being carried back into the still smoldering wreckage of the town, yet nothing more had happened throughout the afternoon.

Off to the west, the sun was dropping low. Would Ha'ark wait till dark? Hans wondered. That would be one way to knock out the cruiser. The troops they were facing now were different. Their loose-fitting black uniforms bore red collars, unlike the traditional Horde leather jerkin of the guards.

If he had trained modern infantry, they must have

some idea of how to mount a night attack, a tactic the Union army had been experimenting with when siege warfare became the norm in '64.

"Flyers are coming up!"

Hans dared a quick glance up over the wall. The two flyers were slowly climbing, swinging out downwind, and at the same moment he heard the distinctive chugging of a train.

"Get ready!" Hans roared.

The first of the two flyers turned into the wind, leveling out, and started toward the fort.

He watched them intently, fascinated by the wings extending from either side. The first flyer finally seemed to hover overhead. It nosed over and started into a dive.

A spray of brick dust erupted in front of Hans from a rifle bullet aimed only an inch or two too low, but he ignored it, unable to turn his eyes away. A fusillade erupted from the defenders aiming at the flyer, and return fire exploded from the opposite wall. A black oblong shape detached from the flyer, which immediately started to pull up.

"A bomb!" Gregory shouted. "A damn big one."

The bomb hurtled down, striking twenty yards to one side of the cruiser. A thunderclap explosion followed. Hans ducked as a geyser of earth sprayed upward, bits of dirt and debris raining down over the wall.

Recovering, Hans scrambled back up, half expecting to see the land cruiser over on its side. The machine was still upright, though dirt covered its side and top.

"The second one," Gregory cried, pointing up.

The next flyer was already into its dive.

"Pour it on 'em!" Hans roared. "Pour it on!"

Cursing, he wished he had arranged for one of the field guns to be rigged for high-angle fire. He picked up his own rifle and fired as well, aware that he could hear the howl of the flyer's engines. The second bomb detached, and he had the sick sensation that it was coming straight at him. He ducked and covered his head.

The bomb impacted just forward of the gate to the town. A thundering shudder ran through the wall, and he saw a column of dirt, debris, pieces of brick, and what looked to be part of a boxcar soaring heavenward and then crashing back down.

He scrambled to his knees and saw that the flyer was not pulling out. Its dive was steepening, the ship coming almost straight down.

"We got it!" Gregory roared. "The pilot. Look."

He thought he caught a fleeting glimpse of the Bantag pilot slumped forward, held in his chair by his safety belt. A second Bantag was struggling with the controls.

The hundred-foot-long ship slammed into the ground alongside the cruiser. An instant later a fireball erupted, flames racing up the fabric sides of the ship, the hydrogen within exploding into a shimmering blue ball of light.

The framework of the ship seemed to stand like a rigid tower above them, and then it crumpled in a shower of sparks, the wings folding in, breaking off. The burning rubble leaned drunkenly, and then pushed by the wind, slowly began to topple, crashing down on top of the cruiser.

For an instant both sides ceased firing, mesmerized by the spectacle. Then a cheer erupted from the human side as the cruiser slowly backed out of the flaming wreckage. But the celebration was short-lived. Suddenly the sound of a train whistle rent the air. The tarp covering the gate was torn aside as a sloping front of black armor appeared, steam billowing around it.

"They must have fixed the drawbridge," Hans snapped. "Damn him! I never thought of this."

The armored car mounted forward of the engine came through the gate, a plowlike blade mounted on the front of it pushing the wreckage and bodies aside.

Completely forgetting where he was, Hans stood up.

"Alexi! Get the hell out!" he screamed.

The land cruiser, still backing away from the burning airship, slowly started to turn. The gun mounted in the front of the armored car fired, an explosion of sparks streaking down the side of the cruiser. An instant later the cruiser fired back. The shot struck square on the front of the armored car and ricocheted straight up with a howling shriek.

In that instant Hans knew what would come next.

"Get out, get out!"

Gregory was by his side, pulling him back down to his knees, while bullets whistled past.

The armored train car fired again. The cruiser seemed to lift into the air from the blow. Steam exploded out of the smokestack and through the gun ports as the shot penetrated the front armor, tore down the inside of the cruiser and burst the steam engine. Seconds later the back hatch of the cruiser was flung open. Horrified, Hans watched as two men staggered out, shrieking and tearing at their clothes.

"Alexi!"

A volley erupted from the far wall, kicking up spurts of earth around the two as they struggled to reach the wall. Both toppled over, screaming . . . and then, mercifully, were still.

Hans watched, cursing wildly, barely hearing Gregory's screams of rage. The train continued forward, its gun shifting, firing straight at the barricade thrown up across the archway into the town. Part of the arch collapsed, the next shot brought the rest of it down.

A solid mass of Bantag now swarmed over the opposite wall and started forward at a run. The four light field guns, which were loaded with canister, swept down dozens of them, but the Bantag, heartened by the destruction they had witnessed, pressed on.

"Sir!"

Hans turned, looking at Ketswana, who was kneeling wide-eyed by his side.

"Get back to your post!"

"Sir, a boat. It's the boat!"

Hans looked at the destroyed archway that cut him off from the north wall.

"We've got to hold, Gregory!" Hans shouted, and following Ketswana, he scrambled down a ladder to the street below. He sprinted past the smoking wreckage of the gate, where several dozen Chin were doggedly holding their position, and ran to the north wall, scrambled up the ladder, and from there made his way out into the projecting bastion.

Coming up the river, and now only a few miles away, an ironclad was just turning the bend. White puffs of smoke swirled around it, and in spite of the roar of battle, he heard the distant sound of a steam whistle.

Grinning, he looked at Ketswana.

"You've got to hold this bastion!" Hans shouted. "It protects the gate down to the river. Once those bastards know the boat's here they'll try to sweep down along the bank and pour fire into the dock."

Laughing with delight, Ketswana nodded. Hans slipped out of the bastion and went back to the street below. He could see another section of the wall crumble, and defenders tumbled off. Running along the north wall, he reached the village temple where the old, young, and wounded were. He burst through the door into the ancient limestone building and looked around frantically until at last he found Tamira. She had Andrew slung over her back while she tended one of the wounded. He raced to her side.

"It's here!"

His voice carried through the temple, and all eyes were upon him.

"Get everyone together and start moving them down to the north gate. When you see the boat reach the dock, open the gate and run. Do you understand me? Run."

"And you?"

"I'll be right behind you."

She stood up and looked into his eyes.

"No, don't even think it," Hans said, trying to block out the cries erupting around him as word spread of the deliverance coming for them. "There's Andrew. You must live for Andrew. Don't wait for me."

The baby, awakened by the shouting, started to cry feebly. She moved the sling off her back and cradled him in her arms, her eyes on Hans.

"You know what to do. Lead these people out of here."

The beginning of a shuddering sob shook her shoulders, but then she braced herself and looked into his eyes.

"For Andrew," she whispered.

He cupped her face in his hands, kissed her lightly on the mouth, and brushed the tears from her eyes. He leaned over and kissed Andrew on the forehead, then disappeared out the door.

"Swing the third regiment around to the north side!" Ha'ark shouted. "I want a volley line down to the river now."

Jamul saluted, and shouting to his staff, he sprinted across the drawbridge, running toward the reserve regiment, which was deployed in column out on the field.

*   *   *

"All hell is breaking loose up there," Bullfinch snapped at Andrew. "It's a hundred-yard run from the wall down to the river. They'll be slaughtered."

Andrew saw the line of Bantag troops deploying out toward the river. A mounted battery came into view, guns bouncing behind caissons as their drivers drove the teams forward.

"Bullfinch, run us past the dock. Take us up to flank that line, tear it apart, then reverse back down."

Grinning, Bullfinch explained the maneuver to his helmsman. Andrew left the bridge and moved to the main gun deck, watching as Bullfinch came down after him, shouting for his port and starboard gunners to load with double canister. The crews leapt to their guns, ramming the heavy charges home, each of the five-inch rifled pieces taking two bags of shot, each bag containing nearly three hundred musket balls, the hundred-pounder forward taking nearly a thousand musket balls of canister. Andrew leaned out one of the gun ports and saw the dock less than a hundred yards ahead. Looking up at the fortress town, he saw the gate swing open, and to his horror a mad rush of people streamed out.

Not yet, damn it. Not yet.

The Bantag troops opened fire. One of the field-pieces, already unlimbered, kicked back, its round of canister tearing through the press of humanity that had started to surge down to the dock. The forward hundred-pound Parrott gun kicked back with a roar, sweeping down part of the Bantag line, but more of the enemy continued to spill around the side of the wall, opening fire, their volleys tearing into the mob.

"Number one starboard, train on the artillery, two, three, and four on the infantry," Bullfinch roared.

The crowd continued to surge forward, though they were dropping by the dozens.

Petersburg raced past the dock, and he could see

the horror on their faces as their salvation passed
them.

Bullfinch turned to face aft.

"Port side engine full astern!"

A shudder ran through the ship as the paddle
wheel on the port side came to a stop and then
slowly went into reverse. The ship began to pivot,
even as its momentum continued to propel it forward. Andrew reached up to brace himself and
jumped when the first gun went off, kicking back
nearly to amidships. The next three guns behind him
fired within seconds, and everything in front of him
instantly disappeared in a wall of coiling smoke. The
ship continued to drift forward, even as it turned.

"Torpedo mine bearing off starboard bow!" The
warning from the forward gun captain had barely
been heard when at nearly the same instant the ship
heaved up, a booming explosion echoing through it.
Andrew found himself lying on his back, stunned.
He could hear the ship groaning, as if it were a living
entity that had just been struck a mortal blow. Bullfinch staggered past him, heading aft, and Andrew
suddenly realized he was soaking wet. The blast had
sent a column of muddy water pouring through the
forward gun port.

The ship was continuing its turn, the stern now
presented to the fort. Regaining his feet, he watched
as the port side gunners, who were still at their posts,
stood poised. The aft gun fired, followed within seconds by the other three. The smoke cleared for an
instant, and he saw that the line had simply disappeared. The field was covered with carnage.

He started aft, following Bullfinch, who was shouting orders for both engines forward and then a
final reverse.

"Deck crew out, rig anchor astern. Marines prepare
to disembark!"

The port side hatch swung open, and a dozen sailors raced out, then the twenty men of the marine detachment. Andrew started to follow them.

A hand reached out and grabbed his shoulder.

"Sir. I'm not bringing your corpse back to face Pat. You, sir, are staying here."

He started to protest but sensed that if he did, he would suffer the indignity of actually being physically restrained.

The engineer scrambled up from below, interrupting the confrontation.

"We're taking water fast, sir. There's a hole about ten feet back from the bow big enough to stick my head through, just below the waterline and cracks springing leaks for ten foot in either direction. Lucky that bastard wasn't down lower or we'd already be settling."

"How bad is it?" Bullfinch asked.

"Like to try and rig a lead sheet patch from the outside. We're going to lose her if we don't patch her."

"Get a crew and get outside then," Bullfinch announced.

He then faced Andrew. "Sir, please don't. If you go out there, I'll order my marines to surround you. I'd rather have them helping get these people in."

Even as they spoke, Andrew could see the rush coming down the hill. Anxiously he searched the crowd as it charged forward, but saw that it was the old, the wounded, and the children.

Of course, he realized, it'd be like Hans to be the last one out.

The pressure was building all along the wall, and he could sense the growing panic.

"This isn't going to be like the Potomac!" Gregory shouted. "You take the first line back, I'll hold there!"

Hans fished in his pocket and pulled out the plug of tobacco Ha'ark had given him.

"Have a chew."

"Disgusting habit, but why not?"

Taking the plug, he bit off the end, and started to chew, gagged but then continued.

"Just get them the hell out, sir. I'll be right behind you."

"It's going to be the other way around, Gregory, and that's an order."

Hans looked over the wall down into the street. The light field gun that had been rolled up to block the gate had been dismounted by the fire from the railroad gun. A second gun was now positioned at an angle away from the gate and twice its blasts of canister at point-blank range had swept the Bantag charges attempting to get through.

"Sir!"

Hans turned to see one of Ketswana's men down in the street, clutching a broken and bleeding arm.

"Everyone from the temple is out. They sent me to tell you it's time to get out."

As the man headed back toward the gate, Ketswana scrambled up to the battlement to join them.

Hans looked down the wall. This was the tough part. A small detachment was going to have to stay behind for at least a couple of minutes. Otherwise there'd be a pile up at the gate, with the Bantag pouring in behind them. He had already detailed off the volunteers, and the orders were for everyone else to load their rifles, prop them up, then get off the wall and run. The crew staying behind would then quickly move from gun to gun, firing, keeping up the sham that the retreat had not yet started.

"Get ready to move!"

He watched down the wall, as everyone reloaded.

"Go!"

He started to turn. "All right Gregory, move your ..."

He barely saw the dark fist of Ketswana coming

at him, catching him on the side of the jaw. The blow knocked him down, stunning him. Steellike arms wrapped around him, lifted him, tossed him to two men waiting below. Ketswana leapt down beside him and grabbed him around the waist. Then he started to run.

Numbed, Hans looked back and saw Gregory on the wall, grinning.

"No! Damn it, no!"

"We're not going to leave you," Gregory roared. "Not now! You're not doing the Potomac to me again!"

Ketswana, stretched his long legs and ran, still carrying Hans.

"Damn you, let me down!" Hans cried, struggling to break Ketswana's grasp.

He could see Gregory still on the wall, directing the fire of the last defenders. Then he was lost to view. Ketswana maneuvered the burning wreckage of the town, jostling and pushing his way to the front of the swarm heading for the gate. The thunder of rifle fire took on a different sound, and Hans realized that the Bantag must be over the wall. Someone next to Ketswana stumbled and fell, and then another.

Around the gate an insane frenzy took hold as people clawed their way through, screaming, pushing, shoving. Ketswana, towering above the rest, slammed into the crowd and burst through to the other side. His strength returning, Hans began to struggle, trying to get free, to get back. Ketswana continued to press forward.

Suddenly a blinding flash of light enveloped them and Hans felt himself falling, tumbling off the pathway that led to the ship, and freedom.

"There he is!" Andrew shouted.

Bullfinch turned away from the incredible press of humanity pouring in through the hatch.

Andrew pushed his way through the gun port before Bullfinch could stop him and grabbed the nearest marine helping to shepherd the crowd off the dock and onto the ship.

"Come on," he roared, as he sprinted to the side of the boat and leapt off. Sputtering, he came up in chest-deep water and started to wade to shore. Looking over his shoulder, he saw Bullfinch standing on the deck, shouting and swearing, pushing marines in after Andrew and then leaping in himself. Andrew scrambled up on the beach, barely aware of the geysers of mud spraying around him. Slipping going down, he came back up, climbed the embankment. Above him, on the dock, the press toward the boat continued, casualties tumbling off into the mud below.

Andrew forced his way through them, grabbing a tuft of grass to pull himself up onto the sloping ground that led to the fort. Crouching low, he sprinted forward toward the gate and then fell to his knees.

"Hans, oh, God! Hans!"

"Andrew, just what the hell are you doing?" Hans gasped.

Andrew reached out and embraced him, laughing and crying at the same time.

"Son, I think we'd better get out of here," Hans growled and for Andrew all the years seemed to fall away, the words almost the same as when he had been a terrified young lieutenant at Antietam, and Hans had looked at him and said it was time to lead the company out of the trap they had fallen into.

Andrew stood up and started to pull Hans to his feet, but Hans stopped and reached down to a wounded black man beside him.

Ketswana groaned, blood pouring from his scalp and arm.

"Come on, my friend, we're going home," Hans

gasped, and at that moment the marines and Bullfinch surrounded them, grabbing Hans and Ketswana, taking them back down to the river. Several of the men positioned themselves between Andrew and the increasing fire from the riverbank, where a new swarm of Bantag was charging into position.

Bullfinch ignored the path and led them straight back down to the river. The three marines carrying Ketswana waded in, floundered momentarily at the side of the boat, and then lifted him up to the sailors who now lined the deck. When they reached the water Hans turned around.

"Gregory! Gregory's back there!" he shouted.

Startled, Andrew looked back at the fort. Half a dozen men came bursting out of the gate, and then no one. Along the north wall Bantag appeared, firing down at them.

And then four more men came through the gate, running hard.

"Gregory! Run, damn it! Run!" Hans screamed.

An artillery round burst on the pathway, knocking the four down. With an anguished cry Hans struggled to get up, but Andrew and Bullfinch restrained him.

Two of the men staggered back to their feet and reached down to pick up their comrades. The marines guarding Andrew sprinted up the embankment again, one of them tumbling back over. They reached the struggling knot of men and helped pick up the two wounded, dragging them down the dock.

"Let's go!" Bullfinch cried, wading out into the river, pushing Hans and Andrew in front of him. Hands reached out to them and hoisted them up onto the deck. The air was alive with bullets striking the iron sides of the ship, ricocheting off, sparks flying.

"Cut the anchor! All engines full ahead!" Bullfinch roared.

Andrew was thrown gasping up on the deck, hustled toward an open gun port, and unceremoniously shoved through.

Turning, he helped to pull Hans through, and the two fell atop each other onto the deck. Bullfinch came behind them, still roaring for full power.

Andrew could feel the shudder running through the ship as it started forward. He looked down at Hans, who was lying across him, bloodied, stunned. There were no words to say. Nothing could ever express what he was feeling or all that he wanted to say. It struck him yet again how one could go for years never really conveying just how deeply he felt, how much love he had for another. But when that person was thought lost forever, one would give all he ever had, even his own life, only to have one precious minute back again.

Hans stirred. "Gregory, Ketswana?"

He sat up and saw Ketswana propped up against a gun carriage, grinning.

"Hans!'

It was almost a scream, and Andrew saw a diminutive dark-haired girl pushing her way through the crowd. Hans staggered to his feet and swept her up into his arms, kissing, hugging her. Hans suddenly realized that those standing around him were silent, and he looked at Andrew sheepishly.

"This is," he fumbled for words, his features reddening, "ah . . ."

"Mrs. Schuder, I presume," Andrew said with a grin.

"And young Andrew," Hans replied, motioning toward the squalling infant cradled between them.

"Sir?"

He turned to see one of the marines, and the memory returned.

"Gregory?" He shouldered his way through the crowd to Gregory, who lay with his men kneeling by his side. The life was already draining from his features. Hans spared a quick glance down to the shattered lower half of his body. He closed his eyes, wishing it away.

"Hans."

He knelt and took Gregory's hand.

"The chew. It made me sick."

Hans tried to smile. "Damn you," Hans whispered. "It was my duty to stay."

"You got me out during the Potomac fight," he sighed. "It was time to repay the favor. Ketswana and I would not let you die."

Then he whispered, "Is that Keane?"

Andrew knelt beside him. "Here, Gregory."

"My wife?"

"Still waiting for you to come home. She never gave up hope. You have a beautiful little girl."

Gregory smiled. "Take me home. Don't leave me here. Please take me home."

"Of course we will, son," Andrew said softly.

He struggled to sit up, but fell back with a sigh.

"We few, we happy few . . ." and his voice drifted away into silence.

"We band of brothers," Hans choked out, reaching down to close his friend's eyes.

Exhaustion, numbness, all of it at last took hold. Sobbing, he stood up. The deck that only a moment before had been packed with people cheering with wild abandon was now silent. All eyes turned to Hans, as he stood with bowed head, long, shuddering sobs racking his body. Andrew could see tears welling up in the eyes of those around him, in sympathy for the one who had been a rock to which they had clung for survival and who now, at last, had time to mourn.

Bullfinch made his way through the crowd, looking for Andrew.

"We got the patch on. We're still taking water and

overloaded like hell, but with luck I think we'll make it now."

Andrew motioned for him to be silent.

Hans stood alone, looking at those to whom he had given life and then back down at Gregory. Tamira came to his side and put her arm around him, and he gazed down at his baby.

Covering his face with his hands he let the tears come, tears for all of them, all those who were lost, who had fallen, and even now for those who were left. He felt a hand on his shoulder, and raising his head, he found Andrew looking at him, bright-eyed.

"Welcome home, Hans."

Chapter Ten

"I wish I could have seen that devil Ha'ark's face, when *Petersburg* cut anchor and was away," Pat laughed. "It'd be nice to hear that those animals turned on him and cut his throat."

"He'll find a way to explain it to his followers," Hans said quietly. "He'll survive."

Andrew looked around the table in the formal East Room of the White House, again feeling a warm and comfortable glow. He had a sudden memory of the first time he had seen this room, coming in with Hans to meet Ivor, the boyar ruler of Suzdal. The man sitting at the end of the table now, the president, had stood with them then, stumbling through a translation and most likely making up most of the conversation as he went along.

Andrew smiled at Kal. Whatever differences had existed between them were gone now, and in spite of the fear of what was coming, he could see that the old Kal had returned. And for that matter, he sensed that he had somehow returned as well.

"Five old comrades," Kal suddenly said. "It's good to be alone with you again."

"I still think, Hans, that you should get some rest," Emil interrupted. "Let's save the drinking for another night."

"In a little while," Kal replied. "It's been a good day. Let's relax a bit before ending it."

The reception Hans had received when the train

pulled in at Suzdal Station came close to rivaling the triumphal return after the Battle of Hispania. Perhaps the only person to complain was Bill Webster, the secretary of the treasury, who claimed that at least two days' worth of work had been totally lost, along with two days in Roum, where the train had stopped the night before. But beyond all else, Andrew felt it was worth it, if only because it had brought the Republic together.

Declared or not, a state of war now existed. A blockade was up along the Bantag coast, and a light sloop had been reported lost when four flyers dropped bombs on it. Petracci was screaming for more airships, beside himself because *Flying Cloud* was down for at least two weeks for repairs after its three missions.

Old regiments were mobilizing, calling back their veteran reserves, and the first brigade of Roum troops had already been dispatched to reinforce the defensive line. Andrew could only hope that the sense of unity engendered by the rescue would endure in the months, perhaps years, of struggle to come.

"And would you look at this?" Pat exclaimed, pulling a copy of *Gates's Illustrated Weekly* out of his back pocket, unfolding it, and putting it on the table.

Emil reached across the table and held it up, looking at the portrait on the cover, and then over at Hans. He read the banner headline: "Our Hero Returns."

Hans, grumbling, took another long sip of vodka.

"I want you to speak before the joint session of Congress tomorrow," Kal told him. "Before I make the formal request for a declaration of war, I want you to tell them everything you saw, everything you experienced."

Hans nodded, and Andrew could see the pain lingering just below the surface.

"And Gregory?"

"He'll be interned with full honors immediately afterward," Andrew interjected softly. "Both Alexi and Gregory will receive the Congressional Medal, and Gregory's widow will always have the special pension supplement."

"Small comfort," Hans whispered.

Andrew nodded. He had met with Gregory's widow immediately after their return, and the anguish of it was almost too much to bear. Nearly four years of his being missing and presumed dead had softened her pain, but now the wound had been torn open again when she learned he had come so close to making it home.

"And Ketswana—I want him appointed a colonel on my staff," Hans said. "His men are to be kept together as well, as part of a headquarters company. Without him, I never would have made it."

"Zulus," Pat said admiringly. "Good fighters. I wish we could find out where they are and bring them in. They'd make a hell of a corps."

"Pull out whomever you want," Andrew said. "Most of these people you brought in will never have a chance to see their real homes again. It would be comforting for them to stay together."

"I wish I could have brought them all out," Hans replied, his gaze drifting as if he were looking off into some unknown land.

"You got out four hundred and twenty-eight," Kal said, "Eighty-three of them from that hellhole you were in. I consider that pretty damn good."

"We broke out with somewhere around three hundred," Hans replied. "We left behind at least three hundred more and thousands who will pay the price for what we did. We picked up at least a hundred on the way, but most of them died. Then there were the townspeople that we dragged into the fight.

There were nearly a thousand people at that settlement before we came."

Andrew leaned forward, fixing Hans with a penetrating gaze.

"You got out, my friend. You might very well have saved the Republic as well, with the information you brought. All of you were dead until the moment you stepped onto the *Petersburg*. How long would all the rest have lived? Another week, a month, a year or two? And then what? Try to convince yourself that they died for something. They were already dead, but by their sacrifice the Republic will live."

"Hard to say that to them now," Hans replied. "Hard to imagine telling them that when they face the slaughter pit for what I did."

"Then, damn it," Emil growled, "tell it to your wife and son. That's why you did it, and in my book it was worth it."

Andrew saw the concern in the doctor's eyes.

"He's consumed with guilt," Emil had told him on the train ride back home. "He admitted he was planning to sacrifice himself in the end, once he knew Tamira and the boy were safe, a sacrifice in atonement, but Gregory and Ketswana guessed what he was up to and stopped him. What makes it worse is that Gregory died so he could live."

Andrew now looked at Hans, who was staring absently into his drink.

"Hans," said Kal softly.

Hans looked up with a strained smile on his face and nodded.

"You came back to us. When all of us here heard you were alive, none of us would have hesitated a second to lay down his own life to save yours."

Hans started to growl a reply, but Kal slammed his open hand on the table.

"Listen to me, Hans."

Hans was quiet.

"And you would have done the same. You were going to do the same for Gregory, but the lad, Kesus grant him peace, knew you well enough to trick you. And I'll tell you this. If we could conjure the soul back into that body resting over in the Capitol building, he would say that he would do it again."

Then Kal continued, his voice dropping, "That is the paradox of war that will always hold me in wonder. It is the most horrible damned thing ever imagined by man or any other race. But it brings out something as well, a nobility of spirit and a love for comrades that nothing will ever break. You taught that to a very young officer named Andrew Lawrence Keane, and he has taught it to this world. And that is why, speaking now not as Kal but as the president, I committed this country to bringing you out, even though it ensured that there would be a war.

"Now I know you are feeling guilty."

Hans stirred and looked helplessly at Emil.

"I don't need the good doctor to tell me. Remember Hans, I survived the coming of the Tugars three times, twice as a terrified peasant. I saw the first girl I ever loved dragged into the pits to have her throat cut. I saw my parents go. I helped trigger the rebellion against the boyars and maneuvered to keep you and your comrades here, not for myself but for the love of my daughter Tanya. The same way I know that underneath it all, the real reason for what you did was out of love for that beautiful young woman you brought back and your precious son."

Hans nodded uncomfortably.

"I know what the guilt is, to survive when others die. I know what it is like to help start a war, knowing that tens of thousands might die, while I"—he paused for a moment, his face turning red—"while I know that I will live because I am the president. During the last war I looked into the eyes of thousands of young boys, knowing they would die. I had to trade jokes with them, reassure, inspire, and then leave. Throughout that war I would have given my soul to be able to stand on the volley line with them, rather than hide behind the lines."

"You did give an arm in the Tugar War," Emil said quietly.

"A convenient excuse to soothe my soul when I lie awake at night," Kal snapped. "But all I'm trying to say is that the only one who will ever blame you is yourself. Forgiveness has to come from within. I know. I've yet to forgive myself, and when I go before Congress tomorrow I know that I will be asking for the lives of tens of thousands more.

"This entire nation thanks Kesus that you are alive, Hans Schuder. All I am asking is that you now thank him that you are alive as well."

The room fell silent. All eyes followed Kal as he stood up and walked around the table and extended his hand.

"It's a long day tomorrow. I suspect your young lady is waiting for you upstairs. Let's get some sleep."

Hans, embarrassed by the overt display of emotion, accepted the traditional Rus embrace, which included a kiss on both cheeks.

Pat, blowing his nose loudly, tried to get up, then accepted Emil's hand.

"Come on, you. I don't understand why I bothered to sew your stomach back together again. You're just trying to drink another hole through it."

"You did it for the glory," Pat replied with a laugh. "And because you couldn't stand not to have me to share a drink with."

Pat came around to take Hans's hand.

"Welcome home, me bucko. And another war to share with you, by God."

Emil, looking into Hans's eyes, took his hand after Pat let go. "We'll talk some more later." And the two left, Pat starting into the latest joke he had heard about the legendary innkeeper's wife, the punch line lost as the door closed behind them.

"And we'll talk some more as well," Andrew said quietly.

Hans nodded, started to say something, and then lowered his head.

"Go on."

"You're all just as I remember," he finally said. "That thickheaded Irishman with the courage of a lion, Emil always worrying about his patients. Kal, maybe more presidential but still the shrewd, wise peasant. And you, Andrew, still carrying the burden of a world on your shoulders."

Hans picked up his glass and drained the last of the vodka.

"Oh, God, how I dreamed of all of you. It was my only hold on sanity at times. I'd imagine myself back with the lot of you, or before then, back on Earth when it was just you and me and the old Thirty-fifth Maine. We'd talk by the hour, remembering together, and saying, at times, the things I wish I'd said."

"Such as?"

Hans tried to force a smile and shook his head. "You know."

"So we'll never say them, then?"

"What can two comrades say? It goes beyond words, Andrew. Beyond words. You haven't changed, and I thank God for that."

"But you have. That's what you're telling me."

"I wonder if I'll ever get home." He sighed. "Not now. Not after all I've seen, all those I left behind."

"We'll go back, Hans. We'll go back and end it. If you hadn't come from hell to tell us all, maybe we never would have gone. That's what you brought back. That and what you've given back to us."

"But me? What of me now?"

"You said you didn't have a home now." Andrew

chuckled softly. "But you do. It's upstairs waiting for you. In the end, that's all we fight for, what's waiting upstairs for you right now."

He put his hand on Hans's shoulder and they left the room.

As they reached the staircase Andrew stopped, again wanting to say so much, but realizing that indeed there were no words for it.

"Thank you, thank you for everything," Andrew said finally. "And thank you for coming back."

Hans forced a smile and reached into his pocket to pull out the shred of a tobacco plug. "Care for a chew?"

Andrew smiled and bit off a piece. Hans pocketed the rest.

"A little memento from an enemy and a friend," Hans said. "I think I'll save the rest."

"Good night, Hans."

"Son, I'm proud of you," Hans replied. The two embraced clumsily and Andrew left him, stepping out into the warm summer night and returning the salutes of the two sentries by the door.

"How is he?"

Startled, he saw Kathleen waiting for him.

"You should have come in."

"No, I think it was time for the boys to have a drink and a chat."

He put his arm around her waist and they started down the steps.

"The children?"

"Tanya and Vincent came over, so all the children are tumbled in together. They'll watch them. I thought it was time we took a moonlight stroll together. It's been a while."

They walked on in silence for several minutes, crossing the great square, passing the occasional reveler who was still out celebrating the holiday for Hans.

"He's wounded in the soul," Andrew said. "It will haunt him. Gregory, Alexi, all those people he left behind. God, what a choice to have to make."

"You would have done it."

"If there was you, the children—yes."

"You would have done it anyway. As long as one lives, as long as one remembers and can tell, the Horde will never win. That's why he had to come back."

Andrew nodded, looking up at the moon again, realizing how precious the moment was and how fleeting it all could be.

"I love you," he whispered. "Always have and always will."

He drew her around to kiss her, and she giggled.

"So now that Hans is back you've taken up chewing again."

Laughing, he hugged her tight and together they walked slowly back to their home.

He looked up at the moon riding high overhead, its companion just breaking the horizon to the east. Absently, he felt in his pocket and pulled out a plug and started to chew.

Something to remember you by, you old bastard, he thought. In the camp below he could hear a scream, a human voice, most likely a servant who had committed some minor offense. The way the scream was cut off told him that the servant would never make such a mistake again.

So now it will start, he thought. Earlier than I had planned, but there will be enough to win. I learned much from you, how your people think, how your Andrew must lead, good lessons to know. And most of all, I know how to beat you. A bit of crisis created by you, Hans. But one that played to my advantage, for all saw just how implacable you were. How fierce in war, how determined to humiliate and destroy us. A few more umen commanders are gone now, conveniently blamed for mistakes they never made, and all will soon thirst for vengeance and for a wiping away of the stain on our honor. For that is now part of the appeal. Before, it was the war of the Merki and Tugar. But now it is our honor, our ancestors who shake their heads and will taunt us, and there will be no stopping us when the blow comes.

He sat in silence, the darkness of the plains below broken by a plume of fire soaring up from the factory where new crews were already at work, laboring as if nothing had ever happened. It was, after all, but a few days' interruption, but now the iron will pour, the guns will be made, the ships and flyers launched, and there will be a grim purpose as well.

Urging his mount forward, Ha'ark Qar Qarth, the Redeemer, rode down into the valley.

As he slipped into the room he saw her asleep in the moonlight, the baby nestled against her naked breasts. He undressed and slipped in beside his family. She stirred, smiling, her hand brushing his cheek, and then she drifted back to sleep.

He drew the two of them close into his embrace.

"We're home," he whispered.

Hans Schuder drifted into a gentle sleep, dreaming of a distant field that looked down on a clear blue lake, and in his dream he finally smiled.

Be sure to catch the exciting

history of the adventures of the

35th Maine. Turn the page

for previews of the ROC novels. . . .

THE LOST REGIMENT
RALLY CRY

TO VICTORY—OR DEATH!

When Union Colonel Andrew Keane led his blue-coated soldiers aboard the transport ship, he could not have foreseen that their next port of call would be in neither the North or South but on an alternate world where no human was free. Storm-swept through a space-time warp, Keane's regiment was shipwrecked in an alien land, a land where all that stood between them and destruction was the power of rifles over swords, spears, and crossbows.

Into this serfdom ruled by nobles and the Church, Keane and his men brought the radical ideas of freedom, equality, and democracy—and a technology centuries ahead of the world they must now call home. Yet all their knowledge and training might not save them from the true rulers there—creatures to whom all humans were mere cattle, bred for sacrifice!

"Some of the best adventure writing in years!"
—*Science Fiction Chronicle*

THE LOST REGIMENT
UNION FOREVER

SPLIT IN THE RANKS
ON A CRACKED-MIRROR WORLD

Colonel Andrew Keane and his blue-coated soldiers were not the first humans time-space-warped to a world so familiar yet not so foreign. Humans abounded on the perverse planet—humans treated like cattle by the alien warrior overlords. Keane's Civil War weaponry defeated the swords, spears, and crossbows of his monstrous adversaries. And part of the human population was freed, but the other part became puppets of the overlords in a vast counterattack. Now it was human vs. human, gun vs. gun, ironclad against ironclad, as the empires of Roum and Cartha clashed in gut-wrenching, soul-stirring struggle for the future of a world beyond time. . . .

THE LOST REGIMENT
TERRIBLE SWIFT SWORD

THE 35TH MAINE HAS LOOSED
THE VENGEANCE OF THE HORDES

After four years of fighting the Rebs, Keane's battle-hardened boys discovered that the creatures' crossbows, swords, and spears were no match for Union rifles. But it didn't take long for the odds to even up. The humans fought hard and bravely, and after defeating their adversaries on land and on sea, Keane and his troops had hoped to live in peace. But it was not to be.

Thanks to a human traitor, the aliens acquired a decisive edge—air power. And in their bloodthirsty quest for vengeance, they plotted to crush the humans once and for all—and forever reinstate their bloody reign of terror. . . .

"A wonderful world where Civil War-era Yankees have been tossed in with Medieval Russian peasants, Roman legionnaires, English pirates, Cathaginians . . . as well as a race of nine-foot-tall, flesh-eating aliens whose hordes make Ghengis Khan's mongols look like party guests."
—Raymond G. Feist

THE LOST REGIMENT
FATEFUL LIGHTNING

A WORLD DRENCHED IN BLOOD

Andrew Keane was now leading a mixed force of humans snatched from assorted periods in history on a desperate flight from an enemy more horrific than any nightmare. The alien Merki hordes, to whom all the humans brought to this distant world were cattle to be harvested at will, were mobilizing to destroy the humans in payment for the assassination of their revered warlord. And, his own military lines overextended, Andrew saw no alternative except to retreat, burning the land behind him as he went.

But retreat would offer only a temporary respite. For when the thirty days of mourning their leader were at an end, the Merki slaughterers would sweep forth to conquer, under a bold new warlord—the ruthless, ambitious Tamuka, who had sworn to leave no human alive on the face of the planet!

"The *Lost Regiment* series moves like a bullet. . . . An excellent read!"
—*LOCUS*

ABOUT THE AUTHOR

William R. Forstchen lives near Asheville, North Carolina, and teaches history at Montreat College. He completed his Ph.D. in American history at Purdue University, with specializations in military history, the history of technology, and the American Civil War. His interests, besides anything related to the Civil War, include scuba diving, white-water rafting, and politics.

BATTLETECH®
Loren L. Coleman

☐**DOUBLE-BLIND** The Magistracy of Canopus has been the target of aggression by the Marian Hegemony, and in hiring Marcus and his gutsy band of can-do commandos, it hopes to retaliate. But the fact that the Canopians are armed with technology that is considered rare in the Periphery is the least of Marcus's problems. Marcus and his "Angels" will have to face the real force behind the hostilities—the religious cult known as Word of Blake. This fanatical group has a scheme deadly enough to trap even the amazing Avanti's Angels....   (0-451-45597-5—$5.99)

☐**BINDING FORCE** Aris Sung is a rising young star in House Hiritsu, noblest of the Warrior Houses that have sworn allegiance to the Capellan Confederation. The Sarna Supremacy, a newly formed power in the Chaos March, is giving the Confederation some trouble—and Aris and his Hiritsu comrades are chosen to give the Sarnans a harsh lesson in Capellan resolve. But there is far more to the mission than meets the eye—and unless Aris beats the odds in a race against time, all the ferro-fibrous armor in the galaxy won't be enough to save House Hiritsu from the high-explosive cross fire of intrigue and shifting loyalties....   (0-451-45604-1/$5.99)

REDISCOVER THE 5TAR TREK UNIVERSE

☐ **STAR TREK CREATOR The Authorized Biography of Gene Roddenberry by David Alexander.** Every time you watch an episode of *Star Trek*, you see a piece of Gene Roddenberry. Now this fascinating book lets you see this many-sided man and his multi-faceted life and mind in their enthralling entirety—and in so doing, gives you new focus and fresh feeling for the show that has soared beyond its time to reach the realm of legend and myth.   (454405—$6.99)

☐ **THE BEST OF TREK #18 edited by Walter Irwin and G. B. Love.** This book more than lives up to its fine tradition and offers brand new articles on everything from a one-on-one interview with Robin Curtis about her role as Saavik, a show-by-show rating of *The Next Generation*, and a resolution to the long-standing debate about whether Data is merely a Spock clone. No matter what your favorite topics, characters, or episodes, you'll find something new about them here.   (454634—$4.99)

☐ **THE BEST OF THE BEST OF TREK® Part One. Edited by Walter Irwin and G. B. Love.** Here are the most intriguing, informative, and revealing contributions of the first ten *The Best of Trek®* collections. Selected by editors Walter Irwin and G. B. Love, these not-to-be-missed writings are by fans and experts alike—speculations, histories, analyses, opinions, and ongoing *Trek* experiences that expand our understanding of why *Star Trek* has captured the imagination and hearts of millions.   (455584—$5.50)

*Prices slightly higher in Canada   **RCF60X**

CUTTING EDGE SCI-FI NOVELS